Joan Jonker was born and bred in Liverpool. Her childhood was a time of love and laughter with her two sisters, a brother, a caring but gambling father and an indomitable mother who was always getting them out of scrapes. Then came the Second World War – a period that Joan remembers so well – when she met and fell in love with her late husband, Tony.

For twenty-three years, Joan campaigned tirelessly on behalf of victims of violence, and her first book, *Victims of Violence*, is an account of those years. She has recently retired from charity work in order to concentrate on her writing. Joan has two sons and two grandsons and she lives in Southport. Her previous bestselling Liverpool sagas have won her legions of fans:

'I love your books, Joan, they bring back such happy memories. Keep on writing, I'm eager for your next one' J. Mullett, Lancashire

'Thank you from the bottom of my heart. Your books are a gem' Angela Taylor, Cheltenham, Gloucestershire

'When I open one of your books my family don't see me for two days, then I'm so eager, I can't wait for your next one' Nicky Scott, South Wirral

'Please keep your books coming, Joan. They are the best. You are my favourite author' Deborah Hulme, Hindley, Wigan

'I'm an ardent fan, Joan, an avid reader of your books. As an old Liverpudlian, I appreciate the humour. Thank you for so many happy hours. Looking forward to your next' Mrs L. Broomhead, Liverpool

One Rainy Day

JOAN JONKER

headline

First published in 2005
by HEADLINE BOOK PUBLISHING

First published in paperback in 2006
by HEADLINE BOOK PUBLISHING

6

ISBN 978 0 7553 2606 8

Typeset in Bembo by Avon DataSet Ltd,
Bidford-on-Avon, Warwickshire

Printed and bound in the UK by
CPI Antony Rowe, Chippenham, Wiltshire

Headline's policy is to use papers that are natural, renewable and
recyclable products and made from wood grown in sustainable
forests. The logging and manufacturing processes are expected to
conform to the environmental regulations of the country of origin.

HEADLINE PUBLISHING GROUP
A division of Hodder Headline
338 Euston Road
London NW1 3BH

www.headline.co.uk
www.hodderheadline.com

I am dedicating this book to my late mother and father, who were affectionately known as Marsie and Pop by the four children they raised with love, laughter and happiness.

My sisters, Edna and Elsie, my brother, Joseph, and I had a wonderful childhood and, thanks to the guidance of Marsie and Pop, we've gone on to have a wonderful life.

Hello friends

I hope all is well with you and yours.

I can't wait to tell you what a treat there is in store for you with *One Rainy Day*. I have never enjoyed writing a book so much or been so sorry when I had to draw it to a close for I love the story and the wonderful characters, I just didn't want to say goodbye. I know self-praise is no recommendation, but you should know by now I am not big-headed. I love this book and I know you will too.

Take care.

Love

Joan

PS – Just a little piece of useless information: I do not have a big garden, just a courtyard, and I have a gardener who keeps asking why I haven't mentioned him in my books yet. He's getting quite tetchy about it, so to keep him happy his name is Brian and he is a good gardener. That should stop him from pulling out my plants or cutting down my trees!

Chapter One

It was a pleasant morning when the young man parked his car in the reserved bay at Exchange Station. There was a nip in the air, though, as the wind blew in from across the Mersey, and after locking the car door he slipped the keys into his pocket and set off at a brisk rate towards Castle Street.

Many a female head turned in his direction, for he cut a fine figure: six foot two in height, well built, with jet-black hair and eyebrows, deep brown eyes and an attractive dimple in his chin. He oozed confidence, in his well-cut overcoat, soft kid gloves and handmade shoes of the finest leather. If he had known the thoughts running through the heads of people passing by, he would have been surprised, for since he had been born into one of the wealthiest families in Liverpool confidence came naturally to Andrew Wilkie-Brook, as did wearing clothes made by bespoke tailors, and shoes made by craftsmen.

However, Andrew's mind was on none of these things as he reached the building that housed his father's import and export business, for today was his twenty-fifth birthday and there was much to look forward to. His mother had planned a lavish dinner party for twenty friends from their social circle, and knowing how fussy his mother was about detail he was sure the party would be a huge success. But there was an engagement he was looking forward to far more than the party, and that was lunch with his father at the club. It was a business lunch, his father had said, that just happened to fall on his birthday. And Andrew was chuckling as he took the stone steps two at a time. He loved his father dearly, and respected him, for when he'd asked if he could leave university when he was twenty-one to join the family business his father had brushed aside his wife's wailing over what their friends would say about their son's taking up a lowly position in an office. He had agreed to Andrew's joining the firm, as long as he was willing to accept the terms. That meant starting on the lowest rung of the ladder, so he could learn every aspect of the business from top to bottom. This had brought more tears and protests from his mother, but once again George Wilkie-Brook ignored her pleas. Instead he'd slapped his son on the back and wished him well. And because of his admiration and love for his father, Andrew had spent the last four years learning as much as he could about the business which had been in the family for almost eighty years. And as he learned, his father rewarded him, each year, by promoting him to a higher position. To his mother's dismay, he had cut down drastically on his social life for he was determined to fulfil the promises he'd made to his father. And now because of his diligence, Andrew had taken over the offices on the first floor of the building, and was responsible for the running of an important section of the business. With the help of his own private secretary, a typist and a clerk, his department ran like clockwork, and he had reason to be proud of his success.

So he was in high spirits when he climbed the stairs and knocked on his secretary's door. 'Good morning, Mrs Stamford. I hope you are well this fine day?'

Wendy Stamford looked up from the pile of correspondence in front of her and smiled. 'Good morning, Mr Andrew. And may I wish you a very happy birthday.'

'Thank you. I'm meeting my father at the club for lunch, so I'll have to look sharp.'

'I've been through the post, Mr Andrew, and I've sorted the letters in order of priority, so we should finish in plenty of time. I'll bring it in to you, then while you're looking through I'll make you a nice cup of tea.'

'That's very kind of you, Mrs Stamford, and reminds me why you are such a very good secretary.'

'Flattery will get you an arrowroot biscuit to have with your tea.' Wendy was very fond of her boss, for he was easy to get along with, very friendly, and not at all snobby. And he had a sense of humour. 'In fact, seeing as it's your birthday, I'll make that two biscuits.'

'I know this sounds forward of me, Mrs Stamford, but seeing as it is my birthday, could the biscuits and tea be stretched to include Miss Kennedy and Miss Williams? I would feel mean leaving them out. They have worked well for me over the past few years, and I'd like to show my appreciation.' Andrew hung his coat on the coat stand in his office, then turned a bashful face to his secretary. 'Tea and biscuits don't sound very appreciative, do they? It makes me sound like Scrooge.' He took a wallet from his inside pocket and removed a white five-pound note. 'Would Miss Kennedy go on an errand, d'you think? I'm having lunch with Father, who has a palate for good food and wine. And I wouldn't enjoy my meal, knowing my faithful staff were having a measly biscuit.' He handed her the five-pound note. 'Ask Miss Kennedy if she would go to Cooper's and order a selection of sandwiches and cakes to be delivered here at one o'clock. I would expect no change, so there should be sufficient to include the staff downstairs. If you turn two desks into a table, you could enjoy a nice, friendly lunch.' He looked quite boyish when he grinned. 'And my conscience will be clear.'

'You really don't need to do that, Mr Andrew, but I'm not going to talk you out of it, because I know the staff would be delighted to celebrate your birthday.' Wendy carried the post into his office and placed it, neatly stacked, on top of his desk in front of his brown leather swivel chair. 'I'll see Miss Kennedy and Miss Williams, and tell them that as soon as one of them has ten minutes to spare, she's to go to Cooper's with the order. Then I'll make our tea and we can get down to business.'

Before Andrew had joined the family firm, Wendy had been working as private secretary to George Wilkie-Brook for twelve years. Then, because of her knowledge and experience, Mr George had asked if she would do him a great favour and allow him to transfer her to his son's new offices, so she could help Andrew find his feet. And she had never regretted agreeing. She knew the job inside out, and was proud at how quickly Andrew had taken in everything she'd been able to teach him. She was forty years of age now, but didn't look it, with a trim figure, mousy-coloured curly hair, a good dress sense and a face that liked to smile. It was twenty years since she'd married her boyfriend, Stan, and they were as much in love now as they had been on their wedding day. The only disappointment in their lives was that they hadn't been blessed with children. They were both eager for a baby, but as the years passed they had gradually given up hope. As Wendy said, it was God's will, and there was little they could do about it. She certainly wasn't going to become twisted and bitter. They had each other, so they were lucky.

Andrew raised his eyes from the letter he was reading when his secretary came through the door carrying a tray with two cups of tea on, a huge smile on her face. 'Mr Andrew, your generosity has been very well received by Miss Williams and Miss Kennedy. I could say they were delighted, but that would be an understatement. I think a better word to describe the expression on their faces is delirious.' Wendy placed a cup and saucer beside him, a safe distance from the correspondence in case of an accident. 'I don't think they would like me to repeat this, so don't let the cat out of the bag for they would be embarrassed. Miss Williams said you are now next to Cary Grant on her list of favourite men, and Miss Kennedy has you second to Randolph Scott.'

Andrew chortled. 'Oh, I say, compliments like that are likely to give me a big head.' With a huge grin on his face which made him look a lot younger than his twenty-five years, he looked across the desk. 'Well, come on, Mrs Stamford, who am I next to on your list of favourite film stars?'

'I'm too old for that, Mr Andrew. I'm past the swooning stage. And unless we keep our mind on the work ahead of us, you're going to be late for your meeting with Mr George.'

Andrew squared his shoulders and picked up the letter on top of the pile. 'Quite right, too! How lucky I am to have a conscientious secretary who keeps my shoulder to the wheel. Off we go, and there'll be no break now until we've finished. So, pencil poised, and I'll dictate to your speed.'

For the next half-hour, there was silence in the room except for Andrew's voice, and the occasional rustle as his secretary turned over a page on her notebook. They were halfway through the letters when the phone rang in Wendy's next-door office, and Andrew tutted in exasperation. 'Get rid of them quickly, Mrs Stamford. If it's me they're after, tell them I've slipped out of the office on business.'

With her notebook gripped in her hand, Wendy left the

office, only to be back within a few seconds. 'It's your mother, Mr Andrew, and she said it's important. If you pick your phone up, I'll replace mine and stay in my office until you call me.'

Andrew's eyes went to the ceiling. He did wish his mother wouldn't ring him at the office so often. He wouldn't mind if there was a reason for her calls, but mostly she rang out of boredom. But she shouldn't be bored today, not when there was so much to organize for the dinner party. He took a deep breath before lifting the receiver. 'Yes, Mother, did you wish to speak to me?'

Harriet Wilkie-Brook had a very cultured voice. Born into a wealthy family, and married to a wealthy husband, she knew very little about what went on in the world. She was, in fact, remote from reality – which would have been apparent to anyone if they'd been in a position to hear the conversation between mother and son. 'It's about the flowers, darling. The order arrived half an hour ago, and they really are lovely. But I'm a little concerned that I may have under-ordered. Perhaps you could ring the florist for me, and ask them to send a further two dozen roses. A mixture of pink and deep red.'

Andrew forced himself to take a deep breath before saying, 'Mother, I am in the middle of dictating to Mrs Stamford, and I really don't have the time. Could Charlotte not ring the shop for you?' Charlotte was his nineteen-year-old sister, who had never worked a day in her life, and was spoiled by both parents. 'I'm sure she's capable of ordering flowers over the telephone.'

'This is a very busy day for Charlotte.' Harriet Wilkie-Brook's tone said she was not best pleased. She wasn't used to refusals. 'This is very thoughtless of you, Andrew. You should understand that your sister had, and still has, many things to do. This morning she had an appointment at the hairdresser's, then a fitting for shoes, next a visit to the manicurist's to have her nails cut and polished. Right now she is in town with one of her friends, picking up the dress she's had made for the party tonight.' Then Andrew's mother became exasperated at having to make excuses. 'This is most unkind of you, Andrew, and it is no way to talk to your mother. I'm sure your father will be horrified when I tell him you refused to do me a tiny favour.'

'Father understands that I am very busy this morning, Mother, because I have to get through a day's work in half a day. You see, I'm meeting him for lunch at the club. It's a business lunch. I'll tell him you phoned, and about your request. And I'll explain that as I was inundated with work I asked my secretary to ring the florists and order the two dozen roses you requested for tonight. Now, as your mind should be at rest, am I allowed to return to the many letters that need my attention?'

There was silence for a few seconds, then in a coaxing voice Harriet said, 'There is one little thing, my darling, but I'm quite sure it will meet with your approval. Annabel was on the telephone earlier, and I promised her you would pick her up in your car at seven fifteen.'

Andrew's brows were drawn together in puzzlement. 'But I was under the impression Mr and Mrs Barford had accepted the invitation to the party?'

'Yes, of course they have. They have never turned down an invitation to one of our dinners. Actually they were the first to reply.'

'Then surely Annabel can accompany them in their car? She always has before, and I would have thought it was obvious that she should do so now! It would be ridiculous for the parents to arrive in their car, then their daughter to arrive in another.'

7

'The poor girl would be so disappointed if you refused, Andrew. She was delighted when I said I would ask, for she really is very fond of you. And she is such a sweet thing, so pretty and very charming.'

'Mother, under no circumstances will I pick Annabel up, and I'm surprised at your even suggesting it. She is pretty, and charming, as you say, but she is also only nineteen years of age. And a very young nineteen at that. Her parents treat her like a child, and they've never allowed her to grow up, which I find very sad. For while she is always happy and pleasant, she is very innocent. Her conversation goes no further than clothes, perfume, and nights at the theatre. I know you had hopes for Annabel and me, and perhaps I should have spoken sooner, but it would never work, Mother, so would you please not give her any encouragement. I like her as a friend, I am fond of her as a friend, but it ends there.'

'You are twenty-five today, Andrew, and have never had a proper girlfriend. Heaven knows there are enough eligible females around who have set their sights on you over the years, but you show no interest. And I still say you could do a lot worse than Annabel. She comes from good stock, and she would be faithful, for she adores you.'

'Mother, when I fall in love it will be with a girl who is right for me. It hasn't happened yet, but one day she will come along. I'm prepared to wait for that day.' Andrew could feel a headache coming on, and rubbed his forehead. 'Mother, I really must go now, I have so much to do. We will talk about this subject at length some time. But I promise that when I do meet a girl I want to spend the rest of my life with, you will be the very first to know.'

His mother's voice was subdued when she answered, 'I'll ring Annabel and tell her you are unfortunately not able to call for her this evening, and she should accompany her parents. And Andrew, my darling, don't mention this conversation to your father, for he has so much on his mind, he'll think it petty.'

George Wilkie-Brook was in the smoking room of the members-only club when his son came through the door. He quickly left his chair, and with an extended arm, and a huge smile on his face, he went to greet his son. 'Come in, my boy, come in.'

'I'm sorry I'm a little late, Father, but there was a lot of correspondence requiring my attention.' Andrew grinned. 'I must tell the truth and say that if it hadn't been for Mrs Stamford, I would still be at my desk. She really is a treasure.'

'Would I give you anything but the best, my son?' George Wilkie-Brook had a loud, confident voice. A voice used to being listened to, and obeyed. Not that he was an arrogant man, for he was far from that. He was very down to earth, treated everyone as an equal, and was blessed with a good sense of humour. He never boasted about his success, but his bearing, dress sense, and easy-going manner in any company were signs that here was a man of means. 'Will you have a glass of whisky before we go into the dining room, Andrew? I must toast you on your birthday.'

'You have a whisky, Father, but I would prefer a glass of claret if you don't mind. Whisky goes to my head, and I don't think Mother would be pleased if I arrived home in a state of intoxication.'

George's laugh was hearty, and turned a few heads. 'You wouldn't bear the brunt of your mother's displeasure, my son, I would! But to make sure we both escape unscathed, claret you shall have.' He lifted a hand to summon a waiter standing nearby. 'One glass of your finest claret, John, and the usual whisky for me.'

'If we're going in for a meal, Father, we could take our drinks through with us.' Andrew was feeling rather peckish, having eaten very little at breakfast time. Usually it didn't matter what time he arrived at the office and he could breakfast at his leisure, but today was special and he had wanted to get in early to ensure that everything ran smoothly.

George laid his cigar in the large, round, solid crystal ashtray before saying, 'I'll have John bring the drinks through.' He put a hand on his son's arm as they walked into the quiet, select dining room. 'I've made enquiries about the menu, dear boy, and the poached salmon and asparagus was recommended.'

Andrew rubbed his hands together. 'That sounds very tempting, Father. I'll join you. I won't have the soup, though, delicious as it always is. I need to leave some room for the mountain of wonderful food Mother will have made especially for my birthday. After all her hard work, she'd be so disappointed if I refused to eat until there wasn't a crumb left.'

George chortled. 'Andrew, my son, your mother will not have seen the food until it is all spread out on the tables. She may know the name of every dish and every cake, and every bottle of wine, but if you asked her to toast a piece of bread, she wouldn't know how. It isn't her fault, for she's been shielded from reality since the day she was born. She doesn't know any other sort of life. Pampered by her parents, and then by myself.' He swirled his glass and watched the golden liquor lap the sides. 'I love your mother dearly, but I am not blind to her lack of knowledge regarding what goes on outside our close-knit social circle.'

Andrew took a deep breath before saying what had been

on his mind since the day he became aware of how the Wilkie-Brook family lived. 'And Charlotte, Father? Are you not afraid she is being spoilt? My sister is a lovely girl, beautiful to look at and full of fun, and she has loads of friends. She's a good daughter and a loving sister. But what about when she gets married, Father? Will her husband be prepared to pamper her as you and Mother do?'

'Don't think I haven't given that a great deal of thought, my son.' George was suddenly serious. 'I keep telling myself to be more firm with her. To cut down on her ridiculously high allowance so she learns to appreciate money. But I'm a coward where Charlotte is concerned, and keep putting it off. I admit I'm putty in her hands.'

'We all are, Father, and that's where the danger lies. You have to be realistic, for Charlotte's sake. What if she married someone who wasn't prepared to put up with her idleness and her love of spending money? What if she married a bully? She'd be devastated, absolutely lost. No one has ever raised their voice to her, or told her there was something she couldn't have. Wrapped in cotton wool since the day she was born, she is ill prepared for any knocks that might come her way. And this is not jealousy speaking, Father. I am not jealous of my sister, I love her. And I'm afraid for her. She is nineteen years of age and the day is not far off when some man will claim her. I believe she should be taught more about life outside the rich society circle.'

'How long have these thoughts been in your head, my boy?'

Andrew pulled a face. 'The last couple of years, I suppose. When I first came home from university and joined the firm, I didn't have time for anything but trying to take in all that was being taught me. Then gradually I noticed what an empty life both Mother and Charlotte had. Mother I can understand;

her life is settled. But not my sister. Hair appointments, fittings for dresses she doesn't need, afternoon tea dances, friends who are the same as herself, who have appointments with the same hairdresser. What an aimless life that is, Father. It doesn't tax the brain or teach them anything about the ninety per cent of the population who are not in the same social circle. It is not a life I would want. It would bore me stiff.'

A waiter appeared with their food, and there was silence as he served the salmon and asparagus. Then, after making sure everything on the table was perfect, he nodded his head, clicked his heels, and said, 'Enjoy your meal, gentlemen.'

'I say, this looks and smells delicious, Father.' Andrew shook his napkin open. 'I am really going to enjoy it.'

George grunted his agreement as he tucked his own heavy linen napkin into the neck of his shirt. He didn't reach for his knife and fork, but studied his son's face across the table. 'The pampered life wasn't for you, was it, Andrew? It would have been if your mother had got what she wanted. And I have to say that when you left university and joined the firm, I thought it was just a fad and you would soon tire of the routine. In my heart I hoped you were serious, but I couldn't be sure. So you can imagine my delight, and pride, when you not only turned up for work each day, but seemed to enjoy it.'

'Oh, I did enjoy it, Father, and I still do. I know self-praise is no recommendation, but I have to admit I'm as proud of myself as you are. You'll never know how grateful I am that you gave me the chance. It salves my conscience that I have worked for most of the money you pay me. Oh, I know I don't contribute towards the beautiful house I'm lucky enough to live in, but I don't squander the wage I earn, I do have a healthy bank account. And I am very happy, Father, thanks to you.'

'You deserve what you have, my boy; you have worked

hard for it, and I am very proud of you. But let us enjoy our meal, then we can retire to the smoking room and discuss business. My brain works better when I have a cigar between my fingers.'

George was in a thoughtful mood during lunch, as he tried to marshal into order the thoughts running through his head. His son had opened his mind to many things he'd been aware of, but was too cowardly to act on because of the disruption they would cause. His home was running smoothly, with no ripples to upset Harriet, his wife. And he probably would have let things carry on as they were if Andrew hadn't been honest and outspoken. Now he realized changes had to be made, for the sake of his beloved daughter. Because he loved her, he had to prepare her for whatever the future held for her, while still protecting her from the harsh realities of life.

'That was delicious, Father.' Andrew patted his lips with the napkin. 'Shall we have our coffee in the smoking room, and you can enjoy one of your cigars?'

'Good idea, my boy. I have much to discuss with you regarding business and staff.'

When they were seated facing each other in the deep comfortable leather chairs, Andrew said, 'You mentioned staff, Father. Does that mean you are taking more people on, or cutting down? I hope mine are safe, for we work very well together.'

'We'll discuss what I have in mind for staff later, Andrew. First I would like to talk about your views on how best to help Charlotte lead a more meaningful life. I don't want to go at the subject like a bull in a china shop, but you have alerted me to the pitfalls she may encounter as she approaches marriageable age. Have you any suggestions?'

'I really don't want to interfere, for I don't want my sister or mother to turn against me. I said what I felt in my heart, for I love Charlotte dearly, and would be devastated if her life was ruined because she knew nothing about the big bad world outside. She sees life as all milk and honey, and we both know that is far from the truth. Except for the very rich, who have never worked a day in their lives, and haven't a clue how ninety per cent of the population live.' Andrew sighed. 'I'm sorry I got carried away, Father. I'm not a communist, far from it. I don't begrudge anyone their money – how could I when I've lived in luxury all my life! You've worked hard to build up the business, and you're entitled to everything you have. And I'm happy to say I earn a living now. But Charlotte doesn't even give a thought to where the money comes from to keep her in luxury. And that is wrong. She should know money has to be earned, it doesn't grow on trees.'

George tilted his head. 'You've never talked about it before.'

Andrew shrugged his shoulders. 'I suppose my time at university brought home the fact that life is not always fair. I had plenty of money to splash around. You were very generous and I was able to live the good life down in London. It took a while for me to understand that other blokes weren't as fortunate. Their families were struggling to pay their fees, and unlike myself and the blokes I had chummed up with, there were no nights out on the town for them. And after a few years, I decided I would like to earn a living. The rest you know, Father, and I think you've heard enough from me. I hope I didn't sound as though I have been anything but grateful to you for everything. You made me what I am.'

'Nonsense, my boy, you proved your worth with your dedication and hard work. And now we have established that fact, I think we should get down to business. As I said, I wish to discuss the matter of staff. We'll start with your office, shall we? Are you satisfied with the people you have, or dissatisfied?'

'Oh, I am quite satisfied. The office runs like clockwork thanks to Mrs Stamford and the two typists. We get along very well with each other, and I wouldn't wish to change anything.'

George and his son were alike in looks, except that George was a few inches shorter, and his black hair was lightly flecked with grey. The dark brown eyes were the same, as were the thick black eyebrows. And the eyebrows were drawn together now as he stroked his chin. 'So, you wouldn't welcome any changes in your office, then?'

'That is difficult for me to answer, Father, for you are the boss. If you want to make changes, then of course I'll fall in with your wishes.' Andrew's boyish grin appeared. 'I have to say, though, that I would be sorry to lose any of my staff, for we really work as a team.'

'I wasn't thinking of removing a member of your staff, dear boy, I was of a mind to increase it by one.'

Andrew looked surprised. 'I don't require any more staff. We manage very well.' Then he added, 'But of course it is up to you, Father. What have you in mind?'

'You have a spare office on your floor. I was thinking of making use of it for your filing cabinets. You will have need of more filing space when I transfer some of our clients' business over to you. And of course, a young clerk will be required to be in charge of the files.'

'This comes out of the blue, Father. How long have you had this change in mind?'

George tapped his chin. 'Let me think. It must have been on my mind for a year now. I told myself that your hard work should be rewarded, and that on the day of your twenty-fifth birthday, I would transfer some of my business over to you. And on the same day you would become a junior partner in the firm.' He laughed with pleasure at his son's astonishment. 'Well, have you nothing to say, my son?'

Andrew's face was white, and although his lips were moving it was a few seconds before any words came. 'I can't believe it, Father, and I certainly didn't expect it. I had no idea; you never hinted at such a promotion. When did you decide?'

'As I said, it was probably a year ago. You were dedicated to your work, never late and never taking time off. And your loyalty deserved to be rewarded. Are you pleased?'

'Pleased, Father, I'm flabbergasted! I never in my wildest dreams thought of this.'

'I'm glad you like your present, dear boy. Happy birthday.'

Andrew left his chair to shake his father's hand. 'Am I allowed to tell our guests tonight that I am now a man of importance, or is it to be a secret for a while?'

'Good heavens, no! You can shout it from the rooftops if you wish.' There came a muted guffaw from George. 'Not from our rooftop, of course, for your mother would be mortified.'

'If you see me with an inane grin on my face, and a faraway look in my eyes, you will do something to bring me out of my trance, won't you?'

'I most certainly will! You have to live up to your new status, my boy. Cool and confident at all times.'

Still trying to take in the unexpected, but wonderful, news, Andrew managed a smile. 'It may take a few days for me to manage that, but I will get there, Father, you have my word on it.'

Chapter Two

George and his son talked long into the afternoon, each at ease in the other's company. Andrew felt close to his father as they discussed future plans for the business. He would have been content to sit there longer, and was disappointed when his father took out his fob watch and said it was time to make their way home.

'I'll leave my car here overnight and travel with you. It will save time, and we can talk some more.' George chuckled. 'Besides, I can't say I enjoy driving.'

As they walked towards Exchange Station to pick up Andrew's car, he said, 'If you don't enjoy driving, Father, I can bring you in each day, and drive you home. I would be more than happy to.'

Again George chuckled. 'Ah, well, you see, my boy, your offer is much appreciated, but it would put me in a dilemma. I would have to ask myself whether I would enjoy being driven to work each day, or whether I would prefer the extra half-hour in bed. Being senior partner gives me some privileges, and one is that I am not tied to time.'

'What would be your answer to yourself?' They were nearing the bay where the car was parked, and Andrew felt in his pocket for the key. 'Comfortable ride into the office each day, or a comfortable half-hour extra in bed?'

George waited for the passenger door to be opened, then slipped into the seat. 'Decisions, decisions, dear boy. How much easier life would be if we didn't have to make them.'

His hand on the open door, Andrew bent down until his face was on a level with his father's. 'Let me tell you what I would choose if I were in your position. I would give it some thought, then decide the winner was half an hour extra in bed. And I would tell myself it was only what I deserved.'

'Sound advice, my son. Now let us make for home, or you'll be in danger of arriving late for your own birthday party, and your mother would be most displeased.'

As Andrew drove out of the city towards the outskirts, the conversation returned to business. And they were still on the subject when he drove through the tall impressive pillars fronting the Wilkie-Brook estate. There was a large front garden, with mature trees partly hiding the imposing house from passers-by. Andrew drove down past the side of the house to where the family cars were kept. The building had, many years ago, been used to house a horse, a carriage, and sleeping quarters for the groom. It now acted as a garage for George, Andrew and Charlotte. The back garden was huge, with lawns, flower beds, trees, bushes and an orchard. And it was immaculate, having a full time gardener to tend it. His name was Jim Woods, and he'd been tending the Wilkie-Brooks' garden for ten years. He tended it with a passion that caused many a row with his wife. She accused him of loving the garden more than he did her. He denied it, of course, but alone in the garden on a summer's day, when all the flowers were in bloom, he had to admit the pink roses were much prettier than she was. And they never answered him back, or kept talking when he wanted to be quiet.

When the car was parked, George and Andrew walked back down the side of the house to the front door. They had to pass the kitchen, and the sounds that reached them told of the hectic activity inside. 'Your mother will be busy ordering the staff to do this that and the other,' George said. 'And she only makes things worse. If she would just sit back and let them get on with what they do best, life would be much easier for all concerned.'

'I can understand Mother, though,' Andrew said. 'She wants to see with her own eyes that everything is going to plan. She's a perfectionist.'

George chortled as he climbed the high step into the vestibule, which boasted beautiful stained glass windows. 'I'm afraid she will be a very angry perfectionist, my boy, for I promised faithfully that we would be home before five o'clock. It is now ten minutes to six. So batten down the hatches, we could be in for a rough ride.'

Andrew shook his head. 'Don't forget it's my birthday, and everyone has to be nice to a person on their birthday.'

George winked at his son before opening the door to the large, magnificent square hall. The wide curved staircase caught the eye first, the stairs being covered in the same thick maroon carpet as the floor. Paintings lined the walls, a huge antlered mahogany coat stand had pride of place by the door, and a crystal chandelier hung over the highly polished round table which stood in the centre.

One of the four doors leading off the hall opened as George was removing his gloves, and his wife, Harriet, walked in. Her nostrils flaring and her hands clasped across her stomach, she faced her husband. 'I hope you have a reasonable excuse for being late, George, and breaking your promise?'

Andrew quickly moved forward. After all, she couldn't be

angry with him on his birthday. 'It's all my fault, Mother. Don't blame Father for us being late.' He took hold of her hands and gently squeezed them. 'This has been the most wonderful day of my life, Mother; please don't spoil it. Firstly, you are working very hard to give me what I know will be a most lavish party, that will have our friends green with envy. And while I was looking forward to this evening, unaware of what Father had in store for me, he presents me with a birthday gift I would never have expected in my wildest dreams.'

Harriet looked past him to where her husband was standing. 'Have you been keeping a secret from me, George? You know I dislike secrets. Had I known you were buying a present for Andrew, I would have been delighted to help you choose a suitable one.'

'I didn't buy Andrew a present, my love, I gave him something far more important. But as it's our son's birthday, I'll let him tell you himself.'

'Look at me, Mother.' Andrew put a finger under her chin and turned her to face him. 'You are the first person to have the privilege of meeting the junior partner of Wilkie-Brook's.'

Harriet turned to her husband, her mouth open to tell him she should have been informed before the deed was done. But the words died on her lips as the significance of what she'd heard sunk in. How much nicer it would be to introduce her son as junior partner with the firm, rather than say he worked for his father. 'That is very generous of you, my darling, and I'm sure the dear boy appreciates his new status.' She cupped her son's face in her two hands and kissed him on each cheek. 'Well done, dearest. I really am very happy for you.'

George rounded the table and put a hand on Andrew's

arm. 'We are cutting things rather fine, my boy. Our guests will be arriving in an hour, and we have to bathe and change.'

His wife agreed. 'You must be here to welcome your guests, my love; it would be bad manners if you were not. So make haste, the pair of you.'

'Is Charlotte not around?' Andrew asked. 'I haven't seen her for my birthday kiss.'

'There'll be plenty of time later,' Harriet said, waving her hand towards the stairs. 'Be assured she hasn't forgotten you. She is very excited, and will be wearing a beautiful new dress in your honour.' Once again she waved her hand. 'Make haste, now; I don't want to make excuses to our guests for your absence.'

'Have faith, Mother. I shall be at the door to greet them.' With that, Andrew took the wide stairs two at a time.

George was ready before his wife, and he wandered downstairs and headed for the kitchen. To say it was busy would be an understatement, for the staff were running to put the final touches to dishes that not only looked delicious, but would bring sighs of pleasure from the owners of appreciative palates.

The housekeeper, Frances, was a bonny woman, with a well-rounded body, rosy red cheeks, mousy hair and an ever-present smile. She ran the house and staff like clockwork, and her eyes missed nothing. She had worked for the Wilkie-Brooks for ten years, and had her own bedroom and sitting room.

Jane the cook came in at ten in the mornings and worked until eight o'clock, except on Sunday which was her day off. She had a wonderful happy personality, and her cooking had to be tasted to be believed. She was a wizard in the kitchen, and even the housekeeper wouldn't dare to interfere or criticize. They were good mates, and Jane would always stay late to help Frances when there was anything special happening, like a birthday party.

Then there was fifteen-year-old Rosie, a young housemaid. She worked from eight until five, and lived with her parents and younger brother. She'd only been employed there for nine months, and was still in awe of the house and its occupants.

There was also a daily cleaner, Kate, who tackled all the heavy work six days a week. She was seventeen years old, from a poor family who relied on her wages. She was very pretty, being slim with auburn hair and hazel eyes, and her ever-ready smile made her a favourite with all the staff and family members. The only exception was the mistress, who didn't acknowledge the two young people on her staff.

'I haven't come to nose, Frances,' George said, 'just to see if you require anything, or need a helping hand? Not that I'd be allowed to roll my sleeves up and get stuck in, but it's just a friendly enquiry. If the delicious smells are anything to go by, our guests are in for a gastronomical delight.'

'All of the tables have been set and decorated, Mr George. As you can see, Jane has everything under control. As soon as the guests are seated, the food will be ready to serve.'

'I hope you and Jane, and the girls, set a table for yourselves out here. Andrew would be very happy if you celebrated his birthday too. He'll be out to see you later, when you are less busy, to thank you.' George was about to turn away when he had a thought. 'Oh, Frances, I know you don't need me to tell you, but you won't forget to share the food that isn't eaten with the rest of the staff, will you? I know you must all have worked very hard, as you always do, and I would like to think you shared a little of the pleasure my son will be having, thanks to you, on his birthday. So try to have a little respite, with a few goodies and a bottle of sherry.'

'Thank you, Mr George. We will toast Mr Andrew because we are all fond of him. And I'll not forget to see that Kate and Rosie take some food home to their families.'

George gazed round the kitchen. 'Where are the young ones?'

'They're in the laundry room, changing into their uniforms. And they're loving every minute, Mr George. It's a wonder you can't hear them giggling. They're thrilled because they're helping with waiting on the tables, and they're wearing the black dresses with the lacy aprons and headdress to match. I heard Rosie saying she felt "proper posh" in uniform.'

'I bet they'll look very pretty. But I have to go now, Frances, for I've heard two cars arriving. Miss Harriet doesn't like it when I'm not on hand to welcome the guests.' He patted her arm. 'You and the staff have my appreciation for the extra work you're being asked to do. I'm sure Andrew will be coming himself to thank you.'

Andrew would have liked to relax longer in the bath and once again go over the events of the day. But knowing what a stickler his mother was on etiquette, he didn't linger. There were four bedrooms on the first floor – one was used for visitors – and each bedroom had its own bathroom and dressing room. When Andrew stepped out on the large square landing, it was to find his father coming out of his bedroom, struggling to fasten his cufflinks.

'Confounded things,' he growled. 'They refuse to fasten.'

'Here, let me.' Andrew had them fastened in a few seconds. 'They always seem to know when you're in a hurry, and then they become obstinate. Still, no panic. We should be down before our guests start arriving and remain in Mother's good books.'

'Oh, I've been down,' George told him. 'I paid a visit to the kitchen to have a word with Frances, and lo and behold, your mother cornered me. She spotted I wasn't wearing her favourite cufflinks and insisted I change them. No one else would have noticed the blasted things, or been in the least interested whether I was wearing cufflinks or not. Anyway, it's always best to give in right away. Saves any argument and much easier than facing a stern face all night.'

They skipped side by side down the wide staircase, and reached the bottom just as the young maid, Rosie, opened the door to the Barford family: Robert, his wife Gweneth, and their daughter Annabel. Robert handed his coat and scarf to the young maid, who was overawed by the occasion, and walked towards George with hand outstretched, grinning broadly. 'Nice to see you, George.'

Andrew intended to greet Gweneth first, but was forestalled by Annabel who, after handing the maid her coat, ran towards him with outstretched arms. 'Andrew, darling, happy birthday.' He managed to catch her arms before they reached his neck, and he kept a tight grip on them. 'How pretty you look, Annabel! Stand back and let me see you properly.'

Like a child, Annabel did a twirl, then a curtsy, before saying, 'I'm glad you like my dress, Andrew. I wanted to look nice for you.'

Her mother was irritated that her daughter was acting in an unseemly manner. 'Annabel, do give Andrew and me a chance to say hello.'

It was George who saved the situation and the Barfords' embarrassment. 'When you have made Gweneth welcome, my boy, there are other guests in the drawing room waiting for you.'

Robert Barford tried to mask his discomfort. 'We're not the first, then, George?'

'No, old boy, the Parker-Browns are here, the Hedleys, and the Simpsons. The Braithwaits rang to say they'd be a little late. We'd better make our way to the drawing room. They'll be wondering what's keeping Andrew.'

Gweneth took her daughter's arm. 'Come, Annabel, and please behave yourself.'

The girl looked downcast and Andrew took pity on her. 'I'll take Annabel through, Gweneth. She can take my arm.'

'Can I sit next to you, Andrew?' Annabel's wide eyes looked up at him appealingly.

'I'm afraid not, my dear. You see, I'll be sitting between my parents, and Charlotte will be next but one. I'm sure you'll find someone to talk to, though, you look so pretty.'

Walking behind them, George mentally gave his son full marks for being straight, and also being kind and not making a fuss, which would embarrass Robert and Gweneth. But really it was time they took their daughter in hand and treated her like a grown-up. A grimace came to George's face when he told himself he was a fine one to talk. He spoilt his own daughter, who was the same age as Annabel, by giving her everything her heart desired, indulging her every whim. A sigh left his lips. This wasn't the time to worry about Charlotte, not on his son's birthday. Tomorrow, perhaps?

When Andrew entered the drawing room the talking and laughter ceased, while all the guests moved to shake his hand and congratulate him. To his delight, his sister, Charlotte, was the first to reach him. She was brimming over with happiness for him, and as she hugged him tight she whispered, 'My wonderful brother, you look so handsome and I'm proud of you.' Then in a voice everyone could hear, she said, 'I often wish you weren't my brother, for then I could marry you.'

'Oh, I don't know about that, my darling sister. I really don't think I could afford to keep you in the manner to which you are accustomed.'

Charlotte, beautiful to look at, and dressed like a dream, giggled. 'We could live in a garret, and I could go out in the streets selling oranges.' She put a hand to her heart and struck up a dramatic pose. 'We might be poor, and starving, but we'd have each other.'

The only person not amused was Harriet. 'Really, Charlotte, that is most unbecoming in a young lady.'

George's guffaw sounded over the laughter. 'You know I felt quite optimistic for a few seconds. Had Andrew not been your brother, Charlotte, I would have gladly given him a princely sum to take you off my hands.'

Charles, the twenty-year-old son of Jeanette and Toby Hedley, piped up. 'Oh, I say, Mr George, that is a very handsome offer. I can assure you that with a princely sum at my disposal, I could take jolly good care of Charlotte. If she would have me, of course.'

Her eyes alive with laughter, Charlotte told him, 'You have a taste for very expensive cars, Charles, and I fear I would come second to an automobile.'

'That's typical of a woman, that is,' Charles said, his round chubby face trying not to smile. 'A minute ago you were prepared to walk the streets selling oranges for Andrew. Now you're turning your back on rides in the country in a red open-top sports car. It shows how fickle the female sex are.'

The rest of the invited guests arrived then, and the room became noisy with greetings, chatter and laughter. And as glasses were refilled with whisky, claret, port and white wine, the level of chattering and tinkling of glasses increased.

The quietest person was Harriet, who loved parties but wasn't a party person. Apart from the odd remark, she was quite happy to sit back, listen, and congratulate herself on being an excellent hostess. The noisiest person was her son, Andrew, which was unusual, for he wasn't a party animal by nature. But today had been a wonderful day and his head was in the clouds. He'd left it to his father to tell their friends about his promotion, for he was afraid if he did it himself it would sound like boasting.

The happiest person was Charlotte, which wasn't unusual for she always shone in company. Tonight she was happy for her brother, and very proud of him.

Dressed in a neat black dress, with her hair combed back into a bun at the back of her neck, Frances entered the drawing room. She moved quietly round the revellers to where her mistress sat talking to Jessica Parker-Brown. After coughing discreetly, she said, 'Dinner is ready to be served, Miss Harriet. Shall I announce it?'

'Please do, Frances. And suggest Mr Andrew leads his guests through to the dining room.' Harriet knew it was an unnecessary question, but she asked it out of habit. 'Is everything going to plan?'

The housekeeper nodded. 'Everything you requested, Miss Harriet. I'm sure the guests will be more than satisfied.'

Jessica leaned forward to touch Frances on her arm. 'I'm sure we will be green with envy, Frances. There is not a kitchen in the city that can compare with yours. A dinner at

27

the Wilkie-Brooks' is a great honour. Much looked forward to and talked about for weeks afterwards.'

'I'll pass your words on to the staff, Mrs Parker-Brown. I'm sure they will be pleased.' Frances inclined her head slightly. 'And now to find Mr Andrew.'

Andrew was holding the floor with the male guests. His face was flushed, and even though he was aware he was talking too much, he couldn't stop. His excitement over the events of the day was still high, and the wine was fuelling his tongue. Frances came up behind him and tapped him on the shoulder. 'Your mother asked me to tell you dinner is ready to be served, Mr Andrew. She asked if you would lead your guests through?'

Looking bashful, Andrew ran a hand through his hair. 'I'm a little tipsy, Frances, but have no fear, I am quite steady on my feet and capable of walking upright.' Once again he ran a hand through his hair. 'I would like Charlotte to take my arm. Where is my lovely sister?'

'I'm right behind you, my darling brother.' Charlotte came round to his side. 'I've been keeping an eye on you. Now, give me your arm and I'll be honoured and delighted to have you escort me. Please don't fall, though, for I should hate it if my new dress was torn. I had it made specially for your birthday, but was rather hoping I would be allowed to wear it on more than one occasion.'

Andrew chuckled. 'You have my promise I will not even stumble. The odd hiccup can't be avoided, however, for that is out of my control.'

George had been watching his son with some amusement, and was pleased to see brother and sister acting the goat and enjoying each other's company. It brought a lump to his throat, and he mentally called himself a sentimental fool. It would be some time before Andrew allowed himself to relax like this again. He'd become very serious of late, even bringing work home with him. He could do with a little of his sister's love of life, while Charlotte would ease her father's worries if, like her brother, she opened her eyes to reality, and the world around her.

Moving away from the group, George approached his wife and took her arm. 'Allow me to escort you, my darling. I can see Michael coming to claim Jessica, so we four sober and responsible citizens can go in together.'

Harriet linked her husband's arm. 'Jessica has been telling me about their baby, George. It seems like only yesterday he was born, but he is now six months old.'

'It's seeing the children grow that makes us feel old. Days pass so quickly, it's frightening.'

Michael Parker-Brown joined them, and put his arm round his wife's slim waist. 'What is frightening, George? Business is booming, is it not?' He and his wife were a handsome couple, and very well off. 'You are an astute business man, old boy, with a son who is going to be equally astute.'

His wife patted his cheek. 'My darling, no one was talking about business. Our baby was the topic of conversation.'

'Ah, yes. Have you asked them yet?'

'Not yet, darling. I wanted you to be here when I do.' Jessica smiled at George and Harriet. 'We are arranging to have the baby christened in the very near future, and we would like to ask if you would stand as godparents? We would consider it an honour if you would.'

George glanced down at his wife and saw a smile on her face. 'I would be delighted, and indeed honoured. And while I can't speak for Harriet, I'm sure she feels the same.'

'Oh, it would be an honour. Thank you for asking us.' And

indeed Harriet was pleased. 'Have you chosen a name for the boy?'

Jessica nodded. 'Charles Leo. After Michael's late father.'

'How thoughtful,' Harriet said. 'When you set the date, you must call and furnish George and me with the details. Now, however, we must go in for dinner.'

The dinner was a happy affair, with flowing wine, delicious food, and lively conversation. It was when the meal was over, and the guests were retiring to the drawing room, that George whispered to Andrew that he should visit the kitchen before all the staff left. His son didn't need telling twice, for the glowing comments from the guests had reminded him that a lot of work had gone into making his birthday party a huge success. He excused himself from the table, and was on his way to the kitchen when his sister caught up with him. 'Wait for me, Andrew. I would like to thank Frances too!'

Andrew pulled up sharp. 'Charlotte, it wasn't Frances on her own who made all that delicious food. Jane must take the glory for almost everything on that table. Every course was down to her wonderful knowledge of cooking and baking. The others would have worked hard washing and cleaning, and Rosie and Kate waited on table as well! They all worked hard to make the dinner a success. Each one deserves our gratitude and thanks. So include everyone, Charlotte. They deserve it, and it will tell them we appreciate all their hard work.'

'Am I a selfish person, Andrew?'

'Of course you're not, Charlotte. Perhaps you just don't think, that's all. But come now, help me to show my appreciation to a wonderful staff for a wonderful birthday party. And I'm sure they'd love to see you looking so pretty in that delightful dress.'

When his sister hung back, Andrew pulled hard on her arm and she found herself in the kitchen facing the staff. She was shy, not knowing what to say. She knew them all by name, and would acknowledge them if she encountered them while they were cleaning her room, or the staircase. But she had never held a conversation with them, or learned anything of their life outside the big house.

While Andrew was thanking Frances and Jane, the two young maids were staring at Charlotte's dress with wonder in their eyes. Then young Rosie plucked up the courage to say, in a timid voice, 'That's a beautiful dress, Miss Charlotte. It doesn't half look nice on yer.'

Andrew turned. 'Yes, it suits her, doesn't it, Rosie? Come here, Charlotte, and let the girls see the back of it. Do a twirl for them.'

To say Charlotte was reluctant would be an understatement. But she knew to refuse would be childish. So she turned round slowly, and some of her shyness fell away when the young maids, and the cook, clapped and raved over the dress. So she did a proper twirl, before taking the hand her brother held out to her. 'We have to go now to bid our guests farewell,' he said. 'But you each have my sincere thanks for all the hard work I put you to. I'll see you tomorrow at breakfast.'

As the couple moved towards the door, Charlotte turned her head and smiled. 'Thank you. The party was lovely and the food delicious.'

On their way back to their guests, she said, 'The dinner went well, Andrew. Have you enjoyed your birthday?'

'More than you'll ever know, Charlotte. It's been wonderful, and Father's gift was the best present I could have asked for.'

'I haven't bought you a present yet,' his sister said. 'I thought I would take you out for a meal to a good restaurant. Just the two of us. Would you like that?'

Andrew didn't answer right away, as his mind was busy. Was this the opportunity, he asked himself? He might never get another. 'There is something I would really like you to do for me. Something that would make me very happy.'

'Anything, my darling brother. Just tell me what it is.'

'I don't want you to think I'm big-headed, Charlotte, but I am so thrilled at being made a junior partner in the firm, I want to show off. I'd love you to come down to my office one day, to see how I work, and where I work. And I'd like to introduce my staff to you and show you round the office. Then I could take you for lunch after I'd bored you stiff with my boasting. Would you do that for me?'

Charlotte didn't hesitate. 'Of course I will, silly boy. It's not much of a birthday present, but if it's really what you want . . .'

'Thank you, my dear sister. We'll set a date tomorrow, but right now we must say goodnight to our friends.' He kissed her cheek. 'I'll look forward to your seeing where I work. And you must show how impressed you are.'

Chapter Three

It was Monday morning, four days after the party, when Charlotte slid into the passenger seat of Andrew's car. 'Do you always come out at this unearthly hour, Andrew? Surely not?'

'It's a quarter to nine, Charlotte, and about three-quarters of the population will be out and about. Workers on their way to the office or factory, and children going to school.' Andrew backed the car out of the garage and manoeuvred slowly past the side of the house. Then, as he changed gear, he grinned. 'The fresh morning air is good for you. Wakes you up and starts the brain ticking over.'

'But it's cold and miserable.' Charlotte shivered. 'Why couldn't we have gone in later, like Father?'

'Because I like to be at my desk by nine o'clock. I aim to set a good example.' Andrew turned and reached behind for a knitted rug that was folded neatly on the back seat. 'I can't expect the staff to be good timekeepers when I'm not.' He handed her the rug. 'Here, put this over your knees. It'll keep you warm.'

'I do hope your office is warm, Andrew, or I'll be sorry I agreed to come.'

Andrew drove through the gates, then, after making sure the road was clear, set off towards the city. 'We do have heating in the offices, Charlotte, and facilities for making tea.

Perhaps I was wrong to ask you to come if you're really not interested. I just thought you would enjoy seeing how the family business is run. After all, there must have been times when you've given thought to how Father makes the money to keep us in luxury?' He slowed down to glance at his sister, and saw that she was looking distinctly downhearted and miserable. 'Look, I'll turn back and take you home.' He pulled in to the kerb and turned the ignition off. 'I just wanted to show you how I spend my days, and introduce my staff to my pretty sister. And I thought it would be a lovely surprise for Father if you walked into his office unexpectedly. He would be so happy. But I can see you have no heart for my plans, so I'll take you back home.'

Charlotte quickly put a hand on his arm. 'No, don't do that, Andrew. I made a promise and I'll keep it. I will come with you, so drive on or you'll be late.'

But Andrew wasn't satisfied. 'No, Charlotte, I can tell it isn't to your liking. Besides, if I were to introduce the staff to my sister, I would like them to see her smiling, and looking happy to be there.'

'Of course I'll smile! You didn't think I'd go in with a long face, did you?' Charlotte sat up straight in her seat. 'I will brighten up, I promise you. Please understand, Andrew, I'm usually still in bed this time in the morning.'

Andrew tapped his fingers on the steering wheel. 'I won't think any the less of you if you don't come, Charlotte. And as Father doesn't know anything about your proposed visit, no one will be any the wiser. It is entirely up to you, dear sister. Do we go into the city, or will I take you back home?'

His sister's lips formed a straight and determined line. 'I intend to visit your office, Andrew, whether you take me there or I call a taxi.' She leaned sideways to kiss his cheek.

'Under my own steam or yours, brother dear. To use one to our father's sayings, I will get there come hell or high water.'

Andrew smiled. 'Now, that sounds more like my sister talking. And as there are no taxis to be had, and you seem to have made up your mind, I suggest we get a move on. Keep hold of that rug and tuck it round your legs to keep the cold out.'

'Funnily enough,' his sister giggled, 'I don't feel cold now. In fact I really am wide awake.'

'That's what the fresh morning air does for you,' Andrew said. 'You should try it more often; it's good for you. It's also good for your complexion. Sitting around all day in a warm house will do you no favours. You'll end up with a huge bottom and a sallow skin.'

Charlotte turned her head to the window so he wouldn't see her smile. 'That could have its advantages, my dear brother. If I had a big bottom and horrible skin, you wouldn't be so eager to have your staff meet me. That would really give them something to talk about. Just think, they'd be whispering behind your back that they feel sorry for you. You so handsome, and your sister fat and ugly.'

'That's more like it,' Andrew said, chortling. 'You sound more like my sister now. My hopes are high again that a very pleasant morning is in store for everyone. Especially our father. He will be so pleased.'

Charlotte took her brother's arm as they left the car and headed for Castle Street. 'Oh, it is busy here, isn't it? And everyone seems to be in a hurry.'

'A lot of firms have offices in this area of the city.' Andrew felt good walking with his sister. And in the back of his mind he was thinking what a pleasant surprise it would be for his father when Charlotte walked into his office for the first time. 'A lot of the people you see have already been into work, and are now delivering letters or messages to customers of theirs. It is quicker to deliver post by hand if the contents are important. I love the bustle. It keeps my adrenalin flowing.' They were nearing the offices of Wilkie-Brook's now, and Andrew told himself it was ridiculous for his heartbeat to quicken simply because Charlotte was seeing for the first time the place where their father had worked for many years to build up a thriving business. 'Here we are, my dear sister. Are you ready for my staff to give you the once-over?'

'Of course I am! They can't eat me!' But that was nervous bravado, and Charlotte quickly added, 'You won't leave me alone, will you?'

'I promise I won't let you out of my sight. But I only have three staff, so I'm sure you can cope with that. And they'll be so happy to meet you, you'll find yourself relaxed in no time. And enjoying yourself, I hope.'

'Do you think Father will be pleasantly surprised, or will he think we should have told him yesterday?'

'He will be delighted, I promise you. He'll make a big fuss over you, you'll see. And I couldn't tell him yesterday, for I wasn't sure whether you would back out when the time came.' Andrew turned her to face the steps. 'Don't look so apprehensive, dear. One would think you were walking towards the gallows. Take a deep breath, put a huge smile on that beautiful face of yours, and off we go.'

Wendy Stamford raised her brows in surprise when Andrew walked in with a young lady hanging on to his arm. Fancy him not mentioning he had a girlfriend, she thought. But the reflection was fleeting, and a smile soon appeared on her face. 'Good morning, Mr Andrew.'

'Good morning, Mrs Stamford.' Andrew withdrew his arm from his sister's. 'I would very much like you to meet my young sister, Charlotte. She's come to see where I spend my time and energy.'

Wendy laid down the morning's unopened post. 'Oh, how nice to meet you! We've heard so much about you from Mr Andrew, it's lovely to see you in person.' Her warm smile and hearty handshake melted Charlotte's shyness, and the girl's face lit up.

'I hope my brother told you only the good things about me? If he didn't, then in my own defence I have to say you must not believe half he told you.'

'To hear him talk, Miss Charlotte, you are not only very pretty, but also kind, caring, funny, and the best sister in the world.'

'Good grief, I find myself blushing. But we do get on very well, except Andrew is far more clever than I'll ever be.'

Andrew was standing behind his desk, and he beckoned his sister over. 'Come and sit in the junior partner's chair and see if it makes you feel important. But take your coat off first, so you look the part.'

Wendy helped Charlotte with her coat, and couldn't help feeling the quality of the material. She didn't feel envy, just admiration for the style and colour. 'I'll put this on a hanger for you, Miss Charlotte.'

'Thank you, Mrs Stamford, but I don't want to put you to any trouble.'

'It's no trouble. I'm just so pleased you are here.' Wendy caught Andrew's eye. 'Shall I make a pot of tea, Mr Andrew? I'm sure you and Miss Charlotte have a lot to talk about.'

It was Charlotte who answered, as she sat in Andrew's chair and placed her hands on top of the desk. 'While I'm in this chair, Mrs Stamford, I think I should give the orders. As my brother said, it does make me feel very important.' With that she spun round in the chair and her laughter filled the room. 'You'll have to fight me to get your chair back, Andrew. I love it.'

He winked at his secretary. 'She's still a little girl at heart, so I'll pamper her this once. If it comes to a fight over the chair, though, I would remind you that as my secretary you will be obliged to help me separate her from it.'

Wendy laughed as she made her way out of Andrew's office into her own. 'I'm afraid fisticuffs are not in my contract, Mr Andrew, so I'm afraid you're on your own.' She popped her head round the door. 'Making a good cup of tea is, though, and it will be served in ten minutes.'

Charlotte waited for the door to close before saying, 'I like your secretary. She's very friendly and seems good fun. Are you going to explain what she does for you?'

Andrew sat on the corner of his desk, delighted at the way things had gone so smoothly. Swinging his leg, he began to explain Mrs Stamford's duties, and his sister's eyes grew wider as she listened. 'You mean she can write as quickly as you speak, and then she types all the letters? She must be very clever.'

'Very efficient, Charlotte. She keeps this office ticking over like clockwork. Not alone, of course, for there are two typists in the other office who are very efficient also. But Mrs Stamford is very much in charge of everything that goes on. She worked for Father until I took over some of the business. Then he kindly gave her to me to help me familiarize myself with the many aspects of running an office. And I have to say I'd have floundered without her. She's an absolute gem.'

Charlotte was taking in what Andrew said, and she was

thinking he must be very clever. 'Can I meet the rest of your staff, Andrew, or would I be interfering with their work? I would very much like to meet them, then I'll be able to tell Mother all about it. I must say I am very impressed, and I believe she will be, too!'

Andrew quickly got to his feet, pleased that his sister was showing some interest. 'Of course you can meet them. That was my intention. Come now, before Mrs Stamford brings the tea in.'

To say Nita Williams and Letty Kennedy were taken aback when Andrew walked into their office with a girl on his arm would be putting it mildly. Their fingers hovered over their typewriters as they wondered whether they should carry on working or not. Andrew's introduction and Charlotte's friendly smile quickly broke the ice, though, and soon the clerks were chatting while they made a mental note of the clothes their boss's sister was wearing. The wage they earned was average, and didn't run to such fine, high-fashion clothes. But that didn't stop them appreciating and admiring them.

Charlotte was quite happy asking questions and would have stayed longer, but Andrew didn't want to keep the women from what they were doing. 'I think Mrs Stamford will be ready for us now, so let's not keep her waiting.' He was really proud of his sister as she shook hands and told the clerks she was delighted to have met them. And at the door she turned and wagged a finger. 'You look after my brother, now, or I'll be forced to pay another visit to reprimand you.'

Nita and Letty were delighted. The visit had really made the day special for them. And although they chatted non-stop, their fingers moved as fast as their tongues and the work didn't suffer because of the short break.

* * *

When Wendy Stamford left the office to take the cups and saucers out, Andrew smiled at his sister. 'Are you glad you came, or not?'

'I've enjoyed it, Andrew. You have a very nice staff and I feel a little envious because they are really fond of you. I'll have a lot to tell Mother when I get home, for it has been very interesting and enjoyable. I'll tell her how very clever her son is, and ask why I wasn't born as brainy.'

'Of course you are as clever as me, Charlotte. It's just that you have never been called upon to put your brains to use.' Andrew was of the opinion that his sister had gained something today that she would dwell on. To push it further, unless she showed interest, would serve no purpose. 'I'll take you downstairs to Father's office when Mrs Stamford returns. You can spend some time there, he'll be absolutely delighted, and you can meet his staff. I have correspondence I must attend to this morning, but if you would like I could take you and Father for lunch. There's a very small restaurant I know not far from here. It is in a basement, and only regulars are allowed. Quiet, discreet, with an excellent menu and wonderful food.'

Charlotte pulled a face. 'In a basement, Andrew? Oh dear, it sounds like one of those dives I've heard about.'

His head back, Andrew chortled. 'Oh, my dear sister. You know so much, and yet so little. This restaurant can be so fussy about their customers, there is a possibility they will turn us away because we are not suitably dressed.'

'Now you intrigue me. I will definitely come to lunch with you, and dare anyone to turn me away.'

'Ah, here's Mrs Stamford ready to set to on replying to the mound of correspondence in her arms. I'll take you downstairs and you can be entertained by Father until I pick you up at twelve.'

'Don't forget your coat, Miss Charlotte.' Wendy held the coat while Charlotte slipped her arms in. 'You'll need it when you go out, because it's started to rain.'

'Oh, I haven't brought my umbrella. Aren't I stupid?'

'I have a huge brolly,' Andrew told her. 'Big enough to cover both of us. Besides, the rain may have stopped by then.'

Wendy watched Charlotte walking towards the door, and on impulse called, 'It's been nice meeting you, Miss Charlotte. I'll be able to see you in my mind now, when Mr Andrew talks about you.'

'And I shall be asking after you, Mrs Stamford. Who knows, I may pop in again sometime if my brother allows. Bye-bye for now, though. I have to go and surprise my father.'

George Wilkie-Brook looked up from his desk when he heard the rap on the door, and called, 'Come in.' When his son and daughter walked in, he looked blank for a few seconds, as though he couldn't believe what he was seeing. Then Charlotte giggled and he jumped to his feet. 'My dear girl,' he said, rounding his desk. 'I couldn't believe my eyes. What a pleasant surprise!'

Charlotte ran towards him, her arms outstretched. 'Hello, Papa.' She hadn't called him Papa for years, and he was so moved he gathered her to him.

'I thought it was my imagination at first, but it's wonderful to see you.'

'This is all Andrew's doing, Papa. He wanted to surprise you.'

George looked over her shoulder to where Andrew was standing, a smile on his face. And the look in the eyes of father and son said the same, that this could be the start. 'Why wasn't I informed, or is this a spur of the moment visit?'

'I invited Charlotte to come and see my place of work, as

a birthday present to me. And she very kindly agreed. Mrs Stamford and the others were delighted to meet in person the sister I'm always talking about. And Charlotte, of course, wouldn't come to my office and not to yours. She's been on pins wanting to come down. So I've suggested she stays with you, to be shown around, while I attend to correspondence.'

'Wonderful,' George said. 'It will be my pleasure to give my lovely daughter a tour of inspection.'

'I'm taking Charlotte to lunch, Father, and we'd very much like you to join us. Twelve o'clock on the dot.'

The smile on George's face faded. 'Oh, I am so sorry, but I won't be able to join you! I have a client coming here at half past twelve, and I can't break the appointment because the client confirmed it just ten minutes ago. If only I had known yesterday, I could have made it another time. But it isn't good business to cancel an appointment, especially with one of our biggest customers.'

'Don't worry, Father,' Andrew told him. 'We can make it another time. I'm sure Charlotte can find room in her diary to fit in a lunch with the two men in her life.' He gave his sister a peck on the cheek. 'Work awaits, my dear. I'll call for you at twelve.'

'Don't forget to take your brolly, Mr Andrew.' Wendy Stamford watched him putting his coat on. 'It's raining quite heavily at the moment.'

'I won't forget. I can't let my sister get drowned on her first visit to my office. It would take all her enjoyment away.'

When he hesitated, and looked back at his desk, Wendy said, 'I'll make sure all the post goes out, Mr Andrew, and I'll make a note of all incoming calls. If anyone important rings, I'll ask them to ring back or they can leave a message with me. So go on your way with an easy mind, and have a very enjoyable lunch.'

Andrew took the large umbrella from the stand and placed the curved handle over his wrist. 'At the risk of giving you a big head, Mrs Stamford, I have to say once again that secretaries don't come any better than you.' He bowed from the waist. 'All being well I should be back, at the latest, by three o'clock. And now I bid you farewell.'

Feeling carefree, Andrew whistled as he ran down the steps to his father's office. He was pleased to see Charlotte sitting on her father's huge desk, swinging her legs and looking relaxed. 'You look at home, Charlotte,' he said. 'All you need is a notepad in one hand and a pencil in the other. You'd make a very lovely secretary, and I'm sure business would increase if you were sitting within the view of clients.'

Fastening the buttons on her warm, pure wool coat, Charlotte shook her head. 'I'm not very good at spelling, and even worse at arithmetic, so shorthand would be impossible. Far from attracting new clients, I'd drive away the ones you have.'

'Come along.' Andrew offered her his arm. 'I've ordered them to serve the meal at twelve thirty, and I'd like us to have a drink first. I'm sorry you won't be joining us, Father, but we'll arrange something in the near future.'

'You two youngsters enjoy yourselves. It does my heart good to see you together.' George held his cheek for his daughter's kiss. 'Make the most of being young. It doesn't last for ever.'

'We'll take your advice, Father, but perhaps not today. A quiet lunch is as exciting as it's likely to get. However, it will be an excellent lunch, in a select, comfortable and friendly atmosphere. What more can we ask for?'

After closing the office door behind them, Andrew and his sister stepped down on to the bottom step. 'It's raining very hard, Charlotte, really pelting down. As soon as I have the brolly up we'll make a dash for it. So be ready, or your hair and clothes will be ruined.'

Andrew pointed the brolly to the ground while he felt for the lever to release the spring. Then he opened it up and held it out to protect his sister from the rain as they stepped down on to the pavement. To his dismay he felt the large, sturdy brolly push against someone, and then he heard a cry and the sound of items rolling on the pavement. He instinctively threw the brolly back into the entrance of the office block out of the way, then turned to see what damage he'd caused. To his horror, he saw a girl lying on the pavement, attempting to raise herself up by her elbows. Scattered around her on the wet pavement were letters of various sizes, and the contents of an open handbag.

'Oh, I am so sorry. I was clumsy and thoughtless. It was my fault entirely, and you have my sincere apologies.' He held out his hand. 'Here, let me help you up.'

The girl ignored his hand. She seemed dazed at first, as she viewed the letters lying near her being drenched by the heavy rain. And to Andrew's amazement she began to chuckle, as though finding humour in her predicament. Then for the first time she looked up at Andrew, and he found himself staring into a face that caused his heart to miss several beats. A wide, generous mouth, cupid's-bow lips, hazel eyes bright with laughter, and white, perfect teeth. Framing this picture was a mass of curly golden hair. Andrew was mesmerized and couldn't tear his eyes away, until the girl spoke.

'As you put me down here, the least you can do is help me up.'

Charlotte had never encounted such a situation, and all she could think of doing to help the girl was to pick up her belongings from the pavement. She had them in her hands when she said, 'Please help the poor girl, Andrew, she will be soaking wet. And her clothes must be ruined.'

By this time Andrew had pulled the girl to her feet, feeling shy and awkward. That wasn't like him; he was usually very sure of himself, and never shy in the presence of females. But then again, he had never met a girl who had had this effect on him. He watched as she examined her white raincoat, and wasn't surprised when she was angry at finding that it was filthy dirty, and had a big tear in the back.

Charlotte couldn't understand why her brother was so quiet, when he really should be making a fuss over the girl after the trouble he'd caused. It was no joke being pushed over and having passers-by gawping at you. 'I've collected the letters you dropped, my dear, but I'm afraid they're wet and dirty. And really you must let Andrew pay for your clothes to be cleaned and repaired. It's the least he can do.'

'Of course I'll reimburse you,' Andrew said. 'But would you like to come inside and clean yourself up while we discuss the trouble I've caused? If your coat is torn, then it would be only right that I should pay for a replacement.'

'I am in working time, and those letters should have been delivered by now.' The girl held her hand out to Charlotte. 'I'll take them off you now, and my bag and contents. And I'd like you to tell your boyfriend that in future he should look where he's going. If I'd been an old lady, he could have caused me a lot of pain.'

As she began to walk away, wiping the letters with the sleeve of her coat, Andrew went with her. 'Please let me make amends for my stupidity. As I have ruined your coat and made you late with your work, surely you'll allow me to ease my conscience?'

The girl turned her head and her eyes met his. 'You have also made me ladder my stockings, so you can have that on your conscience as well. For under no circumstances would I take money off a total stranger. I'm sure my coat will clean up, and I can darn my stockings. I'm more concerned about the letters I was sent to deliver. It won't do much for my reputation that I can't even manage such a simple task.' She eyed Andrew. 'Still, I'll live, so don't waste any time worrying about me.' She was a few yards away from him when she called over her shoulder, 'Not that I think for one moment you'll give me another thought.'

Charlotte walked up to her brother and linked his arm, and they stood close together and watched the girl walk up Castle Street with her head held high. She seemed not to feel the rain that was falling heavily.

'That was most unfortunate, Andrew,' Charlotte said. 'But you didn't do it on purpose, so don't feel badly about it.'

Andrew wasn't concerned about what had happened. All he could think of was that the unknown girl was walking away and he'd never see her again. Suddenly that was important to him. As he stood with his sister he didn't question why he felt sad, he just did.

Charlotte pulled on his arm. 'Andrew, I am getting very wet. Can we go now?'

Andrew seemed to come alive. 'Oh, I'm so sorry, Charlotte. I've spoilt your day. I wanted everything to go well, so you would enjoy yourself. How could I have been stupid enough to knock someone over? I've never been so unthinking or careless in my life.' He ran a hand through his hair, sending a trickle of rainwater down his neck. 'And yours is not the only day I've ruined. What about the poor girl I knocked to the ground? Heaven knows what sort of man she'll think I am. Her coat is ruined, and she wouldn't even let me help her. I bet she's cursing me right now.'

'Andrew, I'm getting very wet right now,' Charlotte reminded him. 'Can we talk about this when you've retrieved the umbrella, and we're on our way to this wonderful lunch you promised me?'

Andrew collected the brolly and took her arm. 'I've never upset a young lady in my life, and today I've managed to upset two. What an achievement!'

'Put it behind you, my dear brother. I'll forgive you. And who knows, you may meet that young lady again and you'll have the chance to make amends.'

'I would think that is a very remote possibility.' Andrew brought her to a halt and pointed to an opening which was quite dark, and the flight of stairs going down even darker. 'Don't be put off by the appearance, Charlotte. I can assure you that when you get down those steps you will be agreeably surprised. Trust me, I wouldn't dream of bringing you anywhere I thought you wouldn't be happy.'

Charlotte stared into the darkness. 'It reminds me of a dungeon, a place where they put murderers and all sorts of unsavoury characters.'

To his own surprise, Andrew chortled. 'For heaven's sake don't let André hear you say that, or I will be banished for ever. He is proud of their reputation as one of the finest restaurants in the city. His customers are envied by many who have been denied entrance because his list of regulars is full. The poor unfortunates have to wait until there's a vacancy.'

Still not convinced, but not wanting to offend her brother,

Charlotte suggested, 'You walk down in front of me as you are familiar with the layout.'

It wasn't until Charlotte's eyes became accustomed to the dim lights that she began to believe her brother's words. For the atmosphere alone was sufficient to tell her that this was indeed a place of excellence. The tables in the centre of the room were beautifully set with silver cutlery, heavy napkins, attractive crockery, a lit candle and a tiny crystal vase holding a single red rose. To one side of the restaurant there were four booths, for those who wanted privacy. Charlotte took all this in while waiting for a waiter to show them to a table. 'You were right, brother dear, this looks very promising. What a pity Father couldn't be with us.'

Her words lifted Andrew's spirits, for although he was upset at knocking over a stranger, he was sad for a different reason. The girl had had an effect on his emotions, and that had never happened before. He sighed inwardly, knowing he would probably never have the chance to see that wonderful face again.

'Mr Andrew, you are very welcome.' The owner of the restaurant, André, shook Andrew's hand while smiling at Charlotte. 'And this lovely lady is the sister you were telling me about? How lucky you are to have such a charming sister, but why have you been hiding her?'

The accent was as attractive as the man, and Charlotte was delighted. 'My brother has been keeping you a secret until now, which was very naughty of him.'

'I can't agree with you in his presence, for he is one of my valued customers. But you are welcome here any time, as long as you ring first. Now let me show you to your table, and Alphonso will relieve you of your coats.'

When they were seated, Charlotte voiced her pleasure.

'This is a charming place, Andrew. Why have you not mentioned it before?'

'I can answer your question with one of my own. Why have you never been to my office before? There was no reason for me to mention a restaurant to you when I didn't think you would ever be down in this neck of the woods.'

A waiter came to the table then, and sister and brother took their time to choose from a menu where each dish sounded mouth-watering. 'Oh, I can't make up my mind,' Charlotte said, 'What are you having?'

'I don't eat much at lunch time,' her brother told her. 'If I did I wouldn't be able to eat three courses again at home. I will skip the hors d'oeuvre, and the dessert, but that doesn't mean you can't have what you like. Everything will be excellent, so whatever your heart desires.'

Charlotte closed the heavily embossed menu. 'I'll have whatever you're having. Frances would be upset if we were to refuse our dinners, and Jane too!'

Andrew handed the menus to the waiter. 'Two fillet steak, medium rare, with all the trimmings. And would you ask the wine waiter for a bottle of his best red wine, please?'

While they were waiting, Charlotte asked, 'Will you be telling Mother and Father about the unfortunate incident with that very pretty girl? Or would you rather put it behind you?'

Andrew took a few seconds to consider. 'Oh, I think I should tell them. They'll probably tell me the same as the young lady, that I should look where I'm going. But my shoulders are broad. I can take a ticking off.' And as he spoke, that unforgettable face appeared in his mind's eye, and his heart flipped.

Chapter Four

As Andrew was describing the events of the morning to his parents in their comfortable drawing room, the encounter was also the topic of conversation in another house on the opposite side of the city, far removed from the luxury of the Wilkie-Brooks' mansion.

Poppy Meadows was standing in the middle of the living room, while her mother eyed the damage done to the back of her raincoat.

'The dirt will wash out, that's no problem. But the tear is jagged and won't be easy to repair.' Eva Meadows put her hand to her chin and let out a sigh. 'I'll have a go, Poppy, and do my best.'

Her twenty-year-old son, David, was looking on. A handsome man, he was eighteen months older than his sister. He was very proud of her, and also very protective. 'Why should Poppy suffer because some stupid bloke doesn't look where he's going and knocks her flying? He should fork out to pay for the damage he's caused.'

'He did offer,' Poppy told him. 'To be fair to the man, he did offer to buy me a new coat.'

'You should have taken him up on it,' David said. 'It would teach him to be more careful in future. He could have seriously hurt you.'

'Well, he didn't hurt me. Except I've probably got a bruise on me bottom, but no one is going to see that. And me pride was hurt. I must have looked so stupid lying flat out on the ground, with me belongings strewn all over the pavement. The post I was carrying was in a right mess, but the clients were very nice about it and said accidents couldn't be helped. In fact one client wanted me to sit down and they'd make me a cup of tea.'

'Well I still think you should have let the bloke reimburse you,' David said. 'He's probably got more money than you.'

'I'm not taking money off a strange man.' Poppy's eyes flashed. 'What do yer think I am?' She was quite indignant. 'He looked like a toff, and I wasn't going to lower myself to him. He was with his girlfriend, and the coat she was wearing must have cost a fortune. They talked like toffs as well.' Then Poppy had a vision of Charlotte, and added, 'The girl was very nice, though, and very helpful. In fact they were both nice to me.'

Eva, a widow of forty-two, worked in a local factory as a seamstress. Her husband had died of TB when he was only thirty-five, leaving her to bring up eleven-year-old David and nine-year-old Poppy. Life was hard then, and she had little time to grieve for the husband she'd adored. Forced to take a full-time job, she had worked all the overtime she could get so they could stay in the six-roomed house that held so many memories of her beloved husband. Still, life was easier now, with her nineteen-year-old daughter bringing in a regular wage, and in a few weeks' time David would finish his apprenticeship as an engineer and start earning a man's wage. Her son was the spitting image of his father, and had the same mannerisms, the same crooked grin and the same sense of humour.

Eva shook her head to clear the memories, and smiled at her daughter. Poppy was still standing in the middle of the room, and she raised her brows questioningly. 'A penny for them, Mam. You were miles away then.'

'No, I was only thinking what we could do with the coat for the best. I could wash it tonight, let it dry for a day or so, then take it into work with me and do the best I can. It won't be perfect because of the ragged tear, but it would do you a turn until you got another.' Eva sighed. 'But what could you wear in the meanwhile?'

Poppy shrugged her shoulders. 'I've got that grey three-quarter-length, though heaven knows that's seen better days. Still, if I wear a colourful scarf to brighten it up, it wouldn't look too bad. Not tonight, though, 'cos I've got a date. I'll wipe the dirt off this coat as best I can, and hope no one notices the blinking tear.'

'Who's the date with?' David asked. 'Anyone we know?'

Poppy slipped the raincoat off and draped it over her arm. 'You don't know him. His name's Pete and I met him at the Grafton. And before yer give me the third degree, he's tall, dark and handsome, and a smashing dancer.'

'Julie usually goes to the Grafton with you,' Eva said, her eyes narrowed. 'Is she going on the date with you?'

'She met a bloke as well, Mam, and she made a date with him. His name is Jim, and they're going to the flicks. But we're not going out as a foursome. I don't know where I'm going with Pete; probably to the pictures.'

'Why don't you ever bring any of the blokes home with you?' David asked. 'You know our mam worries about you, which she wouldn't do if she knew who you were going out with.'

'You're a fine one to talk,' Poppy said. 'What about the girls you go out with? Yer've never brought one home for Mam to see if she approves.' Then her mouth stretched in a smile and her eyes twinkled, 'I know, Mam, it's because the only girls he can get are either cross-eyed or buck-toothed.'

David's guffaw brought a smile to his mother's face. She was proud of both her children, and happy that they got on so well together. 'I'll tell yer what, sis, I'll bring my date home if you'll bring yours.'

'I'm not bringing a bloke home when I've only just met him. If I said I wanted him to meet my mother, he'd think I was serious about him and run so fast I wouldn't see his heels for dust.'

Eva leaned against the sideboard, her arms across her tummy. 'D'yer know anything about this Pete? Tall, dark and handsome isn't enough. I'd rather yer had a steady boyfriend who was honest and hard-working. Being a good dancer doesn't mean a thing. Yer can't spend the rest of yer life dancing.'

'Mam, I'm nineteen! It'll be a few years before I think of courting and getting married. And I don't know how we went from me not having a coat to wear, to me going to the flicks with a bloke who is nice enough to keep me company, but not the sort I'd fall head over heels for. When I do meet someone I really like I'll let yer know. But I warn yer, it might be a long time, because my ideal man would look like Cary Grant, sing like Frankie Lane and dance like George Raft. Oh, and he'd have to be rich enough to keep me in nice clothes.' Poppy took a deep breath, then blew it out slowly. 'That's the longest speech I've ever made, and I'm back to square one with no coat to wear.'

'If you're only going to the pictures, you can wear the raincoat,' her mother said. 'No one is going to see it. It's dark out and dark in the picture house.'

David left his seat to put his arm across his sister's shoulder. 'I go on full pay soon, kid, and although it'll take me a few weeks to sort me money out, I promise I'll go half with yer for a new coat.'

'I'll help out, too,' Eva said. 'The three of us can each put ten bob away for four weeks, and that should be enough for a good coat.'

'I can't let yer do that,' Poppy said, her eyes wet with tears she was determined not to shed. 'You're the best mam and brother anyone could have, and I love yer very much. But I'm a big girl now, and I've got to learn that if I want anything, I've got to save up for it. I can't sponge off you. I earn a wage same as you, and if I have to stay in every night for a few weeks, it won't kill me.' The threat of tears gone, her eyes filled with mischief and she giggled. 'If Pete turns out to be good company, I won't need to use my own money. I'll see if he takes me in the best seats tonight, and if he does I'll know he's not skint and make another date with him. That's if he asks me, of course.'

'You shouldn't do that, sweetheart,' Eva said. 'It wouldn't be fair on the poor man if you lead him on just for the sake of using him.'

'Oh, Mam, I was joking! You should know me better than to think I'd really give any bloke the runaround for the sake of a few bob. I like nice clothes, yer know that, but I'm fussy how I come by them. And if you'll tidy the raincoat up as best yer can, I'll wear it until I've saved up for a new one.'

David left his chair and made a dash for the door. 'I bags the bathroom before you, sis. I didn't realize the time with all the talking. If I don't put a move on I'll be late for my date.' Taking the stairs two at a time, he called down, 'Ten minutes, kid, I promise.'

Poppy stood in the hall with hands on hips and shouted up the stairs, 'You sneak, David Meadows! What sort of man would treat a lady like that?'

'A man who doesn't want to keep a lady waiting, that's who.' The bathroom door closed on his voice promising, 'Ten minutes, kid.'

Poppy put her arms round her mother and hugged her tight. She could remember her father, and knew how much her mother missed him. And she remembered how hard she'd worked to keep the house going. 'I'll stay in tonight, Mam, and keep you company. I know it's mean to let Pete down, but if I ever see him again I'll say I didn't feel well.'

'You'll do no such thing, Poppy Meadows; that would be a mean trick. And you shouldn't tell lies, 'cos God will pay you back if you do. So let's see if we can sponge the dirt off the raincoat and make it presentable. Not that your date will worry about how it looks, anyway. He'll be too busy looking at your pretty face.'

In the kitchen Eva spread the raincoat over the scrubbed wooden table. 'One thing yer have to be thankful for, sweetheart, you've had plenty of wear out of it.' She ran a clean cloth under the tap, then wrung the excess water out. 'If it had been a good coat, I would have agreed with David that yer should have let the bloke buy you a new one.'

Poppy was leaning against the sink, watching. 'I could never do that, Mam; my pride wouldn't let me. Anyway, there's no point in dwelling on it: what's done is done and we can't turn the clock back. At least I was knocked down by a very handsome toff, and not a scruff.'

Eva lifted her eyes from the coat she was wiping down. 'Oh, so he was handsome, was he?'

'Yes, I'd say he was. And his girlfriend was beautiful. Well dressed, make-up perfect, and the perfume she had on certainly wasn't one and eleven a bottle like the one I use. But for all that, both of them were really nice to me. They were genuinely upset by what happened, and even asked me if I would like to go with them to get cleaned up.'

Eva showed her surprise. 'You didn't mention that before, sweetheart! Where were they going to take you?'

'I couldn't tell yer that, Mam, because I just wanted to get away as soon as possible. They came out of one of the office buildings, but I was so embarrassed I couldn't tell yer which one, except it was in Castle Street, on the left hand side going up.'

'Don't you think yer were a little hasty, sweetheart? You weren't pushed over on purpose. It was an accident.'

'I know that, now I can think straight. But it wasn't exactly pleasant lying flat on the pavement and having people gathered around me. I felt really stupid. Hysterical, really. I even started laughing, so yer can tell how hysterical I was. And I took it out on the man and his girlfriend. I was really rude to them, and I'm sorry now. But it can't be helped; it's over and done with.'

Eva lifted the coat off the table and held it up for inspection. 'I'll stand in front of the fire with it while you're getting washed. It's come up all right, so no one will ever notice.'

'You're an angel, Mam.' Poppy gave her a hug. 'I'll run up and get meself ready 'cos I'm late already. I'll wear me blue dress; it's me favourite.'

Peter Broadhurst had been standing by the bus stop for twenty minutes and was giving up hope. Three buses had stopped while he'd been there, and each time he'd had to stand back so the driver wouldn't expect him to jump on board. He was a nice-looking man, over six foot and well built. With black hair, deep brown eyes, a dimple in each cheek and healthy teeth, he was never short of girlfriends. And he wasn't used to being kept waiting. He looked at his watch now and saw it was nearly eight o'clock. He'd never waited this length of time for anyone before. But this date was one he'd looked forward to, and he was disappointed. The girl he'd arranged to meet, who'd said her name was Poppy, was the most attractive girl he'd ever seen. And she wasn't coy or fawning like some girls, which he couldn't stand. Poppy, if that was really her name, had refused when he'd asked her for a date, and it had taken all his powers of persuasion to talk her round. He gave a sigh of disappointment, because he'd been looking forward to seeing her again. Still, he'd been let down and there wasn't a thing he could do about it. He turned the collar of his overcoat up and was about to walk away when he saw her hurrying towards him.

'I'm sorry I'm late,' Poppy said, slightly out of breath with walking quickly. 'I had an accident with my coat, and I almost didn't come because I didn't expect you to wait so long.'

Peter was studying her face as she was speaking, and he told himself she was exactly the same as the vision he'd had of her in his mind since he'd met her at the Grafton. He'd never been as attracted to any girl as he had been to her, and now, by the light from the street lamp, she was even more beautiful than he'd imagined. 'I'd almost given up, but I'm glad now that I waited that little bit longer.' He cupped her elbow. 'You are well worth waiting for. A sight for sore eyes, a vision to delight the eye.'

'Don't overdo it, Pete. I can't stand false flattery.' Poppy grinned, 'Don't take any notice of what I said, 'cos there isn't a female alive who doesn't like to be flattered. By the way, is your name Pete?'

He shook his head. 'I get Peter at home. Only a few of my friends call me Pete, and never within earshot of my mother, who says, "His name is Peter. Had I wanted him called Pete, I would have had him christened Pete."'

'I'm on your mother's side,' Poppy said. 'Peter is a nice name.'

He cupped her elbow. 'Where would you like to go? Dancing or the pictures? Mind you, we would have missed all the shorts at the cinema.'

'Let's go to the pictures,' Poppy said. 'Myrna Loy is on at the Odeon, and I could do with a good laugh. We'd be in time for the big picture. Unless there's somewhere else you would prefer to go? I'm easy.'

'It's what you want, Poppy. I asked you out.' He turned his head. 'There's a tram coming now, or would you prefer to wait for a bus?'

'No, I love the trams. They'll all be gone soon, they reckon, and there'll only be buses. I'll be sorry, 'cos they've always been part of Liverpool and I'll miss them.'

'Then let's make a run for it.' Peter grabbed her hand and pulled her after him. 'Make the most of them before they disappear.'

Seated by the window on the tram, Poppy said, 'You're nothing if not a man of action, are you? You really pulled me off me feet then. For a while I had visions of being flat out on the ground for the second time today.'

Peter paid the conductor for two tickets to Lime Street, then turned to ask, 'What did you mean? Have you fallen over once already?'

A smile hovered around Poppy's mouth. 'I didn't fall, I was pushed. And that was the reason I was late meeting you. My mother had to wash the dirt off this coat and make it presentable.'

'Who the heck pushed you over? Were you larking about?'

'I wasn't larking about, I'm too old for that. No, some bloke pushed me over with his umbrella. He couldn't help it – he didn't see me because he was opening it up. But I landed on the ground looking ridiculous.'

'I don't believe you could ever look ridiculous, Poppy. And by the way, is Poppy your real name? I've never known a girl with that name before.'

'I'm not the only girl in the world called that, it's just that there aren't many in Liverpool. It was my dad who chose the name for me, and my mam gave in to him. I'm glad she did 'cos it means I'll never forget him. I was eight or nine when he died, but I can remember him telling me one day that him and me mam had gone for a walk in the country with my brother David in his pram, and they came across a field full of poppies. My mother was expecting me at the time, and that's why my dad chose the name. So there you have it, Peter: my life story on the tram going into Liverpool.'

'It's a nice story, and I'm on your dad's side. I think it's a lovely name and it suits you.' Peter glanced through the tram window and saw they were passing St George's Hall. He jumped to his feet, saying, 'This is our stop.'

Poppy stood in the foyer of the cinema and waited for Peter as he went to the kiosk for the tickets. When he came back, he handed her a box of Cadbury's chocolates. She felt embarrassed, hoping he wasn't leaving himself skint. 'You shouldn't have bought them, Peter. I'm quite happy coming to the pictures.'

'I have a fairly decent job, Poppy, so you don't have to worry your pretty head about me. And now, if we don't want to miss the beginning of the big picture, I suggest we move ourselves.'

When the usherette showed them to seats in the back stalls, Poppy's mind went back to when she'd laughingly told her mother that if her date took her in the best seats she'd know he wasn't skint. But that had been in fun, and the truth was she didn't like blokes spending money on her, especially if they were on poor pay.

They had only just settled in their seats when the lights were dimmed, and Poppy sat back to enjoy Myrna Loy, one of her favourite stars. She opened the box of chocolates, offered it to Peter, and said, 'Help yourself, save me passing it to you.' Then she fixed her eyes on the screen, and was laughing at the antics of Myrna Loy and her dog when she felt a hand covering hers. She froze for a few seconds, thinking she didn't even know the bloke and he had a bit of a cheek. Then she decided it would be childish and churlish to make a fuss. So she ate the chocolates with one hand while her other remained captive.

When the lights went up, Peter was very attentive. He took the half-empty chocolate box from her, then turned up the seats to make the way out of the row easier. Once outside the cinema, he put his arm round her waist as they walked to the bus stop. Poppy felt he was being over-familiar, but he'd behaved more like a gentleman than many of the men she'd dated, who had straying hands. Some of them thought that when the lights went down in the cinema it was time to get something in return for the money they'd forked out for her ticket. She'd walked out halfway through a film more than once because she couldn't stand being mauled.

'You don't have to see me home, Peter,' she said. 'Not if it's out of your way.'

'Good heavens, Poppy, what sort of man would let a young lady make her own way home after a date? I don't know about any of the other dates you've had, but this date takes the young lady right to her front door, so I know you get home safe and sound.'

Poppy couldn't resist the retort that came to her lips. 'Even on the first date? I mean, I wouldn't mind to the top of the street, but to the front door suggests I'm not capable of looking after myself.'

'Not at all,' Peter told her. 'I believe you are more than able to look after yourself. Perhaps I'm old-fashioned, and if you think that, well, I'm sorry. But that's the way I've been brought up. If I offended you, then I apologize.' He handed her the half-empty box of chocolates. 'If you prefer to make your own way home, I won't stop you.'

Poppy reached for his arm as he turned to walk away. 'Good grief, Peter! What are yer taking the huff over? I didn't mean to insult you.' She waited until he was facing her before she told him what she hadn't even told her mam and her brother. 'I'm not usually so sarcastic, letting me tongue run away with me like that. I told you what happened to me this morning, and I've made light of it to everyone because I didn't want them to feel sorry for me. So, trying to be clever and brave, I put a false face on. And I've done the same with you. The only reason I'm telling you this now is because I don't want you to think I'm rude and sarcastic. The truth is, though, it wasn't only me pride that was hurt, it was the bottom of me back and me two elbows. And it was a shock to me whole body. I ache all over. I didn't tell me mam or she'd be worried sick and fuss over me. And my brother would have insisted on finding the bloke who knocked me over and giving him a piece of his mind.'

'Here comes the bus, Poppy, and I'm getting on it with you, even though it is out of my way. I asked you for a date, you agreed, so let's do what most couples do when they date. I'll take your arm and see you home safely. And in return, you can be nice to me and say that if I ask you for another date, you'll agree.'

Sitting by the window on the bus, Poppy couldn't find any excuse in her head not to like him. He was good-looking, dressed and spoke well, and wasn't big-headed or pushy. 'We could go dancing one night,' she told him. 'I'd have to meet you inside because I always go with my friend Julie. We've been friends for years and I wouldn't let her down.'

'And would your friend object if I joined you? I do want to be friends with you, Poppy. I was attracted to you as soon as I set eyes on you in the Grafton.'

'You are very persuasive and persistent, aren't you? I'm surprised you haven't got a steady girlfriend already. Or do you have half a dozen to choose from?'

'I've had several dancing partners, and one or two girl-friends.' The bus swayed and Peter was thrown closer to her. He quickly pulled away and put a hand on the seat in front to steady himself. 'But I've never had one I liked well enough to take home to meet my mother. Does that satisfy your curiosity?'

Poppy grinned. 'I'm giving you a hard time, aren't I? I'm not always like this, honestly. This just happens to be your unlucky day, unfortunately. But I'll make it up to you at the Grafton, I promise. And in case you haven't noticed, the next stop is where I get off.'

'Correction,' Peter said, standing in the aisle to let her out. 'It's the stop where we both get off.'

Peter wouldn't let Poppy talk him out of walking her right

to her front door. She wasn't too happy about it, for now he knew exactly where she lived. And no boy she'd ever been out with had got any further than the corner of the street. That was because none of them had lit a flame in her heart. Her mother had told her she'd know the man who was right for her as soon as she saw him. If just being near him didn't set her heart beating, then a touch of his hand, or a kiss, would light the flame.

'Shall we meet at the Grafton tomorrow night, then?' Peter asked. 'Although I would prefer to meet you outside and escort you in. And your friend, of course. A casual meeting in a dance hall isn't a date, but if it's the only way I can get to see you, then so be it. But before I bid you goodnight now, will you promise to come out with me again? Just the two of us?'

When Poppy didn't answer right away, fumbling in her bag for the door key, Peter gripped her arm. 'Please say you will, Poppy, then I can go to sleep with a smile on my face.'

'Oh, I'd better agree then,' Poppy said, thinking he hadn't put a foot wrong all night, or said anything she could fault. He'd been thoughtful and attentive, and she wasn't going to tell a lie to let him down. He deserved better. 'I'll see you on Wednesday at the Grafton. And I promise I won't be late this time.' She put the key in the door and pushed it open. 'Thank you for a nice night – I've enjoyed meself.' She stepped into the hall. 'Goodnight, Peter. See you Wednesday.'

Chapter Five

'Well, how did the date go, sweetheart?' Eva searched her daughter's face. 'Was the boy nice?'

Poppy gave her mother a hug. 'Mam, he wasn't a boy, he's a man. I stopped going out with boys when I was sixteen.' She draped her coat over her arm. 'He's about twenty-one or two, I would guess. And yes, he was very nice. Well dressed, well spoken, and just the type you would bring home to meet the family. Not me, of course – I've only been out with him tonight for the first time, so I wouldn't know what he's really like. He could have been on his best behaviour, trying to make a good impression.' Then she felt a stab of guilt. 'I'm being unfair to him, Mam, 'cos he was well mannered and treated me like a lady.' She handed over the chocolate box. 'Not only the best seats, but a box of chocolates to go with them. He did the job properly – even insisted on bringing me home right to the door.'

'He sounds a good person, sweetheart. You should have asked him in. I think I've only ever met one boy you went out with, and although I didn't say it at the time, I really wasn't impressed. He wasn't the sort I would like for a son-in-law.'

Poppy went into the hall to hang her coat up, and she was laughing when she came back. 'Oh dear, Mam, that was years ago. I remember the lad now: his nickname was Ginger 'cos he had red hair. Oh, and he had pimples all over his face. But I didn't go out with him, Mam. I was only sixteen and he walked me home from a dance at the church hall.' To her mother's surprise, Poppy took a fit of laughing. Bent over double, she spluttered, 'He doesn't have pimples any more. What he does have is the last laugh on me, you, and all the other girls around here. I saw him last week and he was driving his own car! He stopped to ask how I was, but I think it was only to make sure I didn't miss the car. His dad used to work in a garage, as a mechanic. He told me his dad owns the garage now, and the car was a birthday present.'

'Go 'way!' Eva looked astonished. 'Driving a car at his age? I didn't think it was allowed.'

'Oh, I think you can drive at seventeen or eighteen, as long as you pass a test. Anyway, Ginger looked the picture of health and very prosperous. And I say good luck to him. He deserves it, after all the ribbing he got at school. The lads in his class gave him a terrible time. That's why I danced with him, 'cos I felt sorry for him. But he's got the last laugh at all the lads who made fun of him.'

Eva nodded. 'You always get paid back if you make fun of anyone worse off than yerself, sweetheart. I hope I've drummed that into you and David. And now would you like a cup of tea, and you can tell me what the film was about? And are you seeing this young man again?'

'I won't have a drink, thanks, Mam. But I am seeing Peter again, so that's one little bit of news for you. I'm meeting him in the Grafton on Wednesday. Yer know I always go with Julie, and I'm not going to let her down. He wasn't very happy about it, but he can't expect me to let a friend down when I've only known him a few days.'

Eva agreed. 'Never let a friend down, sweetheart, because a good friend will be for ever, while a boyfriend can be here today and gone tomorrow. Unless he's the man you want to spend the rest of your life with.'

'I've never met one yet that sent a shiver down my spine.' Poppy tilted her head. 'I remember you saying that the first time my dad looked into your eyes, your feet tingled and your heart beat fifteen to the dozen.'

'I can remember that feeling as though it was yesterday,' Eva said with a touch of sadness. 'And the first time he kissed me I thought my legs were going to give out on me 'cos they turned to jelly.'

'I hope I get that feeling one day, Mam, but I've got plenty of time.'

'I was only seventeen when I fell in love with your dad,' Eva said. 'And I remember my mam and dad telling me I was too young to be courting. They gave yer dad a hard time, I can tell you. I was so embarrassed when they asked him about his family, where he worked, and had he ever courted anyone else before me? It's a wonder he didn't wipe his hands of me.'

'He didn't though, did he, Mam? I was only young, but I still remember that he used to kiss you before he went to work every morning, and when he came home. And when he thought me and David weren't watching, he used to put his arms round you when you were by the sink washing the dishes. Me and David would giggle when you used to say, "Away with you, the children might come in." '

There were tears in Eva's eyes, but they were tears of thankfulness that her children had never forgotten their father, and talked about him openly. How proud he would be now if he could see how they had grown into kind and caring adults.

'You go to bed, sweetheart,' she said. 'I'll wait up for David. He should be in any minute.'

'No, I'll wait up for him, Mam,' Poppy said. 'You have to go out to work, same as us, so you need your sleep.'

They heard the key turn in the lock and smiled at each other. 'Well,' Poppy said, 'here's the man himself, so it saves any argument.'

David came in looking very pleased with himself. 'Did I hear someone saying argument? Surely not! We don't have raised voices in this house, let alone full-scale arguments.'

'Someone is looking very happy,' Poppy said to her mother. 'Is the look on my brother's face the look you were telling me about when love is in the air?'

David was humming as he hung his coat in the hall. 'Can't a bloke be happy without his family thinking there is something wrong?'

'It wouldn't be wrong to fall in love, son.' Eva gave Poppy a sly wink. 'I think your cheerful face and glazed expression speak volumes. So who is the girl who brought all this about?'

Poppy nodded her agreement. 'She must be some girl to have managed that in one night.'

David sat on the arm of the couch, his face still wearing a smile. 'You women don't half have a vivid imagination. And if it wasn't so late I'd hang around just to see how far your fanciful imagination will take you.'

'Me and me mam are both tired and ready for bed,' Poppy told him. 'So why don't you just tell us the girl's name to be going on with? That would satisfy us for tonight, and you could fill in all the details tomorrow.' She gave her mother a gentle dig. 'Such as when the wedding is?'

David's guffaw was loud. 'Oh dear, oh dear! Well, I guess I'm going to have to come clean if any of us are going to get some sleep tonight.' He looked from his mother to his sister. 'I hope you are both strong enough to take this, and won't faint on me.'

'David, so help me I'll clock you one if you don't put us out of our misery. And I mean right now! Me mam has to be ready for work at half seven, and me half an hour later. So, out with it.'

'Right! If you insist, here goes. I have spent a very pleasant evening with a very good friend. And tonight I won the hand of that good friend.'

There were gasps from Eva and Poppy. Surely he would have told them if he was going serious with a girl? But he'd never even hinted at it! 'This is all very sudden, David,' Eva said, with visions of her lovely son getting married and leaving home. 'How long has this friendship been going on?'

David rubbed his chin as though deep in concentration. Then he answered, 'Oh, since we were both in the infants, all the way through to leaving school.' He bit on the inside of his cheek to stop himself laughing. 'You'll remember who I'm talking about, Mam, when I tell yer I used to play marbles with him. Of course you remember Vincent Bellamy. He was never away from our house.'

Not a sound came from his mother and sister, who were looking at him as though he'd gone crazy. 'The hand I said I won was a hand of whist. The first time I've ever beaten Vincent since I've been playing with him. But I beat him tonight, and I feel on top of the world.' He chuckled. 'He looked as if he was ready to cry his eyes out. He's good at cards, but he's a lousy loser.'

Poppy looked at her mother. 'Will you hit him or shall I?' Then, before Eva had time to answer, Poppy had grabbed the evening paper, rolled it up and let fly at her brother's shoulder. He raised his arm to protect himself, but brother and sister were laughing so much they ended up clinging to each other. 'We fell for that all right. Me and me mam thought yer were out with a glamorous girl, and all the time ye're having a game of ruddy cards with a lad yer went to school with!'

Eva was curious. 'When you go out every night, son, saying you've got a heavy date with a girl, are yer telling the truth or pulling our legs?'

'I usually go out with a girl, Mam, but I'm not going steady with any particular one. I don't want to settle down yet – I want to enjoy my freedom while I'm young and fancy-free. But I go to Vincent's at least one night a week, sometimes two. We're good mates, enjoy a game of cards with a bottle of beer, and have a good laugh.'

'I'd like to see Vincent some time, David. I don't think I've set eyes on him since you left school,' Eva said. 'But right now I'm so tired I'm having trouble keeping my eyes open. You two stay down as long as you like. You've got youth on your side, but me, I'm dog-tired and I'm off to my bed. Goodnight and God bless.'

'I'm coming up with yer, Mam. I'm tired meself.' The bottom of Poppy's back was stiff and sore, and she was hoping a night's rest would cure it. 'We'll have a night in sometime, and talk about all our schoolmates and how many of them we still see. But no secrets, our David. We'll be asking you about any girlfriends yer've got or had. But right now I'm going to follow me mam's example and go to bed.'

'I'm going to make myself a quick cuppa,' David said. 'I'm thirsty.' He took his mother's hands, saying, 'Goodnight and God bless, Mam. And when I go on full pay in a few weeks, I want you to pack in your job. You've worked long enough to keep this house going, and it's time for you to retire. Not that you'll be idle, for you'll still have the housework to do, plus the washing, ironing and shopping. But you can do those at your leisure, and sneak off to a matinee when you feel like it. Or go into town with Margie one afternoon to look round the shops and go to Reece's for tea and a cake.'

Eva patted his cheek. 'We'll talk about that tomorrow, son. I'm too tired now. I could do with two matchsticks to keep me eyes open. Try not to make a noise when yer come to bed. I'm hoping to drop off to sleep as soon as my head touches the pillow.'

Poppy linked her arm. 'Me too, Mam. I'm bushed. Good-night and God bless, our kid.'

'Goodnight and God bless, little sister.'

Poppy sat up in bed when her mother called to say breakfast was on the table. She slipped her legs over the edge of the bed and shivered when her feet touched the cold lino as they searched for her slippers. She cursed herself for kicking them off before she got into bed, instead of placing them neatly together so she just had to slip her feet into them. She had a warm dressing gown, thank goodness, and she tied the belt before walking on to the landing. From the bathroom she could hear the sound of running water, and tutted because her brother had once again beaten her to it. The trouble was, she always turned the alarm clock off when it rang, promising herself just another five minutes in the warm bed, and then she'd get up. But on cold mornings it was hard to keep that promise when the bed was warm and the room was cold.

'Good morning, sweetheart.' Eva carried a plate of toast in one hand and a cup of tea in the other. She put them down in front of Poppy, and smiled. 'Your brother beat you to it again, did he?'

Poppy smiled back. 'It's my own fault, Mam. I hate getting out of me warm bed. But our David adds insult to injury when he's singing at the top of his voice while I'm shivering.'

Eva sat facing her daughter with her two hands round her cup. 'Men don't feel the cold like we do, sweetheart. I don't know why, but they don't.'

'I don't mind David going first, really, 'cos he warms the bathroom up with the hot water. So it won't be freezing by the time I get up there.'

'You need to wrap up warm today, sweetheart,' Eva warned. 'I think we're in for snow. It's certainly cold enough for it.'

Before taking a bite out of the piece of toast she was holding, Poppy said, 'I'll put a thick jumper on. My raincoat is fine in wet weather because you can wear anything underneath and nobody knows the difference. They're too busy rushing to get their business done and be back in work out of the rain. But I need a decent coat for when the winter really sets in. It would be warmer than my raincoat.'

'You'd probably get a decent one in T. J. Hughes for a few pound, love, so why don't you nip up there in your dinner hour?'

'Mam, I've only got about fifteen shillings to my name! I'll have to save up for a few weeks to raise enough cash.' Poppy's eyes flew wide as she had an idea. 'I know what I'll do, Mam. If I've got money in my purse I'll spend it, 'cos I've no willpower. So I'll give you ten bob now, and you can mind it for me. And I'll do the same next week, and so on. If I haven't got it, I can't spend it. So do me a favour, and if I try to cadge some of the money back, just refuse me point-blank.'

Eva pushed her chair back and picked up her cup and

saucer. 'It's time I was on my way. But give me the ten bob before I go, then you can't be tempted. And when I get me wages on Friday, I'll add ten bob to your money.'

'You'll do no such thing, Mam, or I'll be annoyed. You haven't had a new coat for years, and you need one more than I do.'

Eva put her dishes in the kitchen, then popped her head round the door. 'You're a young girl, sweetheart, and I'm an old woman. No one would notice if I went out in a coal sack.'

Poppy was indignant, and David came into the room just as she was saying, 'You are not an old woman, Mam, you're in the prime of life! And I'm not going to let you spend your hard-earned money on me. We'll both save up and buy ourselves a coat. And I bet the person who serves us will think we're sisters. So I'll leave me ten bob note on the sideboard, and you can add your money to it. When we've both got three pound, then we'll get the bus down to TJs and buy ourselves a coat.' She started to giggle. 'The neighbours will think we've bought them out of a catalogue and are paying a few shillings a week off them.'

'I've never worried what the neighbours thought, sweetheart, and I'm not going to start now. They don't pay the rent or put food on the table, so why fret about what they think?'

David had plonked himself down next to Poppy, and listened with interest while chewing his toast. 'I heard most of that, but can someone tell me the beginning? I missed that bit.'

Eva went into the hall for her coat, and as she was putting it on she said, 'I haven't got time, son. I'm going to have to run. Poppy will tell you.'

They heard the door close after their mother, then David asked, 'Well, what was all that talk about money for?'

'I can't tell yer word for word, David, 'cos I haven't got time either. But it started with the weather being cold, my raincoat not keeping me warm, and me saying I'll put ten bob a week away to buy meself a new coat. That's why that ten bob note is on the sideboard. If I've got money on me I'll spend it. I'm too weak-willed.' She reached for the teapot and filled up her cup. 'Anyway, mam said she'd put ten bob away with mine, so I could buy my coat sooner. But I wouldn't have that under any circumstances, because our mam has always gone without to make sure we never went cold or hungry.' She pushed her chair back. 'Look at the time! I haven't even washed yet. I'm going to have to run like the devil. You can hear the rest tonight, if you're still interested.'

David left his chair to kiss her cheek. 'You go. I'll clear the table and wash the dishes. And I'm not going out tonight, so we'll have a real family discussion about money. You're right about our mam, she's one in a million.'

Poppy made a dash for the door, calling over her shoulder, 'See yer tonight, our kid.'

Poppy was thoughtful as she sat on the bus taking her into the city centre. The conversation she'd had with her mother had set her thinking that if she'd listened to Eva a few years ago, things would be very different. She'd started working as a junior in the offices of John Sutherland and Son when she left school at sixteen, and at that time she was eager to be as efficient as the older women who worked there. So she'd registered at a local school for lessons in shorthand and typing, two nights a week. But while she loved typing, and soon reached the speed required by employers, she couldn't get the hang of shorthand, and hated it. So against her mother's advice and wishes, she had opted out of the shorthand lessons after a few weeks.

It was too late now for regrets, Poppy thought, looking at the buildings they were passing without really seeing them. Her mam had told her she would be sorry if she didn't stick with the course, and how right she was. To be a private secretary, and earn a good wage, shorthand was essential. And if she hadn't been so headstrong, and had listened to her mother, she'd be earning more money now, and they would be able to afford new coats. Letting out a long sigh, Poppy asked herself if she had the nerve to pocket her pride and register once again for a course at night school. That's if the school was still doing the courses, and if they would sign her up again if she asked.

The conductor came along the aisle and stopped by her side. He'd had his eye on her since she got on the bus. She was certainly a looker, a girl to turn the head of any red-blooded man. 'This next stop is yours, miss.'

Poppy returned to reality. Another ordinary day lay ahead of her, and the prospect did nothing to lift her spirits. 'Thank you.' She smiled at the conductor as she slid off the seat. 'Nose to the grindstone for eight hours.'

He grinned back at her. 'Yer can stay on this bus all day if yer like, and I won't charge yer. It would be a pleasure looking at your face, instead of some of the miserable buggers we get on.'

'I don't think my boss would be very happy if I took a day off without leave. But the offer is very tempting, and I thank you.'

Once off the bus, Poppy stood on the pavement until there was a break in the traffic and it was safe to cross the busy road to the offices of John Sutherland and Son. And standing outside looking up at the windows of the building, a little voice in her head asked if she wanted to spend the next few years being a typist and a messenger. Doing jobs any school leaver could do. All because she was too proud to admit she was wrong. Then she answered the voice in her head. No, she didn't want to waste her life, having to make her clothes last until they were shabby. She would go back to the night school and if it meant begging them to give her another chance, then she would beg. And it was with a determined mind that Poppy mounted the steps to the office.

'Miss Meadows, would you please deliver these two letters for me?' John Sutherland junior stood beside Poppy's desk holding out two envelopes. 'They are really important and they need to be delivered immediately.' He looked down into Poppy's face, and not for the first time he wished he was in a position to get closer to her. He would be delighted to meet her outside office hours, for she was by far the most attractive woman he knew. His interest wasn't in having a serious relationship, as his father would be very much against that because of the difference in their social status. But a clandestine affair was something he'd had in mind for the last year or so. He would love to book a room in a hotel out of town and shower her with silk underclothes, the likes of which she would never have seen in her life. He would be prepared to spend a lot of money to win her over.

Poppy was frowning, wondering why Mr John was standing there just staring at her. She began to feel uncomfortable, and said, 'Is that all, Mr John? I'll finish this letter I'm typing, then deliver your mail.' When he didn't move, she asked, 'Was there anything else?'

'No, that's all, Miss Meadows. Will you wait for replies to the letters, and bring them immediately to my office? Thank you.'

When he'd gone, Poppy felt herself shiver. She had no reason to dislike Mr John, but he had the effect of making her feel uncomfortable. It was as though he was undressing her with his eyes. And whenever he handed her anything, his hand always brushed hers.

Poppy was still thinking of John Sutherland when she put her coat on, picked up the two sealed envelopes and left the office. There had been times when she'd felt like telling him to keep away from her, but the fear of losing her job had always held her tongue. Money was tight enough at home as it was, and if she lost her job the family would really be struggling. Squaring her shoulders and holding her head high, Poppy made herself a promise. She'd make enquiries tonight about night school, and under no circumstances would she talk herself out of it. If she could get a better job, with more money to put towards clothes for herself, and a bigger contribution to the family housekeeping, life would be vastly improved for herself and her mother. It might take six months to master shorthand and get up to speed, but it would be worth it. She could find herself another job and tell Mr John where to go. Let him ogle someone else.

Walking up Castle Street, as she did almost every working day, Poppy's mind was so full that she didn't take any notice of the people passing to and fro. So she failed to see the man walking down the street towards her until he was almost upon her, and then she panicked. She recognized him as the man who had pushed her over with his umbrella, and her one thought was to avoid him. There was no time, however, for Andrew had recognized her and stood in her path.

'Please don't run away. I mean you no harm.' Andrew looked into her face and found his heart reacting as it had yesterday. It pounded so hard, it was a wonder she couldn't hear it. 'I'm glad we've bumped into each other again, for I don't feel my feeble apology for knocking you over reflected how badly I felt.'

Poppy tried to sidestep, but he barred her path. 'You don't need to apologize. There was no harm done. Apart from my vanity being hurt, for I must have looked a complete idiot lying on the pavement and laughing. It wasn't laughter, actually, it was hysteria. But I'm quite all right, so you don't need to have a guilty conscience over me.'

'You could help me ease my conscience,' Andrew said, not wanting her to walk away, perhaps out of his life for ever. 'I really do feel dreadful, causing you so much pain and humiliation. Not to mention the damage to your clothes. I would regard it as a great favour if you would allow me to compensate for my action?'

'I'm sorry, but I couldn't possibly take anything from you. My pride wouldn't allow it. Besides, it was an accident. You didn't deliberately knock me over. You apologized at the time, as did your girlfriend, and I was quite satisfied with that.'

'That wasn't my girlfriend, it was my sister!'

Poppy was flustered. 'I'm sorry, it was an easy mistake to make. She is very pretty.'

'Actually, she said the same about you. She was quite upset on your behalf.'

'That was very kind of her. But I really must go now. I am in working hours, and it is important that I deliver these letters.'

'I'll come with you.' Andrew didn't want to leave her. 'I've left the office to go on an errand for my father. It isn't urgent, so I can walk with you.'

Taking in the quality of his fine clothes, and conscious of the tear in the back of her well-worn raincoat, Poppy shook her head.

'You are very kind, but if you don't mind I would prefer to go on my way alone. You see, this is working time and I can't afford to dawdle. But I appreciate your willingness to atone for the accident, and it's been nice seeing you again. Remember me to your sister.'

Andrew watched her walk away, and he felt sad. But at least he knew she delivered letters daily to somewhere in the vicinity, and his father was always in need of cigars. He would see her again, he had to. She had affected his heart and his mind like no other girl. And he needed to find out why.

Chapter Six

David was in the kitchen talking to his mother when they heard the key in the door. He hurried through the living room and was in the hall when his sister closed the front door. 'Where have you been till this time, Poppy? Our mam's been worried to death. She wanted me to go out looking for you, but I wouldn't have known where to start. She had you under the wheels of a bus, and other things just as dramatic.' He took his sister's coat and hung it up. 'Where have you been?'

'I'll tell you when we're sitting down. I'm not going to tell it twice over.' Poppy patted his cheek, then pulled a face. 'You need a shave, brother. I nearly cut me hand on yer stubble. It's easy to see yer haven't got a hot date tonight.'

Eva's voice came through from the kitchen. 'It's sausage and mash tonight, so sit yerselves down and I'll bring the dinners in. Oh, David, get the HP Sauce out of the sideboard, save you getting up once we're settled.'

When they were seated, brother and sister next to each other and their mother facing, Eva picked up her knife and fork and cut into a sausage. 'Well, sweetheart, are yer going to tell us why ye're so late? You had me worried to death.'

'Let's start on our dinner first, before it goes cold. Ten minutes isn't long to wait, and I hope you'll be happy with what I've got to tell you. Surprised and happy.'

David finished his dinner first, and as he carried his plate out he said, 'I'll put the kettle on for a pot of tea, Mam, then when the tea's made I'll fill it again to wash the dishes. You stay where you are and finish your dinner in peace.'

Finally, dishes were washed, the white tablecloth had been shaken in the yard, and a maroon chenille cloth now covered the table. 'I've sugared the tea, Mam, so all you and Poppy have got to do is drink it. I've spoiled yer tonight, but don't expect it all the time.'

'Your effort has been much appreciated, son, and now if you can manage to stay quiet for a few minutes, we can hear what Poppy has to say. Go on, sweetheart, tell us what you've been up to.'

'It's a long story, so it's a good job we'd all planned a night in. Anyway, I'll start by saying that on the bus going to work this morning, I finally grew up.' When Poppy saw her mother about to speak, she put up a hand and said, 'No, Mam, let me get it off me chest, then yer can ask me anything yer want. What started me off was that ruddy raincoat, and my need for a decent winter coat. And you, Mam, you need one just as much as me. Anyway, I got to thinking that if I had stuck to that shorthand course when I was sixteen, life would be much easier now. I'd have a better job as a secretary, earning a good wage. As it is, typists are two a penny and I'll never get anywhere in life.' Poppy's laugh held little humour. 'I made up my mind that it wasn't too late to start again. I'm still only nineteen. And if I had any misgivings, they soon disappeared when my boss gave me two letters to hand-deliver to another firm in Old Hall Street. I've been a messenger for three years, but today was the final straw. I haven't given me notice in or anything, 'cos I can't afford to. But when I got off the bus tonight, I went straight to the school where they have night classes, and I've signed up for a course, starting next Monday night. Two nights a week, Monday and Thursday, and it's a three-month course.' She faced her mother. 'I'll stick to it this time, Mam, I promise. You were right, I was wrong.'

Eva and her son exchanged glances. This didn't sound a bit like their Poppy, the beautiful girl who was full of fun and always had a smile on her face. 'Listen, sweetheart, there's no need for you to worry about money. We manage, don't we? I know we could both do with a warm coat, and we'll get them, you'll see.'

'I'll make sure you do,' David told them. 'Don't forget, in another few weeks I'll be the man of the house, and responsible for my family being well fed and clothed. They won't be fur coats yer get, the money won't run to that. But they'll be nice coats for the two best-looking women in the street.'

Eva chuckled. 'Ay, don't let Margie Boden next door hear yer saying that, or she'll have yer guts for garters.'

Poppy sounded more like herself when she told her brother, 'Margie is nice-looking, and she is always well dressed. Plus she is the funniest woman on two legs. And her daughters are both very pretty.'

David lifted his hands in surrender. 'Okay, I said the wrong thing. Now, our kid, what else have yer decided that we should know about?'

'There's nothing much I can do, not until I'm qualified for a better job that pays more money. But I'm going to work hard at night school, and practise at home as well. And if my wishes come true, and both you and me are bringing a good wage in each week, David, then our mam can pack in work.'

Eva tutted. 'I wish you and David wouldn't worry so much about me going to work. I enjoy my job, and the women I work with. If I was at home I'd be bored stiff. Besides, I like to earn a wage. I don't want to live off you.'

'Can I add my thoughts on what's been said so far?' David leaned his elbows on the table. 'I know it's two against one, but I'm a lot bigger than you, so by rights that makes us equal. So, while you two have been airing your views and putting the world to rights, I've come up with a solution I believe will suit everyone.'

'Out with it then, son,' his mother said. 'We've got all night to sit and natter. It doesn't happen very often that the three of us sit talking, so we may as well make the most of it.'

'Well, let's take it in stages, otherwise we'll still be sitting here in the morning. First let's get your coats settled. We haven't got the money to buy them now, so it'll be a few weeks at the earliest. I'll put a quid away each week with your ten bobs, so in three weeks you'll have enough to buy the coats. They'll be cheap ones, but they'll do to be going on with. Does that go down well?'

Poppy's head was nodding like mad. 'That would be wonderful, David, and very generous of yer.' She put an arm across his shoulder and hugged him. 'The best brother in the world, bar none, and I love the bones of yer.' She sat back in her chair, feeling happier than she had all day. 'Now you've said your piece, and I'm sure me mam will agree with what I've said, I'll tell yer what's been going through my mind while you were talking. I'm going to give meself four months to be competent enough to apply for a post as a secretary. I'll go to the classes twice a week, and I'll practise at home every night. Not that I'll be missing me nights out, 'cos I won't. But I'll get an hour's practice in before I go out, come what may.'

'Don't build yer hopes up, sweetheart,' Eva told her daughter. 'Even if you pass the course with flying colours, it doesn't mean you'll walk straight into a job. It would be lovely if yer did, but I'm just warning you 'cos I'd hate you to be disappointed.'

'I won't, Mam, don't worry about that. I'll walk the feet off meself until I do get a decent job.'

'At least you'll have a respectable coat to wear for your interviews,' David said, adding in his head that with her looks and figure, his sister should have no trouble finding a decent job.

'Now can I have my say?' Eva asked. 'You both talk of wanting to earn money so I can pack in working. And while your heads have been busy making plans for me, my own mind has been working overtime planning what I'd like to do with my life. I've still got over ten years to go before I should retire officially, and I can't say I relish the thought of another ten years of getting out of bed at half six every morning. Then again, I don't relish the idea of ten years not working. So what I've come up with is a compromise that would suit me down to the ground.'

With the eyes of her son and daughter alive with interest, Eva continued, 'I would like to work part time. Say four mornings a week, if the boss would let me. I am practically certain he would, 'cos I'm the most experienced machinist he's got. That way I would have the best of both worlds. I'd have some free time to meself, and I'd have money of my own.'

'Oh, Mam, that's the perfect solution, if your boss will let you do that. Oh, I feel a darn sight better than I did earlier on. It all rests on me getting meself a good job, but I'm very determined.'

'It sounds good to me, Mam,' David said. 'I wouldn't have to worry about you going out at some unearthly hour every morning in the winter. It's a way to go yet, although my money will improve in a few weeks. Then you and Poppy will get your coats, which will be two things we can cross off our list. The future looks rosy, Mam, and if we had any drink in, I'd suggest we lifted our glasses to toast the future prosperity of the Meadows family.'

'Oh, I've got a little surprise for yer, son, 'cos there's still half a bottle of sherry left from Christmas. It's in the larder on the bottom shelf, but I don't know whether it will still be fit to drink.'

David was off his chair like a shot. 'Alcohol doesn't go off, Mam, it improves with age. I'll get the bottle, and Poppy can get the glasses. We'll have a little family celebration.'

As Poppy walked towards the sideboard where the few glasses they possessed were kept, Eva said, 'At least you'll look respectable when yer do go after another job, sweetheart, 'cos we'll have our new coats by then, please God.'

Poppy stood with her hand on the door of the sideboard, a smile on her face as something came to mind. 'Ay, every time we've mentioned those ruddy coats, I've been going to tell yer about something that happened today. But there's never been a real break in the conversation.' She turned to the kitchen. 'Come in, David, save me going over it again.'

Her brother came in carrying a bottle aloft. 'It's half full, ladies, we're in luck.' He put the bottle on the table and took hold of the three glasses his sister was handing over. 'Sit down, sis, and I'll pour.'

'Only half a glass for me, son,' Eva said. 'Drink always gives me a headache.'

'Half a glass it is then, Mam. And now we're settled, my dear sister can tell us about the other brainwave she's had.'

Poppy stuck out her tongue. 'It was no brainwave, clever

clogs, because me brain stopped working when I bumped into the bloke who knocked me over yesterday.'

Surprised, Eva said, 'Go 'way!' while David swallowed a mouthful of sherry before saying, 'You didn't, did you?'

'Well, strictly speaking, I didn't actually bump into him, but he was standing in front of me and I couldn't walk through him. If I'd seen him coming I would have crossed the road, but my head was in the clouds and I didn't see him until he was standing in front of me. He's very well spoken, very posh, and really good-looking into the bargain.'

'What did he have to say for himself?' David asked. 'I hope you told him about the state of your raincoat.'

Poppy shook her head. 'He was so nice I couldn't bring meself to argue with him. He couldn't apologize enough for being so clumsy, and he wanted to compensate me for any damage to my clothing. I was glad I was facing him and he couldn't see the tear in the raincoat. I have to say I believe he's a good bloke, very kind and understanding. But I couldn't let it go at that, stupid person that I am. I had to be sarcastic. And it served me right when I told him he and his girlfriend had apologized enough, and he informed me it wasn't his girlfriend, it was his sister.'

'Oh, I don't think he'll be stopping you again, sweetheart,' Eva said. 'Fair play to the man if he went out of his way to say again how sorry he was, and to offer financial help for any damage. To be turned down twice is like a snub, so I doubt you'll see him again.'

'I did think about it a few times during the day, and my conscience pricked me. I'm not usually rude to people, but I think I was peeved at the time because it's hard to be dignified when ye're scrambling to get up off the pavement. Anyway, as yer said, Mam, he'll probably give me a wide berth in future.'

Poppy saw her brother filling up his glass, and she passed her empty one over. 'Don't be hogging the bottle, David. You're not the only one with a thirst.'

David held the bottle up to the light. 'Just enough for another glass each.' He grinned mischievously, then relented. 'Okay, kid, a glass full for you, and a half one for me. Then we're quits.'

While Poppy and her brother raised their glasses of cheap sherry, only the finest wine was being poured in the dining room of the Wilkie-Brook residence. The family had finished their meal, and the housekeeper was clearing away the dishes. 'Shall I bring in the coffee now, Miss Harriet?' she asked, 'or would you prefer it a little later?'

'We'll have it now, Frances, please. We've got friends coming for a hand of whist, and we'll be retiring to the drawing room then.'

Andrew waited until the door closed on the housekeeper before saying, 'Don't count me in for the cards, Mother. I'm not a good player and I don't enjoy it anyway.'

'Me neither, Mother, so count me out too,' Charlotte said. 'I find it so boring. I would much prefer to go for a run in the car.'

Harriet was not pleased. 'Really, Andrew, you and Charlotte should know you do not go out when we have visitors. The Hedleys would think it dreadfully rude if you weren't here. I'm disappointed you could even consider insulting them so.'

'Mother, I will willingly be here to welcome them, and also put in an appearance when they are leaving. But I really would like some time on my own. Perhaps, as Charlotte mentioned, a short run in the car.'

Charlotte clapped her hands, her face aglow. 'Oh, that

would be absolutely thrilling, Andrew. Can I come with you?'

Harriet's lips were set in a straight line, which was not a good sign, and George knew his wife would waffle on until she talked the children into giving in to her wishes. And he wasn't in agreement with her. He and his wife, and the guests they were expecting, were a different generation from Andrew and Charlotte, and were quite happy to spend the evening playing cards. But it wasn't fair that the youngsters should be bored. And he approved of Charlotte's going out with Andrew. He was more down to earth than his sister, and would teach her there was more to life than shopping for clothes she didn't need, or playing tennis with friends who also led idle lives. 'I agree. Our children should get out more, Harriet, my love. Andrew is cooped up in the office all day and needs some fresh air. And Charlotte would be good company for him.'

'But our guests, George! What will they think? That they are not good enough company?'

'Harriet, my darling, have you forgotten what you were like at their age? When we were courting you would never consider a night at home having a game of chess with your parents. Every night you insisted on my taking you to the theatre or a dinner dance. You quite wore me out.'

She gave him a stern look. 'We were courting, George, planning on marrying each other. The situation is quite different. Andrew and Charlotte are brother and sister, and single.'

'And that is how they will remain if they are confined to their home every night. They are hardly likely to meet a partner if they're playing cards with people twice their age.' There was love in his smile which melted his wife's heart. Briefly she went back over the years, and she could see herself with George, walking across the ballroom floor at the Adelphi hotel, he so handsome and she in a pale blue, full-skirted evening gown.

'You are quite right, my love. I had almost forgotten what it was to be young and carefree.' And in a rare show of affection in front of the children, she left her chair to kiss his cheek. 'You were very dashing in those days, George, and I was the envy of all my friends.'

George took hold of her hands. 'And you, my love, are as lovely today as you were then.'

Andrew and Charlotte looked on with amazement tinged with emotion. To make light of his feeling of sentiment, Andrew said, 'This is almost as good as sitting in the Playhouse watching a romantic play.'

His father chuckled. 'You may find it hard to believe, my boy, but your mother and I were very much in love, and we weren't afraid to show it.'

Harriet returned to her chair, the stern look replaced by a shy smile. 'Your father is right, I'm turning into an old fuddy-duddy. You should be with people of your own age. So poppy off, the pair of you, and enjoy yourselves. I'll tell the Hedleys you had a previous engagement.'

Charlotte jumped to her feet, her face beaming. 'Can we go to Southport, Andrew, to the Prince of Wales hotel? There may be a dinner dance on.'

'I'm not making any promises, Charlotte, because it would mean my changing into suitable clothes. And I really don't feel like that sort of night out. What I had in mind was a drive into the country, where it would be quiet and peaceful. Not quite up your street, dear sister, but I'm prepared to take you to one of your friends' houses, if you like. You could make a few phone calls and see if there is anything on which would be more to your taste than a drive in the country.'

Charlotte shook her head vigorously. 'No, I would much prefer to come with you, Andrew. We could stop at one of those quaint hotels and have a drink. I would enjoy that very much.'

'No fancy clothes, Charlotte,' Andrew warned. 'We go out in the clothes we're wearing now.'

Harriet's jaw dropped. 'That is unthinkable, Andrew! You've worn those clothes all day! Really, I'm surprised at you.'

George would have intervened, but Charlotte got her words out first. 'Mother, we are going for a drive in the country, and nobody in the country dresses up because they never go out.'

'That's not quite how it is, Charlotte,' George said. 'You do have a lot to learn. People who breed cattle, or work in the fields, play a very big part in our lives. Without them you would have no bread on the table, or meat and potatoes on your plate. Plus, of course, vegetables and fruit. They could not produce those very necessary foodstuffs if they worked the fields in top hat and tails.'

Andrew bit back the words that came to his mouth. His sister would never understand that there were people who didn't possess a change of clothes. She had never known poverty, as indeed he himself hadn't. But he was well aware that there were people who, through no fault of their own, were living hand to mouth. 'Come on, Charlotte, let's go. A breath of country air will do us both good.'

Charlotte wrapped the rug over her knees and tucked it in each side to keep the cold out. 'Where are we going, Andrew?'

Andrew set the car in motion and backed out into the

road. 'I thought we'd drive to Crosby, then on to Southport through all the pretty villages. We can stop for a drink at one of the country pubs, then go along the coast road. I need fresh air to blow the cobwebs away, so we could walk around the lake if it isn't too cold for you.'

'Oh, it won't be too cold. This coat is very warm and I'm wearing a scarf and gloves.'

'Oh, talking of your coat has reminded me of something,' Andrew told her. 'It's nothing exciting, but remind me to tell you when we stop for a drink.'

'It can't be very interesting if it's only about a coat, so you may as well tell me now.'

'I can't take my eyes off the road, Charlotte, and I want to see the expression on your face when I'm telling you. You have the type of face which gives away what you are really feeling, which means you are not good at lying, or hiding your reactions.'

'You've contradicted yourself there, Andrew, and have now got me very curious. First you say it's not exciting, and then you say you want to see the expression on my face when you're telling me. It's nice to know I'm not good at telling lies, for I should hate anyone to think of me as a liar.'

'Have patience, my dear sister, I'll tell all when I don't have to keep my eyes on the road. And don't look forward to my having something of great importance to tell you, because you'll be disappointed. In fact I'm regretting already that I even mentioned it.'

They drove on with little conversation between them, except for pointing out a particularly nice house or garden. Presently they came to a country pub with a thatched roof, and old-fashioned lanterns in the windows which lit up the cosy interior. 'Oh, isn't it quaint?' Charlotte said. 'Please let's go in. It is absolutely charming.'

Andrew laughed at her expression. She was nineteen years of age, but still a little girl at heart in some ways. 'Keep your voice down when we go in, Charlotte, for they're country folk around here and might not welcome toffs in their local. Nor would they appreciate anyone they thought was looking down on them.'

It turned out that Andrew's warnings were not needed, for the manager behind the bar beamed a welcome at them, as did the men sitting at the small round tables with pints of ale in front of them. Weather-beaten faces, rough hands, heavy farming boots still bearing traces of soil, and coats torn and smelling of animals and earth. After a day toiling in the fields, the farmers were exchanging views on the state of the crops and the cattle. Their talking had ceased when the strangers walked in, until the smiles and greeting from Andrew and Charlotte had the men treating them like one of their own, which is the way of country folk.

'Sit by the fire, miss, and I'll put another log on.' The manager came from behind the bar and picked up a log from the pile next to the huge stone fireplace. 'It's a raw night out there.'

The farmers all agreed in their local accent. They weren't used to having customers in their bar who were obviously not from their neighbourhood. They were quite taken with the pretty Charlotte, who had never seen anything like the two-hundred-year-old pub with its old beams and flagged floor. She was intrigued and enchanted, asking all sorts of questions of people who were more than happy to reply. Her smile genuine, her eyes bright with interest, she loved the warmth and the atmosphere. The small pub was like a wonderland to her, and she fell in love with it. And when

Andrew suggested it was time to leave, she begged him to stay a little while longer, reminding him he had something to tell her about. So Andrew gave in, on the understanding that it didn't look good sitting there talking without buying a drink. Not good for business.

When Andrew ordered two glasses of port, and a round of whatever the farmers wanted, plus the landlord himself, there were many voices and glasses raised in thanks.

'That was very thoughtful, Andrew,' Charlotte said, 'and I'm so glad you did it, for they are such friendly people. I bet Father would love this place.'

'You can tell him about it, Charlotte, but don't mention it to Mother, for she wouldn't approve of me bringing you somewhere like this.'

'You will bring me again, though, won't you?' his sister begged. 'If I ask you nicely?'

'Only if you will be quiet while I tell you what happened today.'

'What did happen today, Andrew? Was it something that pleased you?'

'I bumped into the young lady I pushed over yesterday. You remember her, don't you?'

'Of course I do! I could hardly forget such a happening. Did you ask if she had been hurt?'

'She barely spoke to me. I offered to compensate her for the cleaning or repairing of her coat, but she said she would never take money off me, and as she was perfectly all right I shouldn't worry about her. It was an accident and couldn't be helped. And with that she flounced off as though she couldn't get away quickly enough. Oh, she did say my girlfriend had been very kind, and when I said you were not my girlfriend but my sister, she said you were very pretty.'

'That was nice of her, considering the circumstances. Although I have to say she is far prettier than me. I really thought she was quite beautiful.'

Andrew nodded. 'I would very much like to see her again. To get to know her. I really was taken with her, Charlotte, but unfortunately she doesn't want to know.'

His sister leaned across the small table to look into his face. 'I do believe you've fallen for her, Andrew. Or am I imagining it? Has Cupid been busy with his arrow?'

'I've only met her twice, and she's made it quite plain that she would be perfectly happy never to set eyes on me again. And yet I can't get her out of my mind. I have never felt like this about any girl, my dear sister, and I hope I can trust you to keep what I've told you a secret. I don't know the girl's name, or where she lives or works, or if she already has a boyfriend, or even a husband. All I know is that she walks past our office block every day, or has done for the last two days, and she delivers letters for a firm. And while I am very sure that I would like to get to know her, she seems equally sure she doesn't want to have anything to do with me. I'm telling you this because I need to tell someone.'

'How could she not like you?' Charlotte couldn't understand anyone's not liking her brother. He was good-looking, kind, caring and very lovable. 'I'm sure if she got to know you she would like you. If you've met her two days running at the same time, why can't you meet her tomorrow? Wait for her to come along and pretend it's a coincidence.'

'I'm sure she wouldn't fall for that. In fact it would probably cause her to change her route, and then I'd never see her again. I don't even know her name, so how can I find out where she works or lives?'

Charlotte had many ideas running through her head at the

same time, making it impossible to think straight. She'd go over it in bed tonight, and come up with a way to help the brother she loved. 'Can I make a suggestion, Andrew? I know I'm not as clever as you, but if you let a week go by before bumping into this girl of mystery, then she wouldn't think anything of it. She'd put it down to being a pure accident. But don't push her too hard, or she might not like it. As you say, she may already be spoken for.'

Andrew sighed. His sister was right. He couldn't push the girl into liking him. He'd leave it for a week, and then try again. If persistence might pay off, then persist he would.

Chapter Seven

While she was sorting the morning mail into separate piles for the two partners, Poppy kept an eye out for Jean Slater coming out of Mr John's office, where the secretary was at present taking dictation from him. She'd been summoned to his office soon after he arrived, for apparently when he reached his home last night he had remembered a very important letter that should have been answered by return of post. It was from one of the firm's best clients, and he had put it aside, intending to give it special attention after he'd dictated replies to the other letters. However, the matter had slipped his mind. Now he wanted a reply sent off as soon as possible, which meant, of course, that Poppy would be ordered to deliver it post-haste. And he would probably check the times she left the office and returned.

Poppy heard the office door open and Jean came out with pad and pencil in her hand, and a not too happy expression on her face. She rolled her eyes as she passed Poppy's desk, and said softly, 'He slips up, but everyone else has to take the blame. He can be very unpleasant when things don't go his way, and if I didn't need the money I'd have told him long ago to get lost.'

Poppy made sure the office door was still closed before crossing the floor to the secretary's desk. 'If you think you are hard done by, how d'yer think I feel? I'm the sucker who will be expected to deliver that letter, running all the way. Is it any wonder I want to get away?'

'Are you still intent on shorthand lessons?' Jean asked. 'You'd be a fool if you don't.'

'I've already signed up for the full course. Two nights a week for twelve weeks.'

'Good for you.' Jean put a sheet of paper into the typewriter. 'If and when you do qualify, don't take a job here if Mr John offers you one. I've seen the way he looks at you, and you'd be better off with another firm. He likes the ladies does Mr John, and with his money there's plenty of empty-headed females that fall for him. He never tells them he's a married man with children, though; he conveniently forgets that. I feel sorry for his wife.' She gave a sigh as she thought of the long day ahead. 'Anyway, I'll get on with this letter or he'll have something else to find fault with.'

'Just before yer start, Jean, can I have a quick word? Now I've got me mind set on bettering meself, I can't wait to start. So can yer tell me where I could buy a book on shorthand, so I'll at least know a little about it when I go to the first lesson next Monday?'

Jean opened a side drawer in her desk and took out a book. 'You can have this. I don't need it any more. As you can see, it has been well thumbed, but you might learn something from it. And persevere, Poppy, because you deserve better than this. It may take you weeks to get the hang of it, but keep going because it'll pay off in the end.'

Poppy was just closing her desk drawer after putting the book inside when Mr John came through from his office. 'Have you finished that letter yet, Miss Slater? I did tell you it was urgent.' He took a watch out of the pocket of his waistcoat and glared, as though the watch was responsible for his mistake. If the client, who was a very important person, rang his father to complain, there would be a real rumpus. The only person Mr John didn't look down on was his formidable father.

'I shall have it ready in five minutes, Mr John,' Jean said, her fingers flying over the keys. 'I'll bring it in for you to check as soon as I've finished.'

'No time for that. As you get paid for being a competent secretary, there should be no spelling errors. I shall merely sign it, and then Miss Meadows can deliver it by hand as quickly as possible.'

Poppy could see Jean's back stiffen and knew the secretary was finding it hard to refrain from giving her very ungentlemanly boss the answer he deserved. So Poppy spoke up with a smile on her face, hoping to smooth things over. 'If I can run as quickly as Miss Slater types, the recipient will soon have the letter in his hand. She is the quickest typist I've ever seen.'

John stood in front of Poppy's desk, and whether he intended to rebuke her or not no one would ever know, for one look at that beautiful face, with its generous mouth, wonderfully shaped lips and laughing hazel eyes, was enough to restore both his good temper and his appetite for a closer relationship with the delightful typist. 'I'll order a cab for you, Miss Meadows. We can't have you running there and back. As soon as Miss Slater has the letter ready, I shall ring the taxi company.'

Poppy was stunned. But she soon regained her voice when she saw the lust in his eyes. 'Certainly not, Mr John. I get paid to deliver the letters and I wouldn't dream of allowing you to call me a taxi. We can't have the rest of the staff thinking it's favouritism. It would cause me a lot of trouble. Teacher's pet, that sort of thing.' Poppy gave him her brightest smile, thinking she'd gone far enough. The last thing she needed was to lose her job. 'It was very thoughtful of you, and I appreciate that. But I quite enjoy the walk each day.'

Although Jean Slater had been typing at her usual speed, she hadn't missed a word of the conversation going on behind her back. And she gave full marks to Poppy. Most of the typists would have jumped at the offer of a taxi to take them on their rounds, but they would never be given the chance because they didn't have the looks or figure to whet Mr John's sexual appetite.

'The letter is ready now, if you will sign it, Mr John?' Jean placed the letter flat on her desk, and as soon as her boss had signed it she called Poppy over. 'Wait for an answer, Miss Meadows.'

Mr John stood behind the two women. 'And come to my office the instant you get back, Miss Meadows, as the answer may require a response.'

Poppy didn't reply. She picked up the letter, took her coat from the stand and left the office. Once out in the street, with people passing to and fro, she stood for a few seconds shivering. That was the effect John Sutherland had on her. The sooner she didn't have to see his lustful eyes, or feel his breath on her neck when he was leaning closer than necessary, the happier she would be. Roll on the next few months.

Poppy didn't take her usual route up Castle Street, for fear of bumping into that bloke again. She thought she'd heard his sister call him Andrew, but she wasn't sure. Anyway, she'd go a different way today, just in case. It wasn't that she was angry with him – what happened had been a pure accident. And she didn't dislike him, for he seemed a nice, polite bloke. In fact she couldn't put her finger on why she felt uncomfortable in his presence, she just did. Perhaps it was because he was so well spoken and wore such expensive clothes that he made her feel inferior. But Poppy dismissed that idea as she ran up the steps to the office where the letter was to be delivered. There was no reason to feel inferior: she was as good as anyone. Her mother had drummed that into her and David when they were young and money was tight. Clothes don't make the man or woman, she used to tell them. It's what's inside that counts.

'You're early today, Poppy.' The woman sitting at the desk behind the open window smiled. 'An hour early, to be exact.'

Poppy handed the letter over. 'My boss told me to deliver this as quickly as possible.' She pulled a face. 'I didn't mind me mam telling me to run all the way there and back when I was a kid going to the corner shop on a message, but I'm a bit old to be spoken to like that now. If I didn't need the money, I'd have told him to keep his job.'

The woman, whose name was Amy Wright, checked whom the letter was addressed to before saying, 'If I was a betting woman, I'd lay ten to one that your boss is the young Mr Sutherland, and this letter should have been here yesterday. Am I right?'

Poppy nodded. 'I don't know what happened. Mr John must have slipped up. He wouldn't admit it, though – he's too big-headed to confess he'd made a mistake. Anyway, I've got to hang around for an answer, so can I come through and wait? It's blowing a gale and freezing out here.'

Amy grinned. 'It's not much warmer in this tiny cubbyhole. I've only got a one-bar electric fire. Anyway, Poppy, come on through. I'll take the letter up to Mr Fortune and see if he wants to reply straight away or not. Stand near the fire and warm yourself ready for the return journey. I'll be as quick as I can be, but like you I don't have a very understanding boss.'

Amy Wright was back before Poppy had time to feel the

benefit of the pitifully inadequate electric fire. 'I don't know whether I'm better off than you or not, Amy. Half an hour ago I would have gladly swapped places with yer, but at least we have heating in our office, whereas yer could freeze to death in here.'

'The partners here have heating in their offices, but they're too tight-fisted to consider the rest of us.' Amy sighed. 'Anyway, Poppy, there's no reply for you to take back. Mr Sutherland will be getting a telephone call. And if a tone of voice is anything to go by, the conversation is going to be a heated one.'

Poppy chuckled. 'Oh, I hope he gets cut down to size. It's about time someone gave him down the banks. He loves his little self, but God's gift to women he isn't.' She wrapped her scarf tightly round her neck and shivered. 'I'll get going and walk quickly to keep meself warm. And I think I'd be wise to keep out of Mr John's way. If I see him coming, I'll make a dash for the ladies. That's one place he wouldn't dare enter.' She walked out of the door, then waved to Amy through the window. 'See yer tomorrow. Ta-ra.'

Waiting to cross the busy main road to get to the office, Poppy saw Mr John coming out of the building. He was wearing a scarf tucked inside his tailored overcoat, and his hands were being kept warm by fur-lined gloves. Poppy was hoping to avoid him, but unfortunately he had spotted her, and he waited for her to cross the road. There was no smarmy smile on his face now, and his words were clipped when he said, 'See the rest of the mail is attended to, Miss Meadows, as I have an important meeting to attend. It is possible I won't be back in the office until early afternoon. In that case I want you to keep yourself busy going though the filing cabinets and making sure all files are in order. My absence is no excuse for shirking. Is that quite clearly understood?'

'Yes, Mr John,' Poppy said aloud. But in her mind she was saying that understanding didn't mean doing. She wasn't a shirker by nature, but being spoken to as though she was not only lazy but also stupid was hard to take. Nobody, no matter how rich they were, should look down their nose at someone just because they weren't rolling in money.

Back in the office, Poppy found Jean Slater so angry and tearful she could hardly speak. 'Wait until I hang my coat up, and then we can go to the ladies and you can tell me what it is that's upsetting you. There's no hurry, 'cos I've just met Mr John and he won't be back before our dinner break.' Her coat on the stand, Poppy took Jean's arm and steered her from the office.

'I was near to tears, and so angry I wanted to tell Mr John what I really thought of him, and give in my notice.' Jean swallowed hard to try to rid herself of the hard lump that had formed in her throat. 'If I didn't need the money so much, I would have walked out. Ten years I've worked here, and never been late, or taken a day off sick in all that time. And what thanks do I get? None whatsoever.' She rubbed the heel of her hand across her eyes. 'Mr John doesn't know the meaning of the words respect and loyalty.'

Poppy put an arm across Jean's shoulders. 'You're shaking like a leaf, love. Don't let it get to yer. Tell me exactly what happened. Yer'll feel much better when you get it all off yer chest.'

After a few sniffs, Jean said, 'Mr Fortune was on the phone just before you came back, and although I didn't hear every word I heard enough to know that Mr John was being taken down a peg or two. Mr Fortune is a man of very few words, normally, but he obviously didn't like Mr John's attitude on the phone, and threatened to take his business elsewhere.'

'Oh, is that where he's off to now?' Poppy felt as though someone had given her a present. To hear that Mr John had been given a taste of his own medicine lifted her spirits. 'But that should have made you feel good, Jean, not reduced you to tears.'

'It would have done if he hadn't put the blame on me. He told Mr Fortune that his incompetent secretary had placed his letter with some others, and then mislaid it. And he was telling those lies about me when I was standing listening! I mean, how low can you get? According to him, he hadn't done a thing wrong, it was his secretary, and she would be severely reprimanded. So, Poppy, what price ten years' loyalty? Ten years never putting a foot wrong.'

Poppy was shaking her head in disbelief. 'He said that knowing you were there, listening?' When Jean nodded, too full of emotion to put her thoughts into words, Poppy said, 'There is something wrong with that man if he thinks he can do something so evil and get away with it. He's not normal. I don't think he should get away with laying the blame at your door for his mistake. Can't you complain to someone, and make him apologize?'

'There's no one to complain to.' Jean shrugged her shoulders and let out a long sigh. 'Apart from his father, there's no one above him who could reprimand him.'

'I've never spoken to Mr Sutherland senior in the three years I've worked here,' Poppy said. 'Is he all right to get on with, or is he like his son?'

'He's very strict, is Mr John senior, and doesn't have much to say to any of the staff, only his secretary. He's the old-fashioned gentleman type. Raises his blocker to ladies, never swears, and is strictly teetotal. Anyway, there'd be no point in telling him his son is a liar, among other things, because Mr John would turn the tables and say it was me telling lies. I may as well forget the whole episode, 'cos I'd end up out of a job and without a decent reference.'

'Yes, I suppose you're right. Life isn't fair, is it? I wouldn't mind people having more money than me if they didn't think it gave them the right to throw their weight around. I can't stand anyone looking down their nose at me, or talking to me as though I haven't a brain in me head.'

Jean moved away from the wall. 'We'd better get back. If Mr John's meeting doesn't last as long as he expected it to, and he finds the office empty, we'd both lose our jobs. I'm not particularly happy here, but it's better than standing in the dole queue.' They returned to an empty office, and to their relief there was no sound from Mr John's office. 'I'll get these few letters sorted out,' Poppy said. 'Then once they're out of the way, and if Mr John doesn't put in an appearance, I'm going to look at the book you've lent me on shorthand.'

'It'll be our lunch break in fifteen minutes,' Jean said. 'Would you like to come with me for a pot of tea and a sandwich?'

'I'm trying to save up to buy meself a winter coat, so I can't afford to spend much on me lunch.'

'It's my treat, as I invited you. And don't worry about the money, 'cos you can get a sandwich or a bowl of soup for a shilling. And that includes a pot of tea.'

Poppy grinned. 'Oh, I think the bank will run to that. But we both buy our own, right? I'm going to a dance tonight and I need to watch the coppers.'

'I would have thought yer had plenty of lads eager to take you out. A girl with your looks shouldn't have to pay for herself.'

'I'm meeting a nice young man inside the Grafton, if you must know. And he wanted to take me. In fact he was quite upset that I wouldn't go with him. But I always go to the dance with my friend, and I wasn't going to let her down. I might do, after tonight, because last time we were there she paired off with a nice bloke. So who knows? She might have met the man of her dreams and want to see him every night. I'll let you know tomorrow how I get on with my new male friend, and how Julie's date turned out.' Poppy grinned. 'We've talked so much, at least I have, that it is now time for our lunch hour. Come on, coats on and off we pop. A bowl of hot soup seems very tempting right now.'

When they were sitting in the warmth of a small café, a bowl of soup in front of each of them and a thick slice of bread on a plate next to it, Jean asked, 'Haven't you got a steady boyfriend, Poppy? I don't know why, but I thought you were courting strong.'

'I've never been steady with any boy. Been out with plenty, but I've never met one that I'd leave me mam for. I will one day, but how far off that day is, only God knows. In the meanwhile I'll love 'em and leave 'em.'

Jean was enjoying this get-together, for she had little chance of conversing with younger people. Or people of any age, if she was being truthful. She was a spinster, and lived with her elderly mother. So it was a pleasant change to be chatting to a young woman who was outgoing and enjoying life. 'I'm glad to have company. I usually sit here on my own listening to what people at the tables near me are talking about.'

Poppy thought she was having her leg pulled until Jean's expression told her she'd been telling the truth. 'Ay, yer don't have to be short of someone to talk to at dinnertime. Yer can spend the time with me – I'd be glad of the company. And believe me, Jean, I can talk the hind leg off a donkey. I got the impression yer were quiet and reserved, otherwise I'd have been telling yer me life story.'

'Oh, I'd like that, Poppy, but not in working hours. I don't want to give Mr John an excuse to have another go at me.'

'Right then, I'll keep a list in me head of things I get up to, and we'll have a chinwag every day. And as I'm spending an hour every night on trying to learn shorthand, I might ask you for advice. Is that okay with you?'

'As long as you don't mind being corrected. You see, most Liverpool people have an accent, and they don't sound their words properly. That can make for misunderstanding. For instance, you say "me mam" instead of "my mother". And "ye're" instead of "you are". Little things that you never give a thought to. But if you were taking dictation and wrote "me" instead of "my", it could alter the whole sentence. But don't worry about it, you'll be fine.'

Although she was groaning inside, Poppy said, 'Of course I'll be fine. I'll get used to it. It's a case of having to, really. In future, to get used to it, my mother is no longer me mam.'

The two women laughed as they buttoned their coats and paid the bill. And as they walked towards the office, Poppy said, 'Tomorrow you can give me a lesson on speaking English as it should be spoken in return for me telling you how I get on with Peter tonight.' She drew Jean to a halt. 'Ay, that reminds me of a picture I saw a few years ago. Leslie Howard was Professor Higgins and Wendy Hiller was Eliza Doolittle. Oh, it was a smashing picture.' Then she pulled a face. 'Ay, I don't speak as bad as Eliza Doolittle, do I?'

Jean chuckled, and to her own ears it was a sound seldom heard. 'Don't be silly, there's nothing wrong with the way you speak. And if you're thinking what I think you are, then let me tell you I am no Professor Higgins.'

They reached the office steps and Poppy squeezed Jean's arm. 'I've enjoyed meself, it's been fun. Thank you.'

'How did you get on with Jim?' Poppy asked her friend as they combed their hair and powdered their noses in front of the mirror in the cloakroom of the Grafton. 'D'yer like him?'

Julie shrugged her shoulders. 'Yeah, he's okay. Didn't try to get fresh or anything. He's a better dancer than he is a talker, though, 'cos he didn't have much to say for himself. A barrel of laughs he is not!'

'Give the lad a chance, Julie. It was yer first date.' Poppy thought her friend was being unfair. If the lad had talked non-stop all through the picture, or tried to get fresh, then she'd have had something to moan about. She patted her hair, which was curled around her face, then jerked her head. 'Come on. I've kept Peter waiting long enough.'

'How did you get on with him?' Julie asked. 'You're a lucky blighter, you are. You got the best. I would rather have gone out with Peter, but you beat me to it.'

Poppy stopped in her tracks. 'I did no such thing! I've never run after a feller in me life, and I'm not going to start now. Peter did all the running, not me.' They had been friends since schooldays, but only now, looking at Julie's pouting lips, did Poppy realize her friend had always wanted her own way, and would sulk if she didn't get it. 'I'll tell you what I'll do, Julie. If you think you'd have a chance with Peter, I'll swap partners with you a few times and see if you can work your charm on him. I'll have the first waltz with Jim. Okay?'

Julie's smile was more of a smirk. She'd show Poppy she wasn't the only one the blokes fell for. But she tried to play down her excitement. 'Yeah, if that's what yer want. It doesn't bother me who I dance with.'

As soon as the pair walked into the dance hall, Peter left the friend he was talking to and made a beeline for the girl he thought the most beautiful he'd ever seen. And the nice thing about her was she didn't realize the effect she had on men. On him, anyway, and he couldn't help noticing the way all the blokes looked at her. He took her arm. 'You're a little late. I was beginning to think you were going to stand me up.'

'I don't stand blokes up, Peter. If I don't want to go out with them I tell them straight.' Poppy stepped back a little so Julie could join them. 'I think you know my friend Julie?'

Peter nodded. 'Hello, Julie.' His eyes returned quickly to Poppy. 'Come on, let's dance. This slow foxtrot is my favourite, and it's nearly over.'

'I can't dance with my bag over my arm. Give me a chance to put it down.'

'Here, give it to me,' Julie said. 'I'll put it under a chair with mine.'

Poppy was already in Peter's arms on the dance floor when she said, 'Here's Jim coming, Julie, and he looks eager. You said he was a good dancer, so put a smile on your face.'

Peter was a wonderful dancer, and it was a pleasure to be led by him. Long sweeping strides, body swaying to the music, and footwork quick and in perfect time. Poppy was enjoying herself, for she too was an excellent dancer. She was blessed with a sense of rhythm, was light on her feet, and being led close to her partner, she never faltered. They were a well-matched couple, and the envy of many on the floor who were not so accomplished.

When the music faded, Peter took Poppy's hand and led

her off the floor. 'Tonight is the first time I've ever met a date inside the dance hall, and it will be the last. Never again, Poppy, not even for you. Let your friend do what she wants, but she'll not spoil my date again.'

Poppy's eyes sparkled with laughter. 'You are being very optimistic, Peter. Who said there was going to be another date?'

'You wouldn't break my heart, would you, Poppy? Of course you wouldn't. You're too nice to go around breaking hearts.'

Poppy was about to answer when she saw Julie coming towards them, followed by Jim. 'Here's my friend coming now, Peter, and I want you to do me a favour. I'll say it quickly and explain later. To please me, ask her for the next waltz and I'll dance with the bloke she's with. Please?'

The next dance, by coincidence, was a waltz, and Poppy made eyes at Peter. He didn't look very happy, but he made Julie more than happy when he asked her to dance. However, it had to be said that the happiest person by far was Jim. He was quite shy, and couldn't quite pluck up the courage to ask the best-looking girl in the hall if she would do him the honour. So Poppy did it for him. 'Come on, Jim, we can't stand here like wallflowers. Let's show them how it's done.'

Poppy enjoyed the waltz, and she liked Jim. He was a nice bloke, not as good a dancer as Peter, but better than most. And he talked and laughed, certainly not as dull as Julie made him out to be. In fact, Poppy reached the conclusion he was too good for her friend.

Peter wasn't enjoying the partnership at all. Julie wasn't a bad dancer, but they did more walking around the floor than actual dancing. He found himself uncomfortable with her, as she pouted her lips, fluttered her eyelashes and held him too close to be comfortable or respectable. He was glad when the

ONE RAINY DAY

dance came to an end. It had not been a pleasant experience.

The next dance was a tango, and although Julie looked hopeful and told them it was her very favourite dance, Peter looked through her as he led Poppy on to the floor. 'Did you not tell me that Julie was your very best friend?'

Poppy nodded. 'At school, yes, she was. Why?'

'Some friend she is, Poppy. She's a man-eater! Don't ask me to dance with her again because I will flatly refuse.'

A smile and a delightful chuckle had Peter holding Poppy close. 'Why did you put me through that ordeal, you little minx? Was I set up by the two of you?'

Poppy was serious now. 'I would never do that, Peter, and I'm sorry. She was talking in the cloakroom about something I've no intention of repeating, but I don't regret asking you to dance with her, for now I can see her for what she really is. I should have seen it years ago, but I didn't. She's vain, jealous, and selfish. I hope Jim sees through her before he gets hurt. He's far too good for her.'

'Thank heaven you've seen sense,' Peter said. 'Now I can have you to myself and not share you with a friend who isn't a friend. I can make a proper date with you if you'll come out with me again. Please say you will.'

'Yes, I would like that. But I won't be free every evening because I'm taking shorthand lessons two nights a week. However, I'll tell you about that on the way home. You will be seeing me home, or am I taking too much for granted?'

'I'm seeing you right to your door, my dear Poppy. And without sounding forward, or rushing you into something you're not ready for, I'm hoping for a goodnight kiss.'

When the last waltz finished, Poppy waved to Julie but didn't speak to her. They'd been good friends at school, but they were not right for each other as grown-ups.

Later, standing outside her house, Poppy finished the tale she'd started on the bus coming home. She'd told Peter how she wanted to find a better job which would pay a good wage. He heard about her mother's job, and her brother, David, almost out of his time. 'My mam has worked to keep the house going, and to see we were fed and clothed. And now me and David want to pay her back for all she's done for us. We want her to stop work and have an easier life. David comes out of his time in a few weeks, and that will help. But I don't want him to be burdened with too much responsibility, that wouldn't be fair. So, now you know why I'm taking lessons twice a week. And I'm very determined, Peter, so don't try to coax me into skipping lessons, because you wouldn't be doing me any favours.'

'I won't, love, I promise.'

'Right, well now you know all there is to know about me, I'd better get in before me mam sends for the police. I'll see you on Saturday, as we've arranged.'

'But can't I call for you?'

Poppy shook her head. 'Not yet, Peter. I haven't known you long enough.'

'Can I at least have a goodnight kiss?'

'Of course you can. But only one.' Poppy closed her eyes. She felt his lips on hers, and while it was quite pleasing, she found herself being a little disappointed. And when she'd let herself in and closed the door behind her, she leaned back. Had her mother really felt a tingle down her spine the first time Poppy's father held her hand? And was she telling the truth about her legs turning to jelly when he first kissed her?

Poppy hadn't felt any such sensation. Mind you, it had been a fleeting kiss. Perhaps next time, eh?

Chapter Eight

'Why don't you bring this Peter in to meet us, sweetheart?' Eva asked as they were having breakfast on the Sunday morning. 'Yer've been out with him three times now, so yer must like him. And me and yer brother are nosy enough to want to see him for ourselves.'

Poppy shook her head. 'Not yet, Mam. It's too soon. If I brought him home to meet the family, he might take it as a sign I'm serious about him. And I'm not sure how I feel about him meself. Oh, he's a lovely bloke, and I'm sure you and David would like him. He's always well dressed, well spoken, and he must have a good job to be able to afford to go out every night.' Poppy shrugged her shoulders. 'I'm saying he goes out every night, but that might not be true. Although if he had his way he'd date me every night.'

'He sounds too good to be true, sis,' David said. 'Why have you got doubts about him? He hasn't got bad breath, has he?'

Poppy poked him in the arm. 'No, he hasn't, clever clogs. He hasn't any faults that I can see, but nevertheless I'm not getting serious with him. It's too soon. What I'm going to be concentrating on in the next three months is my shorthand lessons, and trying very hard not to strangle my boss before I have another job lined up. The light at the end of the tunnel is giving my notice in to Mr John. I can't wait to see his face. He is so smarmy, he makes my tummy turn over.'

'Well, it won't be for long now, sweetheart,' Eva said. 'Let's hope everything turns out as yer hope it will.'

'I'm going to say a prayer every night, and I'm not being a hypocrite 'cos I do say a little prayer every night. Only this time I'm going to put me heart and soul into it.'

David was watching his sister's face, fascinated by the changing expressions. She was beautiful, and he was proud of her. No wonder this Peter wanted to see her every night. If he could find a girl like Poppy, he'd want to see her every night too. He wouldn't let her out of his sight. 'Ay, sis, this bloke yer've been seeing, Peter, where does he work, d'yer know?'

'I don't know where he works, no. And he doesn't know where I work, either! I've only been out with him three times, David. Yer don't expect me to know his life story, surely? Next yer'll be asking me what he has for his breakfast.'

'I'll ask him that myself, if I ever get to meet him. No, I was just wondering, with you saying he was always well dressed, nicely spoken, and didn't seem short of money. I'm just curious, that's all. You are my only sister, after all, so it's only right and proper that I look after you, and care about your well-being. We can't have you going out with every Tom, Dick and Harry.'

Poppy's infectious laughter filled the room. 'Don't be giving me ideas, David. I've never been out with a Tom, Dick or Harry yet, but I'll try to get round to it 'cos I'd hate to miss out on anything. Any other names, so I can make a list?'

'Take no notice of him, sweetheart, 'cos he's a fine one to talk,' Eva said. 'He's out every night, and he can't fool us by saying he's playing cards. Yet he's never brought a girl home to meet us.' She gave some thought to her next words before she spoke. 'It's different with men, though, sweetheart, 'cos they're more able to look after themselves. Not that you can't look after yourself, but I think you should know a little about the boys you go out with. At least where they live and work. I'd feel happier in my mind if I knew who you were dating. When are yer seeing him again?'

'On Tuesday. He wanted to meet me outside the school tomorrow night, but I told him it wouldn't be worth it. And I might not be in the best of moods if I can't make head or tail of what the teacher is telling us. I couldn't last time. I just couldn't get the hang of it.'

'That's because you've no patience, sweetheart. Just take it nice and easy, and anything you don't understand ask the teacher to go over it again with yer. Everyone has to learn, and I'm sure the teacher will understand. You won't be the first to pluck up the courage to ask for help.'

'Mam's right, Poppy. Everyone has to learn. When I first started as an apprentice, I was as thick as two short planks,' her brother told her. 'I'd never even had a screwdriver in me hand before. But after a few weeks everything started to slot into place. Just keep a picture in yer mind as an incentive. You standing in front of the stuck-up snob of a boss you've got, and telling him where to put his job.'

Eva chuckled. 'In the nicest possible way, of course.'

'Ay, Mam, you saying that has reminded me of something the woman I work with in the office told me. Jean, Mr John's secretary. She said, in a nice way, that my English would have to be good. I couldn't write as we Scousers speak. For instance, I call you me mam, when I should say my mother. We had a good laugh over it, but she was trying to say, without hurting my feelings, that I should concentrate on losing my accent. So, in future, ye're not me mam, Mam, you're my mother.'

'I'm sure she was only trying to help yer, sunshine. I can understand that if yer want to be a private secretary, than yer'll have to live up to it. Neatly dressed, hair always tidy, and well spoken,' Eva said, her head nodding in agreement. 'I imagine that in the course of a job like that, yer'd be dealing with well-educated people. And yer wouldn't want to have them looking down their noses at yer.'

David added his view. 'You don't speak with a thick accent, Poppy; in fact you have hardly any accent. It's just the way most people in Liverpool speak, and it's what we're all familiar with. When your friend in the office mentioned it, she didn't mean that you were as common as muck, she was just being helpful. I often say things like "where's me coat", or "is me dinner ready". It's habit, but all it needs is a little thought before speaking. I'll do it with you, when we're in the house. You can correct me, and I'll correct you. It would soon make us more careful, and I'm sure neither of us would get a cob on over it.'

'All I can say is, leave me out of it,' Eva told them. 'I've spoken like this all me life, and I'm too old to change. Besides, I wouldn't want to. I'm comfortable when I'm talking to anyone, and I would hate to have to think every time I opened me mouth.'

There came a heavy pounding on the front door and the family looked at each other with surprise. 'Who can this be at ten o'clock on a Sunday morning?' Eva's eyes went to the dirty dishes on the table. 'Whoever it is, they've got a ruddy cheek! Just look at the state of the place.'

Poppy pushed her chair back and made for the hall. 'Don't be such a worry, Mam. I won't let them in.'

The woman standing on the step grinned up at Poppy. 'It'll take more than you to keep me out, queen,' said Marg Boden, their next door neighbour. 'I'll go through you like a knife through butter, 'cos this is an emergency.'

Poppy quickly stepped aside to let their neighbour pass. 'What on earth has happened, Marg? Is somebody sick?'

Marg was having great difficulty keeping her face straight. 'It's my feller, queen. He's doubled up with pain in his tummy. You're the only ones I could think of to come to for help. All the other neighbours are miserable buggers.'

'If it's an emergency, sweetheart,' Eva said, her face showing concern, 'then it's a doctor yer want.'

Marg's face split into a wide grin. 'I don't think the surgery will be open on a Sunday morning, queen. And even if it was, I don't think he'd let me have a cup of sugar.'

'Sugar!' Eva's voice was shrill. 'Yer mean yer nearly took the front door off its hinges for a cup of sugar? You've got some nerve, Marg Boden, disturbing a family's breakfast on a Sunday morning.'

'I know, queen, and I agree with every word yer've said. If I was in your shoes I'd say I had a bleeding cheek. In fact I'd go further, and call meself a cheeky cow.'

'You are a cheeky cow, Marg, and ye're looking for trouble, too! Telling us poor Ally is doubled up in pain, well, that's tempting fate, that is. For there's many a true word spoken in jest. It would be the price of yer if yer get back home to find him really ill. Then yer'd be laughing the other side of yer face.'

'Oh, he'll be doubled up, queen, I'm sure of that. But it won't be with pain, and it won't be because he's ill. It'll be after I've told him how yer fell for me cock and bull story. He'll enjoy that, 'cos my Ally loves a joke.'

Eva raised her brows. 'And he's got a sweet tooth, your Ally, if I'm not mistaken?'

'Oh, yeah, he's got a sweet tooth all right,' Marg said, her two hands resting on the back of a dining chair. 'He bought me a box of chocolates for me birthday a few weeks ago, and after I'd made a big fuss over him, and given him a big hug, I opened the box to find he'd eaten half of the bleeding chocolates on his way home from work. And to add insult to injury, he'd only gone and eaten the Turkish delight ones, what are me favourite.'

'Well, yer can get yer own back on him now, sweetheart,' Eva said. 'Tell him he'll have to drink his tea without sugar in, 'cos I've none to spare.'

David opened his mouth to say there was a sugar basin full to the brim in the kitchen, but he kept silent when he saw the look on his mother's face. Their neighbour's joke was about to backfire on her.

'What d'yer mean, yer've got no sugar?' Marg's eyes had lost their gleam. 'I was with yer yesterday when yer bought a pound bag from Irwin's. Yer can't possibly have used it all so soon.'

'Oh, I know I bought a pound yesterday, Marg. I haven't lost me memory. But I made a batch of fairy cakes for after our tea last night, and they take a lot of sugar.' Eva didn't look at her two children, for she knew if she did she'd give the game away. 'And I was up early this morning and heard the milkman putting my two pints of milk on the step. Then d'yer know what, sweetheart? I suddenly got the urge to make a rice pudding to have after our dinner today. So I did no more than put the rice in a basin, covered it with milk, added plenty of sugar, a knob of butter and some grated nutmeg. And I'm sure yer can smell the tasty aroma it's giving out. I certainly can, and me mouth is watering. By the time we've had our dinner, it will be ready to eat, with a lovely brown skin on the top.' Eva shrugged her shoulders. 'So I'm afraid I can't oblige, sweetheart. Yer should have knocked before the milkman came, then I wouldn't have made the rice pudding and yer could have had the sugar for your feller.'

Marg's eyes became slits. 'Oh, I'd have been very welcome if I'd knocked on yer door at seven o'clock. I can just imagine the reception I'd have got. So I waited until a respectable hour so I wouldn't embarrass yer by catching yer sitting with yer hair in rollers, and wearing yer pink winceyette nightdress.'

Eva feigned horror. 'I don't need to put curlers in. My hair is naturally curly.' She patted her hair, while giving David a gentle kick to tell him she needed a little help on this one.

David recognized her request, and said, 'If you're stuck, Marg, I'll let you have my spoonful of sugar for Ally's tea.'

Poppy's vigorous nods sent her curls swirling around her face. 'I take two sugars, Marg, and you're welcome to them. Every little helps. It won't hurt me to go without for once.'

Marg glared at Eva. 'All I need is for you to say yer take three sugars, Eva Meadows, and I'll have enough for me, Ally and the girls to have a decent cup of tea with our toast.'

Eva tutted. 'I don't take three sugars as it happens, Marg, I'm not that well off. But so yer won't go round the neighbours pulling me to pieces, I'll see what I can do for yer.' Eva pushed her chair back and stood up. 'While I'm counting the grains of sugar I'm lending yer, why don't yer pull the chair out and sit down? Ye're making the place look untidy standing there, especially with a look to kill on yer face. If my rice pudding wasn't in the oven, out of sight, yer'd have curdled the milk.' With that, she made her way to the kitchen where she stood for a while with a hand over her mouth to silence her laughter. She'd been a neighbour of the Boden family for about twenty years, and she'd lost count of the number of times she'd fallen for Marg's jokes. So it was time to get her own back. And whatever she came up with would have to be good if she wanted to get the better of her neighbour.

She leaned back against the sink, her chin in her hand. She could do with a bit of help, but if she called one of the children out, Marg would smell a rat. At the moment she was busy telling David and Poppy a tale that had them in stitches. She was a born comedienne who liked to see people laugh, even when she was pulling their leg. But there was a soft side to her, and she would go out of her way to help anyone in trouble.

A burst of loud laughter brought Eva out of her reverie. She'd better think of something quick, or Marg would twig she was up to something. Her eyes searched the kitchen walls for inspiration, and it was when they landed on the bag of sugar that an idea came to her. Popping her head round the door, she said, 'Yer don't seem to be in a hurry, Marg, and as I was about to make us a fresh pot of tea when you knocked, would you like one? Or do yer think yer should be getting back to Ally and the girls? They'll be spitting feathers now if they haven't had anything to drink.'

Marg swivelled in her chair to face the kitchen. 'One minute you're telling me yer've got no sugar, and now ye're offering me a cup of tea. Make yer mind up, queen.'

'I'm asking you out of courtesy, Marg, 'cos I could hardly take three cups in and leave you without. Besides, the spoonful of sugar in the cup of tea would be taken off what I intend to lend yer. It's up to you. Whatever yer want, it's no skin off my nose.'

'Talking about skin, which I know we wasn't but I'm curious. How come I still can't smell that bleeding rice pudding yer were on about? It's either you're telling fibs, or I've lost me sense of smell.'

Eva, with her hand on the kitchen door, tutted as she shook her head. 'Why do yer always change the subject, Marg? I've never known anyone like yer for hopping from one subject to another. So, before it gets time for us to go to bed, do yer want a cup of tea or not?'

Marg's eyes rolled. 'Oh, go on, seeing as yer twisted me arm. If my feller has a cob on when I get back, I'll say you weren't well and I was looking after yer.'

'You'll do no such thing, Marg Boden. That's tempting fate, that is. Why don't yer tell Ally the truth, that yer were busy talking?'

'I don't need to tell him that, queen, 'cos we've been married long enough for him to know I only ever stop talking to take a breath every now and then. He reckons I've got a mouth as big as the entrance to the Mersey Tunnel.'

'Ah, that's a bit of an exaggeration, sweetheart. You're not that bad. The person I would say fits that description perfectly is Florrie Lawson across the street. She's got a mouth on her like I've never known before. And her language is disgusting. Half the things she comes out with are beyond me. I haven't a clue what they mean.'

'Always come to me if yer get stuck, queen, because I know the meaning of most of her words. In fact, I could probably teach Florrie a few, come to that. But I won't tell yer what they are, 'cos I know yer don't like bad language.' Marg suddenly banged her clenched fist on the table and made them all jump. 'What about this cup of tea, Mrs Woman? Am I getting one or not?'

Eva stood quickly to attention and saluted. 'Aye, aye, sir, one, two, three, sir!' She winked at her daughter. 'Poppy, come and give me a hand. David can keep Marg company for five minutes.'

Out in the kitchen, Eva put a finger to her lips. Then very quietly she said, 'I want to pull a fast one on Marg for a change, 'cos it's always her getting one over on me. So help me think of something. Some trick to play on her over the sugar. I think she's pulling my leg about running out, because I was at the shops with her and she bought the same as me. So help me get one back on her for a change. And it'll have to be quick or she'll know we're up to something.'

Poppy closed her eyes so she could think clearly, and a few seconds later a slow smile spread across her lovely face. 'Mam, salt looks very much like sugar, doesn't it? You couldn't tell the difference just by looking at them, could you?'

'Sugar is a bit finer than salt, but you'd never notice unless yer had reason to think there was something amiss. Anyway, I'll put the kettle on for the tea, then we'll put our heads together.'

Poppy rubbed the side of her nose. 'I know Marg loves a laugh, and she gets a kick out of playing jokes on people. But how would she react to being the butt of a joke? Would she take it in good part?'

Eva chuckled. 'There's only one way to find out. Tell me what yer've got in mind.'

Five minutes later, Poppy was handing her mother a wooden tray with four cups of steaming tea on. She gave her mother a gentle kiss on the cheek, then pointed a finger at the tray and whispered, 'Don't forget the cup with the salt in is the one in the top right hand corner. Can yer remember that, or shall I carry the tray in?'

'I'm not helpless, sweetheart. I can manage.' Eva looked down at the tray. 'The one in the top right hand corner.'

With that she marched with confidence into the living room. However, her confidence didn't help her at all, for what she needed badly was a sense of direction. She hadn't taken into account that when she put the tray down on the table and turned to sit down, the tray didn't turn with her, and the cup meant for Marg ended up in front of David. Eva didn't think anything of it. As far as she was concerned it was a mission well carried out. And Poppy, following her mother a minute later with a plate of biscuits, didn't spot the mistake, and was in a happy frame of mind when she sat down. 'Would you like a biscuit, Marg? They're custard creams.'

'I'd love one, queen, but just hang on till I put me cup down.' With the tea in front of her, and a biscuit in her hand, she said, 'Ay, this is the life, eh? Sunday morning tea and biscuits, yer can't beat it. I always said I should have been born into money.' She lifted her cup and took several sips before placing it back on the saucer. She seemed unaware of the surprised looks being exchanged between Eva and Poppy, and carried on talking, as only Marg could. She was noted for being able to chat for hours about nothing in particular and everything in general. Today she chose David as her target. And because she was looking into his face, he didn't like to be ungentlemanly by turning his eyes from hers while she was in full flow.

Mother and daughter didn't know quite what to do. Three cups of tea were still on the tray, each one in a corner. Eventually, and mentally telling herself she'd never again agree to be involved in pulling a trick on someone, Poppy reached for one of the cups. Her tummy was turning over at the very thought of drinking a mouthful of salted tea. But they couldn't sit there much longer, for the beds hadn't been made yet, or potatoes peeled for their dinner. So she took a tentative sip of the tea with her eyes closed and her tummy preparing itself for an invasion. The first sip was fine, so she took another, which was also fine. She touched her mother's arm and whispered, 'This isn't the one, Mam, so it's down to you and David.'

'Pass one of the cups over, David, save me stretching across the table.' Eva held out her hand.

'Which one is yours, Mam?' David asked. 'Or are they both the same?'

When his mother nodded, David handed a cup and saucer over, then turned to listen once again to their neighbour. 'What were you saying, Marg? I missed the last bit.'

'I've lost track now, lad, so give me brain time to get back on the rail.' As she was talking, Marg was watching Eva out of the corner of her eye. She noticed Eva's smile when she'd sipped her tea and saw her nod at her daughter. So when David lifted his cup, Marg said, 'I wouldn't drink that if I were you, lad. Yer wouldn't like it.'

While Eva and Poppy sat open-mouthed, both blushing with guilt, Marg told a very surprised David that his tea didn't have sugar in, only salt. 'But you're drinking your tea and it's all right,' the lad spluttered, 'and so are me mam's and Poppy's.'

Poppy jumped from her chair. 'I'll get yer another cup, David. Marg is right. Me and me mam were trying to play a trick on our friend from next door, but we made a proper mess of it. That cup wasn't meant for you.'

David, looking perplexed, leaned across the table. 'How did yer know what they were up to, Marg?'

'Listen to me, lad, and I'll tell yer the signs to look out for first. To be able to read the mind of a prankster, yer need a good sense of smell. That was yer mam's first mistake. No smell of rice pudding. Secondly, yer need a good pair of ears to hear the whispers and very low voices. And the word "salt" is easy to pick out. Your mam's real mistake there was repeating what Poppy said. That the cup meant for me was the one in the top right hand corner.' Marg couldn't keep the laughter back any longer. In between chuckles that brought smiles to all three faces, she said, 'But didn't yer mam put the tray down facing the wrong way, and the bleeding cup with salt in landed in front of you! And they still thought their plan was running smoothly until I picked up me cup, took a swallow, and didn't bat an eye. If only they could have seen the looks on their faces! I was wishing I had a camera with me.' Hitting the table with both hands, Marg doubled up with laughter. She rocked to and fro, tears running down her cheeks. 'Oh, I haven't laughed so much since the night Ally came back from the pub rotten drunk and I had to help him up to bed. Then didn't the silly sod have to get up to go to the lavvy, and he took the wrong turn and fell down the bleeding stairs.'

That was one piece of information David had never heard before, and he was all agog. 'He didn't, did he? It's a wonder he didn't kill himself.' Then he suddenly remembered Marg's gift for leg-pulling. Grinning sheepishly, he said, 'I almost fell for that. Wouldn't yer think I'd have learned by now?'

Taking two or three sniffs before answering, Marg said, 'Yeah, yer should take everything I tell yer with a pinch of salt, lad.'

Marg's quick wit was met with more laughter. It would take a good one to get the better of her. 'Well, that's helped pass a very pleasant morning,' she said, pushing her chair back under the table. 'It certainly beats watching my feller reading the paper while rubbing his chin to see if he really does need to shave. I'll bet a pound to a pinch of snuff he hasn't moved off the chair since I came out of the house. Lazy bugger, he is.'

'I don't know why ye're always pulling Ally to pieces,' Eva said, 'when yer know yer've got a wonderful husband, and yer love the bones of him.'

'I know when I'm well off, Eva, but I'm not daft enough to tell my feller that. Anyway, it's about time I got back to him and the girls. It's time to start getting the dinner on the go. But I'm not going without the sugar you offered to lend me.'

'I'll get it,' Eva said, hiding a smile. 'Six spoonsful, wasn't it?' She stopped short of the kitchen door. 'No, yer've already had one spoonful in that cup of tea, so that makes it five.'

'It's not worth wasting yer shoe leather to fetch it, queen, so we'll call it quits. It means me opening a pound bag, but what the hell, it's got to be opened some time. So I'll thank yer for a pleasant morning, and love yer and leave yer. Ta-ra for now.'

'I'll see you out,' David said. 'Then yer can't tell the neighbours I'm not a gentleman.'

No sooner had the front door closed on their visitor than Eva and Poppy set to. 'I'll clear away and get the dinner on the go,' Eva said, 'while you nip up and make the beds.'

Poppy took the stairs two at a time, followed closely by her brother. 'I'll see to my own bed,' David said. 'Then I'll peel the spuds for me mam. But it's been a good laugh, sis, hasn't it? I've never known anyone as quick-witted as Marg. She doesn't miss a trick.'

'Me mam doesn't stand a chance with her.' Poppy grinned. 'Her trouble is, she's too nice. She's tried dozens of times over the years to get one over on Marg and not once has she been successful. She definitely thought she was on to a winner today, but once again Marg was too good for her. If I was me mam, I'd give it up as a bad job.'

David chuckled. 'I don't know, sis, it's always a good laugh whichever way it goes. And Marg has been good for our mam. She's always been there when help was needed. We couldn't have a better friend or neighbour.'

'It's not only Marg – the whole family are nice. Ally's a husband in a million, and the two girls are smashers. Sarah and Lucy have grown up to be very pretty.'

'Yeah, I've noticed,' David said. 'How old are they now?'

Poppy frowned in concentration. 'I believe Sarah is eighteen in a few weeks, and Lucy, I'd say, is about sixteen and a half.' She was plumping her pillow when she said, 'Go and do what yer said yer'd do, David. Your bed, and peeling the spuds. I want a couple of hours to meself after dinner, to go through this book on shorthand. I won't feel as nervous or stupid as I did when I was sixteen. Jean from the office has explained some things to me, and I'd like a few hours on me own, nice and quiet, to see if I can remember what she told me. I'm determined to get a decent job, so I can do what you're going to do in two weeks. And that's to give me mam extra housekeeping money. That's my priority, and if it means me sitting up all night to get the hang of half moons, dots and dashes and lots of squiggles, then I'll sit up all night.'

'There's another light on your horizon, sis,' her brother reminded her. 'In twelve days you and Mam can go shopping for your new coats.'

Poppy's eyes lit up at the thought. 'Yeah. I've been busy in me head trying to decide what colour to get. I'll miss the old raincoat, though, 'cos I've had good wear out of it. The only thing is, it's not as warm as a coat.'

She suddenly realized she was wasting time, and she shooed

her brother out of her bedroom. 'That's enough, now let's both get down to work. The quicker we move, the sooner it's done.'

David popped his head back in. 'That makes sense, sis.'

'Get out, David! Vamoose, scram, disappear.' But Poppy was smiling as she slammed the bedroom door shut.

Chapter Nine

Poppy was in high spirits as she walked out of the school, hugging her notebooks to her chest and strolling between the two girls she'd sat next to in the class. They were roughly the same age as herself, and their names were Joy and Jane. It was their third week at the night school, so they were ahead of Poppy. This information had been gleaned during a short break in the lesson. Joy was small in stature, with dark hair and a face which was a perfect partner for her name, as she had an ever-ready smile. Jane, though, was the complete opposite. She was very tall, slim with mousy-coloured hair, and quite manly in stature and walk. She was also very intellectual.

'I hope I'm as quick at learning as you are,' Poppy said as they neared the gates. 'Although Mr Jones did say I'd done very well for my first lesson, and I feel really chuffed with myself.'

The trio paused at the gates to bid each other goodnight, then they parted to go their separate ways. Poppy had only taken a few steps when she heard her name being called. She turned her head to see Peter. 'What are you doing here?'

'I wanted to see you.' He cupped her elbow. 'How did the lesson go?'

Poppy's first inclination was to tell him he had no right to be there when she'd told him not to be. But she dismissed the thought, and admitted to herself that she was glad to see him. 'It went very well, thank you, even though I do say it meself. Mind you, I had spent hours yesterday afternoon trying to get my head round it. And I'm glad I persevered because it really was a big help.' She turned her head to face him. 'I know it sounds like I'm bragging, but I'm so pleased with meself I don't care. When the teacher, Mr Jones, told me I'd done very well, I felt like kissing him.'

Peter held her arm tighter. 'Hey, if you ever feel like kissing anyone, make sure it's me.'

Poppy asked, in a teasing way, 'Oh, but what should I do if you are not available? If you were busy elsewhere, I would have to remain kissless.'

Peter chuckled. 'You're in a very light-hearted mood tonight, Poppy, and I hope you remain so until we reach your house. Then I feel sure that tonight, taking into account your carefree mood, I will be allowed a proper kiss.'

'Don't get your hopes up too high, Peter, 'cos we've only met three times and I think a hug and a kiss on the cheek is about right.'

'In one way I'm glad you said that,' Peter told her. 'But it's really like cutting off my nose to spite my face by telling you. I'm happy you haven't had a lot of serious boyfriends because I'd like to think I was the first one you really had loving feelings for. Would I be wrong to go on hoping, Poppy?'

'Everyone should have hopes, Peter. Life would be very dull if we didn't have something to look forward to. But sometimes our dreams take a little longer to come true, and we have to be patient.' Poppy sensed Peter's disappointment, and added, 'Can't we just enjoy getting to know each other? I would like to do it that way.'

'I'll go along with whatever you want, Poppy, as long as you're not planning a two-year courtship.'

'Oh, I'm not thinking anything so far ahead. My one immediate aim is to get myself qualified to apply for a good job. I'd like to be able to buy myself new clothes when I need them without having to save up. The main reason, though, for wanting a better job is to get away from my present boss. He's a womanizer who believes money can buy him anything he wants. The way he looks at me turns my blood cold, and he can never hand me a letter to type without his hand touching mine. He makes me cringe, and the day I am in a position to tell him what to do with his job will be the happiest day of my life.'

Peter moved his hand from Poppy's elbow to allow him to put an arm round her waist. 'Haven't you reported him to anyone? He should be warned to watch his behaviour.'

'There's no one to report him to, for his father owns the firm. And it's not only me he thinks he can treat like a slave – yer should hear the way he talks to his secretary. And Jean can't afford to tell him what she thinks of him, for she looks after her elderly mother and needs her wages. She's a spinster, you see, so she can't afford to upset him.'

'Oh, dear, your place of work seems far from a happy one.' Peter pulled her close. 'Marry me, and you'd never have to work again. I have a good job and earn a very good wage.'

Poppy chuckled. 'I didn't mean to overstate my case to such an extent that you would marry me to get me away from it all. I may not be rubbing my hands in glee every morning when I sit on the bus taking me to work, but it's better than being a kept woman. Or has the word "mistress" gone out of fashion?'

Peter pulled her to a halt, turned her round and kissed her firmly on the lips. It was so unexpected, Poppy was taken by surprise and stood motionless for a few seconds. Then she asked, 'What was that in aid of, may I ask?'

'I thought it was the only way to stop you talking, and the only way my lips were going to come into contact with yours.' He tilted his head. 'Just out of curiosity, did you find the kiss unpleasant?'

Poppy was laughing inside, but she didn't want him to know in case he thought he could make a habit of it. 'Had you given a warning of your intention, then I would be in a position to answer that question. But I was taken by surprise, and in all honesty I don't know how I felt. You wouldn't want me to lie, would you?'

'Of course not!' Peter was trying hard not to move too quickly, for he could see she was a girl who didn't fool around with a bloke's feelings, and he admired her for that. But he couldn't help himself when he gazed into her beautiful face. He just wanted to take her in his arms and hold her. 'Do you agree that you should give it another chance? After all, if you were so surprised, it is possible you were feeling numb. So will you give me the benefit of the doubt, and when we get to your house, and we're saying goodnight, will you try another sample of one of my kisses? Otherwise, I will never be able to sleep, and I'll spend the rest of my life with an inferiority complex.' He put his hands together and added a few sobs to his voice for good measure. 'You wouldn't want to be responsible for ruining my life, would you? It would be a heavy burden for one so young to carry.'

'You are crazy,' Poppy said, laughter in her eyes and voice. He was such a lovely man, it would be hard to fall out with him. 'Okay, you win. I'd hate to see a grown man cry. One kiss, mind, and it doesn't mean we're courting in earnest. Three dates and a kiss don't make for a courtship. I want to do something with my life before settling down.'

Later, outside Poppy's house, Peter claimed his kiss and found it had been well worth waiting for. As for Poppy, while the kiss didn't send her into raptures, it didn't displease her. But she still didn't feel that shiver run down her spine, and wondered why. Had her mother exaggerated her memories? Or was Peter not the man for her? She liked him, felt comfortable in his company, and knew he was a decent man who would never take advantage of her. So did the fault lie with her? Perhaps she wasn't capable of loving someone in the same way as her mother had loved her dad? The thought didn't bear thinking about. She could still remember the love shown by her parents to each other, and that was what she wanted. And she wouldn't settle for less.

On the far side of the city, in the Wilkie-Brooks' dining room, Charlotte was trying to coax her brother into going for a drive in the country. But so far, Andrew was standing firm. 'I'm really not in the mood, Charlotte. Perhaps another night?'

'We can go in my car, and I'll drive,' Charlotte said. 'You could sit back and enjoy the scenery. You haven't any engagements tonight, have you?'

Andrew shook his head. 'I have no engagements, but I brought some work home from the office to go through.'

George looked across the dining room to where his son was sitting. 'You shouldn't need to bring work home with you, my boy. If the extra clients I have passed over have made your workload too heavy, then you should say so.'

'Certainly not, Father! My office and my staff run like clockwork. I enjoy my work, we have no problems and there's no stress. The only reason I brought some correspondence home with me was because I had no plans for tonight and thought it would pass the time.'

'Then pass the time with me, my dear brother,' Charlotte fluttered her long eyelashes, which brought a smile from Andrew. 'We could go to that little inn we found, the one we both fell in love with.'

George showed interest. 'I've often wanted to see the inside of one of the pubs we pass on the way to Southport, or out towards the Lake District.' He chuckled. 'Did you have a glass of beer there?'

Harriet gasped. 'You didn't take your sister into a pub, did you, Andrew? You, and indeed Charlotte, should have more sense than to enter such a place.'

Andrew was about to protest, but his sister got in before him. 'Oh, Mother, it was a beautiful place, and I loved it! It was hundreds of years old, and was once a hostelry for coaches and horsemen. It was like a fairy tale, and I loved it. Wasn't it quaint, Andrew?'

'It was more than that. A log fire roaring up a stone chimney, beams overhead and a stone-flagged floor.' Andrew smiled as his words brought up memories. 'There were some farmers in there who'd come straight from work in the fields, and they were very countrified. But they were pleasant and friendly, as was the manager. It was like going back to a time when there were no cars on the roads, only horses.'

'I'm of a mind to come with you,' George told them. 'I'm sure I'd find it most interesting.'

'But you can't go tonight, my dear,' Harriet said. 'Have you forgotten Michael and Jessica are coming to confirm the arrangements for the baby's christening?'

'Oh, I'm sorry, my love, it had completely slipped my

mind.' George turned to his son. 'One night next week, then, shall we say? You have aroused my interest now, and I shall look forward to it. But that doesn't mean you and Charlotte can't go tonight. Take your sister for a run in the country and relax a little. And for heaven's sake, leave all thoughts of work behind you. At twenty-five you should spend far more time enjoying yourself than you do. Life is for living, dear boy, so enjoy it while you're young.'

Charlotte stood behind her brother's chair and put her arms round his neck. 'You heard what Father said, Andrew, so do as you are told. Big brothers are supposed to look after their little sisters, and make sure they come to no harm.' She ruffled his hair. 'So you can't let me go out on my own tonight in case I get kidnapped.'

Andrew caught hold of her hand. 'You were a little horror when you were younger, always wanting your own way.' He smiled up at her. 'I remember you used to stamp your feet if Frances tried to feed you porridge for breakfast. And you haven't changed a bit. But you don't need to stamp your feet or cry tonight, because I know when I'm beaten. We'll go for a run in the country, but we won't go to the inn we went to last time, we'll keep that for when Father is with us. We'll find another place that takes our fancy. But there is one condition attached.'

'Oh, and what is the catch?' Charlotte's eyes were dancing. 'Do I have to pay a forfeit?'

'No, my dear sister, no forfeit. But I am putting my foot down for once. I insist we go in my car, for you drive far too fast for my liking. Is that a deal?'

Charlotte pulled his head back so she could give him an upside down kiss. 'It's a deal, and I promise to behave.'

'Right. I'll give you a start to get ready. I'll count to ten, then follow you,' Andrew said. 'Last to the car pays for the first drink.'

After his son and daughter had left the room, George reached for his wife's hand. 'Andrew is good for Charlotte. When she's in his company she's more grown up. She'll learn more about life from him than she will from any of her friends, who spend their days doing absolutely nothing, apart from playing tennis, or having their hair and nails done. A complete waste of young lives.'

Harriet didn't agree. 'Charlotte doesn't sit around all day doing nothing, George, and you are being very unfair to her. I've seen her making up her own bed with Frances, and carrying the dirty linen down to the laundry. She potters in the garden when the weather is fine, and she excels at embroidery and all types of needlework. She has very nimble fingers, and you must admit she is a joy to live with. Always pleasant, never loses her temper, a daughter to be proud of.'

'I am extremely proud of both my children, my love. And also very proud of my wife, whom I love dearly. If I pass a remark about either of our children, it is only a comment and not a criticism. You see more of Charlotte than I do for obvious reasons, while I see more of our son. And I have to say he has surpassed all my expectations. And whom do I have to thank for these two beloved children? My dearly beloved wife, of course. I am truly a very lucky man.'

Andrew was driving down a country lane when he glanced at his sister and asked, 'Would you mind if we stopped here for a short while? It is so peaceful, with not a soul in sight, and only those two horses in the field. And I would like to smoke a cigarette if you have no objection? I would, of course, open the windows to let the smoke out.'

'I have no objection to cigarette smoke.' Charlotte smiled at him. 'As long as it's not too thick to see through. That would surely spoil the tranquil scene of the horses grazing.'

'Then I will leave the car and smoke my cigarette in the lane. The cool night air will add to the pleasure.'

When Andrew was standing by the fence, enjoying the fresh air and the smell of the countryside, Charlotte watched him from an open window. Her brother worked hard, but he had little social life, and it worried her. At his age he should have a girlfriend and enjoy going to the theatre or dinner dances. He needed romance in his life, not to be so involved with work.

Andrew threw his cigarette on the ground and extinguished it with his shoe. Then he climbed back into the car and turned on the ignition. 'Where to now, little sister? Would you like to stop somewhere for a drink?'

Charlotte shook her head. 'No, I'd rather like to sit here for a little while. As you said, it is very peaceful and it makes me feel really relaxed. So shall we just sit and talk, and enjoy watching the horses grazing and the birds singing?'

The engine was quickly silenced. 'That would suit me very well, Charlotte, and I would have suggested it myself if I hadn't thought you'd be bored stiff.'

'If I get bored, then I will tell you, my dear brother. But it is very unlikely, for we see so little of each other, apart from mealtimes. It will be nice to chat for a while, and bring ourselves up to date with any news.' Charlotte settled herself comfortably before saying. 'Tell me how your secretary is getting on. Is she still looking after you well? I really liked her, and I've promised myself I will visit you again soon and have a chat with her. It's Wendy, isn't it?'

Andrew was surprised at his sister's interest, and really

pleased. 'It would be hard to replace Mrs Stamford; I really would struggle without her. I don't have to ask for anything: she knows precisely what I want, and it's handed to me before I've even mentioned it.' He was now completely relaxed, and chuckled. 'I've told her she's wasting her time as a secretary. She could earn more money as a mind reader.'

'I'm glad she's there to look after you,' Charlotte said. 'To make sure you are warm and mollycoddled. Give her my regards and tell her I'll call and see her soon. And the two girls in the typing room were nice too! If my memory serves me right, they are Miss Williams and Miss Kennedy. I imagine they are a lot of fun.'

Andrew was even more surprised now. 'Fancy you remembering their names! I imagined you would have forgotten them by now.'

Now Charlotte chose her words carefully. 'I remember everything about that day, Andrew, because it was a day of change for me. Change from the dull routine of my life. I can picture your office in my mind, where your desk and chair are, and where Mrs Stamford's office is. I can picture her face, and also the two typists. Then I was in Father's office for the first time, and that was exciting.' She put a hand on her brother's arm. 'And I also clearly recall the girl in the raincoat. I can see her face now, and she is very pretty. Beautiful, in fact.' She tried to sound nonchalant when she asked, 'Have you seen her since, by any chance?'

'Only the once, which I told you about, when she wouldn't even listen to me. I know she still passes our office every day, for I happened to be standing by the window on Friday and saw her.'

'It was a pity she wouldn't allow us to help her,' Charlotte said. 'But I can understand her reasons, and admire her for them. Taking money from us would have made her feel like a beggar, and she was obviously a girl with too much pride to be bought off. I still think it was a pity, though, for she is so lovely, and I bet she is a fun person.'

'That is something we will never find out.' Andrew turned the key in the ignition. 'Perhaps we should head for home now. Michael and Jessica will be there explaining to our parents what their role will be at the christening. Remember they have been asked to be godparents, and Mother is delighted. She and Father are taking their role very seriously. Second parents to the baby. To be there for the child if help is ever needed.'

'We've been invited to the church for the ceremony, and also for the luncheon afterwards,' Charlotte reminded him. 'And it is customary to buy a gift for the child. Something in silver, usually, with their name inscribed on it.'

'I have been puzzling about that,' Andrew said. 'There's very little you can buy for a boy. Do you have any thoughts on the matter?'

'Yes, I have, my dear brother, and if you agree with my choice, then we can buy it between us. I was getting worried because it is difficult to buy for a baby boy. A girl is easy, as a bangle or necklace is an ideal gift. Anyway, I had this brilliant idea, and rang Jessica. When I told her what I had in mind, she was utterly delighted.'

Andrew slowed the car down to look at his sister's face. 'Well, come on, are you not going to tell me what this brilliant idea was? I can't agree to anything if I don't know what it is.'

'I'm surprised you didn't think of it yourself.' Charlotte's eyes were bright with excitement. 'I want you to tell me what you have in your bedroom that you most cherish? Something you've had since you were two years old, and would never let me play with.'

Andrew's foot came down hard on the brake, and the car came to a standstill. 'My rocking horse!' His face was more animated than Charlotte had seen it in a long time, and she felt cheered. 'Of course,' Andrew said, his open palm hitting the steering wheel. 'How clever of you, Charlotte. It is the perfect gift. I used to get such fun from mine when I was young, pretending I was a cowboy riding the prairie. I have so many memories of the pleasure it gave me, I would never part with it. It will stay in my bedroom until I have a son of my own.'

'Oh, that's lovely.' Charlotte put her arms round his neck. 'I'm so happy I thought of it as a gift we can give from both of us.'

'Have you seen one that is suitable, Charlotte? Time is running out. The christening is on Sunday.'

Charlotte's face was radiant. She was always happy when she pleased someone, but doubly happy when it was the brother she loved. 'I'm way ahead of you, Andrew. I don't dally when I know something needs doing. The rocking horse is being specially made, and the shop has promised faithfully it will be delivered to the Parker-Browns' house on Friday.' She tweaked his ear. 'And I added a bit on the order. I've asked the shop to put a small sign on the side of the horse, almost out of sight, to say it was from Uncle Andrew and Aunt Charlotte, and the date. Now don't you think I've been not only clever, but thoughtful as well?'

'I think you have done a terrific job, and I am very proud of you. When you meet your knight on a white horse, fall in love and marry him, I will make sure your first son is given a rocking horse as a christening present.'

'First things first, brother dear. You need to find a wife, and I need to find a husband. And as you are the oldest, it's up to you to start the ball rolling.'

'You may have a long wait, dear sister, for there is no one on the horizon.'

'Oh, you never know, brother, for I've heard that love can take you by surprise. It will hit you when you're not looking.'

Chapter Ten

'I must congratulate you on your brilliant brainwave, my dear.' Harriet looked across the breakfast table at her daughter. 'Michael and Jessica were beside themselves with pleasure. A rocking horse for their new son is an ideal gift. Jessica has had a room made into a nursery, and she's already making plans on where to stand it.'

Mother and daughter were lingering over a late breakfast, George and Andrew having left for work over an hour ago. 'The person most thrilled was Andrew,' Charlotte said. 'He has so many happy memories of his own rocking horse, he was delighted when I suggested a joint present from us both for baby Leo.'

'An inspired choice, my dear girl. Well done!'

'I'll be going out later, Mother, after I've bathed and dressed.'

'Oh, are you meeting someone for lunch? A male friend perhaps?'

'No, Mother.' Charlotte kept her eyes on the piece of toast in her hand. She couldn't face her mother and tell a lie. 'I'm going down to the shop to make sure the horse will be delivered to Jessica's on Friday. And I've asked for an inscription to be put on, so I need to check on that as well. It would be so disappointing if it wasn't perfect.'

'Your father is picking our gift up today or tomorrow. As you know, we chose to buy a silver rattle and small round tray, both inscribed with the baby's full name and date of birth.'

'Yes, you did tell me, Mother, and I'm looking forward to seeing them. When he's old enough to understand, he can be told all about the day he was christened. How all his parents' friends were there, and how proud his godparents were.'

When Charlotte pushed her chair back and stood up, her mother asked, 'Will you be having coffee before going out?'

'No, Mother, I'll go straight out when I'm ready. I may spend some time looking round the shops, so don't worry if I'm a little late getting back.'

'On your way to the stairs, would you call in the kitchen and tell Frances she can have the table cleared now?' Harriet dabbed the heavy linen napkin on her lips. 'I'll retire to my room now.'

Charlotte was a nervous driver, and was never really happy behind the wheel except in the country, where there was little traffic and she could put her foot down. She hated driving in Liverpool, where there were trams and buses to cope with as well as cars, so she decided not to go into the heart of the city, and parked her car in a side street off London Road.

The walk into the city centre was downhill, and there were lots of shop windows to gaze in, displaying wares of every description. Looking in one shop, Charlotte couldn't believe you could buy a pair of shoes for just five shillings! And she was even more bewildered when the clothes shop next door had quite a pretty dress in the window for only twelve shillings and elevenpence! Her eyes were moving to another dress in the window when she saw a clock on the wall inside the shop, and it told her it was turned eleven o'clock. She would have to hurry if she was to stand any chance of being successful in completing her mission.

Charlotte's plan was a secret. She had told no one, for she knew she would be talked out of it. Even she knew in her heart that what she had in mind was far-fetched, but she was willing to make a fool of herself for the sake of her brother. The girl in the raincoat wouldn't talk to Andrew, but it was possible she would talk to his sister. If she did, all well and good, and if not, then nothing had been lost. So Charlotte positioned herself at the bottom of Castle Street in a spot from where she would see Andrew if he came out of his office for any reason and have time to hide from him, and she would be able to see the girl in the raincoat whichever direction she came from. It was a gamble, but she'd once heard her father say 'You won't get anywhere if you don't try' and she was trying. If she didn't she would always regret it.

It was a cold day, and Charlotte had left her scarf and gloves in the car. So with her coat collar turned up, and her hands in her pockets, she braced herself against the wind coming in from the Mersey. She'd stay until twelve o'clock, and if there was no sign of the girl, then she'd give up and go home.

Charlotte had no sooner set the time in her head than she saw the girl walking in her direction. She knew it was her right away, because there weren't many people lucky enough to have such an abundance of golden hair. And besides, she was wearing the white raincoat. There was no time to rehearse what she would say, or what excuse she could give for being where she was. Taking a deep breath, Charlotte started walking towards the girl, who, as last time, was clutching several items of post.

Few people would have succeeded as Charlotte did. She was by nature very naïve and trusting, and when she stood in front of Poppy with an innocent smile on her pretty face, it would have taken a hard-hearted person to brush her aside.

'Oh, I say, fancy bumping into you! Do you remember me?'

Poppy was suspicious, and made sure Charlotte was alone before answering, 'Yes, I remember you. I have good reason to, don't you think?'

'Oh, yes, of course you do. But it was an accident, and my brother and I were devastated.' Charlotte's smile was so innocent it would have melted the hardest heart. 'I am so glad to have met up with you again.'

'What are you doing here?' Poppy asked. 'I'm sure you don't work, do you?'

Charlotte shook her head. 'No, I don't work.' She had early on decided it would be wrong to tell the girl a pack of lies. She wouldn't be very impressed when she found out, and anyway it wasn't a crime to be rich. Charlotte's father had worked hard for what he had. He hadn't stolen it. 'My family don't think I should work. They're afraid I'd get lost in this big bad world. The reason I'm here now is because some friends of ours are having their baby christened on Sunday, and I've been seeing to the present.'

Poppy looked into the girl's open, friendly face, and couldn't bring herself to be abrupt. But she had letters to deliver and it was her job. 'Look, it's very nice seeing you again, but I really must get about my business.' She held the letters out. 'I have to deliver these on time, or I'll be in trouble. So I'm afraid I'll have to press on.' She put a hand on Charlotte's arm. 'Please don't think you or your brother have to keep apologizing for last week. It was simply an accident. And now I really must leave you.'

'Oh, can I walk with you? I promise I won't keep talking and hold you back. It's just that I don't have anything to do now, and I don't often get a chance to talk to a girl who is about the same age as myself. My name is Charlotte, by the way.'

'Mine is Poppy. And I must say you would find what I do very boring. But if you want a bit of company, then I don't mind if you walk with me.'

Charlotte's face lit up. 'Oh, that is kind of you. And what a lovely name you have. Poppy really suits you.'

As they walked, Poppy explained how her name came about, and smiled at her companion's enthusiasm. It was obvious they were from divergent backgrounds, but she couldn't help warming to the girl who was used to such a very different lifestyle.

When they reached the offices Poppy visited every day, she said, 'I am usually in here for about twenty minutes. Would you not be better going home?'

'I don't mind waiting for you. I'd like to walk back with you, for as I've said I don't often get the chance for girls' talk. I'll wait here for you, if I may.'

'Oh, you don't have to wait out in the cold,' Poppy said. 'You can come in with me, but there'll be no chairs to sit on or fire to warm you, I'm afraid. So, be it on your own head.'

The next half-hour had Charlotte learning more about the real world, and how other people lived. Poppy passed the letters over to the receptionist, Amy, and they were taken through to the main office, where they would be read by the various solicitors, and Amy would be notified whether there were to be replies or not. During the wait, Amy and Poppy enjoyed their usual exchange of opinions on the men they worked for. Charlotte was so quiet they forgot she was there, but the girl was soaking up the conversation and the atmosphere. How different it all was from her own quiet, aimless daily routine.

When a clerk came with a message to say there were no replies, Poppy jerked her head. 'Come on, Charlotte. I have to get back to the office.' As she pulled her gloves on, she told Amy, 'I'm hoping not to be doing this much longer. I've started a shorthand course at the local night school, and I'm determined to move on. To better meself. But I'll keep you up to date with how I'm getting on. I'll be around for a while yet.'

'If you manage it, kid, I might have a go myself,' Amy said. 'This is a dead end job, and I'm chocker. Go in one of the offices upstairs and it's lovely and warm. If they want anything they don't even have to get off their backsides. They just ring a bell and anything they want is put in front of them.'

'Fair play to them, though, Amy, they spent years swotting for the jobs they've got.' Poppy chuckled. 'I'm as jealous as hell of them. They say if you can't lick them, then join them. And that is what I intend to do. So that is today's lecture over, and I'll have a new one ready for tomorrow. Ta-ra for now, Amy.'

Before following Poppy out, Charlotte smiled at Amy. 'Goodbye, and thank you for letting me stand in from the cold.'

Amy was talking to a filing cabinet when she said, 'I don't know her from Adam, but that girl's got breeding.'

Outside, Poppy said, 'You don't have to walk back with me, Charlotte. Why don't you go home where you'll be nice and warm?'

'Oh, it's so boring at home, with nothing to do.' Charlotte walked sideways so she could look Poppy in the face. 'Why don't you let me take you for lunch? What time do you have your break?'

Poppy paused. 'Oh, I'm sorry, Charlotte, but I promised to have lunch with a woman from the office. She only has an elderly mother and no other family, so she lives a lonely life. I wouldn't let her down, not when she'll be looking forward to it.'

'No, I can see you couldn't let her down. You are too caring to hurt someone. But if you would allow me to, I could take you both for lunch. I would like that very much.'

Poppy was shaking her head. 'We don't go to a restaurant, Charlotte. We go to a little café because it's cheap. Anyway, doesn't your brother work in Castle Street? Wouldn't he take you out for lunch?'

'Of course he would. My brother is a wonderful man. And I love him dearly. But we see each other every day at breakfast, then again for dinner. I need some female company.'

'You mean your brother doesn't know you're in town?'

'No, he doesn't know. There was no reason to tell him. I had that call to make over the delivery of the christening present, and then I saw you! Andrew would be very surprised if he knew I was so near.' Charlotte was trying to keep count of the lies she was telling, so that when she said her prayers in bed she could say an extra one for each lie. Not that they were hurting anyone, for she was only trying to help. But she'd say her prayers to make sure. 'I'm so happy I bumped into you, and I've enjoyed having someone my own age to talk to. And I'd love to take you and your colleague to the little café you mentioned. I know I'm childish for my age, but that's because I've never been given any responsibility. But I am not a snob, Poppy, I'm really not.'

Looking into the pretty face, a thought ran through Poppy's head. Her mother had told her once that money doesn't always bring happiness, and she was now seeing it for herself. She couldn't be cruel enough to throw the girl's kindness back in her face. 'You can come to the café, Charlotte, I'm sure Jean would like some extra company. But I insist we all pay for our own meal. It won't be what you're used to, but it's a warm, friendly place, and it's very clean.'

Charlotte was delighted. 'Oh, you are so kind, Poppy. I really do hope we can be friends.'

Poppy knew there was no chance of their ever becoming real friends, but she just didn't have the heart to say so. Anyway, it was only a flash in the pan: Charlotte would soon tire of the difference in their circumstances. It was all a novelty to her now, but it wouldn't last long. They'd probably never see each other again after today. 'I'm afraid you'll have to hang around for half an hour. I wouldn't be allowed to let you wait inside. But if it gets too cold for you, then I'll understand if you're not here when Jean and I come out. Standing in the cold too long with that bitter wind, you could end up with pneumonia. And I wouldn't like to be responsible for that happening.'

'I'll be fine,' Charlotte said. 'My coat is very warm, and I'm stronger than I look. Don't worry about me, Poppy, I won't get blown away.'

Poppy felt guilty, but there was little she could do: her work came first. Anyway, the girl wouldn't last half an hour in that weather. She'd be gone by the time she and Jean went out to dinner.

However, Poppy hadn't reckoned on Charlotte's determination, which was now stronger than ever. She had started out hoping to find a way for Poppy and Andrew to get together, for she was a romantic at heart. But now her mission was twofold, for she really would like to have Poppy as a friend. She was straightforward and down to earth, and much more interesting than the girls who were members of her social circle. But even Charlotte's determination wasn't going to keep the cold wind from making her teeth chatter, so she hailed a passing taxi to take her back to her car. She asked the driver to wait until she'd picked up her gloves and scarf, and then he drove her back to where she'd started from. The gloves and the heavy scarf kept the cold at bay, so it was a chirpy young girl who greeted a very surprised Poppy and her colleague, Jean.

'I thought you'd have gone home by now,' Poppy said, shaking her head. 'Either that or you'd have been turned into a block of ice. Anyway, this is my colleague, Jean, and Jean, this is Charlotte . . . er, a friend of mine.'

It wasn't far to the small café, and once inside Charlotte was all eyes as they found a small table for three. The café was very busy, for it was noted for serving good food at a reasonable price. When Charlotte saw the menu she almost commented on how cheap the food was, but she remembered in time that her circumstances were vastly different from those of the people around her. 'The soup smells very tempting, Poppy. Shall we order that?'

'I think it would be our best bet,' Jean answered her question. 'It's usually very tasty and you get a slice of bread with it.'

A whole new world was opening up for Charlotte. The customers in the small café were working-class people, wearing working-class clothes and speaking with working-class accents. But she wasn't looking down her nose at them;

on the contrary, she was finding the warmth and friendliness very heartening. And she had to admit the soup was delicious and the thick slice of bread very fresh. She wouldn't be telling Jane or Frances though, for then her little outing would become known to her mother, who would certainly be horrified and put a stop on any further outings. Besides, Andrew would find out, and she didn't want him told until there was something to tell. When she got to know Poppy better, then she'd find a way of arranging an accidentally-on-purpose meeting. It would be wonderful if they fell in love with each other. How marvellous it would be to have Poppy as a sister.

'What pleasant thoughts are you having that are bringing such a smile to your face?' Poppy asked. 'You look as though you'd lost a shilling and found half a crown.'

'I'm smiling because I'm happy, Poppy. It's been a very pleasant morning for me, meeting two of your colleagues. So different from my usual routine, which you would find very dull. I do hope you will allow me to join you and Jean again, sometime soon. I won't be under your feet every day, just when I happen to be in town. Would that be all right with you?'

'I suppose so, but as you heard me telling Amy, I'm hoping that sometime in the near future I'll be looking for another job.'

Jean thought Poppy was being very optimistic. After she'd passed the shorthand course, it would take a long time to get her speed up. 'Oh, I think you'll be at Sutherland's for another few months, Poppy. You still have a long way to go.'

Charlotte was sensible enough to know when pushing herself would be the wrong thing to do, so she spoke casually. 'I'm sure I'll see you both again before there are any big changes. I've really enjoyed your company; you've been very kind. But it's time for me to be on my way home, so I'll leave you to have another cup of tea. I'd like to stay, but Mother worries if I'm out too long and she doesn't know where I am.' She wrapped the scarf round her neck and picked up her bag and gloves. 'Goodbye, Jean. It's been a pleasure to meet you.' Then she bent and kissed a startled Poppy on the cheek. 'Goodbye for now, Poppy. I hope to see you again soon.' With that she went to the counter, paid for her own lunch, then with a wave and beaming smile walked out of the door and was lost to sight.

'What a lovely girl!' Jean said. 'You've never mentioned her before. How long have you known her?'

'I don't really know her,' Poppy said. 'We met last week by accident. I never expected to see her again.'

Jean was curious. 'How do you mean, by accident?'

Lost for words, Poppy said the first thing that came into her head. 'I bumped into her in Castle Street last week. Or was it the week before? I can't remember now. But we only spoke a few sentences, then we went on our way.'

'She's out of the top drawer, Poppy, you can tell. Her coat probably cost more than we earn in a year. But she's a very likeable girl; you couldn't fall out with her. She's friendly, and not a bit stuck up.'

Poppy chuckled. 'You mean she didn't once look down her nose at us?' She was sorry as soon as the words left her lips, and could have bitten her tongue off. 'That wasn't funny, and I shouldn't have said it. She is a lovely girl, and she doesn't deserve my sarcasm. All she wants is to be friendly.'

'Well I thought she was very nice, and I'd like to see her again.' Jean reached for her purse. 'What I enjoyed was seeing her tucking into the bread and soup.'

* * *

Charlotte flagged down a taxi, and was soon back where her car was parked. She was feeling a warm glow inside, really happy that things had worked out so well. But in order that the tale she was preparing to tell her mother would not be all lies, she decided to drive to the specialist shop where the rocking horse was being made, for she'd been informed over the telephone yesterday that it was almost finished. All they had to do was add the inscription Charlotte had asked for. But she decided to see for herself that everything was to her liking before the firm delivered it to Jessica's house.

The shop was on the outskirts of the city, and they specialized in making rocking horses that only the wealthy could afford. There was one on display in the window when Charlotte pulled up, and she could feel her excitement grow. She had been told that the man who made the horses was a perfectionist, and only took one order a month. Gazing at the model in the window, Charlotte could understand why. It was a work of art, so lifelike that any child would be thrilled to own it. Charlotte's mind went back over the years, to when she used to pull on Andrew's arm, pleading with him to let her have a ride on his horse. He always gave in to her in the end, but she was only allowed to play on it when he was in the room, watching her every move.

Charlotte looked to see if there were any people near, and then put a hand over her mouth to stifle her laughter. For a picture had come into her mind of herself and her brother. She must have been about three years of age, and Andrew nine. And in this picture, which was very clear, she was offering her doll to Andrew in exchange for a ride on his horse, and he was pushing her away, telling her boys didn't play with dolls. Poor Andrew couldn't get away from her. She dogged his footsteps everywhere.

Some people walked past, and their chattering brought Charlotte out of her reverie. With a shake of her head, and a quiet sigh, she opened the shop door, setting off the tinkling bell fastened above the lintel.

A man came through from a back room, wearing a beige overall over his clothing. He recognized Charlotte immediately, as it wasn't often they had a pretty young girl in the shop. 'It's all finished. Would you like to see it?'

'Oh, yes, I can't wait! Did you have the inscription put on? I want the baby to always remember that my brother and I were thinking of him on the day he was christened.'

'Come through and see for yourself. I'm sure you'll be more than satisfied.'

And the man never spoke a truer word, for the horse was a masterpiece. As she stroked the mane and tail of real hair, Charlotte had tears in her eyes. 'It's beautiful. The reins, stirrups, everything is just wonderful. Leo is a very lucky boy. Now, my brother settled the account with you this morning I believe?'

'Yes, miss, the bill has been paid, and Mr Wilkie-Brook also gave me the address where the horse has to be delivered to. It will be there sometime between ten and eleven o'clock on Friday.'

'Thank you.' Charlotte shook his hand. 'You've been very helpful, and you are very clever. I could never be as creative as you. I don't have any talent at all.'

The man, middle-aged with a receding hairline, smiled. 'I may have the talent, but you have the beauty.'

Charlotte blushed. 'There are a lot of girls prettier than me.'

He chuckled. 'Then I must need glasses. Are you sure I've put the horse's tail on the right end?'

Charlotte was laughing as she walked towards the door. 'The baby is only a few weeks old, and he won't notice. But don't be surprised if he brings it back when he's older.' She turned and thanked him again. 'I'm more than delighted with your work. I shall go home now and sing your praises.'

'Where on earth have you been all this time?' Harriet asked. 'I have been quite concerned about you.'

'I wandered round the shops for a while, but didn't see anything I liked. Then I had a light lunch in a small café, which I enjoyed. Then I went to the shop to make sure all was well with the rocking horse.' Now there were no more lies to be told, Charlotte told her mother how pleased she was with the christening gift. 'Oh, Mother, it far exceeds my expectation. The man is an artistic genius. But you will see it for yourself on Sunday, after the christening. And I'm so looking forward to seeing Andrew's face when he sets eyes on it. I'm sure he'll be thrilled.'

Harriet smiled at her daughter's enthusiasm. 'I'm glad you feel satisfied, my dear, and I'm sure you have good reason to be. Now, be an angel and ring for Frances. I think we could both do with a cup of tea, and one of Jane's delicious cakes.'

Chapter Eleven

'Guess who I bumped into today?' Poppy asked as she sat at the dinner table, next to her brother and facing her mother. 'Have a guess?'

'How many guesses do we get?' David asked. 'I mean, there must be nearly a million people living in Liverpool, and this could take ages. Just give us a clue.'

Poppy frowned in concentration for a while, then her face lit up. 'The clue was in the question.'

Eva tapped an open hand on the table. 'Do I get a prize if I get it right first time?'

'There's no prizes, Mam, but me and David will wash the dishes if you win. If he gets it right first, you and me do the dishes.'

'It was the bloke who knocked you over last week,' Eva said. 'Am I right?'

'You're warm, Mam, but not right.'

David was getting impatient. 'Come on, sis, tell us who it was and get it over with.'

'It was the bloke's sister.' Poppy didn't want to go over the whole episode, or they'd think she was crazy. 'She's a really nice girl, and she even came to the café with me and Jean for some lunch. And before you start, David, she did offer to pay for me and Jean, but we wouldn't let her. As I

154

said, she's a lovely girl, very pretty and very friendly, so I couldn't be rude to her. Anyway, I'll probably never see her again.'

David leaned towards her. 'You told us she was well off, and now you tell us she's very pretty. You don't happen to know if she's got a boyfriend, do you? From the sound of things, she seems like the girl I've been searching for.'

Poppy patted his cheek. 'Unfortunately, my dear brother, you wouldn't be in a position to keep her in the manner to which she is accustomed.'

With a cheeky grin on his handsome face, David answered, 'I'm very adaptable, sis. I could easily get used to the manner to which she is accustomed. I would have no qualms about being a kept man. In fact the idea appeals to me.'

'You might not, son, but wouldn't the young lady in question have a say in the matter?' Eva asked, a smile hovering around the corners of her mouth. 'Or do you think your looks are so devastating she'd fall at your feet?'

'It has been known for girls to give a second glance when they pass me. In fact, two girls were walking past me just today, and they both stopped in their tracks to stare at me. It was quite embarrassing really. I could feel myself blushing.'

'Oh, dear, the poor girls must be hard up for boyfriends, that's all I can say.' Poppy winked across the table at her mother. 'Are yer sure there wasn't another bloke walking beside yer that they were looking at?'

David stroked his chin. 'Let me think now. Yes, I do believe there was someone sharing the pavement with me. It was a young mother with a baby in a pram.'

'Then that accounts for the girls stopping. All women, young and old, are suckers for babies.'

'Blast and damnation,' David said. 'Here's me thinking I'm

God's gift to women, and my own mother and sister kick the legs out from under me.'

'Enough about you, David,' Poppy told him. 'I want to spend an hour on brushing up my shorthand before I go out. So let's finish our dinner, or I won't have time to do all I want to do. Like getting washed and making myself look pretty.'

'What's on tonight, then?' Eva asked. 'Have you got a date?'

Poppy nodded, 'I'm meeting Peter. It's either the Grafton or the pictures, I don't mind one way or the other. But I'm determined to spend an hour trying to make a sentence out of the dots, dashes, and half-moons in my notebook. I want to be able to show Mr Jones that I'm not as thick as I look.'

'You are not thick,' David said. 'I bet by the end of the month you'll be top of the class.'

'I appreciate your faith in me, brother. And without wanting to sound big-headed, I do have a little faith in meself. That's because I'm getting help off Jean in work. What I get through tonight, she'll check for me tomorrow. And I don't mind her telling me where I've gone wrong, not like I would Mr Jones. I felt a bit daft asking him to explain something twice, but not Jean.'

'Don't blame me if you're late,' David said. 'You're the one doing all the talking. And another thing. We said last week that we would correct each other's grammar, but we haven't, not once!'

'Oh, dear, it's very hard trying to do so many things at the same time. I'm quite happy with the way I speak, and no one has ever pulled me up over it before.'

'Well, we wouldn't would we, sweetheart, 'cos we all speak the same. Like Londoners, who have a cockney accent, or people from Birmingham, or Newcastle. They all speak the local dialect. It's nothing to be ashamed of.' Eva leaned forward and put a finger under Poppy's chin. 'Go and do what you want to do, or you'll end up being late for your date. It's one thing keeping a man waiting ten minutes, but half an hour is going too far.'

Poppy stood up. 'I'll get washed and change me dress, first, then I'll get me nose in the book until a quarter to eight. I'm meeting Peter at eight.' As she was passing her brother's chair, she asked, 'Where did I slip up?'

'Only twice, kid, which wasn't bad.' David put a hand on his sister's arm as she started to walk away. 'By the way, what did you say the girl's name was?'

'I didn't say, clever clogs. But if you are so interested, her name is Charlotte. And before you ask, I haven't the foggiest idea what her second name is. So unhand me and let me get moving.'

Peter hurried towards the bus when he saw Poppy standing on the platform. He held her hand as she stepped down, saying, 'You're late again. I thought you weren't coming.'

'I'm sorry, Peter, but by the time I'd had my dinner, chatted to my mother and brother for a while, and spent some time on homework, well, the time seemed to fly over. And I had to get washed and changed. So don't shout at me, or I'll cry.'

Peter cupped her elbow and whispered in her ear, 'If you're going to cry, please do it on my shoulder so I'll have an excuse to hold you tight. I could even kiss your tears away.'

'Don't push your luck, Peter, or I'll set my brother on to yer. He's as tall as you are, and he packs a powerful punch.'

'He wouldn't see us sitting in the dark in the back row of the stalls. The rendezvous of courting couples.'

'Some hope you've got,' Poppy huffed. 'The only thing

I'm courting for the next few months is my homework book and the night class teacher.'

'You're really serious about changing your job, aren't you? Why this sudden urge?'

'I've never been more serious in my life. I messed up when I left school, but I'm not going to mess up again. I'm going to stick at it this time.'

'If your job doesn't suit you, then look for another one. I might be able to help you get an office job. My father has a small business; I could have a word with him.' Peter squeezed her arm. 'I'm sure my father would find you work you enjoyed.'

Poppy shook his arm away. 'I don't want just an office job, Peter. I've already got one of those and I don't like it. I want a change, and a chance to better me . . . er, myself. So if I'm late for one of our dates, then you'll have to put up with it. Either that or tell me to get lost. That may be the best for you.'

'You won't get rid of me so easily, Poppy, so you may as well calm yourself down and tell me whether we're going to the flicks or dancing?'

'Let's go dancing, please. If we go to the pictures and it's a sad film, I'll only cry me . . . er, my eyes out.' Poppy's shoulders began to shake with laughter. 'I may as well finish off by saying that if the band start playing a sentimental slow foxtrot, you'll have to lend me your hankie 'cos I didn't bring one with me.'

'You little minx,' Peter said, laughter in his voice. 'Have you been having me on since you got off the bus? And like a fool I fell for it! I even offered to ask my dad if he could give you a job! And all the time you've been having the time of your life, laughing up your sleeve at me.'

'A minx I might be, Peter, but little I am not. Five foot five is not small for a girl.'

When they reached the entrance of the Grafton, they could hear the strains of a waltz, and Peter said, 'They always have a slow foxtrot after a waltz, so don't stay long in the cloakroom. My feet are itching to get on the floor.'

'I've only got to hang my coat up and give my hair a quick comb. I can do that in less than a minute. Is that quick enough for you?'

'Don't waste time asking me questions, my five foot five minx, be on your way.'

Poppy was smiling when she pushed the cloakroom door open, thinking Peter was a very easy bloke to be with. She was hanging her coat up when she heard her name being called. She turned. 'Hello, Julie. How are you? Are you still going out with Jim?'

Julie wrinkled her nose. 'No chance! I thought I told yer last time I saw yer that I wouldn't waste me time on him. I've got better fish to fry.'

Poppy had no intention of being drawn into any further conversation, because she thought Jim was a really nice bloke. Too nice for Julie to pull to pieces. 'I'd better go. I told Peter I wouldn't be long.'

'Still going out with him, are yer?' Julie asked. 'Courting strong?'

'I wouldn't say that.' Poppy could hear sarcasm in the voice of the girl who was once her best mate, and she thought it best to walk away. 'We're good friends who enjoy each other's company. And I better hadn't keep him waiting.'

But Julie wasn't going to be put off. 'Yer were dead lucky getting in front of me that night. If yer hadn't, I'd have got Peter, and you'd have been left with soft lad Jim.'

Poppy spun round. 'Jim is a nice bloke, far too good for you. He's had a lucky escape. And now I would be grateful if you went your way and allowed me to go mine. Please keep away from me in future.'

'Oh, Miss Hoity-Toity now, eh? Aren't I good enough for yer?'

'I used to think you were,' Poppy said as she walked on. 'But people change, it's only natural. We all grow up sometime.'

Peter was waiting with a hand outstretched. 'That is the longest minute I have ever known. What kept you?'

Julie was passing at that moment and she sniggered. 'She's been looking at herself in the mirror. No one else could get a look in.'

Peter raised his brows as he took Poppy's hand. 'Lucky old mirror. It must have thought it was its birthday, seeing such a beautiful face.'

Poppy pulled him towards the door of the dance hall. 'Come on, or the dance will be over.'

'What's got into your friend?' Peter asked as he took Poppy in his arms. 'She's not exactly full of the joys of spring. Do I detect jealousy rearing its ugly head?'

'Oh, take no notice of her. I'm not going to let her spoil my night. And earlier on you said yer feet were itching to get on the dance floor, so let's enjoy the dance.'

'My arms were itching too, Poppy. They couldn't wait to wrap themselves round you.'

Poppy found herself relaxing and enjoying the strains of the sentimental song. Peter really was a very smooth dancer, and it was easy to follow his steps. And if he was holding her very close, and stealing the odd kiss on her cheek, well, there was no harm in that. He would never take advantage of her: he wasn't the type.

It was when they were dancing the waltz that Poppy suddenly remembered what Peter had said about his father's helping her to get a job she liked. She had to ask. 'Peter, what did you mean when you told me your father might be in a position to help me get a job? I don't need him to help, and I'm not being nosy, but I just wondered.'

'My dad has a business, and I thought he might be able to help. I really thought you were upset, but you were having me on. In future I'll have to keep my eye on you, and learn to know when you're pulling my leg.'

'I do have an odd mad half-hour now and again, but most of the time I'm quite sane. And I am never dangerous.' The music ended then, and Peter was leading Poppy off the floor when she asked, 'What sort of business does your father have? Just out of interest – you don't have to tell me if you don't want to. In fact, thinking about it, it was rude of me to ask, so forget I did.'

Holding on to her hand, Peter answered, 'I don't mind you asking questions, Poppy, because it means you are interested in me. And dad's business is no secret. He deals in property.'

'Oh, that sounds interesting.' Poppy had a grin on her face. 'The only deal I've ever done is when I deal a hand at cards. And I'm dead unlucky. I never win.'

'You are not unlucky, Poppy, not in anything. Certainly not in looks or personality. And when I said my father deals in property, I meant he owns some houses in the Walton area, and around Bootle. He has an office in Walton, employs a couple of men as rent collectors, and has two women working in the office.'

'Do you work for your father?'

'I work with him, not for him.' Peter put an arm round her waist and walked her towards the dance floor, where couples were spacing themselves for a tango. 'Dance now and talk later, sweetheart.'

'Oh, you can't call me that!' Poppy met his eyes. 'That's what my mother has always called me, ever since I can remember.'

'I'll think of another name for you while we're dancing. I wouldn't dream of copying your mother.' They had only gone a few steps when Peter asked, 'How about pet? Would you like that?'

'I might if I was a dog or a cat. But as I'm not, you'll have to think of something else. Although I don't know what's wrong with calling me by my proper name.'

'I love your name, and it really suits you. But I'd like to have a special, more romantic name for you.' Peter had pressed his cheek close. 'One that no one else is allowed to use. One which means you are my girl and out of bounds to any other bloke.'

'You might be able to do that in a few months, Peter, but not yet. It's too soon. When I've found myself a decent job, and I'm settled in my mind, then perhaps we can talk about pet names and going steady.' The music came to an end and she led him off the floor. 'You are too nice to be messed about, Peter; that's why I'm being honest with you. To have the life I yearn for, I've got to go for it, or I'll never forgive myself. I want to feel I've accomplished something, so I'll know I've done the best with whatever gifts I've got. And my aims are not all for myself: it's not all selfishness. As I told you, my mother had to go out to work when my dad died, to keep my brother and me. And she's never once complained. My brother can start making it up to her the week after next, when he comes out of his time. We won't be so strapped for money then. And I want to pay her back for the sacrifices she's had to make over the years. To do that I need to earn more than I do at the moment. So now you have the list of my aims. If you don't want to wait six months or more, then I'll understand. You deserve more than I'm prepared to give right now. You'll have no trouble finding yourself a nice girl.'

'Oh, I know that, for I've found myself one.' Peter stroked his chin as his eyes rolled to the ceiling. 'If it's only for six months, how about me calling you "babe", or "honey"? Would either of those suit until I can call you "darling"?'

How could you fall out with him, Poppy asked herself. Perhaps in six months, when her life was more settled, she would grow closer to him, and when he touched her the missing ingredient would appear, as her mother said. 'I think I'll settle for "babe". I rather like that.'

Poppy's dream of advancing her prospects was strengthened the next morning when Mr John stood at the side of her desk with some letters in his hand. He didn't speak, just stood there, staring at her face, and the swell of her breasts he could see down the front of her dress. He stood for ages, just staring. Poppy kept her head down, but she felt sick in her tummy as she imagined him licking his lips. In the end she could stand it no longer. 'Do you want something, Mr John?'

'Is that an invitation, Miss Meadows? If so, I would be very happy to take advantage of your offer.' Conscious of his secretary sitting a few yards away, he kept his voice low. 'Lunch perhaps? I know a very comfortable hotel not far from here. I would make sure you were well satisfied and back at your desk on time.'

Poppy raised her eyes. How she would have enjoyed telling him exactly what she thought of him. The very thought of him touching her was enough to make her cringe. 'I'm meeting a friend for lunch, Mr John. It's a regular thing. We meet every day.' She lowered her eyes while raising an open hand. 'I'll take the letters, shall I? I wouldn't like to be late with them.'

The letters were put down with a heavy hand, and a very angry Mr John strode to his office. As he opened the door, he called, 'Miss Slater, my office, now!'

Poppy pulled a face as Jean passed her desk, notebook and pencil at the ready. 'I'll see you later. We can talk at lunchtime.'

'He may have money, but he certainly doesn't have any manners,' Jean said. 'I can understand why you want to get out.'

Poppy put the cover over her typewriter before donning her coat and picking up the letters. It wasn't raining, that was a blessing. And as she made her way up to Mr John's client's office, she was deep in thought, oblivious of the people passing either side. So when she felt a hand on her arm, she gave a start.

'I'm sorry, I didn't mean to startle you.' Andrew Wilkie-Brook had watched Poppy walking towards him, and had been in two minds whether to greet her. He desperately wanted to, for she was constantly in his thoughts, and he might never get another opportunity. 'I just wanted to ask if you are recovered from the unfortunate accident?'

Poppy was flustered. First the sister, and now the brother! But perhaps she shouldn't mention Charlotte in case the girl hadn't told her family she'd been in the city. 'Oh, I'd quite forgotten, but now I know who you are. Of course I have recovered. I wasn't hurt. One or two bruises, but nothing to worry about.' Poppy looked into his face, and without realizing she was doing it, she asked herself why she felt strange being near him. She'd had the same feeling the day he bumped into her. Then she had thought he was a toff, looking down on her, but he wasn't looking down at her now, he was looking straight into her face. 'How is your sister?'

'Charlotte is very well, thank you. I will tell her you asked.' Andrew was lost now. He had no idea how to talk freely to a girl. He waved his hand towards the building behind him, and said, 'This is where I work, if you ever need anything. Just ask for Andrew, Miss . . . er . . . I'm sorry, I don't know your name.'

'Poppy. Poppy Meadows. But I won't be troubling you. I will have no need. And now I really must go, Andrew. Goodbye.'

'Goodbye, Poppy. I hope you don't think I'm being forward calling you Poppy, but it's such a lovely name.'

'Thank you. But I really must dash or I'll be getting the sack.'

With that she was gone, leaving Andrew cursing himself for being so shy. He was used to dealing with hard business-men, yet couldn't hold a conversation with a girl. How his father would laugh if he knew. It was different with Charlotte's friends, and other girls from their social circle, for they were very easy to talk to. Their conversations were usually about hairstyles and clothes, nothing more serious.

And while Andrew was disappointed in himself, Poppy was wondering whether she'd done the right thing by not mentioning she'd spent time with Charlotte. Still, it was too late to worry now. What was done was done, and couldn't be undone.

'Only a couple of letters today, Amy.' Poppy squeezed into the tiny box of a room the receptionist worked in. 'How is life treating you?'

Amy held the letters aloft. 'I'll take these through first, then

165

we can have a natter.' And within minutes she was back, saying, 'They'll ring if a reply is needed. If they haven't rung in ten minutes, Mr Simon said you could leave.'

'Don't you freeze, sitting in here all day with no heating?' Poppy asked. 'My teeth are chattering after five minutes.'

Amy grinned. 'My hands feel the cold, but not the rest of me. I got meself well wrapped up this morning in one of me mam's thick vests, a pair of her fleecy lined drawers, and thick lisle stockings.'

Poppy's jaw dropped. 'You don't mean bloomers, do you?'

Amy nodded, her face creased with laughter. 'I don't care if it snows today, I'm as warm as toast. The only little worry I have is getting run over. I'd die of humiliation if I ended up in hospital and the doctor saw me bloomers.'

Poppy thought it was hilarious. 'I didn't think you could still buy bloomers. I've never seen them in the shops. I thought they were a thing of the past.'

'Me mam gets them from the market. And I'll tell yer what, Poppy, I'd rather be warm and out of fashion than freeze in the skimpy briefs the girls wear these days.'

'Ay, don't be putting years on me.' Poppy laughed. 'You can grow old if yer want, but me, I'm with the skimpy briefs.'

'Oh, before yer leave, do tell me who the young girl is. You know, Charlotte. She's a lovely girl, and I really liked her, but it sticks out a mile that she's not one of us. How do you know her?'

Oh, dear, a little voice in Poppy's head said. You can't get away from brother or sister. They've got me telling fibs now. 'Oh, I just bumped into her one day, and we got chatting. She's not one of us, as you say, but that doesn't mean she's not a nice person. I've only met her twice, but I really like her.'

'What's her name, apart from Charlotte?' Amy was curious. 'And where does she live?'

Poppy raised her brows. 'You are very nosy, Amy. And I'm sorry to disappoint you, but I don't know her full name, or where she lives. And I really don't care one way or the other. I'm certainly not going to ask about her private life, even if I do ever see her again. Which I very much doubt. The times I've met her were both by pure accident.'

Amy wrinkled her nose. 'Pity that, 'cos I've never met anyone really wealthy. If yer do meet her again, will yer bring her to see me?'

'I can't promise anything, Amy, but we'll see if she turns up again. Right now I'm more interested in my own life than anyone else's. That's why I'm going to love you and leave you now. I'm getting some help with my homework from a secretary where I work. She's helping me in our lunch break.'

'So ye're sticking to it, are yer? I wish I had the guts to get out and find meself something better, but I'm too slow to catch a cold. I'll be in this ruddy job when I'm due to draw me old age pension. That's if I live that long.'

'You'll live to a ripe old age if you keep wearing fleecy lined bloomers.' Poppy chuckled. 'You'll never get a feller, but you'll always have yer knickers to keep yer warm.'

Poppy was wearing a smile as she walked back to her office. She couldn't believe Amy was wearing old-fashioned fleecy bloomers. Still, if she had to work in a freezing office all day, she might sing a different tune. Having to work in those conditions in this day and age shouldn't be allowed.

She was halfway down Castle Street when she felt her eyes sliding sideways to the office buildings across the street. Charlotte's brother had come out of one of them, and waved his hand towards it when he said it was where he worked. But there were two buildings with entrances very close together, and she didn't know which was the one he meant. Then she mentally pulled herself together when a little voice in her head asked what difference it made where he worked. It had nothing to do with her, and she wasn't interested anyway.

By the time she got back to her office it was lunchtime, so she made no effort to take her coat off. There was no sign of Jean, but she could hear Mr John's raised voice and gathered he was in a temper and taking his spite out on his secretary. A minute later, when Jean came out of his office, Poppy knew she was right by the look of disgust on her colleague's face. 'Don't let him get to you, Jean,' she said. 'Put your coat on and let's get out of here.'

Once out in the fresh air, Jean gave a sigh of relief. 'He is a dreadful man. I'm beginning to hate the sight of him. He has no manners whatsoever, and God knows how his wife puts up with him.'

Poppy linked her arm. 'That's her lookout. But you can bet a pound to a penny that whatever she puts up with, it'll be in the lap of luxury.'

'Let's forget about work for a while and talk about something more interesting.' Jean was pushing the café door open when she turned her head to ask, 'Did you bring your notebook with you?'

Poppy swung her handbag. 'It's in here. I spent an hour on it last night, but if you're not in the mood we can leave it until tomorrow.'

Jean found a table for two and sat down. 'I think I'll have the soup again. It's always tasty and filling. And there'll be time to go over your homework.'

'I'll have the same,' Poppy said. 'I'll put the order in, and it's on me today. Just a little thank you for helping me out.'

After they'd finished their lunch, Poppy poured out two cups of tea before passing her notebook to her friend. 'And the best of British, Jean, 'cos it's my first try and I couldn't really understand what I was writing. So if I couldn't understand what I'd written, there's no chance for you.'

When Jean had pushed the door of the café open, she'd been really down in the dumps, fed up with life in general. But going over Poppy's homework was as good as a tonic, and she laughed so much it brought tears to her eyes.

Poppy didn't know whether to laugh with her or cry. 'It's not that bad, is it?'

'I find it really funny,' Jean said, wiping a tear away. 'But I don't think Mr Jones will see the funny side. What I suggest is that I write down in shorthand the lines Mr Jones has written in longhand. That way you can keep looking at mine until you've learned the shorthand for each word he has written. And don't look so downhearted, Poppy, because everyone finds it difficult at first. You'll soon catch up with the rest of the class because you are doing extra homework. And you'll have two teachers. I can't do much for you, but even fifteen minutes in our dinner hour will be a good help. I bet in a month's time you'll find it's all clicked into place.'

Poppy was feeling good, inspired by Jean's words. 'I'll press on if it kills me, Jean. I am so determined, nothing will stop me. The sooner I can tell Mr John where to put his job, the better. And you're not too old to look for another place, either! I bet there's plenty of firms would take you on with your experience. Just think of Mr John's face if we both gave notice. Ooh, I'd look forward to that.'

Chapter Twelve

On her way to night school on the Thursday night, Poppy didn't know whether she was looking forward to handing in her homework or not. Even though she'd spent hours on it herself, and she'd had help from Jean over lunch for the past two days, she still didn't feel confident. And when the school gates loomed up, her mind went back to when she was a little girl and didn't want to let go of her mother's hand outside the gates of the school she attended.

Poppy took a deep breath, told herself she was no longer a little girl, and strode across the playground. The school was mostly in darkness, for only two of the classrooms were used for the evening classes. There was a hum of conversation as pupils exchanged notes, and Poppy headed towards Joy and Jane, the two girls she had befriended. They waved when they saw her, and Joy called, 'We've saved you a seat.'

'How far have yer got, Poppy?' Jane asked. 'Did yer manage to get the hang of it?'

Poppy rolled her eyes as she sat down. 'Only Mr Jones will be able to answer that when he checks my homework. I did my best, spending time on it every night, but I'll have to wait for his opinion. I won't be as advanced as you two, seeing as you had a two-week start on me, but I'll catch up, given time.'

A hush descended when the teacher entered the room. He

170

170

was a middle-aged man, with a round pleasant face, and he wore his glasses halfway down his nose, so he could see through or over them. After greeting the pupils, he said, 'I will write tonight's homework on the blackboard, and you can start to copy it into your notebooks. The couple who were late joining the course, I will check your homework first before you begin to copy what is on the board.'

'Oh, crikey,' Poppy moaned, 'that means me. I hope he gives me good marks.'

'There wouldn't be much point in him giving you good marks if you don't deserve them,' Jane said. 'You'd never learn if he did that. Which would mean you never getting the good job you've set your heart on.'

There was silence in the room, except for the sound of chalk grating across the blackboard. When he'd finished, Mr Jones said, 'You may start now. Late starters to my desk with their homework.'

Poppy joined the other girl walking towards the teacher's desk. 'Just leave them there,' Mr Jones said. 'You can begin copying what's on the board while I check them.'

Poppy sat down and picked up her pencil. 'I can't stop me hand shaking,' she said in a whisper. 'Anyone would think it was a matter of life or death. I'm letting it get the better of me, and that's daft.'

'Stop talking, Poppy,' Joy said, 'everyone is giving yer daggers. They can't concentrate when you're gabbing away.'

A loud tut-tut came from Jane. 'You're making more noise telling her to keep quiet than she's making!'

Poppy saw the funny side, and it was with great difficulty that she stifled her laughter. As she started to copy what was on the blackboard, a little voice in her head told her to pull herself together and act her age, or she'd never get a decent job.

However, when she was called over to the teacher's desk, her tummy started to do cartwheels. She'd die of embarrassment if Mr Jones told her she was wasting his time as well as her own. But the teacher said she was doing fairly well, seeing it was her first attempt. 'Keep at it, Miss Meadows,' he said. 'You have a way to go yet, but your homework shows promise. Well done!'

Poppy almost skipped back to her seat, she was so pleased. She had been given the incentive to carry on now, and carry on she would. No one would be allowed to knock her off course, and that was a rule she would stick to. If she ever felt herself weakening, she would just conjure up Mr John's face with his searching eyes. That would do the trick if nothing else did.

'We're ready to go, Poppy. Are yer coming?' Jane asked. 'It's taken you ages to write the homework down, so will yer put a move on, please?'

'Is yer boyfriend meeting yer?' Joy sounded eager. 'Is he?'

'What boyfriend are you talking about?' Poppy looked puzzled. 'I don't have one.'

'Oh, don't come that with us.' Jane laughed. 'We don't miss much, do we, Joy? We saw him meet yer the other night. He's a smashing-looking bloke.'

Nosy beggars, Poppy thought. I don't want them knowing any of my business. 'Oh, I know who you mean. But he's not my boyfriend, just someone I know.'

'In that case,' Jane said, 'if he's not spoken for, introduce him to me and Joy. We're both on the lookout for a feller.'

'He wouldn't be any good to you, I'm afraid.' Poppy found herself telling lies again. 'He's married with two children. And his wife is a real beauty, the image of Doris Day.' She was thanking her lucky stars that she'd told Peter she definitely didn't want him to meet her tonight. She could just imagine these two fawning over him. 'I might as well walk with you to the bus stop. I don't like being on my own in the dark.'

'Do yer live far?' Joy asked. 'Me and Jane only live two streets from each other.'

'Two bus stops, that's all. I could walk it in ten minutes, but as I said, I don't fancy walking in the dark.'

'If you're frightened, we'll come with yer,' Joy said. 'We wouldn't mind, would we, Jane? Half an hour is neither here nor there, and it wouldn't take any longer than that.'

'Yeah, we wouldn't mind coming with yer for company.' Jane nodded agreement. 'I'm not too happy about walking alone in the dark meself: that's why me and Joy stick together.'

Poppy felt terrible. She'd lied to them, called them for everything in her mind, and here they were being so kind to her. God would punish her for being a hypocrite. 'That's very kind of you, and I do appreciate it. But I couldn't take you so far out of your way. If you see me on the bus, then I'll be fine. The stop I get off is just at the top of the street I live in. I've only got to cross the road and walk about twenty yards.'

'Well, if you're sure, we'll just see you on the bus,' Jane said. 'I won't be sorry to get home meself. My feet are freezing.' The couple walked either side of Poppy and linked arms with her. 'A hot water bottle tonight without fail. It can be warming the bed while I'm drinking me Horlicks.'

'Oh, hot chocolate for me,' Joy said. 'Horlicks is too sickly sweet for my liking.'

'Mine's a cup of tea,' Poppy said, as they gathered at the bus stop. 'You can't beat a cup of tea.'

'Here's your bus,' Joy said, freeing Poppy's arm. 'You'll be home before we are.'

'Thanks for walking with me.' Poppy jumped on the platform and turned to add, 'You're good mates.'

The two friends waved. 'See yer on Monday.'

Poppy sat on the first seat inside the bus, and waved to the two girls before sitting up straight and pulling her skirt down over her knees. She noticed a man sitting in the seat opposite looking at her, so she turned her head away. He was well dressed, in a smart overcoat and trilby hat, and was probably on his way home to his wife and children.

As the bus neared the second stop, Poppy felt in her pocket for the two pennies she'd put there in readiness for the fare. The conductor was standing by the driver, and Poppy passed the coins over when the bus came to a halt. 'Thanks, love,' the conductor said. 'Here, take yer ticket.'

Accepting the ticket, Poppy stuck it in her pocket and jumped off the platform. She stood on the pavement waiting for a lull in the traffic, and then hurried across the road into her street. There was a bitterly cold wind out, and she pulled the collar of her coat up to cover her ears as she moved swiftly past houses darkened by drawn curtains. It was very quiet, the only sound being Poppy's high heels on the pavement. Suddenly she felt her body stiffen, and she sensed someone walking close behind her. Filled with fear, she moved faster, now only six doors from her house and safety. But she was pulled up sharp when an arm went round her waist and another round her neck, cutting off her breathing. Her brain wasn't working, and it was by instinct that she brought her right leg forward, bent her knee, then kicked her foot back as hard as she could. Her heel caught the shin of her attacker and he squealed in agony, allowing the arm across Poppy's throat to relax. She took a deep breath, then screamed at the top of her voice. And luck was with her, for at that moment one of her neighbours was leaving his house to go to work on the night shift at Seaforth docks. Ally Boden had just closed the door when he heard the scream, and he was out of the gate in seconds. He quickly took in the scene: Poppy bent double, breathless and crying, and a bloke running fast up the street. He was quick-witted was Ally, and he knew it was a choice between helping Poppy or going after the man. His anger took him sprinting up the street after the coward who had picked on a lone woman.

Inside the Boden house Marg stood in the middle of the room, her ears cocked. 'Did you hear a scream, Sarah, or was I hearing things?'

'I thought I heard something,' her elder daughter said. 'Just before me dad banged the door after himself. But it might have been the wind.'

'I'll have a look,' Marg said, 'put me mind at rest.' She walked through the hall and shivered when she felt a draught coming from under the front door. 'The number of times I've asked Ally to get a draught excluder for this door, and he still hasn't done it. I might as well talk to meself.'

It was dark outside, and it took Marg a few seconds for her eyes to focus properly. Then she heard someone sobbing, and she switched the hall light on before stepping down on to the short path.

Poppy saw the light go on in her neighbour's hall, and she called, 'Marg, can you give us a hand?'

'In the name of God, what's happened?' Marg saw Poppy's bag and contents strewn across the pavement, with papers fluttering in the wind. 'Did yer fall over, queen?'

Poppy shook her head. Her throat was sore, for the bloke had been really rough with her. 'Some bloke attacked me.

Thank God Ally came out when he did, or it might have been a lot worse.'

'Where is Ally?' Marg asked. 'He hasn't gone off to work and left yer like this, has he? I'll break his bleeding neck for him!'

'No, he ran after the bloke, Marg! I don't know what's happened to him. I've only just got me breath back. I really thought the bloke was going to choke me.' Poppy bent down to retrieve her bag. 'I suppose he was after me bag, but he would have got his eye wiped 'cos there's only coppers in it, and a bit of make-up.'

'Are these books yours, queen?' Marg picked them up and handed them over. 'They'll be dirty, so watch yer coat.'

'It's homework from night school,' Poppy said, a quiver in her voice. 'I told yer about the shorthand course.'

'Here's Ally coming now,' Marg said. 'I'll give yer mother a knock.'

'He got away, the bastard.' Ally was out of breath. 'I got as near as touching him, but he was too quick for me.' He held out a trilby hat to Marg as she passed him. 'I managed to knock this off, and I only wish his head had been in it.'

Eva came hurrying up, followed by David. 'Oh, sweetheart, what happened to yer?'

Seeing her mother brought Poppy's tears. 'Oh, Mam, he gave me the fright of me life.'

Ally touched her arm. 'I'll have to go, love, or I'll be late for work. I'm sorry I didn't catch the bugger. I would love to have belted him one.'

'I'm just glad you came out when yer did, Ally,' Poppy told him, ' 'cos heaven knows what would have happened if you hadn't. I managed to give him a kick, but I was no match for him.'

'You go to yer work, Ally,' Eva said. 'We don't want yer getting yer wages docked. But I can't thank you enough. We're beholden to yer.'

'Yes, you go, love,' Marg said. 'I'll go to Eva's to make sure Poppy's all right.' She stood on tiptoe and pecked his cheek. 'See yer in the morning.'

Back in the Meadows' house, Eva and Marg fussed over Poppy. Her coat was taken off, and a chair was placed by the fire to warm her through. She was shivering, partly from the cold, but mostly from shock. Eva put her arms round her daughter, while Marg went to the kitchen to put on the kettle. The one person who hadn't uttered a word was David, for he was too angry. And his anger was directed at himself, for he felt he'd let his sister down. There was no logic to his thoughts, for he couldn't be with Poppy everywhere she went. But all that was going round in his head was that he was the man of the house, Poppy's older brother. He was supposed to protect his mother and sister. 'Did you know the man, sis?' He finally found his voice. 'Had you seen him before?'

Eva rubbed her daughter's back. 'Don't talk about it if it's going to upset you, sweetheart. Give yerself time for yer nerves to calm down and get over the shock.'

'I'm all right, Mam, don't you worry about me. It was a real shock, and me nerves are shattered, but I'm not badly hurt, and I haven't been robbed. Things could have been worse, and after a good night's sleep I'll feel better. Anyway, what was it you asked, David?'

'If you had seen the bloke before, and if you'd know him again?'

'I'm all confused in me head. I never saw his face but I'm sure it was nobody I know. There was a bloke on the bus I noticed looking at me, but I can't remember him getting off the bus with me. And anyway, he didn't look the type to attack a woman.'

David leaned forward. 'Would you know him if you saw him again?'

'Not really.' Poppy sighed. 'All I noticed was he was wearing a good overcoat, and he had a trilby on.'

Marg came out of the kitchen carrying a cup of tea in one hand, and holding a trilby hat aloft with the other. 'Was the hat anything like this? Ally managed to knock this off the bloke's head.' She handed the tea to Poppy, and the hat to David. 'Pity he couldn't have caught the bugger. He'd have knocked the stuffing out of him. He's handy when it comes to fighting, is my Ally.'

David held the hat in front of his sister. 'Does this look like the trilby he was wearing?'

'It could be,' Poppy said. 'But I couldn't be sure because I didn't take that much notice. And lots of men wear hats like that. It would be impossible to pick one out.'

'You get that tea down yer, queen,' Marg said. 'I made it sweet 'cos sweet tea is good for the nerves. And if yer don't need me to do anything for yer, I'll get home. Sarah will wonder where I've got to. I'll give yer a knock in the morning, just to see how things are.' She squeezed Poppy's arm. 'Goodnight and God bless, queen.'

As Marg walked into the hall, Poppy called after her. 'Thank Ally in the morning for me, Marg. If he hadn't come to my rescue, heaven knows what the blighter would have done. I could have been really hurt.'

When the door closed on their neighbour, Eva said, 'You can thank Ally yourself in the morning, sweetheart, because yer won't be going in to work.'

'Of course I'll be going in to work, Mam! I can't afford to take a day off.'

'The firm wouldn't dock your wages if they knew why you took the day off,' David said. 'You're entitled to so many paid sick days every year.'

Poppy was agitated. 'I'm not taking the day off! I'll be fine in the morning, you'll see. I'm not going to let some thug change my life.' She pointed to the table where her night school books were looking the worse for wear. 'I've got homework to do, and Jean in work helps me with it. I learn more in five minutes with Jean than in a whole lesson. There's over twenty in the class, whereas I get private tuition off Jean. It was thanks to her help that the teacher said my homework was promising. So while I'm doing well, I want to keep at it.'

She stared at the flames licking the pieces of coal in the grate, and her mind was turning over. 'D'yer know, I've never been really frightened of being out on me own in the dark, but tonight has been really weird. First, Peter wanted to meet me outside the school to walk me home, but I said I definitely didn't want him to. And there's two girls I've made friends with in the class, who walked to the bus stop with me and saw me on the bus. They offered to walk home with me as well, but I said there was no need to, 'cos I'd be fine. That's some coincidence, isn't it? The one night I turn down two offers of help, I get attacked! That's what I call uncanny.'

'I'll meet you outside night school in future,' David said. 'Then no harm can come to you. Otherwise me and our mam will worry ourselves sick every night. If you're five minutes late, we'll be tearing our hair out. So I'll be there, at the school gates, to meet you.'

'No, I'll let Peter meet me. It's no good you losing two nights of yer social life when Peter wants to do it. It's not for ever, only until the course finishes, and the nights will be lighter then anyhow. But it's taught me a lesson. I'll be on me guard in future. Night time or day time, I'll have eyes in the back of me head. But what's the world coming to, when a girl can't walk the streets in safety?'

'All men are not thugs, sis. This was a one-off. I think he was the bloke on the bus. He saw yer were alone, noticed yer had a handbag, and with it being dark he took a chance. He probably thought he'd grab yer bag and run. But you and Ally foiled him.'

'All he would have got for his trouble was about a shilling. That's all I had on me. I'm skint until I get my wages tomorrow.'

'Life isn't all misery for you, my lovely sister,' David said, smiling into her face. 'Only one day to go before Saturday, then you'll feel on top of the world. Or as the saying goes, the world is your oyster.'

'What's got into you, soft lad?' Poppy thought her brother had picked a bad time to pull her leg. 'What have I got to look forward to?'

Eva left her daughter's side and sat down. There was a smile on her face, for she knew David was about to cheer Poppy up. And he'd chosen the perfect way to do it.

'Have you forgotten about Saturday?' David asked. 'Here's me getting all excited for you, and you don't even remember.'

'What are you on about, David? This is hardly the time for practical jokes. I've got a splitting headache.'

'I'm sure you won't have a splitting headache on Saturday, when you and our mam go into town with eight pound between you to buy two nice warm winter coats.'

Poppy's face became animated. She knew her brother wouldn't be pulling her leg over this. He wouldn't be so cruel. 'Where did the eight pound come from? It'll only be six pound when me and mam add our ten shilling this week, and I thought we were waiting till next Saturday to buy the coats.'

Eva leaned over to pat her hand. 'David's put two pound to our money for the last two weeks, so we'll have four pound each. We should get a decent coat for that.'

Poppy put a hand on each of her brother's cheeks. 'Ooh, you little love. You are the best brother in the world. That has really bucked me up – something good to look forward to. But I hope yer haven't been leaving yerself skint just to please us?'

'Ay, don't forget I come out of my time at the end of next week,' he told her, 'so you're not the only one with something to look forward to. I did cut down on spending, but it didn't do me any harm. And after next week I go on full pay, so I'll be three pound a week better off.'

Poppy was more relaxed now; the knots in her tummy had eased off. She smiled at her mother. 'So, life isn't all bad, Mam! Me and you will be swanking on Saturday in our new coats. Have you thought about what colour you'd like?'

'It won't be a bright colour, that's all I know at the moment, sweetheart. Probably navy or black. As long as it's warm I'm not fussy. What about you? Do you have a colour in mind?'

'I'd like a colour that'll look good in summer as well as winter. I'll need to get good wear out of it until I'm earning a better wage. But if money was no problem, I'd go for a rich deep red, or a medium blue.'

'You'll be able to wear it on Saturday if you're going out with Peter,' Eva said. 'Yer can doll yerself up to the nines.'

'I'm seeing Peter tomorrow night, Mam. We're going to the pictures, I think. But I'm determined to get an hour done on my homework first.'

'You should let him call for yer, sweetheart, after what happened tonight. I'll not rest when I know you're out on your own.'

'Where are you meeting him tomorrow night, Poppy?' David asked. 'Outside the picture house?'

'No, only a five-minute walk from here. He would call for me, but I don't want to get too serious with him 'cos I haven't known him long.'

'I'll walk with you tomorrow night,' David said. 'I'm going out myself, but I'll take you to meet Peter first.'

Poppy sighed. 'Whoever the bloke was who attacked me, he's got a lot to answer for. He's disrupted this whole household. And what did he gain? Not a ruddy thing! In fact he was the loser 'cos he's got no hat now.'

'If he's a married man, he'll have a problem explaining to his wife how he came to lose his trilby,' Eva said. 'I know there's a wind out, but I don't think it's strong enough to blow a hat off.'

'Just wishful thinking on my part,' Poppy said, pushing a lock of hair out of her eyes, 'but I hope he tripped up after he got away from Ally, and broke his leg. I know it's a wicked thing to say, but he's more wicked for trying to steal from someone. There's all sorts going through my head of what might have been. Say it was a Friday, I had me wages on me, and he managed to steal my bag? I know I wouldn't starve because I've got you two. But what if I was older and had no one to help? The more I think about what happened, the more I hate him. I don't know how he can live with himself.'

'I know it's easy for me to talk because it didn't happen to me,' David said. 'But I'd try to put it out of my mind as quick as I could. He's not worth losing sleep over, because he's a no-hoper. He won't have many friends, not like we have, because his mind doesn't work like ours. There is a saying that thieves never prosper, and it's true. Whoever he is, I bet he doesn't lay his head on a pillow at night and have a peaceful sleep, because he's a sad loser. And yer're not going to waste your time thinking about a sad loser, are yer, Poppy?'

Their eyes locked for a few seconds, then Poppy answered her brother in a very determined voice. 'No, I am not going to waste my time thinking about a sad loser. I'm going to get on with my life. And I'm starting right now by having a look at the homework I've got to do. I'm not going to attempt to make a start on it, I'm too tired. But if I have a look at it, I'll know what to ask Jean tomorrow. So, another cup of tea, fifteen minutes trying to figure out what Mr Jones has written, then I'll be ready to climb those stairs to my bed.'

Eva shot up from her chair. 'Kettle's been on a low light, so tea will be ready before you've got yer pencil out. And we can stretch to a custard cream each.'

When Eva was in the kitchen, David moved his chair nearer to his sister. 'Neither of us are doing very well in the good grammar department. If we both intend to seek good jobs, we need to look and speak the part. I know it's not the best time to bring it up after what you've been through, but you could bear it in mind.' He glanced towards the kitchen and lowered his voice. 'I haven't mentioned it before in case it doesn't come off, but my boss has told me he has plans to open another warehouse and will need a supervisor and someone to deal with customers. It will be almost six months before it is up and running, but he hinted he would be looking for someone who dressed smartly and could converse with important clients. It would be an office job, no manual work involved, and if I can prove I'm up to it, the position is mine.'

Poppy's mouth opened wide. 'Oh, that's wonderful! Your boss must think a lot of you, and you've never said a word!'

'I've always been one of Mr Rankin's blue-eyed boys. Since the day I started, he's said I'm the best apprentice the firm has ever had. And I have worked hard, Poppy, and always kept my nose clean, for I knew I had to keep the job because of our mam. And it looks as though it's paid off.'

This made Poppy more determined than ever. 'If you can do it, then so can I. We'll make our mam so proud of us.'

David put a finger to his lips. 'Not a word to her yet, until it happens. I don't want to disappoint her.'

'Who knows, David, I may land a better job before you. I guess mine, as a secretary, wouldn't be as grand as yours, but I'll be very happy. And while I'm learning shorthand, I'll watch me grammar at the same time.'

David grinned. 'It's not "me" grammar, Poppy, it's "my" grammar.'

They were both chortling when Eva bustled in carrying a tray. 'Tea up.'

Chapter Thirteen

On Friday morning, sitting on the bus taking her into the city centre, Poppy made up her mind that she would not tell anyone about the ordeal of the night before. Not even Jean. Because it only needed a whisper of gossip, and it would be round every office in the building. And she didn't want people asking questions and talking behind her back. Or adding their own version of what happened until it grew out of all proportion. She wanted to put the experience behind her and get on with her life.

So after hanging her coat up, Poppy took the cover off her typewriter, flexed her fingers, and started working on the correspondence lying on her desk. And she kept her head down, and her fingers busy, until Jean came out of Mr John's office after taking dictation.

'You've been very quiet since you came in, Poppy,' Jean said. 'You appear to be preoccupied, as though you have something on your mind.'

'I'm fine, Jean, but you're right, I do have something on my mind. I've been dreaming of the new coat I'm going to buy meself tomorrow. I can't make up my mind what colour or style to look for.'

'Oh, if you're anything like me, you'll know which coat you want as soon as you set eyes on it. It's not often I can afford to buy a new coat, mind, but when I have, I've always found that the first one that took my eye was the one I bought in the end. It's just like choosing a boyfriend. I know it sounds soppy, but a look, or even just a touch, can tell you a certain lad is the one for you.'

Poppy was amazed. She had never expected anything like that from Jean. 'I was under the impression you never bothered with members of the opposite sex. You surprise me.'

'Oh, I had my moments when I was younger. I used to go dancing, went on a few dates, and met a lad that I really fell for. Went out with him nearly every night for a year, then my father became ill. Nobody thought what he was suffering from was life-threatening – we had no idea. But he died two days after he was taken into hospital. My mother was absolutely devastated. Out of her mind. I couldn't go out and leave her on her own, so it was a choice between my boyfriend and my mother. I chose my mother. I've never regretted it, for I love her dearly. But there have been times when I've thought of the boyfriend, and wondered what my life might have been like with him.'

'You did the right thing, though, Jean,' Poppy said. 'My dad died when I was about nine, and my mother had to go out to work to keep me and my brother. We both idolize her. We're lucky because there's two of us, so she'll never be left on her own. Besides, she's only in her early forties, and she still goes out to work. She keeps herself young that way, mixing with other women every day.' Poppy suddenly remembered she had to deliver the day's correspondence, and she pulled a face. 'I'll have to get cracking or I'll be late with the mail. We can talk at dinnertime.'

'How did you get on at night school?'

'Not bad. I was quite pleased with meself.' She pulled a face. 'I mean "myself", not "meself".'

Jean was chuckling when she walked to her desk. Her colleague really was determined to get on in the world. And as she put a piece of paper in her typewriter, she muttered, 'And good luck to her.'

'You don't mind if I bring this with me, do you, Jean?' Poppy held up her notebook. 'I'm going to be cheeky and ask you to look at the homework I've been given, to see if you can give me any advice.'

'I don't mind,' Jean told her. 'I'll be glad to help.'

'You'll be glad when it's over and you can see the back of me. But I can't promise how soon that will be. Perhaps I'm too stupid to ever get the hang of it, and I'll still be in the same job this time next year.'

'I won't be glad to see the back of you, Poppy. In fact I'll be sorry when you leave. I'll miss you.'

Poppy felt a bit sad herself, for Jean was a good friend. 'Oh, you won't get rid of me easily. If and when I get another job, it's bound to be near here, so we can still meet for lunch every day, and swap gossip. I don't like Mr John, but I'll like to hear any news about him. Like if he loses a good client because he's too big for his boots. Or if he comes into work one day with a black eye, given to him by his wife because she finds out he's got himself a mistress.'

'Oh, what a lovely thought.' Jean entered the café and unwrapped her scarf before sitting down. It was warm inside, and she'd feel the benefit of the scarf more when she went out into the cold if she took it off now. 'I think everyone, in every office in the building, would give a cheer if that happened, for no one likes him. If he wasn't his father's son, he'd have been out long ago. I often wonder if his father doesn't see him as everyone else does, or if he doesn't want to see.'

'A bit of both, I should think,' Poppy said. 'The old man is a real gent, one of the old school type. But it would be very hard for any father to sack his son. Impossible, really, what with the wife and grandchildren. Anyway, let's not dwell on work. Give ourselves a break. Is it soup again today?'

Jean nodded. 'May as well finish the week on it. I was thinking Charlotte might have been down today. I'd like to see her again.'

'Perhaps one day next week. But don't be surprised if we don't see her again. She probably has other things in her life to keep her busy.'

'Yes, I suppose you're right. Anyway, Poppy, leave the notebook with me while you put our order in. I'll glance through it and see how best to help you. Then when we've eaten we can talk it through.'

Poppy pushed her chair back, oblivious of the looks of admiration from the male customers. But Jean noticed them, and told herself that one of the things she liked about Poppy was her lack of vanity. She had no idea how beautiful she was. There were a few good-looking girls in the building, but they couldn't hold a candle to Poppy, even though they wore a lot of make-up and more fashionable clothes.

'You'll be happy to know it's tomato soup today: your favourite.' Poppy put the plate down in front of her friend. 'And the bread is lovely and fresh. I'll go back for mine, because the staff are busy. The girl said she'd bring it over, but I said I'd save her the trouble.' She was turning away when she noticed the open notebook on Jean's knee. 'Leave that until after you've had your lunch. It's bad enough me asking you to help, without spoiling your meal. Put it away and enjoy the soup, which smells delicious.'

The friends were quiet as they ate their meal, but Jean's mind wasn't idle. She had Poppy's notebook propped up in front of her, and held steady by a salt cellar. It didn't interfere with her enjoyment of the delicious soup and fresh homemade bread, though, for which Poppy was grateful. She felt guilty, as though she was taking advantage of her friend's good nature, but when she'd voiced her unease Jean had told her not to be soft and gone back to her reading.

When the meal was over, Poppy took the plates back to the counter and ordered a pot of tea for two, which the waitress said she would bring to the table. 'Tea is on its way,' she told Jean when she got back to her chair. 'The staff are run off their feet, so we may have to wait a while.'

'We're all right for time, don't worry.' Jean had laid the notebook flat, and she tapped a finger on it. 'What I'm going to do, Poppy, which I think will be the best thing for you, is translate this shorthand the teacher has written into longhand. Keep going over what I have written and then read the shorthand. Try a sentence at a time, and keep at it. I promise you it's the quickest way to learn. If you bring it in on Monday, I'll give you a short test to see how you've done.'

'Jean, you're an angel,' Poppy said. 'I can't tell you how grateful I am. But I will make it up to you, I promise, even though it may take a while.'

'I wish you wouldn't keep on about it, Poppy. I'd be a poor one if I didn't help a friend. It's not costing me anything, and I am really hoping things work out for you. Actually, you've done more for me than I've done for you. Having your company every lunchtime has meant a lot to me. I've never made friends with any of the staff because I'm older than most of them and they've sort of formed a clique. I have friends where I live, though, women who have been neighbours for years, so I'm not what you'd call a loner, or a recluse.'

'I never for one minute thought you were,' Poppy told her. 'The only reason we've been slow in becoming friends lies in the office of Mr John. He certainly doesn't agree with anyone being happy in their work. You never see a smile on his face, and a hearty laugh would kill him. He's a miserable so and so, and he makes everyone else miserable. If I do manage to get meself another job, the only person I'd miss from there would be you.' She frowned, then asked, 'Jean, did I just say meself, instead of myself?'

'Yes, you did, Poppy, but I wouldn't worry about it. Your shorthand won't suffer, you'll see. That is the main thing to concentrate on. Except for the pot of tea which is now coming our way. You can pour while I start writing. I'm not going to do much here, for by the time we've drunk our tea it'll be time to scoot back to the office. But if you'll let me take the book with me, I can slip out to the washroom and finish it off.'

'Don't get into trouble on my account, Jean, or I'll worry myself to death. Helping me is one thing, getting the sack for it is another. Don't take any chances. It's not worth it.'

'Drink your tea and stop fretting,' Jean told her. 'Ten minutes' writing, that's all. And I'll pass it to you at the end of the day. Now I can only advise you to take it slowly. Take a sentence at a time, comparing mine with your teacher's. It may seem like a foreign language at first, but with patience it will fall into place. If you find you can't make head or tail of it, bring the book in on Monday and I'll see if I can help you, before you show it to your teacher.'

The friends put on their scarves, paid at the counter for the pot of tea, and then linked arms for the walk back to the office. Poppy was in a happy frame of mind, feeling more positive about her ability to reach her goal. And it was all down to Jean. A woman who had devoted her life to her elderly mother, and who worked for a man who didn't appreciate her skill and loyalty. A man who treated her with scorn. Jean deserved better than that, and Poppy vowed that she would find a way to repay her, and let her know that she was appreciated. And no matter what happened, she would always keep in touch.

'You don't have to chaperon me, David,' Poppy told her brother as she combed her mass of golden, glossy curls. 'Peter will think you're being nosy, or that you don't believe I'm capable of looking after meself . . . er . . . myself. I'm nineteen, going on for twenty, not a child.'

'You can talk until you're blue in the face, Poppy, but I'm still coming with you. I'm sure Peter is a fine upstanding man, but you've only known him a matter of weeks. And I'm not going to give him the third degree by asking how much he's got in the bank, or what his intentions are towards you.'

Poppy's mouth gaped in horror. 'Don't you dare, David Meadows, or I'll never speak to you again. And I mean that!'

'Oh, come on, sis, where's your sense of humour? I was only joking.' David stood behind her and spoke to her reflection in the mirror. 'I'll just introduce myself, shake his hand, then leave you in his care.'

However, his sister wasn't satisfied. 'I still don't see any need for you to come with me. It's early evening and there'll be plenty of people about, so I'll be safe enough. Anyway,

David, put yourself in Peter's shoes. How would you feel if one of your dates turned up with a brother in tow?'

'I'd tell him he could come to the pictures with us, as long as he paid for himself.'

Eva, who was sitting at the table listening, chuckled. 'Why don't you pick your girl up on the way, David, and make it a foursome?'

Poppy tutted. 'Don't you egg him on, Mam, he's crazy enough as it is.' She put the comb in her handbag and reached for her raincoat, which was draped over the arm of the couch. 'Thank goodness I'll have a decent coat to wear tomorrow. I'm not half looking forward to walking down the street dressed to the nines and looking like Lady Muck. What about you, Mam?'

'Oh, I don't fancy looking like Lady Muck, sweetheart. Mae West, perhaps, but that's where I'd draw a line.'

'Mam, you're only half the size of Mae West,' David said. 'She'd eat you for dinner. How about Jean Harlow? She's more your size.'

Poppy gave one more glance in the mirror, turned up the collar on the raincoat, and picked up her handbag. 'I'm off, David, and if you insist on coming with me, then put a move on. And don't forget, not one word about what happened last night. You're just on your way to the shops for a packet of cigarettes.'

David followed her out of the door, saying, 'But you know I don't smoke.'

'You do for tonight, brother. I'll make that the excuse, you just shake hands with Peter, give him a big smile and then be on your way.'

Eva called after them, 'I'm going next door for a game of cards. But don't worry, I don't need a chaperon either.'

Peter was standing in front of a sweetshop window when he saw Poppy crossing the road. She was linking a tall, good-looking bloke, and Peter's heart sank. Then he curled a fist and punched it hard into the palm of his other hand, telling himself that's what he'd like to do to the bloke who was laughing down at Poppy.

'I'm sorry if you've been waiting long, Peter,' Poppy said, 'but you can blame it on David here. He kept me talking.'

David held his hand out. 'David Meadows, this young lady's big brother.'

Peter let out the breath he'd been holding in. 'Peter Broadhurst. For a minute I thought she had come to tell me she was sorry but she'd double-dated and I was the loser.'

David chortled. 'I'm not brave enough to walk a girl to meet a bloke she was letting down. No, I've got a date myself and I'd better be on my way. It was nice meeting you, Peter, and no doubt I'll see you again.' The men shook hands and David hurried away.

'You caused my heart to stop beating for a minute, babe, and I hope you don't make a habit of it.' Peter cupped her elbow. 'Dance, or back row of the stalls?'

'I'm not dressed for a dance, and I haven't brought shoes with me. So it's the back row of the stalls, if you promise to behave yourself.'

'I'll be as good as gold.' Peter's heart was back to normal and he felt ten feet tall. 'I mean, holding your hand, or putting my arm round you, that couldn't come under misbehaving, could it?'

'It could if I stretched my imagination,' Poppy told him. 'But because I was late for our date, I'll let you off.'

'Your brother seems an easy bloke to get along with. Is

193

your mother as easy-going, or will I have to wait until you introduce us to find out?'

They were nearing the picture house when Poppy said, 'Don't rush things, Peter. I'm keeping my priorities in order. Or at least I'm trying to. And my first priority is my career – if I'm going to have one. But it won't be for want of trying if I don't.'

'I wouldn't care if you scrubbed steps for a living, Poppy. You'll suit me whatever you do.'

They walked into the foyer, and Poppy waited as Peter went to the kiosk for the tickets and a box of Cadbury's Milk Tray. He chuckled when he handed her the box. 'These are to take your mind off me stealing kisses.'

The usherette was shining her torch on two vacant seats on the back row when she heard Poppy answer, 'This girl is not one to be bought with a box of chocolates, Peter Broadhurst. A mink coat, perhaps, but nothing as ordinary as a chocolate. Even if it is Cadbury's.'

In the light from the torch, Peter saw the usherette smile, and he whispered, 'My girlfriend is playing hard to get, but deep down she loves me.'

'I heard that,' Poppy said as she pulled the seat down. 'You'll be getting me a bad name.'

'I wouldn't dream of it. Poppy Meadows is a wonderful name, and it suits you.'

She gave him a dig, and whispered, 'The people in front are giving you daggers, so be quiet and let us all enjoy the picture.'

Peter's right arm went across her shoulders, and his left hand covered hers. In a very low voice, he said, 'Let's go dancing tomorrow night, babe. I can hold you tight without you telling me off. Is that a date?'

Poppy nodded. She was looking forward to going into town with her mother tomorrow, to buy the coats they'd waited so long for. But she wasn't going to tell Peter; she wanted it to be a surprise. He'd only ever seen her in the raincoat that had seen better days, and she hoped he'd be pleasantly surprised.

'Where shall we try first, Mam? London Road, or Church Street?'

Eva smiled at her daughter, whose face was alive with excitement and anticipation. 'We could try TJs first; it's probably the cheapest. Then we could walk down to Lewis's and Owen Owen's. We've nothing to hurry back for, so we may as well look around.'

'Okay, we'll get off the bus in London Road. We can compare quality, choice and price, then decide which shop offers the best value for the money we've got.' Poppy saw a bus coming and squeezed her mother's arm. 'Here we go, Mam, and the best of luck to both of us.'

Two hours later, tired and weary, mother and daughter faced each other. 'No luck so far, sweetheart,' Eva said. 'I can't go on much longer without resting me feet. They're nearly dropping off.'

They were standing in Lime Street after having traipsed round all the big stores. They'd seen coats they'd liked, but they'd been well over their budget. 'There's a little café over the road, Mam. Let's go and get a cup of tea. Take the weight off our feet for a while.' Poppy grabbed her mother's arm as she was stepping off the pavement. 'Mam, there's a bus coming! You should look both ways before crossing a busy road. You nearly got run over.'

'Don't blame me, sweetheart, blame me feet. They heard yer mention a sit-down, and they were all for it.'

Poppy's heart was all of a flutter, thinking of what the consequences could have been if she hadn't acted quickly. 'It's not funny, Mam. Yer gave me the fright of me life.'

'I'm sorry I gave yer a fright, sweetheart, but I wasn't thinking straight. Me feet are giving me gyp.'

'Oh, I'll let you off this time.' Poppy led her mother across the street and into the nice warm café. It wasn't a posh place, but it served the purpose, and Eva's feet were very grateful to have the weight lifted from them. When the tea came, with two scones, mother and daughter began to feel decidedly more cheerful. 'You can't beat a cup of tea, can you, Mam? It's a cure for all ills.' Poppy was looking out of the window at the row of shops facing. 'Look at that shop opposite, Mam. There's some lovely bride's dresses in the window.'

'It's been there some years, that shop,' Eva said. 'They seem to do well.' Her eyes narrowed. 'I'm sure there's a clothes shop a bit further along. Can you see from where you're sitting?'

Poppy craned her neck. 'I can see the shops, but I can't see what's in the window, not from this chair.'

'When we've finished here, it wouldn't hurt to cross over and look in the windows. Yer never know yer luck in a big city. We might just find what we're looking for.'

'Could be, Mam. It's worth a try. But hadn't you better ask your feet if they're up to it?'

'I'll give them another five minutes, sweetheart, just to show there's no ill feeling. We'll finish the tea off, then make a move.' Eva lowered her voice. 'Have you paid the bill?'

'Yeah, I paid when I put the order in. It was only one and six for the both of us. You couldn't fall out with that, could you?'

Eva nodded. 'Cheap at half the price, sweetheart. Let's hope that luck stays with us.'

And luck did indeed stay with them. For two shops past the one selling bride's dresses, they found a gem of a shop which cheered mother and daughter no end, and even improved the mood of Eva's feet.

There was only one assistant in the shop, and she proved to be both friendly and efficient. Poppy expected the smile to fall from the woman's face when they told her they only had four pound each to spend on a coat, but instead the assistant told them she was sure she could find something they'd like within their price range.

Eva tried on a navy blue coat in a warm wool material, with collar, wide revers, and deep cuffs. She felt so comfortable in it, after seeing herself in the full-length mirror, that she declared she didn't want to look any further, as she was perfectly satisfied. And Poppy didn't try to coax her to look at others the assistant was willing to show, for she thought her mother looked very smart. The coat really suited her.

'And now you, my dear,' the assistant said. 'Have you a style or colour in mind?'

Poppy shook her head. 'A friend told me I'd know the coat I really want as soon as I set eyes on it. So perhaps if you would be kind enough to show me what you have in stock, I'll see if my friend was right.'

'With your colouring, my dear, I'd say you want a warm colour. Not vivid, but not dull either. I have two in stock which I think you might like. I'm not going to suggest or persuade, because I'm sure your friend was right when she said you'd know the coat you're looking for as soon as you see it. They're in the back room, so do you want to come through, or shall I bring them in one at a time?'

'Ooh, I'm getting nervous and excited at the same time. It's a while since I bought a new coat, and I'm like a child with a penny for sweets. Nose pressed against the shop window, wondering if the man behind the counter will mix a few of me favourites in the one bag.'

The assistant smiled. No matter what coat this young lady bought, it would never outshine her beautiful face. 'Come with me, my dear. You can try them on and see what you think.'

When her daughter disappeared through the curtains which covered the opening, Eva crossed her fingers for luck. She would be so disappointed if Poppy didn't get a coat she liked. The conversation behind the curtains was indistinct, leaving Eva with fingers crossed and a prayer on her lips.

'Are you ready for the mannequin parade, Mam?' Poppy called. 'Sit up straight now, for exhibit number one.'

'Oh, sweetheart, that looks nice on yer.' Eva eyed the deep maroon coat, which buttoned up to the neck. It had a mandarin collar, and there were deep cuffs to the sleeves. 'It suits yer, sweetheart, and the colour is nice and warm.'

'Don't reach your verdict until you've seen the other one, Mam. I like this one myself, but I'm waiting to see what else this kind lady has to offer before I get excited about it.' Poppy gave a twirl, then disappeared once again through the curtains. But seconds later Eva heard her daughter cry out, 'Jean was right! Oh, wait until my mam sees this.'

Eva called, 'I can't wait, sweetheart. Hurry up!'

The curtains parted and Poppy stepped into the shop. And her mother thought she had never looked so lovely. The coat was a deep turquoise, in a velour material, with a nipped-in waist, flared skirt and round collar. The assistant didn't say as much, but she was thinking the young lady looked like a film star.

'Do you like it, Mam?' Poppy didn't wait for an answer. 'Ooh, I do. I'm delighted and I love it.' She rubbed a hand lightly down the velvet-like velour. 'You'll have to pay the bus fare home, Mam, 'cos the coat is ten bob more than I bargained for. But I'll pay you back.'

'You look a treat, sweetheart, and I'm wondering what the neighbours will say when they see us both dolled up. Not that I care, mind. Why should we worry what people say?'

Three happy women stood in that shop feeling very proud of themselves. Two of them had bought coats they liked, and were over the moon. The third was happy because she was the one who had put those smiles on their faces.

Chapter Fourteen

When Peter saw Poppy coming across the road towards him, he let out a low whistle. She looked absolutely gorgeous. 'Wow, babe, what a sight you are.' He couldn't resist a quick peck on her cheek. 'You always look lovely, but tonight you look adorable. I'll be the envy of every red-blooded man in Liverpool.'

Poppy was delighted with his reaction. Now she knew she looked as good as she felt. But there was a little niggle in her head. She almost hadn't put her new coat on, for as they were going to the Grafton it meant she would have to hang it in the cloakroom, and she didn't fancy that at all. It wasn't a big cloakroom, not for the number of people they got in. Especially on a Saturday night, you could hardly move, the place was heaving, and it would be easy for anyone to walk off with a coat that didn't belong to them. The man on the door wouldn't know what was happening; he couldn't be expected to keep tabs on everyone. Poppy had passed her fears on to her mother, who said surely there must be a cloakroom attendant. Well, there was, but she disappeared once the hall was full, and only came back to give the coats out when the last waltz was playing.

Peter glanced sideways as they walked towards the bus stop. 'You're very quiet, babe, and that's not like you. Have you got something on your mind?'

'Yeah, I have as a matter of fact. If I tell you, you'll say I'm crazy, but I'm going to tell you anyway.' So Poppy started the tale about how she'd only bought the coat that day, and how delighted she was with it. When the bus came she kept on talking, and Peter was told about her fear of leaving it in the cloakroom. He thought it was hilarious, but he kept his laughter at bay until the bus stopped near the dance hall. He helped Poppy down off the platform, cupped her elbow as they neared the door, and steered her towards one of the two men standing at the entrance. 'Bill, would you do me a big favour?'

'Of course I will, Peter. You know I'll always oblige. What's the favour?'

'Well, it's like this.' Peter put his arm round Poppy's waist. 'This young lady is a good friend of mine, and this afternoon she bought this coat. Naturally she's afraid of anything happening to it. So would you ease her mind by putting it in the office until the dance is over?'

'No problem, Peter.' Bill called across to the other doorman. 'Hey, Mike, keep an eye out for a minute. I'm just nipping to the office. Two minutes, tops.'

'You better make it snappy,' Mike called back. 'I've only got one pair of eyes.'

Poppy was looking from one to the other. She couldn't believe what was happening. It was like something from an American gangster film, and she was the gangster's moll. Peter took her coat from her, folded it carefully over Bill's arm, and watched the man carry it through to an office. 'Come on, babe. Your coat will be perfectly safe, so you can relax and enjoy yourself.'

'What's going on, Peter?' Poppy asked. 'How come you know this man, and why would he be so eager to do what you ask? It's all very mysterious.'

'Oh, what a vivid imagination you have, babe,' Peter said. 'There's nothing mysterious about me wanting to stop you from worrying about your new coat. Which, incidentally, suits you beautifully. And Bill is no stranger to me, for he works for my father. He's a rent collector by day, and a doorman by night. He's married with three children, so the extra money comes in handy. And now, if I have answered all your questions to your satisfaction, can we go into the dance hall and trip the light fantastic?'

'I'll change my shoes first. I can't dance in these. But I'll do it in the hall and leave these under a chair.'

'I can ask Bill to put them with your coat if you like?'

'Don't you dare, Peter Broadhurst. I don't want any more favours. Besides, I wouldn't really worry about these shoes being pinched. I've had my wear out of them.'

They danced every dance together, except for one 'excuse me' quickstep when Jim tapped Peter on the shoulder and claimed Poppy. It has to be said that it was with great reluctance that Peter allowed himself to be parted from her. But Poppy liked Jim and thought he'd been shabbily treated by her ex-friend Julie. 'How is life treating you, Jim?' she asked. 'Any girlfriend on the horizon?'

He grinned. 'Could be. I've been out a few times with a girl from where I work. We get on well, but she can't dance. Not yet, anyway, but she's going to a dancing class twice a week, so it won't be long before she feels good enough for here.'

'Oh, that's good, Jim. I'm glad for you. I'd like to meet her when she's ready, so I can tell her she's got a good one in you.'

The music came to an end, and as Jim was leading her back to where Peter was standing he said, 'I see you're courting strong, Poppy?'

'Oh, I wouldn't go that far. Not yet, anyway. It's still early days. But Peter's a nice bloke and we get on well together.'

'Don't make a habit of that, Jim.' Peter put on a straight face. 'This girl is spoken for.'

'Hey, Peter Broadhurst, I'm not a puppy in a shop window,' Poppy said. 'I can speak for myself. And as Jim is a friend of mine, he's welcome to ask me for a dance.'

Peter added a low growl to his straight face. 'Only once in a while, though. If you make him too welcome, he'll make a habit of it.'

Jim chortled. 'Scouts honour, I'll stick to just once in a while. And I won't forget, 'cos that's my favourite song. I'm always singing it.'

'Just as long as you're not singing it in my girl's ear, that's all. And as they're playing a slow foxtrot now, do I have your permission to take part?'

Poppy let herself be led on to the dance floor, saying over her shoulder, 'Take no notice of him, Jim. He has these moods now and again.'

His arms round her, and his lips close to her ear, Peter said, 'Don't encourage him, babe, or every other bloke here will be doing it. The only way I can think of stopping that is to put a placard on your back saying "Off Limits" in big letters.'

'Peter Broadhurst, for a feller, you don't half talk a lot. Could you close your mouth and let your feet do the talking? It's my favourite dance and I'd like to enjoy it.'

Dancing was in Peter's blood, and he enjoyed the feeling of freedom as he covered the floor with long strides and easy body movements. And Poppy followed his steps so perfectly, anyone would think they'd been dancing together for years, rather than weeks. 'This is heaven,' he said, his cheek brushing hers. 'In fact I'm holding heaven in my arms.'

'You are a very poetic and romantic man, Peter.' Poppy moved back to look him in the face. 'Can I ask how old you are? I know so little about you.'

'I'm twenty-five, babe, and if you have any questions, just fire away.'

'I don't want to sound rude or nosy, but I'm a little surprised you are not courting seriously at your age. Or even married. Have you never had a steady girlfriend?'

'I've had a few casual girlfriends, and there was one girl I became attached to, but for one reason or another it didn't last.'

'Did you really like this girl?' Poppy was curious. 'I mean, not just like, but did you have feelings for her?'

'Can we change the subject, babe, because I really don't want to talk about it.'

'The wounds are still raw, are they? I've never had a steady boyfriend, so I don't know much about courting or being in love.'

'Being in love can be very painful, because it leaves you open to the whims of other people. But when two people truly love each other, then there is no greater happiness.'

'This conversation is getting too deep for me, Peter, so do you mind if we change it?'

'You were the one who started it, babe, not me!'

'I know I did! But how was I to know I was digging up old wounds? I'm more used to a girlfriend than a boyfriend, and I'm beginning to think it's less trouble.'

They were walking off the floor when Peter said, 'It's very unusual for two people to meet, fall in love, and live happily ever after.'

'My mam and dad fell in love when they first met. And they loved each other until the day my dad died. I was only a kid, but I could see they were crazy about each other. And while I was growing up, it was always in my mind that I wanted a man I could love as much as my mam loved my dad.'

'I'm open to offers, babe, and I'm not a bad catch. All you have to do is say the word.'

'I'm not even considering any romantic entanglements right now.' Poppy nodded for emphasis. 'Career first, then romance.'

'How long are you going to keep me waiting? Some careers take a long time, Poppy.'

'The course I'm on is a three-month one. That's not very long, is it? Then hard slog for a month to get my speed up, before I can apply for a private secretary's position with any hope of success.'

'I can help you there,' Peter said. 'I have connections in the business world.'

Poppy raised her brows. 'There's a lot I don't know about you, isn't there, Peter? You're a man of mystery.'

'There's nothing mysterious about my feelings for you, babe. I've been very open about them.' Peter cocked an ear. 'This is the last waltz. Do you want to dance, or pick up your coat before the mad scramble?'

Poppy chuckled. 'I know you think I'm crazy worrying about the coat, but I waited a long time for it, and it'll be treated like the crown jewels until I've had my wear out of it.'

'Wait until you've got this career job you're so keen on,' Peter said, 'then you'll be able to afford a whole new wardrobe. Just as long as you never change in your heart, Poppy, that's all I ask.'

'Come on.' She linked his arm. 'Let's get my coat before your friend Bill takes a fancy to it for his wife.'

'His wife is twice the size of you. And as I did you a favour in having the much talked of coat guarded, I think you owe me a favour in return.'

'Such as?'

'Introducing me to your mother.'

Poppy slipped her arms into the coat Bill was holding up for her. And after smiling her thanks, she turned to Peter. 'A favour you said, so that means one. I'll let you choose what you would prefer. To meet my mother, which would be a privilege, or a goodnight kiss from me?'

Peter thanked Bill before steering Poppy towards the door. 'You drive a hard bargain. But it's rather late to disturb your mother, so I'll be considerate and settle for a kiss.'

At two o'clock on Sunday afternoon, the son of Michael and Jessica Parker-Brown was to be christened. Thirty guests had been invited, including family members and friends. They stood in groups talking as they awaited the arrival of Michael, Jessica and the baby. George and Harriet Wilkie-Brook had been first to arrive at the church, taking their role as godparents very seriously, and they'd been closely followed by Andrew and Charlotte. And to say everyone in the congregation was well groomed would be a huge understatement. The ladies were dressed in the height of fashion, with dresses and hats costing a small fortune, while the men sported handmade suits and silk cravats. They represented the cream of Liverpool society.

'Jessica is cutting it fine, my love.' George spoke softly, as one usually does in a church. 'Or perhaps we were early?'

'It's a big day in their lives. Everything needs to be perfect,' Harriet said. 'I'm sure they'll be here any minute.'

George gazed around the groups of guests, and his eyes

lighted on Andrew and Charlotte, who were chatting with three of his daughter's friends. The three girls were making a fuss of Andrew, each one attempting to outdo the other. Any one of them would be over the moon if he showed a preference for her. They hung on to his every word, and although George would be delighted to see his son settle down, he could understand his reluctance to get involved with any of the females in their circle. Oh, they were nice enough girls, but too empty-headed for Andrew. If you asked any one of them who the Prime Minister was, the look on their faces would be blank. His own daughter had been the same until recently, when, thank goodness, she had started to show some down-to-earth sense. And that was down to Andrew, who preferred not to be a member of the idle rich.

A hush came over the congregation when the vicar appeared, followed closely by Michael and Jessica, carrying the baby. The vicar indicated that George and Harriet should stand by the baby's parents at the font, as they were to be godparents, and the rest of the guests should form a circle.

The baby was wearing a christening robe of heavy satin covered by layers of lace, which had been worn by every baby born into the Parker-Brown family for the last seventy-five years. Christened Charles Leo Parker-Brown, the baby behaved himself throughout the ceremony. He didn't cry as most babies do when they are splashed with cold water, and his parents were enormously proud of him. Harriet, now Leo's godmother, was allowed to hold him, and she was so emotional her eyes filled with tears. 'Steady on, old girl,' George whispered in his wife's ear. 'This is supposed to be a happy occasion. You and I have a godchild now, and that will enrich our lives. And we have a responsibility towards him.'

Charlotte appeared and leaned over to look into the baby's face. 'Oh, isn't he sweet. He's like a little doll.'

George chuckled softly so Leo's parents couldn't hear what he was saying. 'You were just as sweet when you were christened, my darling. I think it lasted for a month or so, then you learned how to cry when you wanted to be picked up and nursed.'

Charlotte pouted. 'Oh, Papa, I was never a crybaby. The nanny I had said I was as good as gold.'

'She meant you were as good as gold when you were asleep, my dear, and of course you were.'

Harriet was swaying, as people do when holding babies. 'George, don't tease Charlotte. Both she and Andrew were good babies.'

'Well, she will find out for herself one day, when she is married and has children of her own. And I am sure you are as eager as I am to have grandchildren.'

'I think you should talk to Andrew about that, Papa, for he is older than me.' Charlotte looked across to where her three friends were keeping Andrew talking. Several times he'd made to move off, only to have a hand laid on his arm to detain him. And he wasn't the type of person to be rude and walk away. 'He will meet the right girl one day, Papa. And when he does, she'll be someone really special.'

The baby had gone to sleep in Harriet's arms, so she kept her voice low. 'And what about you, young lady? You appear to have lost interest in the boys you went around with. And several of them would have made an excellent husband. You would have wanted for nothing.'

'When I do get married, Mother, it will be for love, not for money.' Charlotte gave her father a saucy wink. 'I'm sure you wouldn't see your daughter living in a garret, with no coal for the fire and the larder bare, would you, Papa?'

George forgot where he was for a moment, and the chortle had left his lips before he could stop it. He raised his bushy eyebrows in apology to those who had turned their heads, then tutted at his daughter. 'You would make a good actress, you little minx. An empty grate and larder, in a garret no less. You don't know what a garret is.'

'Well, not in real life, Father, I have to admit. But when I was little, only about six or seven, I think, Nanny Barbara took me to a picture house one afternoon. I'd never seen a film before. Mother was having friends in, and she told Nanny to take me out for a few hours. I'll never forget that afternoon because it stayed in my memory for ages. In fact I can still see the film in my mind. It was very old, and the woman in it was called Mary Pickford. She was very poor, and she lived in a garret with no coal and no food.'

Harriet gasped. 'You were never allowed to go to picture houses when you were so young! I would never have permitted it. They were dirty places, filled with common people. I don't believe you, Charlotte. I think you've made it all up, and I must say it is in very bad taste.'

Charlotte was feeling full of devilment. 'That must have been why Nanny Barbara made me promise not to tell you where we'd been.'

Jessica arrived at that moment and relieved Harriet of baby Leo. 'We'll see you back at the house. Most people are going to their cars now. It all went off beautifully, don't you think, Harriet? Leo was a little angel.'

'It was perfect, my dear,' Harriet said. 'And I'm so glad Michael brought a camera. It will be lovely to have photographs to look back on.'

'You will be given copies,' Jessica assured her. 'You must have photographs of your godchild. But don't dally.

The tables will be set out for a light meal and a drink.'

'We'll be there directly, my dear.' Harriet waited until the church was almost empty, then glared at Charlotte. 'Now, young lady, I want the truth.'

George rolled his eyes at his daughter, a sign for her to behave. 'I believe our daughter made up a very likely story, which I found rather amusing. But perhaps this wasn't the place, or the time, for frivolity.'

Harriet's face broke into a smile. 'I am not completely without humour, my dear. Charlotte's make-believe story was funny, and I remember the Mary Pickford film very well. You see, not long after you had the television installed, several very old films were shown in the afternoons. In fact, because we were the first of our set to have a television, several of my friends would come to see what they called "the afternoon matinee". We watched all the old movies, with Laurel and Hardy, Charlie Chase and Ben Turpin. Oh, we did have some fun.'

Charlotte was more surprised than her father, and absolutely delighted. 'Mother, you have stolen the spotlight from me! Nanny Barbara would be horrified if she knew I was using her as one of the characters in my web of lies. Of course she didn't take me to a picture house when she knew how displeased you would be. Everything I said was make-believe, except one thing, which I am sure you will remember if you cast your mind back. It was not long after father had the television installed, and you began entertaining a few of your friends in the afternoons. I'd been in bed with mumps, and because you felt sorry for me, you allowed me to watch the television while lying on the couch. Do you remember?'

Harriet nodded. 'And that was where you saw the Mary Pickford film. The memory is vague, but there none the less.'

George was becoming impatient. 'I do think we should make a move. We are the only ones left in the church, apart from Andrew who is being kept prisoner by your friends, Charlotte. Please rescue the poor man immediately, before he is torn limb from limb. I'm sure he will thank you for freeing him. He's far too polite for his own good.'

'I'll tell them he is coming in our car and there'll be no room for them. They will have their own cars anyway, and there'll be a fight over who can coax Andrew into hers. But I'll say you need to speak to him urgently, and I'll drag him away if necessary.'

Andrew's fixed smile relaxed when his sister linked his arm, saying, 'I'm taking my brother, for he and Father have something to discuss.' She ignored the protests and pulled hard. 'Come on, Andrew, it's quite important.'

When they were far enough away not to be heard, he let out a deep sigh. 'I'm sorry, Charlotte, I know they're your friends, but I've been bored rigid. They don't appear to have a brain between them. I missed the baby being christened, for they weren't in the least interested. All they came for, as far as I heard, was to weigh up what the guests were wearing, then find fault and pull them to pieces. If I see them bearing down on me when we're at Jessica's I'll plead a headache and leave.'

'I'll see to it that they don't,' Charlotte said as they quickened their pace to follow their parents out of the church. 'I'm not going to allow them to spoil the day for you, so as soon as we get to Jessica's I'll tell them a whopping big lie.'

'Don't lie on my behalf, Charlotte, for that would make me feel a coward. I'll stay close to Mother and Father, stick to them like glue. Father wouldn't entertain the type of conversation I've put up with. He'd soon send them packing.

I was congratulating myself that Annabel was being kept away by her parents, but at least she isn't rude about people.'

'They are my friends, or used to be, so I'll put a stop to them bothering you. And I know the best way to do it, so they won't ever trouble you again. I'll tell them you have a girlfriend and are serious about her. She's gorgeous to look at, with an hourglass figure, and you are crazy about her.' Charlotte climbed through the car door her father was holding open for her, while Andrew slid into the far seat. 'That should do the trick.'

George closed the car door, and then climbed into the driver's seat. 'Just to satisfy my curiosity, Charlotte, what will do the trick, and who won't bother whom again?'

Harriet turned her head and smiled at her impetuous daughter. 'Could you tell your father the true facts, without any embellishment? I would like to arrive at the Parker-Browns' before nightfall.'

Charlotte narrowed her eyes in thought. Then she sat upright and grinned. 'Right, Mother, you shall have the situation in as few words as possible. My three friends made a nuisance of themselves and cornered my dear brother, Andrew. Bored him stiff with stupid conversation. So now they're going to be told he has a gorgeous girlfriend, with an hourglass figure, and he's crazy about her. Then, exit three brainless women, and enter freedom for Andrew.'

George guffawed. 'Well done, my daughter! And when are we to meet this gorgeous girlfriend with the hourglass figure?'

Charlotte leaned across the seat and kissed her brother soundly on the cheek. 'As soon as he's found her, Papa. He's still looking.'

Chapter Fifteen

Eva stood at the bottom of the stairs on the Monday morning and called up to tell her children it was time they were out of bed. She had barely finished calling when Poppy came bounding down the stairs. 'Good morning, Mam.'

'My goodness, that was quick.' Eva was wide-eyed with surprise. 'Did yer not sleep well, or are yer feeling out of sorts?'

'I slept like a log, Mam, but I woke early. I think it was because I had that homework on my mind. I spent so much time pawing over it, I was cross-eyed when I went to bed. But I feel quite chuffed with myself, and I bet Jean will be surprised at how well I've done. I hope so, anyway, 'cos if Mr Jones doesn't say I've improved, I'll go mad.'

'You're rushing things, sweetheart, wanting things to happen too quickly. Try to be patient; learn to walk before yer run.'

'I know, Mam, I should jump before I leap. I went over all that last night. I am going to try very hard to be patient, and not dwell on something I can only achieve given time. So to cheer myself up, and take my mind off shorthand, I'm going to give myself a treat today, and wear my new coat to go to work in. Apart from wanting to show off, it will give the office staff something to talk about. They've only ever seen me in the old raincoat.'

213

Eva was bustling in and out of the kitchen during the conversation, setting the table and making tea and toast. 'Give David a shout for me, sweetheart. Yer know he takes ages to get ready. He takes twice as long as us.'

Poppy defended her brother. 'We don't have to get shaved every morning, Mam, thank goodness. I think if I was a man I would grow a beard, rather than have to go through that palaver every day.'

She jumped when a voice behind her said. 'Oh, I don't think you would suit a beard, Poppy.'

'Oh, you daft nit! Yer gave me the fright of me life then. I nearly jumped out of my skin! Why didn't you say something so I'd know you were there?'

'I didn't want to interrupt the intelligent conversation you were having on the merits of beards.' David yawned. 'I also heard you saying you were wearing your new coat to work today. Is it a celebration?'

'You don't miss much, even though you still look half asleep.' There was fondness in Poppy's eyes. 'If I had anything to celebrate, my dear brother, you would be the first to know. After my mam, of course, but that goes without saying.'

'The toast is ready, and the water boiling for tea,' Eva told them, 'so sit yerselves down. If yer keep on yapping you'll be late for work.'

Poppy made a dive for the kitchen, to get there before her mother. 'I'll see to the tea, Mam; you sit down and eat your toast. You shouldn't be waiting on us – me and David are old enough and ugly enough to look after ourselves. So go on, sit down. You go to work same as we do.'

Eva did as she was told and sat down, but it didn't feel right. She was used to seeing to the children, making sure they had a decent breakfast before going out, and old habits die hard. 'I don't have as far to travel to work as you and David. I can walk to the factory in fifteen minutes.'

'Poppy is right though, Mam, you shouldn't be running around after us. You've spoilt us, that's the trouble. We're so used to you waking us up every morning, and having our breakfast ready, we take it for granted. And that is not right. It should be the other way round. You have an extra half-hour in bed, and we'll make the breakfast.'

'But I don't want an extra half-hour in bed. I'd only be lying there counting the cracks in the ceiling, bored stiff. I've got to be active, it's what I'm used to. So don't you and Poppy make me old before me time, 'cos I wouldn't thank yer for it. And I'm not being miserable or ungrateful when I say that, because I know you only want what is best for me. But I'll know when it's time for me to start taking things easy: my body will tell me. And I'm hoping it won't be for a long time yet.'

Poppy put a cup down in front of her mother. 'I've put sugar in, Mam, and stirred it.' She pulled a chair out and sat next to her brother. 'Mam, there's nothing old about you. You certainly don't look it, and you're not old in the head. But you should be getting a bit more out of life than you are. The only social life you have is a game of cards next door. That's hardly exciting, is it?'

Eva chuckled as she spread butter on a piece of toast. 'Funny you should say that, sweetheart, because when I told Marg about me new coat, she said it wouldn't do the coat any good being stuck in a wardrobe. It needs fresh air, she said, or the moths will get at it. So next Saturday me and her are going into town to look round the shops. If she can talk Ally into mugging her to a new coat, I told her I'd take her to the shop we got ours from. We were very lucky. We got real bargains.'

David swallowed his tea, then pushed back his chair. 'Good for you, Mam. You'll enjoy yourself with Marg, She's good company. And now I'm going to get washed and shaved before my dear sister bags the bathroom.'

'Don't be long, David,' Poppy said. 'I need to get ready as well. My hair could do with washing, but it'll have to wait until tonight now.' She ran her hand through the curls, which bounced back into place. 'I should have done it yesterday.'

'Your hair looks fine, sweetheart, it always does. And the colour of yer new coat goes well with it. Yer couldn't have found one that suited you better if yer'd paid ten pound.'

Poppy began to stack the breakfast dishes. 'I'm not telling anyone in work how much I paid for it. It's none of their business.' She carried the dishes out and put them on the draining board. 'There's some hot water left in the kettle, Mam, so I'll make a start and see what I can get through before David comes down. You go and get ready for work; it's no good the two of us hanging around. We're not running late, so there's no panic.'

'I'm not running late, sweetheart. I had a good wash before I called you. My clothes are laid out on the bed, so I can be dressed, comb my hair, and be out of the door in five minutes. It's you I'm worried about. You've got further to travel.'

They heard David's heavy footsteps on the stairs, then his voice. 'Bathroom empty, ladies, but don't kill each other in the rush to get there first.'

Poppy patted his cheek as she made for the stairs. 'It's only a rush of one, 'cos Mam got washed before we were up. So you can finish the dishes off, like a good boy. I've washed most of them, so there's no need to pull a face.'

In the end the three of them left the house together, with Poppy walking between her mother and brother. She was feeling self-conscious, wearing a new coat to go to work in, and was glad they didn't encounter any near neighbours.

When they reached the top of the street, where they would part company to go their separate ways, Poppy admitted, 'I'm sorry I didn't put my old raincoat on now. I'll stick out like a sore thumb when I get to the office.'

'Don't be silly, sweetheart,' Eva said. 'You look very smart.' She turned her head away as a cloud of sadness engulfed her. Not for the first time, she wished her husband was alive to see the two fine children he'd fathered. He would be so proud of them. 'If anyone says otherwise, then put it down to jealousy.'

'Mam's right.' David squeezed his sister's shoulder. 'You go in that building with your head held high, and knock 'em for six.'

Poppy could see surprise on the faces of staff as they passed her on their way to the many offices in the building. Some raised their brows, and others, more friendly, smiled a greeting. But no one passed a comment, until she entered the office she shared with Jean. Then the reaction of her friend brought a smile to her face. 'Oh, you look beautiful,' Jean said, with sincerity. 'When did you buy that, and where from? It's a lovely colour and suits you down to the ground.'

'I bought it on Saturday.' Poppy couldn't bring herself to lie to someone who had been good to her, so she skirted round the implied question. 'I got it from a small shop my mother took me to, where the clothes were a lot cheaper than the stores in the city.' She hung up the coat carefully, then sat at her desk and took the cover off the typewriter. There were no letters for her to type with it being Monday, so to give herself something to do she decided to go through the files and make sure they were in order. Then when Mr John had opened his post and dictated replies to Jean, Poppy would be required to hand-deliver the letters.

'How did you get on with the homework, Poppy?' Jean asked, her eyes watching Mr John's office door. 'Did any of it make sense to you?'

'I'm going to sound very big-headed now, Jean, especially after swanking in my new coat. But I have to say I feel very proud of myself regarding the homework. I spent all day on it yesterday, and thanks to you I can see some light now. Your work was much easier to follow than Mr Jones's! Not that I haven't made any mistakes, 'cos I probably have. But all those squiggles that looked so hard to me before are beginning to make sense. I'm not there yet, not by a long chalk, but I am learning a bit more each day, thanks to you. You're a pal.'

Jean put a finger to her lips and mouthed, 'Here comes his lordship. We'll talk at dinnertime.'

There were only two letters to be delivered by hand, and both were for the offices where Amy worked. Poppy glanced out of the window as she pulled her gloves on and was glad to see it wasn't raining. She hadn't got an umbrella with her, and wouldn't like the idea of getting her new coat wet. So, after putting her homework notebook in the drawer, away from prying eyes, she left the office and stepped into the street. She pondered on which of the two streets facing she should use. Without having made a conscious decision, she found her feet crossing over the main road, then into Castle Street. She automatically smoothed down the front of her coat and pushed a wayward curl behind her ear. If she met that bloke again, Charlotte's brother, at least he'd know there was more to her than an old raincoat. Not that she was particularly worried what he thought; she wasn't a snob. But as she neared the buildings where he worked she slowed down, so if he came out she wouldn't miss him. However, telling herself she couldn't walk any slower or she'd be standing still, she set her feet moving faster. She was disappointed, though. Not because she was interested in him, even though he was probably a nice man. It was just that on the few occasions she'd seen him, he'd been very well dressed, a real toff, while she had that old raincoat on. She'd felt at a disadvantage, as if she was inferior. It was daft to think like that, 'cos her mother had always drummed it into her and David that they were as good as anyone, and better than most. And he, Charlotte's brother, was the only one who had ever made her feel like that. So if she had bumped into him today, knowing she looked good in her new coat, she would have felt they were on an equal footing.

'My God!' Amy said, eyeing Poppy up and down. 'The state of you and the price of fish! When did yer get the coat?'

Poppy did a twirl. 'On Saturday. D'yer like it?'

'It's beautiful! Have you come up on the pools?'

'That would take a miracle, Amy, and they don't happen very often. You see, I don't do the pools.' Poppy could see Amy was gearing herself to hear all the details, so she quickly pointed to the letters she'd put on the counter. 'I think you'd better take those upstairs. Mr John seemed to hint they were important.'

The letters were snatched up and Amy opened the door. 'I'll not be long. It depends if an answer is needed.' She was gone in a flash, leaving Poppy in the tiny room, afraid to move around because there was dust everywhere and she had to be careful with her coat. Mind you, if she was going to be frightened every time she went near anything, she'd be better leaving it at home and wearing the old raincoat for work.

Amy came back with an envelope in her hand and a very flustered expression on her face. 'Mr Simon wants this taking to Mr John right away. I don't know what your boss had written, Poppy, but whatever it was, he's got Mr Simon hopping mad.' She passed the envelope over. 'If I were you, I'd stand well away when you give him that.'

Poppy huffed. 'They're worse than children! Why can't they meet up and discuss their business in a civilized manner, over a meal or a drink? I mean, how childish can you get? They could even lift up the phone and sort out their differences. Why have me running back and forward when they can talk to each other without getting off their backsides?' She walked to the door. 'I'm surprised they've got the sense to make money. Then again, what's the use of having money if you don't enjoy it? My Mr John wouldn't know what a joke was if it hit him in the face. I've never heard him have a good belly laugh in all the years I've worked for him.'

'Same here, girl! Mr Simon would split his face open if he smiled. Miserable pair of buggers, and you and me are lumbered with them! Anyway, you'd better hurry. I'll see yer tomorrow.'

Poppy was deep in thought as she walked back down Castle Street. Her boss, Mr John, was a solicitor, following in the steps of his father and grandfather. And she happened to know, from the letters she typed, that he earned a lot of money by charging exorbitant fees. If she needed a solicitor, she certainly wouldn't go to him. And she had a feeling that Amy's boss, Mr Simon, was complaining about the fees, and those complaints would be in the letter she was carrying. What a pity they had nothing better to do. Two very rich men whose only thought was making more money. Oh, Mr John did have one other thing on his mind . . . he was a womanizer.

Poppy was telling herself she would rather be skint and happy than rich and miserable when a figure blocked her path. She was about to sidestep, thinking she was at fault, when a voice said, 'Hello, Poppy.'

She stared at Andrew, her face blank. Then she gathered her thoughts together. 'I'm afraid I was miles away then. I didn't see you.'

'I could see your mind was elsewhere. I do hope I didn't alarm you?'

Her brow furrowed, Poppy was asking herself why this man had an effect on her. She hardly knew him, yet for some reason she didn't feel at ease with him. 'No, you didn't alarm me.' A passing thought brought a smile to her face. 'And you didn't knock me down, either. I'm glad you don't make a habit of doing that.'

Her smile had Andrew's heart pounding. He was absolutely captivated by her, but too shy to do anything about it. There were words whirling around in his head, but he couldn't summon up the courage to speak them out loud. Twenty-five years of age and unable to say what was on his mind. He was standing in front of a girl who had stolen his heart when he first set eyes on her, yet he was too much of a wimp to ask her for a date.

'Look, I'll have to go,' Poppy said. 'My boss will wonder where I've got to.'

'One minute won't matter, surely?' A little voice in Andrew's head was urging him on. 'Would you think it was forward of me if I said you were looking very smart? That coat really suits you.'

Again Poppy's smile sent his heart into a spin. 'No girl would object to a compliment, and I thank you, kind sir.'

'Please call me Andrew.' He waved to the offices across the

street. 'I've told you where I work, and I'd be delighted if you would call in one day and have a cup of tea with me.'

'I don't have time during office hours, Andrew, but thank you for the offer. And now I really must be on my way. I can't afford to get the sack.'

As Poppy moved forward, Andrew put a hand on her arm. 'The offer is always open, Poppy. You would be very welcome.' With those parting words, he spun on his heel and crossed the road, leaving Poppy staring down at her arm with a puzzled expression on her face. She'd felt a tingle, causing her to shiver. But it couldn't have been Andrew: he'd barely touched her. It must have been the cold wind, or, as her mother would say, it was someone walking over her grave. That was a very old saying, but not one that Poppy liked. In fact it brought on another shiver, just as she walked into the office, and almost into the arms of Mr John, who was standing by her desk. It was obvious he'd been awaiting her return and was becoming impatient. But Poppy's appearance saved her from his vitriolic tongue. He stared at her, his eyes travelling upwards from her feet to her flashing eyes. Making no attempt to hide his lust, he stripped her naked in his mind. 'You are looking very fetching today, Miss Meadows.'

I don't have to put up with this. Poppy's pride rose to the fore. *Who the hell does he think he is?* So she held his eyes, saying with a coolness she was far from feeling, 'My boyfriend is always telling me how fetching I look. It gets quite boring, really.' She brushed the envelope she was holding across his chest. 'Mr Simon said to make sure this was put in your hand.'

Jean had been watching and listening with an expression on her face that defied description. On the one hand she applauded her friend for having the guts to stand up for herself, but on the other she was afraid it might cost Poppy her job. Mr John had been in a foul mood all morning, and she should know because she'd borne the brunt of it.

However, much to Jean's astonishment, Mr John watched Poppy walking towards the coat stand with a half-smile on his face. Little did she know that her boss was promising himself that one day he would get through to his typist. Money would do the trick. Few women could refuse the offer of a gold watch, or rich satin underwear. No matter how much it cost, it would be worth it for one hour with the beautiful Miss Meadows. He would take it slowly, confident she would rise to the bait in the end. His other conquests had been so easy he soon lost interest in them. But Poppy now, she was a challenge.

Jean watched Poppy putting her coat on at lunchtime. 'You nearly gave me a heart attack before. I thought you'd gone too far. I really expected Mr John to tell you to pick your cards up on Friday.'

Poppy shrugged her shoulders. 'He didn't though, did he? The man is so big-headed he thinks he's God's gift to women. He thinks he'll wear me down eventually, the silly man.' She linked Jean's arm and walked her to the door. 'When the time comes for me to leave here, it will be me giving in my notice, not the other way round, so don't look so worried. Let's go and have some lunch.'

'Have you brought the book with you?'

Poppy patted her handbag. 'It's in here, Jean, but don't worry about that on top of all the other things you worry about. It's time you gave some thought to yourself, never mind me or Mr John.'

They were walking down the steps of the building when Jean said, 'Oh, look, here's Charlotte! What a lovely surprise!'

'Are your family checking up on me?' Poppy had a smile on her face when she spoke, for the girl looked so happy to see her and Jean, she couldn't not be nice to her. 'I was talking to your brother half an hour ago, did he tell you?'

'I haven't seen Andrew; he doesn't know I'm in town. I came to go for lunch with you in that nice little café. You don't mind, do you?'

'Of course not. It's lovely to see you.' Poppy bent her elbow for Charlotte to link. 'Jean was only saying the other day that she hoped you hadn't forgotten us, weren't you, Jean?'

'Yes, I was,' Jean said. 'And am I right in saying a friend of yours was having her son christened yesterday?'

'Oh, yes, and it was lovely.' Charlotte's cultured voice was eager. 'The baby, Leo, was a perfect angel. He never even whimpered.'

'Can we find a table and sit down?' Poppy said. 'Then we can talk in comfort.' She looked around and spotted an empty table by a side window. 'You two nab that table while I put our order in. And as we don't have a lot of time I'm ordering three bowls of soup, with bread, and a pot of tea. Is that okay?' She waited for their nods, then pushed her way to the counter.

When Poppy returned to the table it was to see Charlotte and Jean talking and laughing. 'Oh, that's nice, I must say! I bet I've missed all the news now.'

'No, you haven't, Poppy. I was only telling Jean how happy my parents were yesterday, becoming godparents.' Charlotte put a hand on Poppy's sleeve. 'What a lovely coat! And it suits you. The colour is perfect with that mop of golden curls.'

'Listen, Charlotte, if I keep being flattered, I won't be able to get through the front door when I get home, my head will be so big.'

224

'When you saw Andrew, did he flatter you?' Charlotte's eyes held devilment. 'I'd be very surprised if he did, for my brother is quite shy with girls.'

'He did say I looked very smart. Oh, and he invited me to his office any time I was passing, for a cup of tea. Your brother does seem to be shy with females, Charlotte, but I think that's rather nice. The word I would use to describe what little I know of Andrew is chivalrous. But don't you dare tell him I said so, for he'll think I'm comparing him with the knights of old.'

Their soup and bread arrived at that moment, and it put an end to conversation. It's difficult to talk while eating soup, particularly when you are wearing . . . *the* coat. But as soon as the plates were cleared and stacked ready to be picked up, Charlotte went back to where they had left off. 'When you go for tea to Andrew's office, could I come with you? I would like that very much, for I am very proud of my brother, and love him dearly.'

'Oh, I won't be calling on him for a while, Charlotte, for it would be in my working time and my boss wouldn't take kindly to my taking time out.'

Jean pushed her chair back and stood up. 'I'll take these plates to the counter and fetch the tea. You two carry on. I won't be long.'

Poppy smiled at Charlotte. 'Your brother is nice, and I can understand you being fond of him. But you know I am going to night school to learn shorthand, and that's a priority with me, for I'm not happy in my present job. So everything else has to take second place for the next few weeks or months. It depends on how quickly I pick it up.'

'You are not spending all your free time poring over books, are you?' Charlotte had been eager when Poppy told of her meeting with Andrew, and now she felt sad. 'You need some social life.'

'Oh, I am having some social life, Charlotte, but I'm not out every night like I used to be. I have a male friend I go to dances with, or the pictures, two nights during the week. So I've not turned into a recluse.'

Charlotte's heart sank. 'You have a steady boyfriend, do you, Poppy?'

'I wouldn't say he was a steady boyfriend, for I've only known him a matter of weeks. And as I've said, my heart is set on training for a new job, so courting is out of the question for a while.'

Hope flared once again in Charlotte's heart. 'When you are settled, with all your plans bearing fruit, then will you come with me to Andrew's office and accept his offer of a cup of tea? I have only been there once, which is a bit mean of me for I have nothing to do all day but lounge around. I get bored sometimes, and feel lonely. So say you'll come with me, Poppy, and I'll have something to look forward to.'

How could she refuse, Poppy asked herself, looking into Charlotte's eyes. She could spare half an hour, if it made the girl happy. But not for a while. First things first. 'When I'm more settled I'll come with you, Charlotte, I promise. And you can tell your brother I'll expect a cake with the cup of tea.'

Charlotte was delighted. Wait until she told Andrew tonight! He would be overjoyed. 'How are you getting on with your shorthand? Are you close to mastering it yet?'

Jean reached the table with a tray bearing cups, saucers, and a pot of tea. 'Ooh, it's a crush trying to get through the queue at the counter. And that tray is heavy.'

'I'll take it back when we've finished with it,' Poppy said.

'And I'll be mother and pour out the tea. While I'm doing that, you are the best one to answer Charlotte's question. She asked if I was close to mastering the art of shorthand yet. You tell her.'

Jean delved into Poppy's bag for her notebook. 'Give me ten minutes and I'll tell you both whether Miss Meadows goes to the top or the bottom of the class.'

'I can't bear the suspense.' Poppy laughed. 'While you mark my homework, Jean, I'll ask Charlotte how the rocking-horse was received by the baby's parents.'

The three women left the café in high spirits: Poppy because her homework had been passed with flying colours, marked by Jean at eight out of ten; Charlotte because she had two pieces of news for her brother which would please him. One, Poppy had promised to accept his offer of tea in his office, and two she wasn't courting. And Jean was happy because she was in the company of two good friends.

Chapter Sixteen

Charlotte was in the kitchen chatting to the housekeeper and cook, while watching them preparing for the evening meal. She often spent time in there now, finding it warm and homely, and she was happy chatting to the staff. And she wasn't above pinching a cake as Jane was taking a tray out of the oven, or testing the after dinner trifles, which were rich with a variety of fruits and covered in fresh cream. Sitting at the huge scrubbed table, her arms folded, she watched Jane's quick, sure movements. 'How did you learn to be such a good cook, Jane?' she asked. 'Did your mother teach you?'

'Good heavens, no, Miss Charlotte. My mam could make a good pan of stew, and she could make an apple pie that had us kids drooling at the mouth. And her fairy cakes were so light they could float in the air. But we couldn't afford those luxuries very often, 'cos with five children to feed and clothe, and a husband what only earned coppers every week, well, she was always pushed for money.' Jane picked up a thick cloth to cover her hands before opening the oven door to make sure the piece of lamb was cooking to her satisfaction. Then, after rubbing her hands down the side of her long pinny, she smiled at Charlotte. 'My mam had to go out cleaning to earn enough money to keep the wolf from the door. But I'll say this for her, God rest her soul, she was a good mother. We might have gone hungry at times, but we never starved. She saw to that. What we lacked in food and clothes, she more than made up for with hugs and kisses, and telling us how much she loved us.'

Tender-hearted Charlotte was ready to sympathize. 'Were you very poor, Jane?'

The cook was about to give a truthful answer when a knowing look from the housekeeper caused her to think twice. 'Oh, no, Miss Charlotte, we weren't poor. Our house was noted in the street, because there was always singing and laughter coming from it. My mam and dad were both good singers, and they would sing all the old songs. We had some fine times. I've taught my kids all the songs from my childhood days, Irish, Scottish, cockney, I remember them well. So yer see, Miss Charlotte, yer don't need money to be rich in happiness and love. It comes free.'

'Oh, that's lovely, Jane. Those songs will always bring back happy memories of your mother and father. You'll never forget how much they loved you.'

At that moment a light passed the kitchen window, and Charlotte was off her chair like a shot. 'Oh, that is Andrew's car, Frances. I'm going to meet him.'

'No, Miss Charlotte, don't go out without a coat on,' Frances said. 'It's very cold out; you'll catch a chill.' But her words fell on empty air, for Charlotte was out of the door like a streak of lightning. 'If she catches a cold, I'm the one who will get the blame.' The housekeeper shook her head in despair. 'Miss Harriet will say I should have stopped her, but there's no stopping Miss Charlotte when she sets her mind on something. She can be very stubborn at times.'

'I wouldn't worry, if I were you,' Jane said, turning the gas off in the oven. Mr George came home half an hour ago, and now Mr Andrew was home the family would expect to sit down to dinner at half past seven. 'If she catches cold it's her own lookout.' When she opened the oven door, the smell of lamb wafted into the kitchen, and both women closed their eyes and sniffed several times in appreciation.

Outside, walking from the garage to the house, Charlotte was clinging to her brother's arm. 'I've got some news for you, Andrew.'

'Tell me later, when we're inside. You shouldn't be out without a coat on. So into the kitchen, quickly.' Andrew followed his sister up the step, and closed the door behind him. 'What a delicious smell! Jane, I believe you can work magic with a piece of meat. You never fail to set my taste buds yearning.'

Charlotte was fussing over him. 'Give me your coat and scarf, Andrew, and I'll hang them up for you.'

'I'll do it myself, Charlotte, for I want to take my briefcase upstairs.' Andrew smiled at the housekeeper as he passed. 'Doesn't the smell make you hungry, Frances?'

'It does, Mr Andrew, but Jane's fine cooking has its drawback for me. I eat far more than I should, for it is too delicious to refuse. But, oh, dear, it does no favour to my figure. I swear I'm going fatter by the hour.'

Andrew gave her a hug. 'You are just nice, Frances. I don't think you would suit being thin.' He then smiled at Jane, who was as thin as a rake. 'It doesn't seem to affect you, Jane.'

'No, Mr Andrew. And that's because I don't stand still long enough for the fat to settle. I live on me nerves and can't stand or sit for long. Always on the go, that's me. Doesn't do me no harm. I'm as fit as a fiddle, thank God.'

'And we are very grateful you are fit and healthy. Without you and Frances, we would starve, and the house would fall to pieces.' Andrew swung his briefcase. 'I'd better take this upstairs and start getting dressed for dinner.'

As he was passing the cook, Andrew said softly, 'Nice golden brown roast potatoes, Jane, will go well with lamb and mint sauce.'

All the staff were fond of Mr Andrew, for he was so down to earth, and Jane in particular thought he was one of the best, a real gentleman. And he could give and take a joke. 'How many would yer like, Mr Andrew? Any number between one and six.'

'I won't be greedy, so make it five.' Andrew chortled as he made his way out of the kitchen with Charlotte hanging on to his arm. 'I said five because I didn't want to sound greedy, but I hope Jane slips up and I get six.'

Charlotte wondered whether he would mention his meeting with Poppy. Surely he'd be so delighted he wouldn't be able to keep it a secret? But they reached the top of the stairs and Andrew turned in the direction of his bedroom without saying a word. Charlotte didn't think she could sit through dinner with such knowledge running through her brain. 'Andrew, can you spare five minutes? I have something to tell you which you'll be happy to hear.'

Standing with the knob of his bedroom door in his hand, Andrew smiled at her across the wide, square landing. 'And I have some news to tell you, my lovely sister. But it will have to wait. You know how strict Mother is about being punctual for meals. She would be most upset if neither of us were seated when the dinner was served. We may get a chance to talk later.'

'I doubt it, Andrew, because Mother is having one of her card evenings. I know several of her friends are coming.' Then Charlotte put her hands together as an idea crossed her mind. 'We could go for a run in the country. We'd have plenty of time to talk.' She looked at her watch. 'We're going to be late and Mother will be cross. So say you'll agree to a drive in the country, and we can both look sharp and be in the dining room, sitting comfortably, in fifteen minutes.'

Andrew was smiling when he answered. 'You drive a hard bargain, dear sister, but yes, I would enjoy a run in the country. It's stuffy in the office all day, and it will be nice to breathe in some pure air.'

Dinner was over, and the table cleared, when Frances came in with a tall silver coffee pot. She placed it in the centre of the table before saying, 'Jane kindly offered to stay later tonight, to make a small buffet for you and your friends, Miss Harriet. And I have to say she has excelled herself, for it looks very appetizing. Everything is covered and in the larder, so it will keep fresh.'

'That is very kind of Jane,' Harriet said. 'Please tell her I am very grateful.'

George raised his bushy brows. 'Please add that she will be paid extra in her wages, Frances. Extra work deserves extra pay. I'll rely on you to make sure she has an appropriate sum in her packet on Saturday.'

'Yes, Mr George, I'll do as you ask. And now I'll bring in the milk for your coffee.'

'Charlotte and I are going for a run in the country, Mother,' Andrew said. 'So we won't interfere with your card game. I feel like some country air after a day in the office. But we'll be home in time to show our faces before your friends leave.'

George sat back in his chair and hooked his thumbs in his maroon braces. 'Do you intend to pay a visit to the old country inn you told us about? If so, I would very much like to join you. I'm sure I'd find it interesting.'

This announcement didn't go down well with his wife.

'George, you know I have friends coming. They would think it was very rude of you not to be here.'

'They are your friends, my love, not mine. I have nothing in common with them, and while I am prepared to suffer in silence most of the time, I would like leave of absence tonight. I rather fancy a log fire in an inn that was built hundreds of years ago. That's if my children don't mind spending the evening with an old fogey?'

'Of course not, Father. You are the last person I'd think of as an old fogey.' Andrew glanced at his sister. 'We'd love Father to come along, wouldn't we? I'm looking forward to seeing the inn again, and I'm sure it will hold a lot of interest for him.'

Charlotte didn't let her disappointment show. She had been looking forward to being alone with her brother and telling him all she had learned about Poppy, which she wouldn't be able to with her father present. Still, she was being selfish, and selfish people were not nice people. 'Oh, of course you should come with us, Papa. I'm sure you will love it. I'm looking forward to seeing the look on your face when you first set eyes on it. Andrew and I were really taken with the inn, and the people there. They were very friendly, even if they did smell of farm animals.'

George looked into his wife's eyes. 'This is something I would like to do, my love. If it is all that Andrew and Charlotte say it is, I'm sure it will give me great pleasure. And I have to be frank with you, and say I have little interest in watching you and your friends playing cards. Female chatter is something I have never quite understood.'

There was a smile hovering around Harriet's mouth. 'If you did understand female chatter, my dear, then I would have cause for worry. You should have told me this when I first began the card evenings, and you could have made arrangements to go to your club. I suggest you do so in future, starting tonight. Go with Andrew and Charlotte, enjoy yourself, and tell me all about your adventure when we're in bed.' Then her eyes turned away from her husband, and she did a very unusual thing. She winked at Andrew before saying, 'Who knows? If it is as interesting as it sounds, I may have an urge to see it for myself. A family outing, perhaps?'

Charlotte found the idea hilarious, and doubled up with laughter. 'Oh, Mama, that would indeed be wonderful! Oh, yes, we must do that soon. And I insist that Andrew brings a camera along to record the event.'

'I have thought of taking photographs of the inn.' Andrew nodded. 'There are not many such places left, and it would be nice to have photographs to look back on in years to come.'

This wasn't what his sister had in mind. 'You misunderstood me, Andrew. It wasn't the inn I was thinking of when I suggested you brought a camera. It was Mother's face! I believe her reaction would be worth capturing on film.'

'I'm going to suggest that if Mother is serious about seeing the inn, then our family outing should be very soon. When the light nights are here, I think the inn would lose some of its charm. Probably no log fire, and lots of customers out for a drive in the country. It would spoil the atmosphere completely for me.' Andrew faced his father. 'Let's see what you think. Perhaps Charlotte and I were wearing rose-coloured glasses on our first visit and tonight will be a let-down for you, who knows? But there's only one way to find out, so shall we retire to our rooms and change into suitable clothing? Come along, Charlotte.'

George covered his wife's hand. 'Can you bear to be parted from your loving husband for a couple of hours?'

'I think I'll survive, my love. And we'll have lots to tell each other in bed. So poppy off and enjoy yourself. I do hope this much talked of inn lives up to your expectations.'

Andrew and Charlotte were walking up the wide staircase side by side. 'I was hoping we would have a chance to talk to each other,' Charlotte said. 'I have some news for you.'

'And I for you, Charlotte, but it can't be now for we need to have a swill and comb our hair before going out. And we can't keep Father waiting. There'll be time when we get home. I'll come to your room for a chat.'

As Andrew was opening his bedroom door, Charlotte called, 'It is a lady's prerogative to be late, Andrew. We don't just have a swill and comb our hair. We must put paint and powder on. Plus nail varnish and perfume.'

'You've got ten minutes, Charlotte, and if you're not ready then, Father and I will go without you. That is my last word, and now I'm closing the door.'

When Andrew parked the car at the side of the inn, George leaned forward for a better view. There were no other cars there, and the only sign the inn was open was the lantern in the window. He stepped from the car and stood looking up at the thatched roof. 'It's like stepping back in time,' he said. 'I've often wished I'd been alive in the early Victorian years, but this is going back a lot further than the reign of Victoria.'

'Wait until you see inside, Papa.' Charlotte was alive with excitement as she clung to her father's arm. 'You'll love it.'

As he was being led to the door, Andrew advised his father to duck, for the entrance was very low. 'I wasn't looking properly the first time we came, and I almost knocked myself out. I'll go in front.'

George noted the thickness of the wooden door, the old

latch, and the dents made by wear over the years. And when he stepped on to the flagged floor and looked around, he drew in his breath, for the scene was like a tableau. There wasn't a sound or movement. The innkeeper was leaning on the wooden bar, and the farmers sitting at a table with tankards in their hands looked like statues. It was a scene that would stay for ever in George's mind, but in reality it was fleeting. The innkeeper and the farmers remembered Andrew and Charlotte, and they greeted them warmly in their thick country accents. And their welcome was genuine, for they were truly happy to see them. Working in the fields and on the farms seven days a week, they had no time or money for a social life. And when George was introduced, he received the same warm welcome. That he sported a hard bowler hat, wore a suit of pure wool, and was obviously a man of distinction, mattered not. He was treated, as his children had been, as a friend. And being George, he was soon at the bar ordering drinks. There was no selection, just beer and whisky. But that didn't deter him, for he was comfortable in any company. He sat with his children for a while, discussing the wonderful wood-burning fire, the stonework around it black with age, the low wooden beams, and the thickness of the whitewashed walls. 'It's everything you said it was.' George puffed on his cigar. 'I wonder how old it is, and if there's a history attached to it? If you'll excuse me, I think I'll have a chat with the landlord. And I'll get a round of drinks in for the farmers.'

'Can we talk now, Andrew? Exchange our news?' Charlotte asked. 'In case we don't get time later?'

Andrew's eyes were on his father. 'No, leave it until later, Charlotte. I promise I'll come along to your room after supper. Right now I'm enjoying seeing Father showing so much interest. He still works quite hard, you know, so it's nice to see him finding something to engage his interest. And look how he mixes in with the farmers, as though he's known them for ages. Sitting on a roughly made stool, and drinking out of a glass that has a chip in the rim. That is what I admire so much about our father, Charlotte. Prince or pauper, he treats everyone alike.'

Loud laughter came from the farmers' table, where the landlord was delivering a round of drinks. George was holding forth with a tale his children couldn't hear for the babble, and it was their father who was responsible for the bursts of laughter.

'I have never seen Papa so relaxed and happy,' Charlotte said. 'I am really glad we found this inn, and pleased we told Papa. I don't think he is disappointed, do you?'

'Far from it. He's in his element. This little inn is steeped in history. If the walls could talk, they would have many tales to tell of how life used to be hundreds of years ago.' Andrew leaned forward. 'I am noticing far more this time than I did before. The bar counter is thick, rough wood, and going by the notches all over it I bet it's hundreds of years old. On the ground in the corner by the bar is a brass spittoon, bearing dents and scratches from days gone by. And I don't know how I missed that stone alcove with a stone bench at the back of it. I'd say there were no chairs and tables here years ago. The customers must have sat on those stone benches.'

'How uncomfortable,' Charlotte said, with a little shiver. 'I'm glad I didn't live in those days.'

'People wouldn't have known any different,' Andrew told her. 'Except for the very rich, of course. I'd love to know the history of it, and the coaches that stopped here for refreshments, and to water their horses. I imagine they were on their way from somewhere up north, to London. It would be a very uncomfortable journey, as there were no metalled roads in those days.'

Smiles lit up their faces and they turned their heads as their father's loud guffaw was followed by roaring laughter from the farmers, and much slapping of thighs. With his pipe in one hand, and a pint tankard in the other, George felt as free as a bird. 'Should we join them, Andrew?' Charlotte asked. 'It looks as though we're being stand-offish, sitting over here. Shall we move?'

Andrew was quick to press his sister back on the chair. 'I don't think so, Charlotte. It's men's talk, I would imagine by the laughter, and I believe the presence of a lady would not be welcome. You would spoil the freedom of speech that they are enjoying so much. I'm not saying they are being vulgar or obscene, for Father would not allow that. But they are telling jokes, and I believe some of them will be about the opposite sex, hence the laughter.'

Charlotte was silent for a while as she digested what her brother had said. Then, slowly, her eyes began to sparkle. 'I had an idea then, Andrew, but I quickly discarded it. Which was a pity really, for I thought it was very funny.'

'Aren't you going to let me into the secret? After all, I am your dear brother.'

'Yes, I am well aware that you are my dear brother. But I am also very well aware that you are a man, and men stick together.'

Andrew raised his brows. 'Are you insinuating that because I'm of the male sex, I am not to be trusted?'

Charlotte giggled. 'Cross your heart and hope to die, if you repeat what I'm about to tell you.'

Thinking he was as soft as his sister, Andrew nodded. 'This better be good, Charlotte.'

'I thought it was funny at the time, but it probably won't appeal to your humour. The idea was, I thought that if there was such a thing as men's talk, then it should apply to women as well. So how about me coming here one night with Mother? Then we could indulge in women's talk. You know what they say about what is good for the goose being good for the gander.'

Andrew started with a chuckle, and then, as his imagination took over, it turned into full-blown laughter. The further his imagination took him, the louder his laughter grew. With tears rolling down his cheeks, he spluttered, 'Oh, I've got a pain in my side now. Don't say any more or I'll have convulsions, and this is hardly the place.'

The farmers became quiet, looking across the room at Andrew's now shaking shoulders. And although they didn't know the reason, laughter is contagious, and soon everyone was laughing heartily, even the innkeeper and George.

'I don't know what you find so amusing, dear boy,' George said, holding a cigar in his hand. 'But I'd like to be let in on the joke, and I'm sure my friends here would too!'

'We'll tell you in the car on the way home, Father.' Andrew wiped the back of his hand across his eyes. 'It's getting late and we really should make a move, or Mother will think we've had an accident. You know how she worries.'

George nodded. 'You are right, my boy, your mother does worry.' He turned round and faced the farmers and the innkeeper. 'I thank you for a very enjoyable evening, gentlemen, one of the best I have ever spent.' Being an outgoing man, and very sure of himself, George had asked and been told the name of the innkeeper. John Morley, his name was, and he'd been proud and happy to tell George everything he knew about what was once a hostelry for travellers. 'Thank you, John, for telling me the history of this wonderful inn. I will be back again, you can be sure of that. But in the meanwhile, if you will let us have six chickens, plucked and ready for the oven of course, my daughter will pick them up on Wednesday morning. Plus one and a half dozen eggs.'

The farmers were more than grateful, and it showed on their faces. They'd been paid five pounds in advance – more than they would have charged the local people who called to their farms, and a lot of money to men who worked hard for little reward.

George crossed the room to shake hands. 'I can't promise anything definite, gentlemen, but I have many friends who I am sure would be delighted to have farm-fresh poultry and eggs. I'll have a word with them, and see if I can put some business your way on a regular basis. When my daughter calls for our order on Wednesday, she will have some good news for you, I hope.' He placed his hard hat on his head and patted the crown until it was sitting to his liking. 'Now I'll say goodnight and go home to the wife, who, if I am very late, will greet me with a rolling pin.'

This brought forth a burst of laughter, and Charlotte was pleased that these men, who had made them so welcome, had taken her father into their midst. They had given him an evening of pleasure, and she surprised everyone by giving each a kiss on his cheek. George and Andrew stood in amazement, while the farmers were delighted, as well as blushing with shyness.

On the journey home, George talked non-stop. 'One of the best nights of my life, my boy. You were very lucky to have come across such a gem. Did you know there is a stone over the door with the year 1625 engraved on it? John said you have to look hard for it now, because the date was hacked out of the stone and is now very worn. The place has been in his family for nigh on two hundred years, and he has in his possession letters and invoices dating back to the first owners. The paper is very fragile, so he doesn't keep it on display. But he said he would show me some time. Also farm implements that date back centuries.' He shook his head. 'What an amazing find. I feel very privileged to have seen and heard so much about life hundreds of years ago. I will definitely be paying another visit to the inn, and the farms, very soon. But I somehow don't think it is to your mother's taste. What say you?'

Andrew and Charlotte answered in unison. 'Definitely not to Mother's taste, Papa.'

Andrew and Charlotte spent a little time in the drawing room while George told his wife and her card-playing friends about what a wonderful time he'd had, and what a host of treasures there were at the inn. Then, when Andrew thought they had stayed long enough not to appear rude, he excused himself by saying he had one or two letters to write. Charlotte then pleaded a slight headache, and followed him out of the room. 'Yours or mine?' he asked.

'Mine is more comfortable,' Charlotte said, with a cheeky grin. 'Besides which, I can get straight into bed.'

When Andrew had seated himself on the round, blue satin-covered chair, she asked, 'Can I go first, please?' She was now sitting on the end of her bed, with her legs dangling. 'You see, I've been keeping a secret from you. But let me tell my story, and hear me out before passing judgement.'

Andrew looked a little puzzled, but was smiling when he nodded in agreement. 'Go ahead, Charlotte. I'm sure you haven't done anything that will bring disgrace upon the family.'

Swinging her legs, and a little nervous about how her

brother would take her confession, Charlotte began with, 'Well, you see, I have become quite friendly with the girl in the raincoat . . .'

'Poppy Meadows,' said Andrew softly.

'Yes, Poppy. I didn't know she'd told you her name. Anyway, I met her the day I went to see the rocking horse, and I saw her again today. I did this for both our sakes, because I know you liked her, and I've liked her from the minute I set eyes on her. And I need a friend, Andrew, who is more in touch with reality than the set I've mixed with all my life. I get on well with her, even though I've only met her a few times. I did intend to tell you when I was more sure of our friendship, and could introduce you properly.' She paused for a few seconds, and then said timidly, 'Don't be angry with me. I only did what I thought was good for both of us.'

'Of course I'm not angry, Charlotte, and I'm glad you've made friends with her, for as you say she lives in the real world.'

Sighing with relief, now it was all out in the open, Charlotte asked, 'Now tell me how you got on with Poppy today. She told me she had met you.'

'I saw her for a maximum of five minutes, Charlotte, and she really doesn't like me. I know she has a right to bear a grudge for what happened, but her objection to me seems more than that. She refuses to have a conversation with me.'

'She doesn't dislike you, Andrew, and she isn't the type to bear a grudge. I think she is a very straight person, who would say what was really on her mind. I mean, she didn't ignore you, did she?'

Andrew shook his head. 'No, she didn't ignore me, but her reluctance to hold a conversation with me was enough to tell me that she really didn't want to even be in my company.' He sighed. 'I'll have to put her out of my mind. Anyway, with her looks, the chances are she will already have a boyfriend.'

'Don't give up so easily, dear brother of mine. You know the old saying that faint heart never won fair lady, so start being positive and don't despair.' Charlotte was swinging her legs as she gave thought to her next words. 'Do you really like Poppy, Andrew? After all, you don't know anything about her.'

'I feel a bit soppy talking about a girl like this, especially as the girl in question doesn't want to know me. But as I am sure you won't repeat our conversation, I'm going to open my heart to you, Charlotte. It's the way I feel, and I can do nothing about it. The first time I looked into Poppy's face, when I stretched out a hand to help her stand up, my heart stopped beating and I fell in love. I know it doesn't sound possible, but that is what happened. No other girl has had that effect on me, and I can't get her out of my mind.' Andrew's sigh was deep. 'I know I'm crazy, and I realize there's no chance of winning her round when she doesn't even like me.' He shrugged his shoulders. 'It's something I'm going to have to live with.'

Charlotte wasn't going to let her beloved brother go on without any hope in his heart. 'But Poppy does like you, Andrew. She told me so today. And she thinks you are chivalrous, like the knights in the old days. I went to lunch with her and one of her work colleagues, and found out a few things you will be interested in. The first is that she does like you, as I've said. The second is that she does have a boyfriend, but is not serious about him because she is busy learning shorthand so she can get a job as a private secretary. And it sounded as though she was putting the shorthand before the boyfriend.' Charlotte was keeping the best until the last, because she knew it would put a smile on her brother's face. And that was something she hadn't seen for a long time. Oh, he had smiled, but the happiness behind it was missing.

'Do you want to hear any more, Andrew?'

'I don't think so, Charlotte,' he said, loosening his tie ready to pull it from his collar. 'I'm grateful to you for trying, but I have resigned myself to the fact that Poppy will never return my feelings.'

'Oh, what a pity,' Charlotte said, trying not to sound too interested. She wanted to savour the look on her brother's face when she told him there was plenty to hope for. 'Should I cancel the cup of tea, then?'

Andrew had his tie in his hand when he asked, 'What tea?'

'Oh, I must have got it wrong. Poppy said you'd invited her to call in to the office one day, for a cup of tea.'

'I did do, Charlotte, but she refused.'

'Only because she is spending all her time on shorthand lessons. She is very determined to improve her job prospects.' Here Charlotte crossed her fingers before adding, 'She agreed to come with me one day when her lessons finish. It would be a few weeks off, but we did make arrangements. Still, if you don't want us to come, I can cancel those arrangements when I meet Poppy next week. If that is really what you want?'

She didn't hear her brother's answer, for he had lifted her off the bed and was swinging her round. There was a huge grin on his face and he was chortling.

Charlotte was delighted. 'Am I to take it that you do not want me to cancel the tea date? Oh, and Poppy said she would like a cake with her tea.'

Chapter Seventeen

Mr Jones looked over his glasses when Poppy came to his desk to pick up her homework at the end of the lesson. It was two months now since she joined the course and the teacher was on first name terms with her. 'You're doing remarkably well, Poppy – as well as anyone in the class.'

Every time Ernest Jones saw Poppy smile, he told himself she had a face that could launch a thousand ships. And she was smiling now, when she told him, 'And so I should be good, Mr Jones, 'cos I'm spending half my life on it. I used to go out every night enjoying myself, dancing and going to the flicks. Now I go out two nights, and spend the other five, plus all day Sunday, writing out pages from a book to get my speed up.'

'It will pay off in the end, Poppy,' Mr Jones said. 'And when you work hard for something, you appreciate it far more than anything you get for free.' He handed her notebook over. 'I would think another month, and you'll be ready to apply for the position you've set your heart on.'

'I don't drink, Mr Jones, except for the odd sherry now and again. But the day I reach the speed required to take dictation, then I intend to push the boat out.'

Ernest smiled. 'Does that mean two glasses of sherry, Poppy?'

She tucked her book under her arm and smiled. 'At least two, Mr Jones. In fact I might even go mad and buy myself a gin and tonic. I've never had one before, but I am told they are what's in fashion these days. A glass of sherry is for old ladies, so they say.'

She was walking away when the teacher shouted after her, 'Don't believe all you hear, Poppy. And if you enjoy a sherry, then stick with it.'

Poppy waved a hand to show she'd heard, then quickened her steps to catch up with Joy and Jane. They still walked with her to the bus stop, though she had never breathed a word to anyone about the night she'd been attacked. But it had become a habit that her friends saw her to the bus stop, and when she got off the bus at the top of her street Peter would be waiting for her. It was too late for the pictures, but they'd either go to the Grafton or walk to the park. The nights were getting lighter now and it was a pleasant change to see the greenery of the park, and the buds appearing on the plants. Another few weeks or so and spring would be here.

'Mr Jones has got a soft spot for you,' Joy said, linking one of Poppy's arms. 'He never has much to say to us like he does to you. You're his blue-eyed girl.'

Jane was linking Poppy's other arm when she said, 'In case you haven't noticed, soft girl, Poppy hasn't got blue eyes. They go from hazel to green, depending on her mood.'

'I didn't know my eyes changed colour,' Poppy said. 'I know I've got hazel eyes, but I didn't know they sometimes changed to green.'

'Well, you wouldn't be able to see them, would you?' Joy chuckled. 'Nobody is able to look themselves in the face; it isn't possible. You can look in the mirror, but you wouldn't see them changing colour.'

'All this about eyes, just because Mr Jones says a few words to me,' Poppy said. 'It's a pity you two have nothing better to talk about.'

'Nothing happens in our lives which is worth talking about.' Jane sounded down in the dumps. 'We go to work every day, and the only nights we do anything are the two nights we come to evening class. I think if anything exciting happened we'd die of shock. Our hearts couldn't stand it.'

'No one makes you stay in every night,' Poppy said. 'It's your own fault. There's nothing to stop you from going dancing; there's enough places to go to. You don't live far from Blair Hall, and it's nice there.'

'Neither of us can dance,' Joy said. 'I can't put one foot in front of the other. And neither me nor Jane look exactly like film stars.'

'Most boys are more interested in how good a dancer you are than whether you look like Doris Day. Besides, I haven't seen many blokes that look like Clark Gable at the dance halls I go to.' Poppy glanced from one to the other. 'The pair of you want your bumps feeling. Get yourselves out and start enjoying life. If it's your faces that are holding you back, you could always put a bag over your heads, or plaster yourselves with make-up.'

'Oh, you're being very helpful,' Jane said, as they came to a halt by the bus stop. 'We don't look so bad when we've got a decent dress on, nice hair and make-up on. But we can't dance and that puts paid to a social life. More girls meet their boys at a dance hall than anywhere else.'

'Then learn to dance! Ye gods, if you can learn shorthand, you can learn to dance, 'cos believe me it's much easier. There's a dancing school called Connie Millington's, and she's a great teacher. A couple of lessons and you'd be tripping the light fantastic.'

'Ay, that's a good idea,' Joy said, as Poppy's bus drew up. 'Where is it?'

There was no time to talk, for Peter was meeting Poppy off the bus. 'Anyone will tell you,' she shouted from the platform as the bus pulled away. 'Connie Millington's, everyone knows her. I had a few lessons off her myself when I started.' She waved a hand. 'See you next Monday.'

It seemed no time at all between getting on the bus, and getting off again. She didn't have to jump or step off, for Peter was waiting and ready to lift her down. 'How did it go, babe? Did you come out top of the class?'

Poppy didn't think this was a bit funny. Peter had tried every trick in the book to stop her shorthand lessons. He didn't see any sense in a woman wasting her time on learning, when she would eventually marry and have no need of the skills. Well, Poppy didn't agree with him. She wanted to be independent. 'As a matter of fact it went really well, and I'm very proud of myself. The teacher reckons another month and I'll have my speed up to what is required. Then I should be able to look for the job I'm so keen on getting.'

'I still think it's a waste of time.' Peter put his arm round her waist. 'Three months of your life gone, and in a few years' time you'll be wondering why you bothered.'

'It's nice to get encouragement.' Poppy put sarcasm into her tone. 'If I hadn't been so determined, you'd have put me off before I started. A bit of support would be appreciated, but you're too busy making little of anything I've achieved.' She was getting fed up with Peter pouring scorn on what she was doing, and thought him selfish in wanting her to finish night school so she could be with him. He was becoming possessive, and she was finding it stifling. 'When I've completed the three-month course, I'll be fully qualified. I don't have to worry about my typing, as I'm well up to speed with that, after working as a typist for nearly four years.'

'In that case, I can start seeing more of you,' Peter said. 'You can't make homework an excuse not to see me.'

Poppy stopped in her tracks and pulled away from him. 'What do you mean about making excuses, Peter? Do you think that's what I've been doing on the nights I don't see you? If so, you don't know me very well. I don't need to make an excuse not to see you: I tell the truth, and if I didn't want to see you, I would come right out and say it to your face. You don't own me, Peter, nobody does.'

He was immediately contrite. 'I'm sorry, babe, I didn't mean to upset you. It's just that on the nights I don't see you, I feel lonely and pine for you. But, cross my heart, I'll be as good as gold for the next four weeks. It will soon pass, and then we can see more of each other.'

'Peter, you're a smashing bloke and I'm very fond of you. But you have to give me some space, to let me do things I want to do. Like taking my mam to the pictures one night, or seeing a girlfriend. I'm too young to be on a lead. I need to be able to make up my own mind where I go, and what I do. And I don't think you would be prepared to give me that freedom, would you?'

'If I was sure you were my girl, I would, yes. You are not the flighty type, not man mad like some girls, so I would trust you.'

However, Poppy wasn't convinced and so she wouldn't commit herself. She didn't know what, but there was something missing in her relationship with Peter. She'd never been in love – not the kind of love her mother had told her about, anyway. She liked Peter, and was happy in his company. But she didn't think that was enough to keep them together. She was never excited when she was getting ready to meet him for a date. Nor was there a shiver down her spine when he touched her. When she'd known him longer, would she feel differently about him? She didn't think so.

'Snap out of it, babe. Your mind is miles away.' Peter peered down into her face. 'What were you saying before you retreated into your shell?'

'I can't remember now what either of us said. But it doesn't matter, because whatever it was it wasn't earth-shattering.'

'Where are we going then, babe? It's too late for the pictures now, and it's not worth going to the Grafton. Do you fancy a drink? There's a cosy little pub over the road.'

'Oh, yes, that would be a change. It's very seldom I've been in a pub, but a glass of sherry sounds fine.'

The pub was quite busy, but most of the customers were men, and they were three deep at the bar. They say women talk a lot when they get together, but men can outdo them when they've got a pint glass in their hand.

'There's an empty table over in that corner,' Peter said, pointing a finger. 'You sit down while I get the drinks. Is it sherry you want, or port?'

'I'm not really a drinker, so either will do.'

Peter came back with a pint glass in one hand and a glass of sherry in the other. He put them down on the small round table, shook the drops of spilt beer off his hand, then took out a hanky to wipe them. 'It's murder getting to the counter. Some of the blokes stand there the whole night, and they won't move to let anyone get served.'

'Now I was the one letting off steam before, so do you

think we can sit and have a nice chat, minding our own business?' Poppy picked up her glass. 'Cheers, Peter.'

He raised his pint glass. 'Here's to you and me.' After drinking from the glass he ran the back of his hand across his mouth. 'You weren't telling me in a nice way that you wanted to finish with me, were you, Poppy? I got that impression, but I'm hoping you're going to tell me I'm wrong.'

'You and I will always be friends, Peter,' Poppy told him. 'You are a nice bloke who I am fond of. But I am not ready to commit myself to anyone yet.'

'But you'll still go out with me?' His smile was a weak one. 'You're not giving me the heave-ho?'

'We'll still see each other, now you know you have to give me some breathing space. Particularly now, when I've almost reached the goal I was aiming for, and when I'm looking for a job. Not any job, but one I can be happy in.' Poppy took a sip of her sherry. 'And now you know all about me and my life, there's a few things I want to know about yours.'

'Fire away, babe. Ask anything you like.'

'Well, do you still live at home with your parents? What do you work at, and where? That will do to be going on with.'

'I do still live with my parents, and I have a sister and brother still at home. My mother looks after us so well, we're reluctant to move, although my sister is engaged, so I presume she will be moving out in the near future.' Peter put an open hand to his forehead. 'What was your next question? Oh, yes, what do I work at? Well, babe, I told you I work with my father, who owns a lot of property. I don't collect rents, like Bill on the door at the Grafton, but I survey any property that comes on the market in which my father is interested. I worked very hard for many years, and am now a quality surveyor. It is a job I very much enjoy.'

Poppy didn't speak for a while, for she was too busy thinking that he must have trained hard to get the position he wanted, and yet he objected to her achieving her goal. It seemed as though he was old-fashioned enough to think the right place for a woman was at home.

Peter touched her knee. 'No comment, babe? No more questions?'

'Only about your love life. And this is not me being nosy, but me being interested. I know you've told me you've had a few girlfriends, and there was a special one who you refused to talk about. I just wondered why you won't talk about that girl. Did she have two heads or something? Or did she run off with another bloke?'

Peter stared past Poppy to the far wall. He appeared to be unaware of his surroundings, his mind elsewhere, and she thought there was a look of sadness in his eyes. When she touched his arm, he gave a start and seemed to have forgotten where he was. 'Hey, where have you been?' she said. 'You were in a world of your own there for a while. You gave me a fright.'

Peter looked blank for a couple of seconds, then he pulled himself together. 'Sorry about that, babe. My mind, for some unknown reason, went off on its own. Probably to the property I was looking over today, which I've advised my father not to touch with a bargepole.'

Poppy shook her head. 'I'm not buying that, Peter. Your mind was no more on a piece of property than mine was. I've got a feeling it had something to do with the girl you were courting, which for some reason came to an end. It's nothing to do with me, except I know it sometimes helps to talk to people if you've got something that's causing you to fret. So why don't you open up and tell me? It might help, you never know.'

'I told you I didn't want to talk about it, and I still don't,' Peter said. 'But I will tell you so it need not be mentioned again.' He lifted his glass and drank deeply, and then he leaned forward and rested his elbows on his knees. 'I went out with a girl for two years. We didn't see eye to eye on many things, and argued a lot. Then we had a huge row and decided to split up. And that's about it, Poppy. I haven't seen her since.'

'How long ago was that?'

'I can't remember exactly, but it's over a year ago. And I don't want to keep harking back to something that is over and done with. So can we lay it to rest now, babe, please?'

'Of course we can. It's got nothing to do with me anyway. I was just curious, and in future tell me to mind my own business.'

'I hope I am your business, babe, when you settle down and get this desire for a secretarial job sorted out. I've told you I can help you find a job, and I've also told you that you don't have to work anyway. I earn good money, and you could live in comfort for the rest of your life.'

'I don't want to live in comfort, Peter, I've already got all the comfort I need at home. I want to run my own life, do what I want, be my own person. That's my goal, and I'm going to stick to it. I'm nineteen – plenty of time to enjoy what life has to offer before even thinking of settling down. My mam is in her forties, and no matter how much my brother and I ask her to give up work and take life easy, she refuses to pack her job in and settle down. She's young for her age, very independent, and does what she wants to do. I admire my mam. She is my role model.'

'And when do I get to meet this paragon of virtue?' Peter asked. 'I'm looking forward to having her on my side, to instil in her daughter that she has a suitable suitor in me. So when am I going to have the honour of meeting your mother, babe?'

'Don't rush me, Peter. I don't want to take on any more commitments than I've got now. When I am lucky enough to find a position in a good firm, where the boss is at least middle-aged, then I'll really start enjoying myself. Until then I'm going to carry on as I am.'

'Why does this unknown-at-present new boss have to be middle-aged?' Peter asked. 'That's a curious stipulation for a girl of your age. I would have thought you would be happy with a young bloke.'

Poppy's curls swung across her face as she shook her head. 'I told you once about my boss, and how I hated him. Well, he's young, and I don't want another boss like him. He's the main reason I want to be out of that job as soon as possible. Tomorrow wouldn't be quick enough for me.'

'Why is that? I can't imagine anyone not getting on with you, Poppy. You are very easy to get along with.'

Poppy wrinkled her nose. 'I am a very easy-going person, who loves life. I have never had an enemy ever, until I was sixteen and went to work as a typist in that office. There's nothing wrong with the office, which has two departments, it's the junior partner who is the bugbear. Because he's got plenty of money, he throws his weight around, and he is vain enough to expect women to fall at his feet. A lot of them do, as well, the silly beggars. They are wined and dined, given the full treatment, and think he's fallen for them. But from what I've heard, he gives them expensive presents, flatters them so much they can't see the wood for the trees, and as soon as he's had what he wants from them discards them like a worn-out pair of shoes.'

Peter was quick to ask, 'He hasn't tried anything on with

you, has he? I know his sort very well, and I'd break his jaw if he pestered you.'

'I'm not that stupid or naive, Peter. He would if he was let, but I wouldn't let him within a mile of me. No amount of money would entice me. When I do eventually get married, I won't be hiding any secrets from my husband.'

'I am hoping the lucky man will be me, Poppy. You haven't given up on me, have you?'

Poppy drained her glass. At nineteen years of age, she wasn't ready to tie herself down. And she wasn't going to make a promise she wasn't sure she would keep. There was a boy for her somewhere out there, and she was sticking to what her mother had told her, and Jean in the office. She would recognize the man who was meant for her, as soon as she saw him. 'I haven't given up on anything, Peter. I'm just going to take the next few weeks as they come. And try to enjoy myself in the process.' She smiled to soften her words. 'Will you take me home now, please? It's been a long day with work and night school, and I'm ready for bed.'

'Not too tired to give me a goodnight kiss, I hope?'

Poppy was in two minds whether to speak the words that were on her tongue or not. One voice in her head was telling her she would regret it, while another told her to get on with it and stop messing. 'Are you taking me out Saturday night, Peter?'

'I sincerely hope so, babe. I've got my heart set on it. And I know you're not the type of girl to break a man's heart.'

'Then why don't you call for me, and then you can meet my mother? It would save you hanging around in the cold if I'm late.'

Peter looked as pleased as Punch. 'I'd love to, babe! What time shall I call?'

'Where are we going?' Poppy asked. 'Pictures or dancing?'

'I'll do whatever you want to do. But if I was to be honest, I would prefer to go dancing.' He held up an open hand. 'It's your choice, babe. As long as I'm with you I really don't mind.'

'We'll decide on the night, eh? You call for me at half seven and we'll have time to make up our minds then.' She pulled her collar up and left the pub, linking Peter's arm. When they were on the pavement outside, she said, 'Better make it seven o'clock on Saturday, otherwise it would only be a quick in and out, and you'll have no time to talk to my mam. And David should be in then. He doesn't usually go out until nearly eight o'clock.'

Peter had his arm round Poppy's waist as they walked towards her house. 'Anything you say, babe, is all right with me. I don't care how, where or why, as long as you're by my side.'

'Stop being so soppy, for heaven's sake.' Poppy sighed inwardly. She wished he wouldn't be so clinging. 'You're a big boy, Peter. You don't need me to hold your hand.'

They were passing the Boden house when the front door opened and Marg came out. She saw Poppy in the light from the hallway before closing the door behind her. 'Hello, queen. I'm just going to your house to see yer mam.' She nodded at Peter. 'Hello, lad. I've seen yer before, bringing Poppy home. I watch through the window, yer see, 'cos I've got nothing better to do. If ye're thinking I'm a gabby, nosy cow, then you're dead right. I am bleeding nosy.'

Poppy chuckled. 'Let me introduce you to our neighbour, Peter. This is Marg Boden, and Marg, this is Peter Broadhurst.'

'Please to meet yer, lad. I hope I haven't put a stop to your canoodling, but I'm going in the Meadows house, so I'll not be in the way. And I'll not sneak a peep out of the window, either. Not because I don't want to know what you and Poppy get up to, like, but because her mam wouldn't let me.' She banged on the knocker so hard it was enough to wake the dead. And then she lifted the letter box and bawled, 'Are yer bleeding deaf, Eva Meadows? Open the ruddy door.'

Poppy was bubbling inside with laughter. What would Peter be thinking of their neighbour? 'I may as well go in with Marg, save my mam having to open the door again.' She stood on tiptoe and kissed his cheek. 'I'll see you Saturday night at seven.' The front door was open now, and Poppy called, 'Don't close the door, Mam, I'm coming in now. Goodnight, Peter.'

'Ay, queen, your bloke is a bit of all right. If I was a bit younger I'd be giving him the glad eye.'

'I go out with Peter because he's a nice feller and we dance well together. But we are not courting, merely friends.' Poppy went into the hall to put her coat on a hanger. She treasured that coat, for she didn't know how long it would be before she could afford another. When she went back into the living room, Marg was sitting at the table facing her mother. 'Anyway, Mrs Boden, what are you up to, knocking on neighbours' doors this time of night?'

'I've come to see what time yer mam will be ready on Saturday morning. Hasn't she told yer, queen, that me and her are painting the town? My feller had a win on the gee-gees, and he's given me the money to buy meself a coat at last. He said he was so fed up with me moaning about Eva putting me in the shade, he chased the bleeding horse round the course with a stiff brush to make sure it won. And didn't it prance home at six to one.'

Eva smiled at her daughter. 'How did it go at night school, sweetheart? Did all yer hard work pay off?'

'Yes, it certainly did, Mam, and I'm really proud of myself. Another few weeks and I'll be scouring the jobs column in the evening paper. But tell me what you two are up to. Are you making a day of it, or just looking for a coat for Marg?'

Eva didn't get a chance to speak, for her friend and neighbour answered for her. 'We're not rushing there and back, queen, we're going as ladies of leisure. I've told yer mam that when I call for her Saturday morning, I expect her to be dolled up to the nines. I know she never wears make-up, but she'll have it on Saturday, or I'll make her walk behind me. She doesn't make the most of herself, your mam, and it's about time she did.'

'I wouldn't know how to put make-up on, even if I had any, which I haven't. Why would I want to, anyway? A woman of my age, I would look like mutton dressed as lamb.'

Marg opened her mouth, but Poppy beat her to it. 'Don't be daft, Mam! A bit of make-up isn't going to make you look like a tart. I'll do it for you, and you'll see what I mean. You don't have to put it on with a trowel, like some do. Just a trace of powder, a touch of rouge, and a hint of lipstick, that's all you need. You've got a lovely complexion, Mam, and you don't look your age, so go out and enjoy life.' Poppy turned to Marg and winked. 'I hope you don't try to lead my mother astray, Mrs Boden.'

'Ay, listen, queen, if I get the chance to lead yer mam astray, then I will. But I will promise she won't be on her own when she goes astray, I'll be right with her. We're mates, and we'll stick together like glue.' Marg leaned across the table and squeezed Eva's hand. 'You leave it to me, queen, and yer won't go far wrong. I'm fussy I am, and unless we're approached by an Errol Flynn or Gregory Peck lookalike, then we won't bother.'

'I was quite looking forward to a day out,' Eva said. 'But with all this talk of make-up, and being led astray by anyone who resembles a film star, well, I'm thinking twice about it now.' She chuckled inside herself. 'I mean, I don't even like Errol Flynn or Gregory Peck. Now if it was Robert Taylor that would be a different thing altogether. I'd happily walk off into the sunset with him.'

Marg jerked her head and rolled her eyes. 'Your mam doesn't want much, does she? Robert Taylor indeed. If we're talking high stakes here, I'd give her a run for her money. And I'll tell yer what, queen, when it comes to the push, I'm a bleeding good runner.'

Eva gave her daughter a gentle kick under the table, before saying to her neighbour, 'Marg Boden, if you want us to dress up posh on Saturday, best bib and tucker, can yer tell me what good it would do if you're going to come out with language like that? Talk about going into Reece's for lunch, I'd be hanging me head in shame if you said to the waitress, "Where's the bleeding sugar?" I wouldn't know where to put meself.'

'I'll be on me best behaviour, queen, I promise. I won't lick me fingers when I'm eating a cream slice, and I won't drink me tea out of the saucer, either. I know when to use me manners, queen, so yer don't need to worry on that score.'

'Oh, well that's a relief,' Eva said. 'If yer start to make a holy show of yerself, I'll pretend I'm not with yer.'

'Some mate you are then, if ye're going to turn tail and run at the first sign of trouble.'

'I thought the whole idea of going into town was to buy you a new coat, Marg?' Poppy said. 'You're the only person I know who can go from buying a coat to getting into a fight with me mam over Robert Taylor! Not to mention your promise not to swear, lick your fingers in a restaurant, or drink tea out of a saucer. That takes some beating, Marg, even by your standards.'

'It's a habit I've got into, queen, and I don't notice meself doing it. Yer see I started just after I got married. I got bored being at home all day, 'cos we didn't have any children then. So I started going to the pictures every afternoon to pass the time away. But I never told Ally because there were lots of things we needed in the house, and he would have gone mad at me going to a matinee every afternoon when the money would have been better spent on buying sheets or towels, which we were short of.'

When Marg told a tale, she really made a meal of it, and went into every little detail. Not that her audience ever minded, for not only were her tales funny, but so were her facial expressions. She could do more contortions with her face than any acrobat. 'So when he used to come in from work and ask me what I'd been doing with meself, I used to make things up. And I'd keep on talking so he didn't have a chance to get a word in edgeways. And it became such a habit, I've never got out of it.'

'Have yer ever tried, sweetheart?' Eva asked.

Marg chuckled. 'How can I stop talking non-stop after all these years? Ally would think there was something wrong with me if I sat with me mouth shut for any length of time. He'd think I was sick, or he was going deaf.'

Poppy and her mother laughed at their neighbour's expressions. Life was never dull when Marg was around. She had a fantastic sense of humour, and always saw the funny side of life. But there was a serious side to her as well. She was always ready to help in times of trouble, never asking if you needed help, but just getting stuck in. A true friend.

'You don't know how lucky you are with your husband,

sweetheart,' Eva told her. 'There's not many blokes as easy-going as Ally. He's one in a million.'

'Yes, I do know that, queen.' Marg looked at the clock. 'Oh, my God, I didn't realize it was so late! Ally will be doing his nut. It's nearly time for bed, and he won't go up those stairs until he's had a cup of tea, and a last cigarette.' She pushed her chair back, nearly toppling it over. 'Why didn't you tell me how late it was?'

'It's hard to stop you when you're in full flow, Marg,' Poppy told her. 'It would be easier to stop a twenty-two tram than it would be to stop you.' She smiled when she added, 'But we love the bones of yer.'

'Well, before I go back and humour my feller, I'd better tell yer what I came for in the first place.'

Eva and Poppy gaped. 'You told us what yer came for, sweetheart, so hadn't yer better get back to yer husband? I'll be ready at half ten, when yer call for me on Saturday morning.'

'No! I didn't come especially for that! Yer know, sometimes me mouth takes over and I don't know whether I'm coming or going. What I came for was to ask Poppy a favour for our Sarah. She's a bit on the shy side, and she didn't like asking you herself. She wants to know if she could come to the Grafton with you one night? She can dance, but she's never been to a big dance hall like the Grafton. She wouldn't hang on to yer all night, 'cos she knows yer've got a boyfriend, but she needs someone to walk in with. Would yer mind, queen? I know it's a lot to ask when you've got this Peter feller with yer, but it would only be for the one night, just to get over her shyness.'

'Of course I wouldn't mind her coming with me, and I'm sure Peter wouldn't mind. I know a couple of lads there, so I'd see she wasn't left like a wallflower all night. Tell Sarah I'll be going on Tuesday, and if that's all right, I'll call for her. It can't be Monday, 'cos that's one of the nights I go to night school, but Tuesday would be fine. And it's a good night, not as crowded as it is at the weekend.'

'Thanks, queen. Our Sarah will be over the moon. She'll see yer herself before then, anyway. So I'll love yer and leave yer now, and go and soothe my feller's brow. Then I'll put the kettle on and make us a nice cuppa to have with our last cigarette of the day. See yer on Saturday, girls. Goodnight and God bless.'

Poppy saw their neighbour out, and came back to find her mother striking a match under the kettle. 'Tea up in five minutes, sweetheart. Give the fire a poke, will yer, to brighten the room up. It's no good putting more coal on – it would be a waste seeing as we'll be going to bed soon.'

Just then they heard a key in the lock. 'Here's your son and heir, Mam,' Poppy said. 'I'm sure he can smell tea a mile away.'

David came in rubbing his hands. 'It's chilly out. I'll be glad when summer comes, with the light nights.'

'Been out with a girl, have you, brother dear?' Poppy helped him off with his overcoat, and then carried it through to hang it on one of the row of hooks. 'You're a bit of a mystery where your female friends are concerned. You've never brought one home to meet the family.'

'You're a fine one to talk, sis! What about you and Peter? You've never brought him home to meet Mam. I've got a good excuse for not bringing a girl home, and that is because when I do finally bring one here, it will be the one I'm quite sure I want to spend the rest of my life with.'

Eva had poured a cup of tea out for David, and when she

carried it through to the living room she smiled at Poppy. 'Your brother has got it all sorted out the way he wants it.' She put the cup down before asking, 'But what about you, sweetheart? Will you be bringing Peter to meet me? Is he the one for you?'

'As a matter of fact, Mam, you'll meet him on Saturday night, because he's calling for me. But don't read anything into it – or you, David – because calling for me doesn't mean anything. Peter is as nice a bloke as you'll ever come across, but I'm not sure what my feelings for him really are. I'm nineteen and he is six years older than me. He has had the time to do what all young people want to do, and that is to enjoy all the good things that life offers. When I've lived another six years I'll know, through experience, what I want, and who I want it with, for the rest of my life.'

'Don't go out with anyone just because you are afraid to hurt their feelings, sweetheart; that wouldn't be fair to either of you. Go out with boys by all means. Enjoy yourself while ye're young enough to do the things all young people do. Youth is fleeting, sweetheart, so get the most out of it while yer can. But try not to hurt anyone in the process.'

'I wouldn't knowingly hurt anyone, Mam, I couldn't do that. But neither do I want to marry a man who I don't love, but will be tied to for the rest of my life.'

'You're being sensible, Poppy,' David said. 'You've had the same boring, low-paid job since you left school. You haven't lived yet, don't know what life is all about. So give yourself a break and make up your mind to get as much enjoyment out of life as you can.' He chucked his sister lightly on the chin. 'Peter did seem to be a good bloke, steady and reliable. But perhaps it's not steady and reliable you want at nineteen years of age. So don't be talked or persuaded into doing anything you're not happy with.' He waved his hand. 'Like me, wait until the right one comes along.'

Eva was nodding in agreement as her son was speaking. She wanted the best for her beautiful daughter, and the best was true love. 'Don't dwell on it, sweetheart. You've got all the time in the world to worry about settling down. Just remember what I've told you many times. When the right man for you comes along, you'll have no doubts, yer'll know right away. And it'll be the most wonderful experience yer'll ever have in yer life.'

'I've never forgotten what you told me about the first time you met Dad. And I'll never settle for anyone who doesn't measure up to him. As soon as I get that tingle down my spine, and go weak in the knees, you'll be the very first to know.'

Chapter Eighteen

It was Poppy who opened the door at half past ten on the Saturday morning, to find their neighbour looking up at her. And she had to smile when Marg pushed her aside with a cheery, 'Top of the morning to yer, queen. I hope yer mam is all titivated up and raring to go. If she's not, I'll have a cup of tea with yer while I'm waiting.'

Poppy was still in her dressing gown, for she didn't work on a Saturday and always indulged herself with a lie-in, followed by a leisurely breakfast, then a lovely soak in the bath. 'I'm not long up, Marg. I've still got sleep in my eyes. Saturday is an easy day for me; I don't get dressed until the afternoon. So if you're after a cup of tea, you're going to have to make it yourself. Mam is upstairs getting ready; she won't be long.'

'I'll leave the tea, then, queen. I couldn't be bothered putting the kettle on.' Marg pulled out a chair from the table, and plonked herself down. 'Anyway, it's coming to something when a visitor is told to make their own tea. It's not very welcoming, queen, or polite. It's enough to make anyone feel unwanted, like. Could even give them an inferiority complex. If I was the timid type, I'd be cut to the quick.'

'Then I'm glad you're not the timid type, Marg, because Saturday is the day I get to lounge around in me dressing gown, before having me breakfast. I have a routine, you see, and I stick to it.'

'Oh, aye, queen, and what is your routine? If I like it, I might even copy it, 'cos I'm bleeding hopeless when it comes to planning. I promise meself every day that I'll do so-and-so the next day, but I never stick to it. I've got no willpower, yer see, queen. I'm away with the fairies half the time.'

Poppy pulled out a chair and sat facing her neighbour. 'What will Ally have for his dinner when he gets home from work? Have you left anything for him?'

'Of course I have, queen. I wouldn't let him come home from work to fresh air sandwiches. My Ally is easy-going, but he's not that easy-going. The air would be blue if there was nothing to eat, and I'm gadding about town, spending his money. He'd have a duck egg.'

Poppy waited to hear what Marg had left for her husband to eat, but her neighbour appeared to think the subject had been dealt with. So, being curious, Poppy asked, 'What have yer left for Ally's dinner, Marg?'

'A pan of stew on a low light, queen. Lucy said she'll keep an eye on it so it doesn't burn. She's good like that, is our Lucy.' Marg lowered her voice, and her eyes surveyed the room as though what she had to say was for Poppy's ears only. 'I hate to admit it, queen, but our Lucy is a better cook than me. When the stew is ready, half an hour before Ally gets home, she's going to put some dumplings in, and my feller will get a meal fit for a king. When I make dumplings, they're as heavy as lead, but our Lucy's are so light they could float.'

Marg had been so busy talking she hadn't heard footsteps on the stairs, and she was startled when a voice behind her said, 'Don't you ever run out of topics to talk about?'

With a hand on her heart, Marg said, 'You silly beggar! Yer

nearly gave me a heart attack, sneaking up on me like that.'

'Oh, I'm glad yer didn't have a heart attack, sweetheart,' Eva said. 'Just think of the shock Ally would get, if I had to be the bearer of such bad news. He wouldn't enjoy the stew, and it would be wasted. It would have to be thrown in the bin with Lucy's dumplings.'

Marg kept the stern expression on her face. 'How long have you been standing there? I bet you haven't been as thoughtful as me, and you're probably feeling guilty about your David coming home to find no nice smell of dinner coming from the kitchen.'

'Ah, well, now.' Eva smiled. 'Stew is a lovely smell, I agree, and it does take a couple of hours to cook. Whereas bacon, sausage and egg have an equally inviting aroma, and they only take twenty minutes to cook. So Poppy will be serving David and herself an appetizing meal, with fruit and cream for afters.' Eva held up an open palm. 'Before yer say anything, sweetheart, I'll admit the fruit will be out of a tin, and the cream will be evaporated milk, also out of a tin.'

'That's what I like about your mam, Poppy. She can't tell a lie.' Marg pushed her chair back and stood up. 'Or at least if she does tell a lie, she can't get away with it because her face goes the colour of beetroot.' She eyed up her friend. 'I have to say you look very smart, queen. I see yer've got make-up on, as well. It suits yer, and makes yer look a lot younger.'

'Only you could pay someone a compliment with one hand, and take it back with the other,' Eva said. 'I look very smart, but without the aid of powder, rouge and lipstick I'd look as old as the hills.'

'There's only months difference in our ages, queen, so if I insult you, I insult meself at the same time. More, come to think of it, 'cos I've got twice as much powder on as you.'

Poppy tutted. 'If you two don't stop talking, and go out, you'll be little old ladies before you get to the bus stop. So be on your way, vamoose, skedaddle, scram.'

Marg linked Eva's arm. 'I think yer daughter wants to see the back of us, queen, and I don't need the bleeding house to fall on me to take a hint. So, let you and me hit the road, eh? You can take me to the shop where you bought that coat, and keep our fingers crossed there's one there to suit me.'

Poppy went to the door with them, but she stayed inside the hall. They had a neighbour opposite, Florrie Lawson, who was eighteen stone of trouble. She had a husband and two teenage daughters who were as quiet as mice, but Florrie loved causing trouble, and no one, man or woman, was safe from her tongue. She was common, her language was filthy, and she hadn't a friend in the street. When she stood on her step, arms folded across her enormous tummy, people would take a detour and use one of the entries rather than pass her house. So as soon as Eva and Marg stepped on to the path, Poppy closed the door behind them. She didn't go back into the living room, but climbed the stairs and turned the bath tap on. She would indulge herself by lying back in the warm water and think ahead to when she was competent enough to apply for a job with a firm she could be happy working for. Then, after daydreaming for half an hour, she would get dressed and see to the dinner when David was due home. They'd probably have the house to themselves for the afternoon, for she couldn't see her mam and Marg coming home until about five o'clock. Or perhaps a little earlier if her mam's feet were tired, or they ran out of money.

Luxuriating in the warm water, Poppy's mind went through her wardrobe to choose the dress she would wear tonight. It didn't take long because she only had a couple of decent dresses. That would change though when she was on a better wage, for she could add to her wardrobe as she went along. Then, with clothes still in her mind, she thought of Charlotte, who always looked smart and attractive. If she did go to Andrew's office for a cup of tea, as she'd promised Charlotte she would, then a new dress was essential. Not for the world would she turn up like a poor relation. She wouldn't give him the satisfaction of thinking she wasn't as good as him. Charlotte was different. Poppy got on well with her and would like to keep on seeing her, to be a friend. But not Andrew. She'd go to his office, not because he'd invited her, but because of Charlotte's persuasion. She wouldn't let the girl down, but the visit would be a one-off.

David opened the front door and was met by the aroma of bacon and sausage. 'It smells good,' he called as he took off his coat and hung it in the hall. 'I didn't realize I was hungry until I put the key in the door.'

'You have timed it well, David,' Poppy shouted from the kitchen. 'Any later and the egg would have been fried too long, and I know you like the yolk runny.'

David was rubbing his hands as he stood in front of the fire and watched his sister putting the plates down on the table. 'Chief cook and bottle-washer today, are you?'

'Chief cook is right, brother dear, but bottle-washer I most certainly am not! I'm going to leave that privilege to you.' Poppy tilted her head and her curls hung loose around her lovely face. 'On second thoughts, because you're my brother and I love you, I'll go easy on you. I'll wash and you can dry.'

'Suits me, Poppy. It will do me good to do a household task. It's a very small one, I know, but little chores like that will stand me in good stead when I get married.'

Poppy feigned surprise. 'You can't get married before me, David! Daughters always get married first.'

'In that case I could be walking down the aisle when I'm an old man if you hang about. Don't be too fussy, our kid, 'cos I've been thinking about twenty-three or four being a good age for a bloke to get hitched.'

'Have you got anyone in mind? You're very mysterious about your girlfriends, David. You never mention a name, or whether you date anyone regularly. Why is that?'

'Because I don't date anyone on a regular basis. I haven't met anyone yet who sets my pulses racing. I'm too fussy. Still, better to be single than married to the wrong one.'

'I'm not even thinking of tying myself down until I'm turned twenty-one,' Poppy said. 'I want to see a bit of life first. Until then I'm going to love them and leave them. Unless what happened to our mam happens to me. She was younger than me when she met our dad, yet they fell in love with each other right away. One look, one touch, and that was it! Nothing like that has happened to me. Of all the blokes I've been to the pictures with, or danced with, not one has had me seeing stars.'

'Not Peter? He's certainly got it bad where you are concerned. And I think he's of the opinion you feel the same.'

'He's a lovely man, and he'll make a wonderful husband for some lucky girl. But I'm not that girl, David, I'm afraid. The more I see of him, the more I know he's not the man for me.'

David pushed his empty plate away. 'I enjoyed that, our kid. And I'm very relieved to know you can turn your hand to cooking. For if all else fails, and we never find our soulmates because we're too fussy, we could be stuck with each other for life. So if you do the cooking, I'll make the beds.'

Poppy laughed. 'I don't think it'll come to that. I have great hopes that I take after our mam. I don't fancy being left on the shelf, a spinster with a cat for a companion.'

It was David's turn to laugh. 'So have I, sis. I'm pinning my hopes on coming across a very pretty girl, with a good sense of humour, who will fall into my arms and swear undying love. Someone I will feel comfortable with, and love. And she'll come along one day, I know she will.'

For some reason, a mental picture of Charlotte crossed Poppy's mind. 'I know a very pretty girl who has a very good sense of humour, and she fits the description of your dream girl perfectly. Unfortunately, she is way out of your league.'

'Why is she out of my league?' David's eyes showed interest. 'I'm not missing anything. I've got one head, two eyes and ears, ten fingers and toes, plus arms and legs and a face that would pass inspection. What more could any girl ask for?'

'I was only pulling your leg, David, and I'm sorry 'cos it wasn't remotely funny.'

David pretended to be disappointed. 'Just my luck. Here was me building my hopes up with the image of a dream girl floating around in my head, and my own sister bursts the bubble and tells me she was only pulling my leg.' He dropped his head in his hands, and with a long, dramatic sigh, said, 'I had visions of walking down the aisle with a beautiful girl with blonde hair, wearing a flowing wedding dress and a veil on her head held in place by a diamond tiara.'

Poppy was shaking with quiet laughter. 'The girl I had in mind doesn't have blonde hair, it's more an auburn, and it's curly.'

'Is this a real person?' David asked. 'You talk about her as though she's real.'

'Actually it's a friend I've described. But not a close friend, so there's not much chance of my ever bringing her here. She is nice, but there's thousands of girls as pretty as she is. So start looking around, big boy, and I'm sure it won't be long before you're snapped up.'

Poppy reached for her brother's plate and put it on top of hers with the cutlery. 'Come on, dear, you've had your meal and now it's time to pay the bill. But I'll let you off the tip.'

Brother and sister worked in harmony, and in no time at all the dishes were washed, dried, and put away. 'I'll make a pot of tea now,' Poppy said. 'You go and sit down and read the paper you brought in with you. We can have a few lazy hours before Mam and Marg come home.'

'Did they say what time they thought they'd be home by?'

'Mam really didn't get a chance to say much. You know what Marg is like when she's in full flow, no one can get a word in. But she is so funny she really cheers me up. And she's been good for Mam since our dad died. We've got a lot to thank Marg for. When the going is tough, she's always there to help, so I was glad when she asked if I could do something for her for a change. Sarah wants to go to the Grafton, but is too shy to go on her own, so I've promised to take her on Tuesday. I haven't told Peter yet. I don't think he'll be very happy.'

'Anyone can go to the Grafton if they want. It's open to the public, so Peter couldn't stop Sarah even if he wanted to. But surely he wouldn't object to her going. Why should he?'

Poppy didn't want to tell him how possessive Peter was, and how he didn't like her dancing with anyone else. It wasn't fair to him, for although Poppy didn't like him being so clinging, he was a good man and would never overstep the mark. Oh, I'm sure he'll be all right about it. And he'll ask Sarah for a dance if he sees she's not being asked up.'

Brother and sister spent the next two hours reminiscing.

They talked of their dad, how he used to take them to the park and give them turns on the swings and the seesaw. And they remembered how he used to throw his head back when he laughed at something funny. How gentle he was with them, and how he used to tell them every night, when they were going to bed, that he loved them.

They were deep in conversation when David suddenly cocked an ear and held up a hand to silence his sister. 'I can hear voices. It must be Mam and Marg. I didn't expect them back so soon – it's only four o'clock.'

Poppy jumped to her feet. 'There's an argument going on. I can hear Marg's voice, and I'm sure she's shouting at Florrie Lawson over the road.'

David was first out of the front door, with Poppy close on his heels. 'What's going on, Mam?' David took hold of his mother's arm. 'Don't waste your time and energy on Mrs Lawson. She's not worth it.'

However, it wasn't Eva who was shouting, it was Marg and Florrie Lawson swapping insults with each other.

'You two been out on the town have yer?' Florrie looked fearsome, standing with her feet apart, her huge arms crossed and resting on her enormous tummy. She was wearing an old-fashioned mob cap, and a wraparound pinny with a large safety pin keeping it fastened. And on her chubby face there was a look of satisfaction. For Florrie liked nothing better than a fight: it was more exciting than going to the pictures. It wasn't often she got the chance to trap her neighbours into a confrontation, for they kept out of her way. The only one brave enough to take her on in a slanging match was Marg Boden.

'What's it got to do with you where we've been?' Marg asked, putting her shopping bags on the pavement by her feet. 'Get inside and mind yer own business, yer nosy cow.'

David stepped in front of his mother and reached for Marg's arm. 'Come inside, Marg. She's goading you on, looking for a fight. Don't give her the satisfaction.'

'I'll give her more than satisfaction, lad. I'll give her a black eye if she doesn't shut her bleeding mouth.'

'I'd like to see yer try,' Florrie shouted across. 'You and yer mate there come walking up the street in yer new coats and think yer own the place. Talk about mutton dressed as lamb isn't in it. Yer look like a couple of tarts.'

David tried once again to cool things down. 'Mam, will you and Marg come in the house, please.'

Eva shook her head. 'I wouldn't miss this for the world, son. It's about time someone took on Florrie Lawson. I wouldn't 'cos I'm a coward. But I'll help Marg out if she gets stuck.' Eva patted David's cheek. 'Don't worry, lad, no one is going to come to any harm. Florrie's all mouth. She trades insults with everyone from her path. It never comes to fisticuffs, only name-calling.'

Marg was enjoying herself. In all the years she and Eva had lived in the street, they'd put up with the shenanigans of the woman opposite. They'd never really retaliated, only to tell her to shut up. Now she was going to get a taste of her own medicine. 'Yer've set me thinking, Florrie. When yer said me and Eva were mutton dressed as lamb, I got to wondering what animals you reminded me of. And I've fitted you out perfectly. Yer've got the body of a rhinoceros, and the skin of an elephant. And if yer think I'm exaggerating, go inside and take a good look in the mirror. Stand well back, though, 'cos if the mirror cracks with fright, yer might end up getting bits of glass in yer face. And yer really can't afford to look any uglier than you are, or yer'll frighten the postman.'

Florrie was blazing. She wasn't going to let that go, or her status as a woman to be feared would be in jeopardy. She could see curtains twitching and realized half the street was listening, so her reputation was at stake. With a roar like a lion, she stepped down on to the path. 'I'll break yer bleeding neck, talking to me like that. Come on, yer stupid cow, let's see what ye're made of. Yer'll wonder what's hit yer by the time I'm finished with yer.'

'Oh, aye! You and whose army, yer daft cow?' Marg shrugged off David's restraining arm and started to cross the street towards her adversary. 'Stay where yer are, Florrie. I don't want yer to tire yerself out, so I'm coming to you.'

Florrie was waving her arms, the fat swinging from side to side, as torrents of threats, complete with bad language, poured from her mouth. She was going to blacken both of Marg's eyes, break her nose and knock out every tooth in her head. That was until she saw Marg hand her new coat to Eva, then roll up her sleeves as she neared Florrie's gate. It was then the big woman realized she was dealing with someone who was more than a match for her. And she decided she couldn't fight with her false teeth in, in case they got broken and she couldn't afford a new set. To take the teeth out and put them in her pocket would make her a laughing stock. So she did the unthinkable. With a speed she'd never moved at before, she reached her gate before the enemy, and closed it quickly.

'You coward,' Marg said, when she stood outside the closed gate. 'Come out here, and say to me face what yer've been calling me and me mate. Come on, look me in the eye and tell me again what yer said we looked like. A couple of tarts, I think that's what yer said, but correct me if I'm wrong.'

Behind many a curtain, women were waiting with bated breath. Was the street bully about to get her just deserts? There would be no tears shed for her if she did. There wasn't a family in the street that hadn't fallen victim to her vicious tongue. And they would be delighted to see her suffer the same humiliation she'd meted out to others.

They weren't to be disappointed, thanks to Marg Boden. For the determined expression on her face when she leaned over the gate and grabbed hold of the neck of Florrie's pinny caused the big woman to quickly change her tactics. Common, blowsy, and a bully she may be, but a fool she wasn't. 'What the hell are yer doing? It was a joke! Can't yer take a bleeding joke?'

'You're the biggest joke of the lot, Florrie Lawson, and I can't stand yer! It's about time someone brought yer down to size, and I'm just in the mood. If yer'll open the gate, so I don't have to climb over it, I'll prove to yer exactly what size you are.'

But Florrie hung on to the gate like grim death. 'It's coming to something when yer can't even crack a joke without being attacked.' She looked across to where the Meadows family were standing. 'I'm surprised at you, Eva Meadows. Ye're usually as quiet as a mouse. You and me have never had no trouble.'

'Seeing as I've never had a conversation with you, Florrie, it would be difficult for us to have had any trouble. Half a dozen words we've exchanged over the years, and that has suited me fine. I don't like anyone who has a loud mouth, and who thinks being a bully is clever. Hitler was a bully who thought he was clever, but look what happened to him. He lost the war.' Eva picked up the shopping bags and handed them to David to take inside. 'Put her down, Marg, and come in for a cup of tea. I'm spitting feathers and me feet are killing me.'

'I'll put her down gladly, queen, 'cos I can't stand the woman. But I won't come in yours for a cuppa. I'd better get home to my feller, or he'll have a cob on.' She released Florrie and dusted her hands as though to brush dirt off them. 'I'll come in for me shopping, then I'll get off home. My feller is easy-going, but he does have a limit.'

However, when Marg went into the Meadows house, and put her new coat back on for them to admire, she forgot about her husband. The deep mauve coat was military style, with gold buttons down the front, and two on each cuff. It fitted perfectly, and Marg, slim and elegant with hands on hips, paraded it like a professional model.

'It's lovely, Marg,' Poppy said. 'Did you get it from the same shop me and Mam went in?'

'Yeah. It's a little treasure is that shop. A coat like this for four pound, I couldn't believe it.' Marg chuckled. 'Mind you, it cost five pound as far as my feller is concerned, so I don't want any of yer to let the cat out of the bag.'

'That's a lousy trick, Marg,' Eva said. 'Yer sweet talk him out of the money, then lie about the price. I couldn't do it if he was my husband.'

'It won't hurt his pocket, queen. He's not short of a few bob. What he doesn't know isn't going to worry him.'

'I won't tell Ally, sweetheart,' Eva said, 'but if he asked, I wouldn't tell a bare-faced lie. So don't bring me into any discussion over the price of the coat.'

Marg's eyes rolled. 'Ye're too bleeding good to be true, you are, missus. Yer don't drink, don't smoke, and only swear once in a blue moon. It's a wonder yer haven't got a permanent headache with that ruddy halo on yer head all the time.' She winked at Poppy. 'How does it feel to have an angel for a mother, queen? Yer've got a lot to live up to, both you and David, if in later life yer want to hear people say, "Ah, they both take after their mother, she was an angel." '

David chortled. 'Ay, Marg, don't be putting years on us. We've got our lives ahead of us, me and Poppy. And when we've sown our wild oats, and settle down to old age, then we'll start taking after our mam.'

'Marg, will yer go home, sweetheart, to that fine man who is your husband?' Eva started to gently push her neighbour towards the door. 'I don't want him to blame me for keeping you out so long, so don't you tell him I've kept you talking.'

David picked up the two bags, saying, 'These are heavy. Have you had a spending spree?'

'The big bag has me old coat in, that's why it's heavy. The other has some groceries, nothing exciting.'

'I'll carry them to your door,' David said. 'And if Ally tells you off for being out so long, I'll stand like a man and take the blame.'

When they were alone, Poppy reminded her mother, 'Don't forget Peter is calling for me, Mam. Can we get the tea over early and tidy around before he comes? I'm not a snob, but I'd like the place looking nice.'

'It won't take long to make our tea, sweetheart. I've brought some boiled ham for sandwiches, and a tin of pears for afters. And I gave the room a good going over this morning before you were up.' Eva gave her daughter a hug. 'He won't be looking for faults, love. He'll only have eyes for you.'

'Ay, that's the title of a song, Mam! Ooh, I can feel myself dancing to that tune, and the words are really romantic.'

'Yes, I know, sweetheart. I'm not so old I don't keep up with the latest songs. I know all the tunes and the words that go with them, 'cos the girls in work are singing all day.' Eva chuckled. 'I couldn't grow old if I wanted to. I wouldn't be allowed. But I wouldn't have it any different, for life would be very dull if I couldn't keep up with the times.'

'Me and David will make sure you don't ever grow old or lonely, Mam, don't worry about that. We'll both get married eventually, and then you'll have grandchildren to keep you young. There's a lot to look forward to, for the three of us.'

'I know that, sweetheart. I couldn't ask for more loving children than you and David. When yer dad died, I thought it was the end of the world. That's how I felt. I was never going to be happy again, not ever. But I hadn't reckoned on my children turning into kind, caring, loving adults.' Eva didn't mean to be emotional, but tears were very close when she said, 'Your dad will be looking down on us now, and he'll be happy that I'm not lonely, and that I'm surrounded by love.'

Poppy brushed a hand across her eyes. 'Don't set me off crying, Mam. I don't want to go to the dance with red eyes.'

They didn't hear David coming into the room, and looked guilty when he asked, 'What are you two cooking up, huddled together like that?'

'We're not cooking anything, love, we've decided on an easy tea. How does this sound? Slices of lean boiled ham on thick slices of homemade bread from Gregson's bakery? And then pears and cream for afters? Unless yer prefer chips from the chippy?'

David had felt the tension when he'd walked into the room, but was wise enough to let well alone. 'I don't want chips, Mam. I'll settle for what you and Poppy feel like. I'm easy over food, you know that.'

'It's only just turned a quarter past five, so we've plenty of time to have our meal and tidy away before Peter comes,' Poppy said. 'And it doesn't take long for me to get meself dolled up.'

Eva was on her way to the kitchen when she had a thought. 'David, what did Ally think of Marg's new coat? Did he like it?'

'Yeah, he seemed pleased with it. But you know what men are like, they don't make a fuss the same as women. The girls liked it, though. They were taking turns trying it on when I left.'

Eva raised her brows. 'Did Ally ask how much Marg paid for it?'

'I didn't stay long, Mam, because I was expecting Ally to ask, and I'm a coward. Walk away from trouble, that's my motto.'

'That's the best thing to do, sweetheart, then yer can't lose any friends. Not that it makes any difference to Marg; she's got loads of friends. She doesn't keep anything back. If she thinks something, she's right out with it whether yer like it or not. But she gets away with it, and she's popular with friends and neighbours.' Eva smiled. 'Except for Florrie, across the road. Marg can't stand her.'

'I gathered that, Mam,' David said with a chuckle. 'When I saw her nearly choking the woman, I said to myself that she mustn't like Mrs Lawson. And I made up my mind, right then, that I would never get on the wrong side of Marg.'

'Her bark is worse than her bite, David,' Poppy said. 'You should know that by now. She got in a temper today because of what Mrs Lawson said about her and our mam. And it's about time someone gave that terrible woman a taste of her own medicine. I bet all those watching Marg were cheering her on. She had the guts to do what everyone in the street would like to do. I wouldn't 'cos one puff from Mrs Lawson would blow me over. Anyway, I'm going to get washed and changed now before tea. Then I won't be in a mad rush later.'

'This is Peter, Mam,' Poppy said, and watched her mother holding her hand out. 'Peter, meet my mam.'

'Pleased to meet yer, lad.' Eva was thinking what a nice-looking, well-dressed man he was. 'I've heard a lot about yer from Poppy.'

'All good, I hope, Mrs Meadows?'

'Oh, Poppy never speaks ill of anyone, Peter. At least not to me she doesn't.'

'You've met my brother David, who insisted on waiting in to see you. And that is an honour, for he's going to be late for his date with a very beautiful girl.'

Peter had his trilby hat in his hands, and he was running the brim through his fingers. 'Never keep a lady waiting, David, because she may decide not to hang around, and leave you in the lurch.'

'No, no, no!' David drawled in an American accent. 'No dame would leave me in the lurch. They're putty in my hands.' Then he straightened his tie and his face. 'Just to be on the safe side, though, I'll make tracks. You see, it's her turn to buy the tickets tonight.'

'Go on, yer daft ha'p'orth,' Eva said. 'It would serve you right if the girl left you swinging.'

'We'll go out at the same time, Mam.' Poppy gave her mother a kiss. 'Are you going next door to play cards?'

Eva nodded. 'It'll pass the time away, and we have a good laugh. We only play for matches, so it's a cheap night's entertainment. But you lot get off and enjoy yourselves.' She shook hands with Peter again. 'It's been nice meeting yer, lad. Enjoy yer night out. And I'll wait up until yer come in, Poppy. We'll have a cup of tea before going to bed, and yer can tell me what the dance was like. And remember the names of the old songs; I'd like that. It'll take me back to the days I went to a tuppenny hop.' She waved her children and Peter off, then went back to the living room and sank into a fireside chair. She'd have half an hour to herself, then go next door.

Poppy and Peter were earlier than usual, and on the dance floor at the Grafton there were only about a dozen couples enjoying the freedom of movement as the band played a waltz. 'Oh, we'll have to come early in future,' Peter said. 'This is heaven, having room to cover the floor without bumping into other dancers.'

But good things don't last for ever, and half an hour later there was barely room to move. For those who loved dancing, though, it was worth the odd elbow in the ribs, or trodden-on toes. Rhythm was in the blood, and for some it was the greatest pleasure in their lives.

'The next dance is a slow foxtrot, babe, so get ready to be on the floor while there's room to get round at least once in comfort.'

They'd been on the floor a few minutes, both humming to the tune the band were playing, when Peter seemed to lose control of his feet, and he stumbled. 'That's what happens when you've got two left feet,' Poppy said, laughing. Then she looked into his face to find it drained of colour, and his eyes were staring unblinkingly over her shoulder. She got a fright, thinking he was ill, and then dismissed that idea. But they were standing still in the middle of the floor, making it difficult for the other dancers. She'd never known anything like it. It was only a matter of seconds, but to Poppy it seemed an eternity.

'Peter, are you all right?' She dropped her arms, embarrassed because other couples were giving them daggers. 'Peter, what's wrong with you?'

He looked down into her face and stared, as though he

didn't know her, or indeed where they were. Then he shook his head as though to clear his mind. 'I'm sorry, babe. Come on, let's dance.'

'You've just frightened the life out of me, Peter Broadhurst, and if that was your idea of a joke, then I don't think it was funny. I really thought you were having a seizure. You were like a statue – I couldn't even see you breathing! I don't want to finish this dance. Let's get off the floor. You must know something was wrong with you, and I want to know what it was. If you're ill, then you shouldn't be dancing, anyway.' She took his hand. 'Come on.'

'I'm all right now, babe. Don't panic.' Peter's smile was forced, his face colourless. 'I thought I saw a ghost from the past, and it threw me off course a bit. But it was all in my imagination, and it's gone now.'

Poppy found that very hard to believe. There was more to it than Peter was letting on, but surely if he was feeling unwell he wouldn't be stupid enough to step on to a dance floor. 'I think we should sit out until after the interval. You may be feeling better by then. And looking better, 'cos you're as white as a sheet. And I'm not taking any chances, in case you pass out on the dance floor.'

There were chairs lining the walls of the dance hall, and Peter cupped Poppy's elbow as they walked towards them. They'd just seated themselves when a voice said, 'Hello, Peter.'

As Poppy looked up, she heard Peter's sharp intake of breath and turned to face him. He looked exactly as he had on the dance floor. His eyes were unblinking and his face and body were rigid. Then Poppy looked back to the girl who was standing in front of them. She looked to be in her early twenties, tall and slim with dark hair falling around her shoulders, and she was very attractive.

When Peter didn't move or speak, Poppy asked the girl, 'Are you a friend of Peter's?'

The girl nodded. 'I haven't seen him for two years, but yes, we were friends.'

Her voice brought Peter out of his trance. 'What are you doing here, Kate? You're a long way from home.'

'You remember my friend Rita? Well, she told me she'd seen you here, and I thought it would be nice to say hello. For old times' sake.'

'I don't know why,' Peter said, his face set. 'You weren't so concerned two years ago, so why this sudden fit of nostalgia?'

Poppy was surprised at Peter's being abrupt to the point of being rude. But she was also intrigued as to why the girl was here. Then the answer came to her in a flash. This was the girl Peter was reluctant to talk about, except to say they had courted for . . . was it two years he'd said? Whatever the reason for them splitting up, the appearance tonight of the girl had certainly had an effect on Peter.

'I just thought it would be nice to see you again,' Kate said. 'I often think of you. But I see you have a companion, so I won't intrude. Goodbye, Peter.'

Poppy jumped to her feet. 'No, please don't go. I'm going to the cloakroom to freshen up, so stay and talk to Peter. I'm sure he'll enjoy hearing your news after all this time.' She patted Peter's arm. 'I won't be long. Talk to your friend till I get back.'

Poppy spent ten minutes in the cloakroom, then stood at the back of the groups gathered near the edge of the dance floor. She wanted to give Peter and the girl, Kate, time to talk. She was certain that Peter's behaviour on the dance floor, and again when his old friend came over to speak to him, was down to the shock of seeing her after so long. And her excuse of wanting to see him for old times' sake, well, it just didn't ring true.

Poppy found Peter alone when she went back to where they'd been sitting. Sounding cheerful, she said, 'Your friend has gone, then? It must have been nice, seeing each other after such a long time.'

'It was a shock.' That was all Peter said. And he would have remained silent if Poppy hadn't persevered. 'Just out of curiosity, Peter, and don't bite my head off, but is Kate the girl you courted for two years? The one you don't like talking about?'

'Yes, we courted for two years. We fell out, and now she thinks she can walk back into my life again as though nothing had happened. Well, she can't do that, and I've told her so.'

Poppy leaned towards him, to enable him to hear above the music. 'Look, Peter, why don't we leave? You don't look in the mood for dancing now, so let's go somewhere where we can talk. There's a pub not far from here, and we could go there for a drink. I really believe we should talk.'

'Yes, that suits me. You were right, I don't feel like dancing. It was such a shock, seeing her after all that time. I thought she was out of my life for good.'

'Up you get, then, and I'll get my coat. We'll find a quiet spot in the pub, and have a question and answer session. I have a few questions to ask, and I'm sure there are things you need to get off your chest. Come on, let's go.'

Chapter Nineteen

It was quiet in the pub, the customers mostly middle-aged and elderly men, out for their Saturday night pints. The working men would down four to six pints, for Saturday was payday. The older men would make the one pint last them all night, unless one of their younger neighbours had been lucky on the gee-gees, and would mug them to half a pint of bitter.

'Is it a sherry, babe?' Peter asked, removing his trilby and casting an eye around the room. 'Or would you like a change?'

'No, a sherry will be fine. There don't seem to be many people in the snug,' Poppy said. 'I'll go in and keep us two seats.'

Poppy was pleased to see an empty table in a corner, and she waved Peter over when he came through with a glass in each hand. 'It's nice and quiet here. We can talk in peace and privacy.'

Peter put the glasses down. 'I'm glad it's not noisy. I've got quite a headache.'

'That's because you had a shock, seeing a friend you hadn't seen for a long time.' Poppy tried to choose her words with care. Peter was upset, and she didn't want to make matters worse. 'She didn't stay long, did she?'

'She wasn't made very welcome. I'm afraid I was rude to her.' Peter picked up his pint glass, but halfway to his lips he pulled a face and put the glass back on the table. 'I find I'm not in the right frame of mind for beer.'

'Then don't drink it,' Poppy told him. 'Just let's sit quietly and talk. You called her Kate, so what was Kate doing at the Grafton when she doesn't normally go there?'

'She came to say she misses me, didn't think our quarrel was serious enough to break us up, and still loves me and wants me back.'

'That was very brave of her, Peter. She must really love you to have come and told you that. It took guts.' Poppy meant it, for she thought the girl was indeed courageous. And Peter's reaction when he first saw her wasn't the reaction of a man who didn't care. 'You didn't just send her away, did you? I can't believe you'd be so cruel.'

'She walked out on me, babe, after two years of courting. And she broke my heart, all over a stupid quarrel. Now she thinks that after all this time, she can just walk back into my life and I'll welcome her with open arms.'

'Let's not lose our temper and get all worked up, Peter. Talk it through and you'll feel much better. And let me ask you questions without biting my head off. I'm your friend, remember, so let me ask you, did you really love Kate when you were courting?'

Peter sighed, his fingers laced on his knee. 'Yes, I loved her very much. We were to be married. Then this stupid row flared up over who was to be best man, bridesmaids and so on. It ended up with me and Kate almost coming to blows because she didn't approve of the friend I'd chosen to be my best man. He was a good mate of mine; I'd known him since schooldays. I'd already asked him, and he was delighted. So as far as I was concerned that was sorted. But Kate objected to my friend being my best man, for, without telling me, or asking my permission, she had asked the husband of a friend of hers, who I didn't really know!'

Oh, dear, Poppy thought, that was very naughty of her. She should have asked Peter first.

'And that was the cause of you splitting up?'

'I was blazing, and told her she would have to tell her friend that I had chosen a good friend of mine to be best man. She flatly refused, so I walked away. And that was the last time I saw Kate, until tonight.'

'She never came to apologize, or change the arrangement to suit you?'

Peter shook his head. 'I haven't seen her since the day I walked out. She phoned my parents' home a few times, but I refused to speak to her.'

'But you still have feelings for her, Peter, don't you? I could tell by your face when you saw her. And don't say you don't, without giving it careful thought. We're mates, Peter, and mates help each other.'

'You're more than a mate, babe, you're my girlfriend.'

'I'm the girl you've been going out with for a few weeks, Peter. I am a friend who is very fond of you, and who enjoys your company. But we haven't had time to really get to know each other. For all you know, I may not be the happy-go-lucky girl you think I am. I could be selfish and bad-tempered for all you know.' Poppy took a sip of sherry, then asked, 'How did your conversation with Kate finish, Peter?'

'She said she will not give up without a fight. And she asked me to think seriously about us getting back together. She said she couldn't believe that after being so much in love, I could get over it. She can't. She said I'm never out of her mind, she thinks of me all the time.' He huffed. 'It's easy for her to say that now, when she was the one who caused the split.'

Poppy nodded. 'She was in the wrong, Peter, I agree. But don't we all make mistakes sometime that we regret? If I were you I'd give it a lot of thought. After all, it's the rest of your life you're talking about. Are you going to meet her again, to see what your feelings are? Whether they've changed after you've had time to consider?'

'She's coming to the Grafton on Tuesday, after I've had time to think things through. But I told her she's wasting her time.'

'Does Kate dance, Peter?'

'Yes, she's a smashing dancer. Why?'

'Only asking,' Poppy said. But in her mind she had thoughts more serious than she would let on. 'I forgot to tell you that one of the girls who live next door asked if I'd take her to the Grafton one night and I said she could come with us on Tuesday. I knew you wouldn't mind, and Sarah is a nice girl who won't cling to us all night. But I'll put her off, if you want?'

'There's no need to do that,' Peter said. 'If Kate comes she won't be staying long, for I have nothing to say to her.'

That's what you think, Poppy thought. I'm going to play Cupid and find a way to get you dancing with Kate. If there is love in your heart for the girl, then it will surely surface if she's in your arms. At least, it will according to my mam. And I'll put money on my mam being right any time.

'Shall we go, babe?' Peter asked. 'I'm not in the mood for drinking. My headache is getting worse, and I think I'll have an early night. Two headache pills, a good night's sleep, and I'll be fine tomorrow.'

'Very sensible, Peter.' Poppy fastened up her coat. 'A clear head tomorrow and you'll be able to think clearly.'

'I'll still meet you off the bus on Monday night, babe, after night school.'

'That's fine, Peter. I'll have someone to brag to about how clever the teacher says I am.' She linked his arm when they were outside the pub, wondering what the next few days had in store for her, Peter and Kate.

On Monday morning, Poppy came back into the office after hand-delivering the usual correspondence. 'I'm really fed up being dogsbody to Mr John. The next few weeks can't go quickly enough for me. Mr Jones from night school suggested I buy an *Echo* every night and look in the situations vacant column. I think I'll do that, to see how often the services of a private secretary are advertised.'

'You might as well start looking, Poppy,' Jean said, 'because decent jobs don't come along very often. And you don't want to give this job up when the course ends, or you might find yourself out of work. You can't claim dole when you are responsible for making yourself unemployed.'

'I wouldn't do that, Jean. I'm not soft. I won't be giving my notice in until I've got another job to go to.'

'I wish you luck, Poppy, because you deserve it. I never thought you'd stick at it, but you've worked really hard. Your speed is up to my level now, and that's taken some doing in such a short time.'

'I don't know why you won't look elsewhere for work, Jean,' Poppy said. 'You're a fantastic worker, but you don't get credit for it here. You don't get paid enough, either, for the work you do.'

Jean saw Mr John's shadow through the glass panel in his door, and she gestured to Poppy. 'Watch out, his lordship is on the prowl.'

'Then I'm going to the ladies. Tell him, if he asks. He can't follow me in there. And by the time I come out, it'll be lunchtime.'

Poppy had just closed the door behind her when Mr John came into the office. He looked at the empty desk, then asked abruptly, 'Where is she?'

Jean turned her head. 'Miss Meadows has gone to the washroom.'

John Sutherland spun round, and as he walked towards the open door of his office he called over his shoulder, 'My office, as soon as she comes back.'

Jean plucked up the courage to say, 'Miss Meadows was feeling unwell, Mr John. She might not be back until after lunch.'

He growled, a sign he was in a bad temper. 'Women and their blasted monthly stomach pains.'

Jean went back to her typing with a smile on her face. She'd got Poppy off the hook and felt proud of herself. She wished she had her friend's confidence, though: then she'd get out and look for a job she'd be happy in.

Poppy poked her head in the door. 'Come on, Jean, it's time for lunch. Bring my coat, please, I don't want to be caught by his lordship.'

When the pair walked out of the building, they found Charlotte waiting for them. She looked so cheerful, and happy to see them, that neither of the friends could resist giving her a hug. 'It's nice to see you,' Poppy said. 'Are you coming to the café with us?'

'Of course I am! I'm looking forward to the soup and homemade bread.'

'Don't tell fibs,' Poppy told her. 'I bet you would be getting much better fed at home.'

'Well, yes,' Charlotte giggled, 'but I'd much rather be with you and Jean. You're my friends, aren't you?'

Jean was delighted. She had really taken a liking to the

young girl who always had a smile on her face. 'We look forward to seeing you, Charlotte. Your smiling face is in stark contrast to the face of our boss. You see, he may have studied hard to be a solicitor, but sadly for him he never learned how to smile, or even be civil to people.'

The three girls had their arms linked as they walked to the café, and once inside Charlotte said, 'You find a table, Poppy, and I'll put the order in today.'

'That girl is a real charmer,' Jean said, undoing the buttons on her coat. 'She really brightens up the day. Mr John was in a foul temper when he saw you weren't at your desk, and I had to tell him a fib, because he wanted you in his office the second you came back.'

Charlotte slipped into a chair between her new friends, and listened with wide eyes to their conversation.

'What did Mr John say, Jean?' Poppy asked.

'Well, first, when I told him you'd gone to the washroom, he barked, "My office, as soon as she comes back." And when I told him you were feeling unwell, and might not be back until after lunch, he got in a right temper. "Women and their blasted monthly stomach pains." '

Poppy was open-mouthed. 'You actually told him that? I am really surprised, Jean, 'cos I've never heard you answering him back. I've heard him being really rude to you, and felt like telling him to mind his manners, but you've just sat there and not said a word.'

'You know why, Poppy. I can't afford to lose my job. Many times when he's been ranting and raving, I've felt like putting my coat on and walking out, because he is so unfair. Not one word of praise for my hard work in all the years I've worked for him. Never a day off, never late. But he just treats me like dirt and takes everything for granted.'

Tender-hearted Charlotte was really touched. 'He sounds like a dreadful man, Jean. You can't let him treat you like that. He's not very gentlemanly, is he?'

Jean looked downhearted. 'It'll be worse when Poppy leaves. I'll have no friend there at all then.'

'I haven't left yet, Jean, and I've told you I'll always be your friend. Even when I leave, we can still meet every day for lunch.' Poppy leaned forward and looked into Jean's face. 'You won't get rid of me that easily. You have done me a lot of favours, giving me help and encouragement with my short-hand, and I will never forget that.' Her wide, generous mouth stretched into a smile. 'Another thing, Jean. Whether you like it or not, I'm going to do all in my power to get you out of Sutherland's altogether. While I'm searching for a job for myself, I'll be keeping an eye out for one for you.'

Charlotte clasped her hands, her eyes lighting up with excitement. 'Oh, that would be marvellous, Poppy, and you'll do it, I know you will. You are so kind and thoughtful, and helping Jean to leave that dreadful man will repay her for helping you.' Again she clasped her hands together. 'I am so lucky to have you both as friends.'

Poppy chuckled, her hazel eyes changing colour. 'Hang on, Charlotte, I haven't done anything yet. But tonight, on the way home, I'm buying a copy of the *Liverpool Echo*, and am going to look at job vacancies. That will be the start of my search.'

The soup, which was vegetable, arrived, and put a halt to the conversation for a while. When it started up again, Jean changed the subject. 'Are you seeing Peter tonight, Poppy?'

'Yes, he's meeting me off the bus when I come back from night school. Then I'm going to the Grafton with him tomorrow. And one of my next-door neighbour's daughters is coming. She's never been to the Grafton, so I didn't like refusing when she asked if she could come with me.'

Jean looked surprised. 'Peter won't be happy about that, will he?'

'Oh, I've told him, and he didn't object.' Poppy didn't want to tell the whole story, not until Peter had decided what he wanted to do regarding Kate. 'Anyway, I'm not courting him, we're just good friends.'

When it was time to leave the café, the three friends split the bill between them, leaving a threepenny bit for the waitress. Charlotte walked back to their office with them, but as soon as Poppy and Jean had disappeared inside, the girl swiftly made her way to Castle Street, and her father's office.

George was pleasantly surprised to see his daughter. 'What brings you down here, dear girl? Have you a message from your mother, or are you on a shopping trip?'

'Neither, Papa. I've come to see you. Mother doesn't know I'm in town.'

George chortled, stroking his moustache. 'It all sounds very cloak and dagger, my girl. What mischief are you up to?'

Charlotte sat on the edge or his desk and began to swing her legs. 'Have you had your lunch yet, Papa?'

'No, dear girl, I've had quite a busy morning. I'll be eating at the club shortly. Why?'

'I want to have a serious talk with you, Papa, and it will take some time. Can you spare me half an hour?'

George was intrigued. He had never known his daughter have a serious talk with anyone. 'I'm sure I can last out for half an hour, my dear. Even longer, if required.'

'Then I'll sit in the chair opposite you, so I have your full attention, and can tell by the expression on your face whether you are taking me seriously or not.'

George was so amused he had difficulty keeping his face straight. He loved his beautiful daughter dearly, and would never deny her anything her heart desired. She only had to ask for what she wanted, but that surely wouldn't warrant half an hour's serious conversation! Still, he wouldn't interrupt. He'd sit and listen, even if his tummy was beginning to rumble. 'My ears are cocked, my dear, and I'm interested in what you have to say.'

Charlotte swivelled her bottom on the chair before crossing her legs. 'Papa, do you remember Andrew and me telling you about the unfortunate incident where we bumped into a girl and knocked her over?'

'Yes, I remember that, my dear. Is that what you are going to talk about? Is she threatening to sue for damages?'

Charlotte giggled. 'Oh, no, Papa, Poppy wouldn't sue, she's far too nice to do anything like that. Why, Andrew wanted to reimburse her for any damage to her raincoat, or to have it dry-cleaned, and she refused to be compensated. No, I only mentioned the incident now, for that is where my story begins. It's several weeks ago now, but I have met Poppy many times since then, and we have become friends. She is lovely, Papa, and the nicest friend I've ever had.'

George sat forward in his chair. 'I'm going to have to interrupt you, my dear, for you are going so quickly I am a little confused. You say you got to know this girl when Andrew knocked her down with his brolly. She was a stranger to you, am I right?' When Charlotte nodded, George went on, 'So she's gone from being a complete stranger to you to being the nicest friend you've ever had? I'm very confused, Charlotte, and quite concerned. How can you have become friends in such a short time? Does she know who you are, and where you live? And do you know where she lives? Really, my dear, your mother would be very worried if she knew what you were up to.'

'Her name is Poppy Meadows, Papa, and she works in a solicitor's office. I think the solicitor is called John Sutherland, and he sounds a very nasty man. At first Poppy didn't want to be my friend, but now I often wait for her outside the building, and with one of her work colleagues we go for lunch at a little café. Oh, don't be angry, Papa, for I am so glad to have Poppy for a friend. She is much nicer than any other of the friends I've had. And Papa, she is so beautiful, she should be a film star. But I don't just like her for her looks; she's good company and I'm learning more about life than I've ever heard before. I never knew some people had such unhappy lives. There's Poppy's office friend – she's my friend now, too, and she's a really nice person. Her name is Jean, and she's private secretary to this dreadful man, John Sutherland. She is a spinster, but not really old, and she cares for her elderly mother. That's why she can't give her job up. But she's very unhappy there.'

George was shaking his head. 'I really can't take all this in, my dear. I'm losing track of why we are having this conversation. If your mother was here, she would be reaching for the smelling salts.'

'Papa, please don't stop me from coming into Liverpool once a week to have lunch with Poppy and Jean. I do so look forward to seeing them, and I feel alive in their company. I get very bored at home, with nothing to do but hang around.'

'Can I ask you why you have decided to confide in me, dear girl? You know you make me an accessory by doing so. If I tell your mother she will forbid you to see these people again. And if I don't tell her then I will feel very guilty. I really don't think I can allow you to mix with people we know nothing about. I could well end up having cause to regret my lack of action.'

'I didn't come to see you to bring trouble on myself, Papa. I am not so simple. I came to see if you could help one of my friends find a job as private secretary to a man who would treat her with respect. And that friend is Poppy's colleague, Jean Slater. She is very respectable, a good worker, and has been very kind to me. And if I can help a friend, I would very much like to, with your assistance.'

It was all very complicated and confusing, but George couldn't help seeing the funny side. He and his daughter had gone through all that, just because she wanted to help someone find a job. Or at least she wanted George to help someone find a job. Someone he didn't know from Adam. 'Charlotte, does Andrew know these women?'

Looking very serious, his daughter nodded. 'Yes, Papa, he knows Poppy, because, if you remember, he knocked her over. But I don't want you to tell Andrew what I've told you, for I have a secret plan up my sleeve for Andrew.'

George kept his face straight because his daughter wouldn't appreciate his humour right now. 'Charlotte, how can I help someone I have never seen? You say Jean Slater is a private secretary who doesn't like working for Sutherland's. But she would need to be interviewed to see if she is qualified. I have a vacancy for a private secretary, as it happens, because one of the staff is leaving to get married. But I can't say I will give your friend a job, not even for you, my darling daughter. I would need to see her.'

Charlotte was round the desk like the shot of a gun. 'Oh, Papa, I do love you. I knew you would help, for you are so kind-hearted.' Almost choking him, her arms circled his neck. 'I'll bring her to see you tomorrow, my dear wonderful father.

Say one o'clock sharp. And I'll bring Poppy, too, so you can see how nice and respectable my friends are.' After one very noisy kiss, she said, 'You can go for your lunch now. You deserve it. But not a word to Mother, please, or Andrew. I have only told you half of my plan. The rest might take longer, and not be so easy. But I'll see it through, and I know you will be pleased with the result. And very proud of your loving daughter.'

Peter was leaning against a shop doorway when the bus came along, and he hurried forward to help Poppy down off the platform. 'Hello, babe. It's good to see you.'

Poppy had been wondering whether he would be there, what with his old flame turning up at the Grafton on Saturday night and asking him to take her back again. He'd told her she was wasting her time because she was the cause of them splitting up, but Poppy had seen his reaction when her saw her at the Grafton. And she thought he still had strong feelings for Kate, his ex-girlfriend.

'How are you, Peter?' she asked as he put an arm round her waist. 'You were under the weather when you left me on Saturday night. Do you feel better now you've had time to think over what happened? I don't want you to tell me what decision you've come to, that's up to you. I just want to know that you are all right.'

'I didn't go to work today, my head was too full. My mind kept going back to when Kate and I were courting. Then I'd see pictures of you in my mind, and everything got mixed up. I don't feel like going to the pictures, babe. What do you want to do?'

'I'm not fussy about doing anything, Peter. I'd say come home with me and have a drink, but Mam might start asking questions. I don't mean she'd be nosy, it's just because she thinks it's manners to talk to a guest.'

'No, let's just go for a walk. With the fresh air, and a bit of exercise, I might be able to sleep tonight. That's if it's not too cold for you. I'm being selfish, just thinking about myself.'

'We'll go for a walk. I'm not cold.' Poppy yawned and put a hand over her mouth. 'Oh, excuse me, that just came of its own accord. But I do feel a bit tired, so let's just walk to the end of the road and back. And don't talk about Kate. I don't want to know. You'll be seeing her tomorrow night, and I think the pair of you should sort it out between yourselves. Nobody else can do it for you. And Sarah and I won't interfere with you and Kate.'

'I'm going to the Grafton with you, babe, as usual. And I haven't forgotten your neighbour's coming. I'm not altering our usual arrangements to suit Kate. I'll call for you at half seven.'

Poppy didn't argue. She could imagine how mixed up he must be. He was putting a brave face on, and only he knew what his true feelings were. His pride had been dented when Kate did something that he felt belittled him, and to give in to her now would make him appear weak. No man would be happy with that. And Poppy was inclined to agree that what Kate had done was really out of order. But as she'd never been in love, she wasn't in a position to understand. Did true love really conquer all? Or did pride come first?

'Let's turn round now, Peter. We've walked enough.' Poppy pulled on his arm and they did an about-turn. 'You can leave me at the top of our street. I'll be all right. You hop on a bus, go home and have a good night's sleep.'

When they reached the corner of Poppy's street, Peter asked, 'Can I have a goodnight kiss, babe?'

He sounded so sad, Poppy felt sorry for him. 'Of course you can, and I won't charge. You can have it for free.' Their kisses had never been passionate, and that was down to Poppy, for she didn't feel she'd known him long enough to commit herself to him. And tonight she was glad, for he didn't expect more than her usual friendly, boy-girl kiss. 'Shall we meet at the Grafton, Peter, for I'll have Sarah with me?'

'No, I'll call for you. Seven thirty, babe. Goodnight.'

Poppy wondered what the next night would bring. She hoped Peter was prepared to give Kate another chance. A couple don't court for two years if their love for each other isn't strong. And she wanted him to be happy. She would never love him herself, she knew that, for the spark wasn't there. But she was very fond of him, and would always think of him with affection.

When Eva opened the door she looked surprised. 'You're home early, sweetheart. Didn't Peter meet you off the bus?'

'Yes, he did, Mam.' Poppy brushed past her mother and made for the fire in the living room. Winter was nearly over now, but there was still a nip in the air. 'Neither of us felt like going anywhere, so we decided a short walk and then home was the best bet.'

'David's in the kitchen making a pot of tea. He came home early tonight, too. I hope ye're not both sickening for something. Either that or yer've both been chucked by boy and girlfriend.'

David came through from the kitchen carrying a tray. 'I'd have a job getting the heave-ho from a girlfriend when I haven't got one. I've been playing cards tonight with Vincent, and you'll be happy to know I won the grand sum of threepence.'

Eva chuckled as she set the cups and saucers on the table.

'Better than losing threepence, sweetheart. At least it's your bus fare to work.'

'One way, Mam, one way.' David's face was wearing its ever-ready smile. 'Perhaps I should have stayed for another hand and won the return fare.'

As she was pouring out the tea, Eva said, 'Poppy, you haven't forgotten you promised to take Sarah with you to the Grafton tomorrow, have you? She's so looking forward to it.'

'I haven't forgotten, Mam. Peter is calling for us at half seven.' Poppy glanced at her brother. 'Are you going out tomorrow night, David?'

'I've nothing planned, sis, but I'll probably find something to do, or somewhere to go. Why the sudden interest?'

She shrugged her shoulders. 'It was just a thought, my dear brother. I know what your answer will be, but I'll ask just the same. Why don't you come to the Grafton with us, to make a foursome?'

'You must be joking, sis! I've known Sarah since the day she was born. I can't take her out on a date!'

'It wouldn't be a date, soft lad! Sarah is pretty enough to attract partners; she wouldn't have to rely on you.' With a sly wink at her mother, Poppy went on, 'You don't half think a lot of yourself, if you think Sarah would swoon if you asked her for a dance. The only reason I mentioned it was I thought she might feel like a gooseberry with me and Peter.'

'Of course he'll go with yer,' Eva said. 'He's only playing hard to get. Tell yer sister you'll go with them. And try to do it with a smile on your face, sweetheart, so she'll know you mean it.'

'Shall I get down on one knee, as well, Mam?' David asked, adding, 'Just to add a bit of drama to it, like?'

Eva flicked him lightly on the head. 'Don't be sarcastic, son, or your sister will be sorry she asked you.'

'Oh, I've given up, Mam,' Poppy said, knowing it was all in good humour. 'I don't want him to come now.'

'Too late to change your mind, sis, for I've already put it in my diary. Seven thirty Tuesday night, escort Sarah to the dance. And in brackets I've put, as long as she pays for herself.'

'If you don't enjoy yourself, my dear brother, then I will reimburse you for any losses incurred.' Poppy drank the remains of her tea and put the cup on the tray. Then she kissed David's cheek before hugging her mother. 'Would you mind if I went up to bed, Mam? For some unknown reason I feel dead tired.'

'It's a long day for you, sweetheart, going to night school after working all day. How did you get on tonight? Was the teacher pleased?'

Poppy nodded. 'He said the hours I've put in have really paid off, and he'll give me a good reference. He suggested I'm ready to start looking for a job, so I've begun buying the *Echo* every night.'

'You've done well, sweetheart, and I'm proud of yer.'

'So am I, our kid,' David said. 'You've done what you set out to do, and completed it in record time.'

'I've got Jean to thank for that. Without her help and encouragement, it would have taken me twice as long.' Poppy's wide mouth stretched in a yawn. She was tired, but it was more mental than physical. She had Peter on her mind, hoping that things worked out for him. She wanted him to be happy, and prayed tomorrow night would show him the way.

Chapter Twenty

George Wilkie-Brook looked up when his secretary knocked on his office door and poked her head in. 'Your daughter is here, Mr George. Shall I show her in?'

Looking at his fob watch, George saw it was half past twelve. Charlotte had said one o'clock sharp. Still, he wasn't busy, for he had put everything in the hands of his secretary in anticipation of his daughter's visit. 'Show her in, Miss O'Brian.'

Charlotte came in like a breath of fresh air. Smiling and cheerful, she flung her arms round his neck. 'Hello, Papa.' She kissed him on both cheeks. 'I know I'm a little early, but I only called for a quick visit. I'll have to leave in ten minutes to catch Poppy and Jean as they leave their office. They are going to be very surprised because they won't be expecting me.'

'If you only have ten minutes, dear girl, can I get a few thoughts off my chest?' George saw the smile fall from his daughter's face, and he was quick to assure her he hadn't had a change of heart over meeting her friends. He was curious, and doubtful, but would keep his promise. 'If they are not expecting the plans you have made for them, won't they miss having lunch? If I am to interview someone for a position in my office, then it will take some time. I don't employ someone because they have a pretty face, or a nice figure. I run a business, Charlotte, not a charity.'

'I know that, Papa, and I'll make sure, somehow, that they do get some lunch. But I've called in now to thank you for not giving away my secret to Mother. You will see for yourself that my friends are good people. And I want to keep them as friends, Papa, so if Jean is not up to your standard, you will tell her nicely, won't you, that she hasn't got the job?'

George couldn't be guilty of taking the smile off his daughter's face, or dousing her excitement. 'I will be the perfect gentleman, my dear, have no fear on that score. I will even send out for sandwiches, so they won't die of hunger. And Miss O'Brian will sort drinks out for them. Now don't you think you should go, so you don't miss your friends? Oh, but before you do, let me write their names down so I'll know how to greet them.' He pulled a pad towards him. 'Who is the woman you would like me to interview for a position?'

'That is Jean, and she is the oldest. Jean Slater her name is. And my very best friend is called Poppy Meadows.'

'Have you told Andrew what you are up to?'

'Not yet, Papa, but I will do tonight. He doesn't know Jean, but he does know Poppy.' Her infectious laughter filled the room. 'Well, he would do, wouldn't he, Papa, because he knocked her over.' Charlotte had her hand on the office door when she turned her head. 'Don't tell him I told you, Papa, but Andrew likes Poppy.'

With that she was gone, leaving George rubbing his chin. He really didn't know what to make of it all. And he'd never been asked to keep so many secrets in his life. He hoped Jean Slater was qualified as a private secretary, for he would hate to disappoint Charlotte. She had never been so happy or animated as she seemed to be now. And although his wife wouldn't agree with him, his daughter was old enough to choose her own friends. And if he found they were good for her, teaching her about real life in general, then he would welcome them. But now he must ring for his secretary to organize sandwiches and tea. And a selection of cakes from Coopers.

After Miss O'Brian had written down a list of what George thought would be sufficient to quench hunger and thirst, he sat at his desk and wondered what he'd let himself in for. To give his daughter whatever her heart desired was one thing, but employing a private secretary as a favour to her was something else entirely. He thought of asking Andrew if he could offer any advice, but Charlotte had asked him not to tell her brother. Oh dear, he was beginning to dread the afternoon. He really should have been firm with his daughter and refused her request. Still, it was too late now for regrets. At least it wouldn't be a dull couple of hours; Charlotte would see to that.

While her father was wondering what he was in for, Charlotte was standing outside the offices of Sutherland and Son. She was very excited, but also a little apprehensive, in case she had done the wrong thing. She wanted to help Jean, for she didn't like anyone to be unhappy. But if Jean wasn't suitable for her father's firm, Charlotte's action might have sad consequences for her.

There was no time now to worry, as Poppy and Jean were coming down the steps. Poppy was the first one to spot her. 'Hello, Charlotte! Twice in two days! You really must love soup and homemade bread. But it's lovely to see you.'

Jean was about to link arms when Charlotte said, 'Can I talk to you for a minute? I didn't come to have lunch with you. I have some news for you, Jean, which I hope will please you.'

'Oh, ay,' Poppy said. 'This is all very mysterious. And why is Jean the lucky one to have news? Don't I get a look in?'

Charlotte told them her father was waiting to meet them so it would have to be a quick version of what she'd been up to since seeing them the day before. When she had finished, Jean's face was drained of colour, and she was shaking her head. 'Oh, I couldn't do that. You'll have to tell your father I'm grateful but I'll keep the job I've got.'

Poppy stared at her. 'You will do as you are told, Jean Slater, and I say you are going after that job if I have to drag you there. I'm surprised you're not jumping for joy, as this could be a chance of getting away from Mr John. I think Charlotte is wonderful to have gone out of her way to help you, and you're throwing her kindness back in her face! Shame on you, Jean Slater.'

Charlotte didn't know what to say. 'Come and meet my father. He is expecting you and Poppy. He is very kind, and he won't bite your head off.'

'What time did you tell him we'd be there, Charlotte?' Poppy asked. 'We'll drag Jean there, even if she cries all the way. But I think she'll calm down in a few minutes, after the shock's worn off.'

'I told my father we'd be there at one o'clock.'

Poppy gave her a nod. 'You take one arm, I'll take the other. We'll be ten minutes late, but you can say we were late coming out of the office.'

Taking an arm each, Charlotte and Poppy moved so fast that Jean's feet hardly touched the ground. And when they reached the Wilkie-Brook's offices, Poppy took in the names in gold on the window, but shut them out of her mind for the time being. Her friend Jean had the chance of changing her life for the better, and Poppy wasn't going to allow nerves to prevent her from seizing the opportunity. 'For heaven's sake, Jean, straighten up and put a smile on your face. The man isn't going to eat you. And remember, you may never get this chance again. That isn't to say you'll get the job, but at least you will have tried. You are very efficient, and you show him that by walking in there as though you own the place.'

When the trio walked into the front office, the receptionist smiled at Charlotte and said, 'Go through, Miss Charlotte. Your father is expecting you.'

George came from behind his desk to greet his daughter's friends. Jean had been pushed forward by Poppy, with a whispered, 'Look happy, Jean, and make me proud of you.'

'Ah, you must be Miss Slater?' George smiled as he shook hands. 'George Wilkie-Brook.' He waved a hand to one of the chairs he'd brought into his office. 'Please be seated.' Then he moved to Poppy, his hand outstretched. He smiled into her face, and was so struck by her beauty, he was silent for a few seconds. He had never seen such perfection before. Every feature was perfect, as though chiselled by a craftsman. And when she took his hand and smiled, her eyes were bright with laughter.

'My name is Poppy Meadows, and I work in the same office as Miss Slater.'

'Yes, I have your name written down. My daughter gave it to me.'

Charlotte linked Poppy's arm. 'Poppy is my very best friend, Papa. And she's been going to evening classes to learn shorthand.'

'I'm sure your father isn't interested in me, Charlotte. It's Jean he wants to talk to. And we don't have much time because we only get an hour for lunch and an hour soon flies over.'

'I have organized some sandwiches and tea for you and Miss Slater,' George told her. 'My secretary will serve them in her office. If Miss Slater will kindly come back in here when she's eaten sufficient to keep her going, then we can have a chat.'

'I feel like an intruder,' Poppy said. 'I only came to give Jean some moral support, for she is quite shy. I didn't expect to stay, certainly not for lunch. My being here will slow things down, so I'll slip away and leave you to go about your business.'

'You are not intruding, my dear,' George said. 'And I believe you are no stranger to the members of my family. You have met Andrew, have you not? And not in the best of circumstances, I was told. Nevertheless you know him.'

Poppy stared at him for a few seconds, then a slow smile gave way to a hearty laugh. 'Poor Andrew, is he never going to be allowed to forget what was a pure accident? I was mad at the time, I admit, but I soon got over it. No harm done.'

'Don't go, Poppy,' Jean begged. 'Have a sandwich with me, then stay until I'm ready to leave. I am very nervous, even though I have no reason to be. I can't help the way I'm made.'

'Okay, I'll wait. But if we're both late getting back, Mr John will be in a right temper. We could both end up losing our jobs.'

'That won't happen, I assure you,' George said. 'Please go and have something to eat. Charlotte will take you to my secretary's office.'

After several sandwiches, a cake or two, and two cups of tea, Jean was feeling well enough to return to the man she knew now as George Wilkie-Brook. 'You will wait for me, Poppy, won't you? I couldn't face Mr John on my own.'

'I said I'll wait, Jean, and I don't break a promise. All I ask is that you promise me you'll sell yourself to Charlotte's father.

Be confident. You're as good a private secretary as anyone, and more loyal than most. I want you to let that show. But don't forget we haven't a great deal of time.'

Although she hadn't let it show, Charlotte was like a cat on hot bricks. She couldn't wait for Jean to leave so she could put another little plot into play. She'd never enjoyed herself more, or had as much freedom, in her whole life. 'Poppy, you haven't forgotten that you promised to come with me one day to have a cup of tea with Andrew, have you?'

'No, I haven't forgotten, Charlotte, but I've had a lot on my mind, with one thing and another. But I haven't forgotten. I'll come with you one day, when I have time.'

'We could go up now, and surprise him. He doesn't know we're here, or about Jean.'

'We can't just walk in on him, he might be busy. Besides, time isn't on our side. Leave it for another day, eh?'

Charlotte was not going to be put off. She was feeling in a very helpful mood. She'd helped Jean, and now she wanted to help her beloved brother. 'You won't have much time any other day with going to the café for lunch. So why not come up with me now to say hello to him? That's if he's in, of course. If not we'll come another time.' She pulled Poppy off the chair. 'Come on, you know time is running out. Just a quick hello, and out again.'

Poppy was halfway up the stairs and still protesting. 'Charlotte, we can't just walk in. It's very rude, and very annoying if he's busy.'

By this time Charlotte was in Andrew's secretary's office. 'Is my brother in, Wendy?'

'Yes, Miss Charlotte, but he's going out for lunch soon. Shall I tell him you're here?'

'No need, thank you, I'll tell him myself.' Charlotte gave

one sharp pull on Poppy's arm, and before she could control her steps Poppy found herself looking into Andrew's startled face as she stumbled towards him.

He was out of his chair like a shot, with papers floating all over the floor. 'Here, let me help. Did you trip?'

'No, I didn't trip, I was pulled.' Poppy wanted to be angry, but her sense of humour wouldn't let her, and the picture in her head caused her laughter to fill the air. 'Brother and sister, neither of you safe to be near. There's a saying "Did she fall or was she pushed?" and I've had both treatments from you two. I must be allergic to you.'

Charlotte couldn't help seeing the funny side, and had a hand over her mouth to keep herself from laughing outright, for Andrew's face was a mixture of so many emotions. Disbelief that Poppy was standing next to him, laughing. Puzzled that she was there at all, and bliss that he was so near to her. 'Charlotte, will you stop acting silly and bring a chair for Poppy? And what are you doing here anyway? You should have let me know you were coming.'

'It's not Charlotte's fault I lost my footing, Andrew,' Poppy said. 'She has been trying to help a friend of mine, which I think was kind of her. My friend is downstairs being interviewed by your father. She is a fully qualified private secretary, none better. But she has a lousy boss who doesn't appreciate her or respect her, and she deserves better. Apparently a secretary here will be leaving soon, and there will be a vacancy. Jean might not get the job, but I hope she does. And Charlotte deserves a pat on the back for helping a friend.'

'Sit down, Poppy, and I'll have some tea brought in.'

'This is my dinner hour, and I should be on my way back to the office. Besides, your father kindly had sandwiches and tea ready for us.' Poppy looked at her watch. 'If Jean and I are not back at our desks in fifteen minutes we'll both be in very serious trouble. So I'll have to dash. It's been nice seeing you, Andrew. And if Charlotte thinks her actions are not appreciated, then she can think again, for she's a kind and generous girl who somehow has become a friend. And now she can take me downstairs to pick up my colleague.'

'What about the visit you promised?' Andrew asked. 'Will you let Charlotte know so I can be prepared?'

Poppy nodded as she headed for the door. 'I will let her know.' Then she moved fast, with Charlotte beside her. 'We'll be in trouble, and neither of us can afford to lose our jobs. So I'm going to have to drag Jean out, while you thank your father, and apologize at the same time.'

But Jean was already standing by the bottom steps. She quickly explained she'd been asked to go back after work to finish the interview and be introduced to the man whose secretary was leaving. And who, if Jean passed the test, would be her boss.

Poppy was so delighted she gave Jean a hug. 'It sounds promising, from what you say. Oh I'm so happy for you, and I've got a feeling in my bones that you'll get the job. Pity I won't find out until tomorrow, 'cos I'll be on pins wanting to know. I'd stay with you until after the interview, but I've made arrangements for tonight and it's too late to change them.'

'I'll be fine,' Jean told her. 'Mr Wilkie-Brook is very nice, and he soon put me at my ease. And he said the man who will interview me is a Mr Robert Blakemore.'

Charlotte turned them round so she could walk in the middle and link their arms. 'Mr Blakemore is a lovely man. Very friendly, and unlike your present boss he's every inch a gentleman.'

Poppy squeezed her hand. 'If Jean does get the job, Charlotte, it is all down to you. And like me, I'm sure Jean could kiss you right now. You are one very good friend, and I'm glad that your brother bumped into me that day. But don't you dare tell him I said so.'

They came to a halt outside the office block, and Jean said, 'We'll have to be quick. We're five minutes late now.'

'For heaven's sake stop worrying!' Poppy said. 'I'll take the blame if Mr John is there. But he's never back early from his lunch, so to hell with him. This time tomorrow you could be handing your notice in, please God. I'm dying to see the look on his face when you do. Anyway, fingers crossed. You'll know later, while I'll have to wait until tomorrow.' At the top of the steps, Poppy turned to look down at Charlotte. 'When will we see you again, love?'

'Oh, I'll be here tomorrow. I'll know tonight what the news is, for Papa will tell me. But I want to be with you tomorrow, so I can see for myself how Jean feels, and what she intends to do, and when. I'll be waiting here tomorrow, same time.'

That evening around the dinner table of the Wilkie-Brook family, not one word was spoken about the events of the day. It hadn't been planned; it was pure coincidence that the three involved decided it would be better not to mention the matter to Harriet. It was far too complicated for three people to put forward three different versions of events.

However, when the meal was over, Andrew and Charlotte decided to go to their rooms. The decision was passed by several gentle kicks and rollings of eyes: messages sent by Charlotte, and understood by Andrew.

George and Harriet were left alone with their second

glass of wine. George lit a cigar to steady his nerves. If his wife knew their daughter was spending time in Liverpool city centre, making friends with people unknown to her parents, she would have a fit. Added to that, the appeal from Charlotte for one of those friends to be considered for employment, well, it wasn't going to go down well. The very idea alone was sufficient to bring on a bout of indigestion. His best bet was to tone it down a little. Or maybe, on second thoughts, he'd better tone it down a lot. Otherwise he'd get the blame for aiding and abetting.

George cleared his throat. 'Do you remember several weeks ago, my dear, Andrew told us he accidentally knocked a young lady over with his brolly?'

'I vaguely remember the incident, but surely it's more than a few weeks ago? I had completely forgotten. Why do you ask?'

Lies, lies, and more lies, George thought before answering. 'Because I happened to make her acquaintance this afternoon, my love, and she is the most stunning girl I have ever seen. She has the most open face, with laughing eyes and perfect features. And one can sense she is a fun-loving young lady with a remarkable sense of humour.' He patted his wife's knee. 'Of course, my darling, it goes without saying that she can't hold a candle to you. Not in my eyes.'

'How did you come to meet this young lady, who seems to have captivated you?'

'Well, you know Andrew and Charlotte made her acquaintance in circumstances in which many people would actually have sued for damages, claiming they'd been injured, or their clothes ruined. This remarkable young lady did neither. Anyway, I was talking to Andrew outside the office when the young lady came by, and Andrew introduced us.' George turned his head to draw on his cigar, and remembered the saying about what a tangled web we weave, when first we practise to deceive. How true it was. For he was having to lie to his dear wife again. He couldn't risk Charlotte or Andrew's coming in and telling a different story. 'It turned out that her friend was the woman being interviewed to take over from Robert Blakemore's secretary. You remember, I told you she was leaving to get married? Robert interviewed the woman, whose name is Jean Slater, and he was more than satisfied she would fit in very well.'

'The other girl, the one you said was stunning, what is her name and pedigree?'

George turned his head sharply. 'We are not talking about animals, Harriet. That remark was uncalled for and does you no credit.'

'I'm sorry, my love. You are quite right to chastise me. I really meant no harm. Your description of the girl intrigued me, and I wanted to hear more about her. She sounds very interesting.'

'Her name is Poppy Meadows, and I can't speak for her being interesting, for I hardly spent any time in her company. What I can say with certainty is that she would stand out in any crowd.' George could feel a headache coming on, caused by his dislike of telling lies to his wife. He was going to have a good talk to his daughter about this helping hand of hers. He was pleased she was kind and caring, but he must insist she put him in the picture before plunging into her good deeds. 'I need to have a word with Andrew about business, so I'll go up to his room now, before it gets too late.'

When Peter called for her that night, only Poppy saw that his eyes looked a little puffy, as though he hadn't slept well.

Nobody else noticed, for her mother chatted away to him while they were waiting for David to finish shaving. And when Sarah arrived just at the moment when David came downstairs, there was so much talking that no one noticed that Peter's smile held no warmth.

After introducing Sarah to Peter, Poppy headed the foursome out of the door. David walked in front with Sarah, who had known him all her life, and was at ease with him. His presence helped steady the nerves she'd been suffering from all day at the prospect of going to her first big dance hall.

Poppy and Peter walked behind, and they were at the top of the street before either of them spoke. He had his arm round her waist, and he said softly, 'You're very quiet, babe.'

'I didn't think you'd feel like me jabbering away, Peter, for you look tired. Have you not slept well?'

'On and off, that's all. I've had a permanent headache for days now and it just won't go away.'

'I can't say I know how you feel, Peter, only you know that. But my advice would be to take things as they come. You're seeing Kate tonight. Perhaps you'll feel differently after you've been with her for a while. Don't push her out of your life until you are certain of your feelings.'

'She won't let me push her out of my life, babe. She's been to see my parents twice and phoned several times.'

They reached the bus stop then, where David and Sarah were standing, and Poppy turned her head so her words couldn't be heard by them. 'She must love you very much, then, Peter, and unless you are very sure, don't throw that love away. It only comes once in a lifetime to most people, so take heed.'

The bus came then, and David and Sarah opted for the top deck, while Poppy and Peter sat near the door.

'What about you, babe?'

'This is not about me, Peter, and I'd rather not get involved. I don't want to settle down for a few years yet. I have told you that several times. But not wanting to get involved doesn't mean I'm not interested in what happens to you, because I am. I want what is best for you. And I feel the best thing is for you to take your time, and not rush anything. You don't have to decide right away, so take it slowly. A few dances with Kate tonight should help.' But because she didn't want Peter to think she was eager to get rid of him, and was pushing him into Kate's arms, she added, 'But not all the slow foxtrots, please, 'cos you and me do a very professional slow-fox.'

When they walked into the entrance hall of the Grafton, a playful argument started between David and Sarah over who should buy the tickets. 'No girl ever pays for herself when she's with me, even if she does live next door.'

Poppy had spotted Kate standing on her own, her eyes on the entrance, and thought the girl must really love Peter to run after him the way she was doing. She really was wearing her heart on her sleeve. 'Peter, you get my ticket while I sort David and Sarah out. Our David can be as stubborn as a mule when he puts his mind to it. Oh, and will you see if Kate has a ticket? She's standing on her own by the cloakroom.'

When the tickets had been sorted out, Poppy took Sarah along to the cloakroom. Passing Kate, Poppy said, 'Are you coming in, Kate? We may as well stick together. This is a neighbour of mine, Sarah.'

Kate had begun to comb her hair in front of the mirror on the wall before she said, 'It's very kind of you to be so friendly, under the circumstances. Most girls would tell me to get lost.'

'I have no intention of interfering, Kate. You and Peter have to sort your own affairs out. Now let's get back to the men. My toes are itching to get on the dance floor.'

The band were playing a slow foxtrot when the girls pushed open the door of the dance hall, and Peter hurried to Poppy's side. His hand out, he said, 'Come on, babe, this is our dance.'

David hadn't been introduced to Kate, so he didn't think it rude to ask Sarah to dance. He thought she was a novice, and had made up his mind to be patient with her. But he certainly had his eye wiped for she was a fantastic dancer. She floated like a dream, and David was delighted. 'I was under the impression you were a beginner, Sarah, with your mother saying you hadn't been to a big dance hall.'

'My mam always gets things wrong, David, you should know that by now. I've never been here before, but I go to loads of dances.'

Poppy had seen Jim on the dance floor with a girl she'd never seen before, and she had an idea. She waited until they were passing, then over Peter's shoulder she mouthed the words, 'Next dance with me.'

Jim grinned and nodded. He'd be delighted to dance with Poppy. She was a good dancer and fun to be with.

The next dance was a waltz, and Jim was over like a shot to claim Poppy, while David, unaware of the situation, led Sarah back on to the floor, leaving Peter and Kate standing awkwardly a few feet apart. Poppy kept her eyes on them, even while talking to Jim, and she saw Kate close the distance between herself and the man who had once loved her. 'Are you going to ask me to dance, Peter?'

Without a word, Peter reached for the hand she was holding out, and led her on to the floor. And as Poppy watched, he danced as stiff as a board for the first two or three circles of the floor, and then seemed to relax and dance as he always did, steps and rhythm perfect.

'Who is the girl your boyfriend is dancing with?' Jim asked. 'It seems unusual for him to dance with anyone but you.'

'Her name is Kate, and she's an old friend of the family. That's all I know about her, really, except she seems a nice friendly person. With regard to Peter, I've told you a few times, Jim, that we are not courting! Good friends who enjoy dancing and being in each other's company, that's all.'

'So he won't object to my asking yer to dance again, then?'

'Not at all. And the girl our David is dancing with lives next door to us. You're more than welcome to ask her to dance. She'll be delighted as it's the first time she's been here.' While she was talking, Poppy kept glancing at Peter and Kate. They danced well together, and it was easy to see they were used to each other's body movement and steps. So far so good.

'By the way, Jim, what happened to the girl you told me about? I know you said she was going to a dancing class, but surely she should have learned enough by now to come here with you? Once she had the basic steps, you could teach her the rest.'

Jim gave a sigh. 'Woe is me, Poppy. It's just my luck to find a girl I like, then it turns out she can't dance. She didn't learn anything at the classes, because she has no sense of rhythm and two left feet.'

Poppy chuckled. 'That doesn't stop her from being a nice girl, Jim! She's probably good at something else, like baking, or knitting.'

'I'm only twenty-one, Poppy. I don't need fairy cakes or knitted cardigans. I love dancing and don't want to go through the rest of my life not being able to do the thing I like best. You know yerself, when dancing is in yer blood it's hard to stop.'

'I know the feeling,' Poppy said. 'As soon as I hear dance music my body moves in time with it.' She laughed. 'It makes it very awkward when you're sitting in the picture house and start swaying in the seat. I get some funny looks.'

The music came to an end and Poppy moved away. 'Next waltz, please, Jim?'

His face lit up. 'Yeah! You bet!'

When the interval came, Peter stood between Poppy and Kate, addressing Poppy more often than Kate. But David was puzzled by the situation, for the stranger never took her eyes off Peter, even when he was on the dance floor with Poppy. So when the opportunity came to speak to his sister alone, he asked. 'Who is Kate, sis? She seems to have a crush on Peter.'

'I'll explain it tonight when we get home. There is a story attached to her and Peter, but now is not the time to tell it. I'll tell you and Mam about it tonight, over our bedtime cup of tea.' Poppy turned to Sarah and a change of subject. 'What do you think of the Grafton, Sarah? Does it live up to your expectations?'

'Oh, yeah, Poppy. It knocks spots off the other dance halls I've been to. It's much bigger, and the floor is smashing to dance on. I'll be coming here again, that's for sure.' She bent towards Poppy's ear and whispered, 'Ay, your David isn't a bad dancer. I didn't know he ever went to dances.'

'He doesn't go as often as me, 'cos he enjoys a game of cards with his friends. When he does go dancing, he goes to the Tower at New Brighton, or Barlows Lane. Like here, both of them have sprung floors, much better to dance on.'

The strains of a slow foxtrot started up, and Peter held out his hand. 'Our dance, babe.'

Poppy didn't even think of refusing. She wasn't going to push Peter into going back to his old flame; he had to decide for himself. But she was happy when she saw Jim asking Sarah up, and David followed with Kate.

'How is the shorthand going, babe? Are you winning?' Peter slowed down to look into her face. 'I don't want to lose track of events.'

'You asked for it, Peter, so I'm going to blow my own trumpet. The teacher said I'm good enough to apply for a job as a private secretary, and he'll give me a good reference. I'm going to start looking around. It may take a while to get a job, but I'm going to do my best to get away from where I am now. You know the girl I work with, the one I've told you about who has been so good to me? Well, she went for an interview today, and I'll know tomorrow if she's got the job. If she leaves, then I'll leave the same time as her. I'm not staying with a boss like the one we've got. If Jean goes, then I go.'

'I've told you my father could help you find work, babe. Why won't you let me ask him?'

'I want to do it on my own, Peter. I'll get there eventually, you'll see. But thank you for the offer. You're very kind.'

'I'd do anything to help you, babe, you should know that. And no matter how things resolve regarding me and Kate, I don't ever want to lose touch with you. I'll want to know where you are, and what you are up to, all the time. You are a wonderful, beautiful woman, Poppy, and I'll always love you.'

She smiled up at him. 'Love comes in many forms, Peter, remember that. Like the love you had for Kate. That is still there in your heart, you just don't want to admit it, because you were hurt. The girl made a bad mistake, but don't punish her now. I think she's suffered enough. Let yourself go, loosen up, and give her another chance.'

'I'm trying, Poppy, I really am. But I don't want to lose you.'

'You'll never lose me, Peter. We'll always keep in touch and see each other. And let's change the subject for now, until you have sorted your life out. It's not fair to Kate for us to be so close. Be friends with her, and take it from there. At least let her into your life.'

'I'll take her home after the dance, babe, since you'll be with your brother and Sarah. So when will I see you again?'

'I'll be here on Friday, as usual. I'll get David to come with me, so we'll be a foursome.' Poppy raised her brows. 'It's a start, Peter. Give it a chance.'

Poppy waited until they were seated at the table with their bedtime cup of tea in front of them. 'I've got something to tell you, Mam, and you David. It's about Peter. I know you were curious about Kate tonight, David, why she was at the dance with us, and who she was. Well, she is an old flame of Peter's, who I've known about for a while.'

Eva and David showed surprise at first, then settled down to listen in silence until Poppy had told them everything. She had left nothing out.

'How do you feel about it, sweetheart?' Eva asked. 'Are you disappointed, or sad?'

Poppy shook her head. 'No, Mam. I've known all along that Peter wasn't the man for me. I do have strong feelings for him because he's a wonderful person. But the love I feel is like a love for a brother, not a husband. There was no romantic spark there for me. Kate adores him, and I'm hoping Peter will slowly find the love he once had for her seeping back into his heart. She'll be good for him because she really loves him. She hurt him badly, but she shouldn't be punished for the rest of her life.' She sat back in her chair. 'I'm seeing them again at the Grafton on Friday. I agreed because I think Peter needs time to get used to courting Kate again. But we'll always be friends, I've promised him that. So you'll be having visitors when their lives are running smoothly.' Poppy yawned and stretched her arms above her head. 'By the way, David, don't make any plans for Friday, because you're taking your sister to the Grafton.'

Chapter Twenty-One

'Why are you in such a rush this morning, sweetheart?' Eva asked as she watched Poppy pushing her empty breakfast plate away. 'Yer wolfed that toast down so fast yer'll have indigestion all day. And you've got plenty of time, you're not running late.'

'I want to be very early this morning, Mam, not just on time. An extra ten minutes to talk to Jean, that's what I'm hoping for. I can't wait to hear whether she got the job or not. Once we're inside the office we won't be able to talk to each other with Mr John prowling round like a bear with a sore head.'

Poppy stood in front of the mirror and ran a comb through her hair, before turning to face her mother. 'I hope she got the job, Mam, because she's been so good to me, and she's a very good secretary.'

'And a good friend.' David swallowed a mouthful of tea, then went on. 'You've said yourself you couldn't have got so far in such a short time without her. Anyone who will give up part of their lunch break to help . . . well, there's not many would do that.'

'You'll miss her if she does leave, won't yer, sweetheart?' Eva was clearing the breakfast table as she spoke. 'They'll have to take someone on to fill her place, and it won't be the same with a stranger, not after working with Jean for nearly four years.'

'I won't be losing touch with Jean, Mam, not ever! She's the best friend I'll ever have. Like I'll keep in touch with Peter, I'll keep in touch with Jean. We've already said that no matter what happens, we'll meet every day for lunch.' Poppy fastened her coat up and reached to the sideboard for her handbag. 'I'm on my way, Mam. I'll let you and David have all the news tonight. Ta-ra.'

'Tell Jean we were asking after her, sweetheart, and have been keeping our fingers crossed for her.'

'Will do.' Poppy banged the door and walked smartly up the street to the bus stop. And all the way into the city, as the bus swayed from side to side, she kept saying under her breath, 'Oh, please let the news be good, she really deserves it.'

Poppy stood outside the office building waiting for sight of Jean. She was ten minutes early, and hoped her colleague would be along any minute. There'd be no chance to talk once they got in the office, for if Mr John got wind of what was going on he'd sack both of them on the spot on some trumped-up charge of bad behaviour and refuse to give them a reference.

'Oh, there you are!' Jean was puffing, out of breath with hurrying. 'I couldn't see you with all the people passing on their way to work. I'm glad we've got a few minutes to spare. I have so much to tell you!'

Poppy's heart was beating faster. 'You've got the job, haven't you? I can tell by your face.'

Jean had never looked so alive in all the years Poppy had worked with her. Her eyes were bright, and her voice was filled with emotion and excitement. 'Oh, Poppy, I am so happy. Charlotte is certainly my good luck charm. I passed the interview and test with flying colours.' Happiness had Jean wanting to tell her friend everything, so she could be happy with her. 'They were so kind, Poppy, they treated me as though I'm someone special. Mr Wilkie-Brook is one of the nicest men I have ever met. Considering I was a complete stranger, who was only there because his daughter had no doubt talked him into it, well, he was brilliant. He's obviously a very wealthy man, but he's certainly no snob. He is down to earth, treats you as an equal, and has a really good sense of humour.'

'You can fill me in with the details at dinnertime, Jean, but I am so happy for you. If we weren't standing in the street I'd give you a big hug and a kiss. But before we go in, tell me when you're to start the new job?'

'The secretary who is leaving will be going in three weeks. But the man I'll be working for, Mr Robert Blakemore, wants me to start the week before she leaves, so she can acquaint me with the running of the office.'

Poppy's mouth gaped. 'That means you'll have to give your notice in this week! Ooh, I'm so pleased and excited for you. And you are right about Charlotte being your good luck charm. She's changed your whole life.'

'I haven't finished yet, Poppy. Wait until you hear this! I get three pound a week here, and that is for slaving for a man who is ill mannered, bad-tempered, and a devil. In my new job, I will be paid the princely sum of five pound a week, and my boss will be a real gentleman. How about that!'

Poppy began to mount the steps. 'Come on, you lucky blighter, or Mr John will spoil your happiness.' She pulled Jean into the building. 'The day you get your first wage packet, lunch is on you. And because I'm jealous, filled with envy, I'll insist on a cream cake after our soup.'

When they'd taken their coats off, and hung them on the stand in the office, the two friends looked towards Mr John's office. There was no sound from it, and no sign of him through the glass door. 'His lordship isn't in yet,' Poppy said, rubbing her hands in glee. 'I can't wait to see his face when you hand in your notice in two days' time. Oh, how I wish I was in a position to do it with you. Two staff giving their notice in at the same time would have Mr John's father asking the reason why. And I'd be only too happy to tell him the truth.'

They heard a door closing and both girls made themselves busy at their typewriters. But the atmosphere was brighter than it had ever been. Not that a bad-tempered Mr John noticed when he barged in and barked his orders.

Charlotte had been given a good talking-to by her father the night before about being too impetuous, and told she must in future think before she acted. And she agreed, or half agreed, that Papa was right. But all she could think of, as she waited for her two friends to come out of the building, was that if she hadn't been impetuous, Jean would never have got away from that dreadful man. And another thing Charlotte had achieved, which was all part of the plan, was the meeting between her father and Poppy. He'd been very struck by her looks, and when he'd said so Andrew had wholeheartedly agreed. In fact he'd been so wholehearted, Papa had raised his brows.

'There she is, I knew she'd be here.' Jean grabbed Charlotte in a bear hug, tears stinging her eyes. 'Oh, my dear, how can I ever thank you enough for what you've done for me?' Then, after one or two sniffs, she held the girl at arm's length. 'How lucky I am to have met you. Without your help I would never have been brave enough to seek another job. I'm a coward at heart, you see, afraid of my own shadow.'

Poppy coughed. 'Would you mind if we moved on to the café? I'm the only one who doesn't know all the details, 'cos I'm sure Charlotte will have heard them last night from her father.'

'It's my treat today,' Charlotte said, giving a nod to stress she had made up her mind. 'We have to celebrate your good fortune, Jean.'

'It's me who should be treating you, not the other way round. But I can't stretch my pennies that far today, so you'll have to wait two weeks, until I'm in the money.'

'No, let me pay, please.' Charlotte wanted to celebrate her own victory. It hadn't been part of her main plan, but she was delighted she'd had a hand in Jean's change of fortune. 'Andrew gave me the money to buy lunch for the three of us.'

Poppy wasn't happy about that. 'Indeed not! Why should your brother pay for our lunch? He doesn't even know Jean, and he doesn't know me very well.'

'Oh, I met Andrew,' Jean said. 'Yes, his father took me along to his office and introduced us. He thought it would be easier for me if I knew some of the staff. And Mr Andrew's secretary was really nice and friendly.' She smiled at Charlotte. 'Your brother is very handsome.'

'I still don't see why he should pay for our lunch,' Poppy said, with a toss of her head which sent her curls swinging. 'Why can't we pay for our own?'

'Don't you like my brother, Poppy?' Charlotte asked, managing to look upset. Her father had called her a little minx last night, and she was inclined to agree with him. 'I thought you and Andrew were going to be friends.' And, her acting reaching Ethel Barrymore standards, she added, 'But you can't really be friends if you don't like him.'

One look at that innocent face and Poppy knew she was beaten. 'Of course I like your brother, Charlotte, even though I don't know him very well. And to please you, I'll be very happy to allow him to buy our lunch.'

Charlotte cheered up immediately. She couldn't have her plan going off course now, not when yesterday had gone without a hitch. She'd known all along she would have to tread carefully with Poppy, but she did wish events were moving a little faster. 'Come along then, and let's find a table. Oh, and I believe you are partial to cakes, so I'll order three cream cakes to have with our cup of tea.' And smiling as though she didn't have a care in the world . . . which she didn't . . . Charlotte made her way to the counter to order soup and homemade bread for three. To be followed by a large pot of tea and three cream cakes.

Poppy had followed Charlotte's progress to the counter with her eyes. 'That young woman could charm the birds off a tree,' she told Jean. 'I find myself going against myself, just to please her! And I'm not easily talked into doing something I don't want to do.'

'I know what you mean,' Jean said. 'She does have a way with her. I think the word that suits her is captivating. As you said, she could charm the birds off a tree. But whatever it is she has, I'm glad she's got it. If it weren't for her, Poppy, I'd be the same woman today as I was yesterday. And that was a woman without hope, without any future to look forward to. I'll be for ever in her debt.'

Charlotte joined them, looking like the cat that got the cream. 'I know all about your interview, Jean, and how well you passed all the tests. Papa was very pleased with you. I believe you'll be starting the week after next? I'm so pleased you'll be getting away from that horrible man who is so rude to you. But what about you, Poppy? You'll still be working for him. You mustn't let him be rude to you. I will worry about you if you are alone with him.'

'Oh, don't worry about me, sweetheart, I can handle Mr John. If things got too bad, even if I didn't have another job to go to, I'd walk away. My mam and David would look after me until I found employment. I intend to start looking for a post as soon as I have a reference from the night school teacher. I'll get it from him tomorrow night, which is my last night of the course. There'd be no point in asking Mr John. He'd be required to give one, as I've worked for him for over three years. But I know that, for spite, it would not be a glowing reference. So I'll rely on Mr Jones.'

Changing the subject, Jean asked, 'Are you seeing Peter tonight?'

Poppy shook her head. 'No, I'll most likely see him at the Grafton on Friday. My brother came with us last night, which is unusual for David, and he really enjoyed it. So much so, he's coming on Friday.'

'Could I come with you, Poppy?' Charlotte asked. 'I can dance, you know. In fact I'm quite good.'

'Good grief, no! Your father would never allow you to come to the Grafton.' Poppy saw the mouth droop and heard the sigh. 'Charlotte, I don't know where you live, and you mustn't tell me. But I know it won't be anywhere near the Grafton, sweetheart, so it would be out of bounds for you. How would you get there and back in the dark? No, it's not for me to encourage you and get myself into trouble.'

Charlotte didn't argue or press, but a little voice in her head told her to be devious and keep quiet. 'You've called me sweetheart twice now, Poppy, and I like it. No one has ever called me sweetheart before.'

'My mother has always called me that, ever since I can remember. I know I'm a bit old for it, but I wouldn't have my mother any different.'

'What does she call your brother?' Charlotte was hearing things she'd never heard before. 'She couldn't call a boy sweetheart, could she?'

Poppy laughed. 'My brother is over six feet tall and very well made. I don't think he'd take kindly to being called sweetheart. Do you?'

'What does your mother call him, then?' Charlotte asked. Her parents usually called her by her full name, or 'dear girl'. She thought sweetheart was much nicer.

'David used to get called lad, and still does. But mostly he gets son off my mother, and "dear brother" or "our kid" off me. He's really too grown up for a nickname, and he suits the name David better. He's quite handsome, and I'm very proud of him.'

'I wonder if I will ever get to meet David, Poppy? Do you think I ever will?'

'I can't see it, Charlotte, for David has his own friends and is out every night. He's only coming to the Grafton on Friday because I asked him to. He seldom comes into the city centre for he works on the other side of town. You wouldn't know him if you passed each other in the street, so it seems unlikely you'll ever meet him.'

'No, I suppose not.' What came out of Charlotte's mouth didn't match what was running through her mind. She wanted to get to know Poppy better for Andrew's sake. He couldn't chase Poppy, he was too shy, so she would have to do it for him. Her brother was a wonderful, kind and caring man, who wouldn't hurt anyone. He was thoughtful and gentle, and Poppy would like him if she got to know him. But it was proving difficult to get them together, so she'd have to get her thinking cap on.

The housekeeper was clearing the dinner plates and piling them neatly and efficiently on to the large wooden tray. Harriet waited for her to leave the room before addressing her son. 'Andrew, dear, your father was telling me last night that he'd met the young lady who was involved in the unfortunate accident caused by yourself some time ago, when the young lady was knocked to the ground. And he was quite taken with her looks. In fact, he said she was stunning. Is that an accurate description, would you say, or the imagination of a man seeing what he wants to see?'

Geﾟorge snorted. 'Really Harriet, what a strange thing to say! My eyes and ears are in excellent order, I am neither deaf or short-sighted.' He looked across the table to his son. 'Is Miss Meadows stunning, my boy, or was I exaggerating?'

'You were right, Father. Stunning is more of an under-statement than an exaggeration. She really is a very beautiful young lady.'

Charlotte sensed an opportunity to bolster her plan. 'Poppy is not only beautiful, Mother, she is very good company and very funny. When she smiles she is really lovely. I'd say she was better-looking than any film star.' Charlotte suddenly realized her mother wasn't supposed to know about her secret visits to the city. 'I could tell what a lovely person she was the day Andrew bumped into her. She didn't rant and rave as most people would have done. She actually saw the funny side and began to laugh.'

Harriet raised her brows. She knew very little of what

went on outside her own home, where she was pampered by her husband and the servants. She only left the house to go on shopping trips with friends, or to Scotland on holiday, and neither gave her any insight into real life. She was quite happy with her lifestyle and had never questioned whether her children would prefer a different one.

'I would very much like to meet this young lady, Andrew. Would you make arrangements to bring her here? She sounds very interesting, and must be outstanding if she has captured the admiration of all three of you.'

Andrew looked horrified. 'I can't arrange a meeting, Mother. I hardly know the girl. And I'm quite sure she wouldn't even consider an invitation if she were to receive one.' He shook his head. 'It's out of the question, and I would side with her if she did refuse.'

George agreed. 'It would be an insult to invite a girl we hardly know, just because you think she sounds interesting.'

'You keep calling her "the girl" or "the young lady".' Charlotte was ready to do battle. 'Her name is Poppy Meadows, and I don't think she'd come here just to be looked over. She's very independent and proud, and I have much admiration for her.'

'Oh, dear,' Harriet said. 'I do seem to have put the cat among the pigeons. The speed with which the three of you rushed to the young lady's defence has raised my interest in her. I really don't want to just look her up and down because I'm curious. Am I really so bad you would think that of me?'

All three were ready to appease her, for they loved her very much. 'Of course not, Mother,' Andrew said. 'But if you knew Miss Meadows, you would understand what we are trying to tell you. We only met her because of my clumsiness, so you can't expect us to be her favourite people. She is very proud, and would not consider any compensation for my stupidity. So you can imagine if we asked her to come here, to visit a family she doesn't know, she would think we were offering charity. And I have such respect for her pride, I wouldn't insult her.'

'I wonder if this young lady knows that three members of my family hold her in high esteem, while I am not allowed the privilege of making her acquaintance?'

'You will one day, Mama.' Charlotte couldn't bear to see her mother left out. 'I know where Poppy works, so if I ever go into Liverpool to visit Papa or Andrew in their office, I might just bump into her. And I'll ask her to come and see you as my friend. I'm sure she likes me a little bit.'

Harriet laughed. 'There is no one who couldn't like you more than a little bit, my dear. But please don't pester the girl on my behalf. Let us leave it in the hands of fate.'

A knock on the door heralded the arrival of Frances with their after dinner coffee. So all talk of Poppy was ended, or so thought Harriet and George. They didn't connect Andrew's excusing himself from the table after finishing his coffee with Charlotte's leaving five minutes later. Andrew's excuse was the correspondence he'd brought home from the office, while his sister said her wardrobe needed clearing. But on reaching the landing it wasn't her bedroom she headed for, but her brother's.

'Can I come in, Andrew?' Charlotte stood with her hand on the doorknob. 'I want to talk to you.'

'Why do you ask for permission after the event, Charlotte?' Andrew asked. 'You are already in the room.'

She chuckled and closed the door. 'If I'd asked from outside, you might have told me to go away.' She moved to sit on the end of his bed. 'I want to ask you a favour, and I'd like you to be a darling and hear me out before refusing.'

Andrew was shaking his head, and he said in no uncertain terms, 'The answer is a refusal before you start. You've put me in a difficult situation several times over the last day or two, Charlotte, and it's got to stop. I find myself in a very awkward position with both Father and Mother. They had no idea you were going into Liverpool so often to meet up with Poppy.'

'I couldn't tell them, Andrew. You know very well I would have been forbidden to go near the city on my own. But if I have to stay in the house all day with Mother, I'm never going to grow up properly and learn how different people live their lives. And apart from all that, I should be able to choose whom I would like for a friend. And don't tell me there are three suitable girls among Mother's friends who would make excellent companions for me, because I've spent a lot of time in their company and I find them rather dull.'

Andrew sympathized with her, for hadn't he gone to university to get away from the boredom? But while he understood, he couldn't help his sister to go against the wishes of their parents. 'I know how you feel, Charlotte, I've been through it. But because you are a girl, it's only natural our parents worry more about you. And you are a little tinker when the mood takes you. Especially the last couple of days. You know I like Poppy and want to strike up a friendship with her. But dragging her up to my office, with no prior warning, was embarrassing for both her and myself. You are putting her off, not helping.'

'Andrew, you are very sweet and I love you. But as you well know, faint heart never won fair lady! Poppy will be snapped up and married before you pluck up the courage to even ask her for a date.'

'I can't help the way I'm made, my dear sister. It isn't because I haven't had the opportunity to go out with girls, but like yourself I haven't met one I could take to.'

'If you agree to the favour I am going to ask, you could meet Poppy in a completely different situation from any you've been in so far. But I'm not going to try to force you, it's how you feel about it yourself. It's up to you, Andrew. You wouldn't even have to talk to her if you didn't want to. However, you deserve to lose her if you don't make an effort.'

Andrew was torn between wondering what his sister was up to, and his desire to become closer to Poppy. 'What does this favour entail, you little minx? I don't want you making me look a fool in front of her again.'

'Are you free on Friday night, brother dear?'

'Why? Do you want to go for a run in the country?'

'Far from it. In the other direction, actually.' Charlotte was delighted now. She felt very close to getting what she wanted. 'I want you to take me to a dance in a hall called the Grafton. I don't know where it is, but I'm sure you can find out. Poppy is going to be there with her brother, David, and another boy and girl. I gather it's a big dance hall, plenty big enough for Poppy to get lost in if she doesn't want to see us. But she won't, she'll be happy, I know she will.'

'And what excuse are you going to give our parents? Don't expect me to lie, Charlotte, because I won't.'

'I'll tell them I want to go to a dance, and would like you to drive me there, and bring me back home. That won't be telling lies, will it?' Charlotte's legs were swinging like mad. 'In fact, Andrew, I might tell Papa the truth, and he can talk Mother into agreeing.'

'I would feel happier if you did that. I don't like being deceitful, even in the cause of love.'

'Papa always goes to his study for a last tot of whisky and a cigar. As soon as I hear Mother coming up to bed, I'll nip down and have a talk to him. I'll be very careful what I say, Andrew, and I promise I won't tell any more lies. If Papa says I can't go to the dance, I won't try to coax him.' She gave a cheeky grin. 'Well, not much, anyway. And I'm not doing all this for you, my dear brother, I have my own interests as well. Poppy is as important to me as she is to you. I would be sad if I were to lose her friendship. I'd pine, and be very ill.'

Andrew chuckled. 'I don't know whether you're better at getting round Father, making up stories, or being a detective. But I do know there is a fairy godmother out there somewhere, looking after you.'

Charlotte's legs stopped swinging. 'Oh, I never knew about her. Who is she, Andrew?'

'Who is who?'

'My godmother, of course. You just said she was looking after me, so you must know, or you wouldn't have mentioned her.'

'I said your fairy godmother, Charlotte. Like the ones you see in the pantomimes, like Cinderella. Not a real godmother.'

Once Charlotte got her teeth into anything, she wouldn't give up, 'But I must have a godmother, everyone does. Baby Leo has. I'd like to know who mine is. And yours, Andrew. You must have one too.' When her brother didn't answer, she insisted, 'We must both have godparents, and I'm going to ask Mama who they are.' She was halfway to the door when her brother called her back.

'Charlotte, you'll upset Mother very much if you mention godparents. And I'm sure you don't want to hurt her, or make her cry, do you?'

'Of course I don't want to make Mama cry. That would be

cruel, and I'm not cruel, Andrew, I wouldn't hurt anyone. But I don't understand why my asking her who my godmother is would upset her.'

'I will explain to you, if you promise not ever to repeat one word of what I tell you, for, as I have said, Mother would be upset. So sit quietly and listen carefully.' Andrew thought deeply before going on. 'You are old enough to be told now, because you are an adult and have to learn that most people have sadness in their lives. So there must be no crying: you shall act like a grown-up. Mother had a sister called Helen, who was twenty years older than her, and they were devoted to each other. Helen was my godmother when I was christened, and I can vaguely remember her when I was a toddler. She never married, for she suffered from ill health from the time she was born. When you were two weeks old, it was understood that Helen would be your godmother also. Now you must remember, Charlotte, that I was very young at the time, and my memory of those few weeks is very faint. I remember very little. However, I learned over the years from different family members that Helen died a week before you were to be christened. Mother was so distraught, I believe, she refused to allow anyone else to be your godmother. She probably regretted it later in life, but the loss of her beloved sister was something she didn't recover from for many years.'

'Oh, poor Mama.' Tears filled Charlotte's eyes, but she wasn't going to cry, she must be brave. So she clenched her fists so hard she could feel her nails digging into her palms. 'Thank you for telling me, Andrew. It was very thoughtful of you. I have never wondered about a godmother, but I might have done one day, and I would have hurt Mama without knowing.'

'The reason you never wondered, Charlotte, is because you've had no cause to. You have been pampered all your life, given anything and everything you needed. You've never even had to ask, because Mother and Father have doted on you since the day you were born. They did the same for me. I wanted for nothing. But sometimes you can be suffocated by too much kindness. That was why I was so determined to go to university, and it was the best move I ever made. I found I couldn't have everything I wanted just for the asking; I had to work for it. And if you achieve something you have worked for, then believe me, Charlotte, you appreciate it much more than if it was handed to you on a plate.'

Charlotte jumped down from the bed and flung her arms round Andrew's neck. 'Oh, I do love you, and I'm going to do my best to be as good as you are. From this very minute, I am starting to grow up and act my age. I know Mama won't let me go out to work, but she can't stop me going to see you and Papa at the office. I am quite decided that in future, Charlotte Wilkie-Brook is going to be a woman of determination. No longer will I do childish things. Those days are gone.'

Andrew drew her arms from his neck and smiled at the serious expression on her face. 'Charlotte, I don't want you to change. We all love you as you are . . . happy, funny and beautiful. All I ask is that you think before you do anything. Such as bringing Poppy to my office without telling either of us what you were up to. I'm not going to get anywhere with her if you keep pulling stunts like that.'

'I promise I won't do anything like that again, Andrew, but I did help Jean to get a job where she will be happy. That was really my first ever good deed. And I have one more good deed to accomplish before I start being grown up and sensible.

I'm going along to Papa's study now, and if I come back with a huge smile on my face, you'll know I've accomplished part of my second good deed. Keep your fingers crossed for me, my lovely brother, because my smile could bring a bigger one to your face.'

Charlotte listened with her ear to the study door, in case there was someone in with her father. She heard nothing but silence, so, bending her finger, she rapped on the door. 'It's your loving daughter, Papa. May I come in?'

'Come in, dear girl, but you'll have to suffer the cigar smoke I'm afraid. This is the one time of the day I look forward to, when I can sit in solitude with a glass of whisky in front of me, and a cigar in my hand. And no one to tut and wrinkle their nose at the smoke.'

'I'm rather partial to the smell of cigars,' Charlotte told him. 'It's a manly smell. You wouldn't find a wimp with a cigar in his mouth.'

George laid his cigar in the large crystal ashtray. 'Where on earth did you hear the word wimp? You do surprise me sometimes, Charlotte. And frighten me.'

'Papa, don't you give me a lecture. I've just had one off my brother, and even you must agree that two lectures in one day is far more than one person can bear.'

George hid his chortle behind his whisky glass. 'Oh, and what, pray, did you do to deserve a lecture off Andrew? Your brother is far too fond of you to lecture you without good cause.'

Charlotte sat on the edge of the desk and began to swing her legs. In her mind she was telling herself she must go very carefully here, or her mission would not be successful. 'Andrew told me, in a very nice way of course, that it was time I grew up. And he's right, of course, because I do act childishly for my age. I have vowed to change and behave like a grown-up.' She winked as she smiled at the man whose love for her was there in his eyes, for her to see. 'Since I've met Poppy and Jean, I've tried to be as grown up as they are, and I have learned a lot from them. I do hope you and Mama don't try to stop me seeing them, for I would be devastated, Papa. I feel Poppy is like a sister to me; I am really fond of her. Apart from being so beautiful, she is kind, gentle, and really funny. I am at my happiest when I'm with her.'

'You will not be stopped from seeing her, my darling, for I can see for myself that she is good for you. And I know that if your mother met her, she would be captivated by her, and won over. We must try to arrange a meeting. Do you think you could persuade her to pay us a visit?'

Charlotte put on her business head. She would love to bring Poppy to meet her mother, but there was something more important she wanted to do first. And to do this, she needed the help of her father. 'Papa, you know how I asked for your help in giving Jean Slater a job? Well, can I ask for your help again? After all, I did you a good turn with Jean, because she really is a very good worker.'

George was always intrigued by the way his daughter could manipulate him without his being aware of it until it was too late. 'What are you up to now, my dear? I hope you are not going to take me into a situation where I must lie to your mother.'

'Let me tell you what I want to do, and how happy it would make not just me, but Andrew also. You see, Papa, I truly believe that my brother fell in love with Poppy the day of the accident. He was holding out his hand to help her off the ground, and I saw the look on his face. I'm not telling tales out of school, Papa, I'm telling you because I want him to be happy. He's admitted to me how he feels, and I've thought of a way they can meet, without her having an excuse to walk away or ignore him.'

George sighed. 'What do you want me to do for you, Charlotte, that won't involve deceiving your mother?'

'I know Poppy is going to a dance on Friday night, somewhere in Liverpool. She is going with her brother, David, and two other friends. Now if you would help me to get Mama to agree to Andrew's driving me to the dance and back, then he and Poppy could meet socially. I know they would get on well together if they were given the chance.'

George was thoughtful. 'Are you sure Andrew would want this? It's not just one of your ideas, is it, Charlotte? If it is then your brother will be very angry with you, and your mother and myself most displeased. For you would be playing with people's feelings, and that would be most unfair.'

'Papa, Andrew knows I am in here right now, and he knows why. He really, really likes Poppy, but you know yourself he is shy around females. He will never ever run after her, he's not the type. But I know them both, Papa, and I'm certain they would be good together. And where better to get close to someone than in a dance hall? If Andrew is too shy to approach Poppy, then I'll drag him over. And she couldn't really refuse if he asked her to dance.' Charlotte slid off the desk. 'Are you going to help me with Mama?'

'I don't think I need to, my darling. I think you are quite capable of persuading her yourself. I'm not asking you to go against your mother's wishes, but you really don't have to tell her the tale you've told me. You and Andrew are old enough to do as you please, and go where you like. And if you are going together then I can't see any objection from your mother. If there is, I will definitely step in.' George puffed on his cigar. 'And Andrew really likes Poppy, does he?' He nodded his head. 'He's got excellent taste. Now go and tell him so.'

Charlotte knocked on her brother's door, and waited for him to answer before she walked in with her hips swinging from side to side. 'Who did you say was childish, and should learn to grow up? I'll have you know your sister now has all her plans in place.'

A smile covering his handsome face, Andrew asked, 'What have you done with Father? Twisted his arm?'

'He has told me we are both old enough to go where we please, and do as we please. We don't need permission, but it would show respect, and stop any worry, if we told our parents what we were up to. He will take our side if Mama raises any objection to our going to a dance on Friday. As long as I'm with you, there'll be no refusal.' She stood in front of him, devilment in her eyes. 'It'll be up to you on Friday night, Andrew. I've set everything up, so now you'll have to do your part. Which is the easiest, for all you'll have to do is ask a beautiful girl to dance with you.' She kissed his cheek. 'Sleep well, brother dear.'

Chapter Twenty-Two

When Poppy arrived for work on the Friday morning, she found Jean waiting for her by the steps. 'What are you standing here for? The wind is enough to blow you over.'

'I'm a nervous wreck, Poppy. I haven't closed my eyes all night. My tummy is turning over, my head is bursting and I feel like being sick.'

'Why didn't you stay in bed if you feel so bad? Go home, now. You must be sickening for something. You've never missed a day's work since you've been here, so no one is going to tell you off.'

'You don't understand, Poppy,' Jean said, her lip quivering. 'I'm not sick, just afraid! I'll never be able to go to Mr John and hand my notice in. I haven't got the guts. You know how sarcastic he can be, the way he bawls and shouts. I couldn't stand there and listen to him. My legs would give out and I'd end up making a fool of myself by crying.'

'So what do you intend to do?' Poppy felt sorry for her friend, but also a little angry. Jean had been treated like a slave for years, then out of the blue she was handed a new job on a platter. She didn't have to look for it; it was given to her. She should be full of the joys of spring this morning, and instead she was dithering. 'You are going to give your notice in, aren't you? You'll have to do it today or you won't be able to leave next Friday. So come on, Jean, buck up. You can't let Charlotte and her father down after they've been so kind. That would be a terrible thing to do.'

Jean took a deep breath. 'No, I can't let Charlotte down. I wouldn't be able to live with myself if I did. Come on, we'll go in. But if you see me weakening, give me a good telling off.'

The friends walked up to the office in silence, but when Poppy was hanging her coat up, she turned her head to where Jean was taking the cover off her typewriter. 'I can't believe you're frightened of Mr John. You should be on top of the world this morning, looking forward to giving your notice in. I'd swap places with you any day, because your life has been improved in every way. Nice people to work with, and a raise in pay into the bargain. It'll be a pleasure getting out of bed every day.'

'Poppy.' Jean swivelled in her chair. 'You've heard him being rude to me, but he saves the worst until you go out to deliver the letters. Then he looks me up and down as though I'm scum, and his language is foul. That's every day, and it's normal. So what is he going to be like today, when I tell him I won't be working for him after next week? He'll hit the roof.'

'Let him hit the roof. Don't take any notice of him. If he sees you're frightened he'll go on all the more. He relishes seeing someone kowtow to him.' Poppy felt like giving Jean a good shake, but it wouldn't achieve anything: it would make matters worse. 'Don't you want to start your new job the week after next, or have you changed your mind?'

'Oh, I want to go, Poppy. The atmosphere there is so much better than here. And Mr Robert is really nice. I can't imagine him raising his voice, never mind swearing.'

Several unopened letters lay next to Poppy's typewriter. It was part of the morning ritual. The staff in the front office would sort the post out and take it to the solicitor's office it was intended for. 'I'll have to get started on this post, Jean, so we'll talk later. And I've got two letters to answer from yesterday, which I must make sure catch the twelve o'clock post.'

Jean was at the filing cabinet, later, when Mr John came out of his office. 'My office, now!' he barked, bad temper written all over his face. He never passed the time of day with his staff; that was unheard of.

Poppy raised her brows as Jean was passing her desk, and mouthed, 'Tell him now, and get it over with.' She leaned back in her chair to listen to any raising of voices. And she didn't have to wait long, for Mr John was in a foul temper for some reason they would never know, and when Jean told him she was handing her notice in, he went berserk. Poppy was horrified. She heard him laughing like a maniac, asking who would give a dowdy spinster a job. She was an eyesore, she was no good at her job, and he certainly wouldn't give her a reference.

Poppy found she couldn't sit there and let a brute of a man talk like that to any woman, especially a friend. She scraped her chair back and strode towards Mr John's office. She was so angry she didn't knock, but walked straight in and up to his desk, where she stood next to a white-faced Jean. 'How dare you speak to Miss Slater like that? What sort of monster are you to shout at a lady in language fit for the gutter?'

'Get out of here!' The man's face was distorted with rage. 'Who the hell do you think you are to barge in here without knocking? Get out, back to your typewriter, before you find yourself out on your ear.'

Words were racing around in Poppy's head. When Jean left, she would be the one having to put up with being treated like a slave. Could she cope? Oh, no, her pride wouldn't take being spoken to like that by anyone. 'Oh, I'm not waiting for you to sack me. I've come in here to give you notice that I will be leaving at the same time as Miss Slater. We'll be going down to the personnel office to hand in our notice officially at lunchtime. Until we do leave, if you try any of your dirty tricks, or even look sideways at us, I won't hesitate to go to your father and tell him exactly what sort of man his son is. And how badly you treat your staff. He'll find out anyway, because I fully intend to give your behaviour as my reason for leaving.'

John Sutherland's veins were bulging, blue and purple, and beads of sweat were breaking out on his forehead. He looked very threatening, and Jean was terrified. 'Let's go, Poppy.'

'Yes, I'll be glad to get out of here.' Poppy wasn't afraid of the man glaring at them across his desk, but she was disgusted and very angry. 'We'll go straight down to personnel, hand in our notice, and tell them that Mr John's behaviour has upset us so much, we won't be coming back to the office until tomorrow. They'll have to put a temp in for the rest of the day.' She took Jean's elbow and led her out of the room. 'Put the cover on your typewriter, Jean. We won't be back today.'

'Oh, Poppy, what have you done?' Jean's hands were shaking with nerves. 'You can't give your notice in – you haven't got another job lined up. And it's all my fault, too! You shouldn't have got involved. I'd have put up with his insults; I'm used to them. But I've got to say I've never seen him in such a rage. He did frighten me.'

'I wasn't going to sit here and listen to him insulting you, and using foul language. I was so mad, I felt like thumping him.'

'But you'll be out of a job! And all because of me! Oh, dear, I don't know what to say.'

'Don't get yourself in a dither, Jean; it's not worth it. I'll start looking for a job next week. I'll have two weeks' wages to draw next week, with my week in hand. That will keep me going, and my mam and David will help me out until I'm earning again. Peter said he could get me a job – he's told me several times. But I'd rather be independent and find my own way. And don't worry yourself to death, Jean, because I'm not sorry I'll be leaving here next week. I couldn't stand much more of Mr John.'

'Perhaps Charlotte's father knows of a vacancy. He's bound to be in touch with a lot of firms.'

'Don't even think of it, Jean. That is definitely not going to happen. I'll get a job off my own bat, not through a favour from a friend.' Poppy handed Jean her coat from the stand, then reached for her own. 'We'd better go down to personnel and get it over with. And don't contradict me when I say we're so upset by Mr John's behaviour we don't feel well enough to work the rest of the day. Let the word get back to his father, and perhaps whoever takes our place will be better treated than we've been.'

'Are we going to the café for lunch?' Jean asked. 'I don't want to go home too early, for Mother will want to know all the ins and outs, and if I told her she'd only get herself upset.'

'Yeah, we can go for lunch. But I'll go straight home after, 'cos I'm going dancing tonight, and I want to have a bath, iron a dress and wash my hair. And listen, Jean, don't spoil your weekend by worrying. You've got something to look forward to, and next week will fly over. We'll have no hassle from Mr John. I bet you he'll be as good as gold. Two members of staff leaving because of his behaviour, he's got more problems than we have.'

'It's you I'm worried about,' Jean said. 'I really feel bad about you giving your job up.'

'If I'm not worried, I don't see why you should be. I'm not sorry about what I did. The creep had it coming to him.' Poppy didn't want her friend to go home and spend the weekend fretting because of what happened, so she added, 'I'll be too busy enjoying myself tonight to give any thought to this place. And now let's go and officially hand in our notice.'

No arrangements had been made regarding time, but it just happened that Poppy and David arrived at the Grafton at the same time as Peter and Kate. 'Great minds think alike,' David said, nodding to Peter. 'Good to see you again.'

'Shall we go to the cloakroom, Kate, while the men are getting the tickets?' Poppy asked, after returning Peter's smile. 'While we have a chance to get near the mirror before it gets crowded.'

Kate nodded and linked Poppy's arm. 'I don't know my way around here yet.'

Pushing open the cloakroom door, Poppy said, 'You'll soon get used to it.' She was combing her hair, and looking at Kate through the mirror. 'Don't think me cheeky or nosy, Kate, but how are you getting on with Peter?'

'Well, he brought me here tonight, which is something. But I've got stiff competition from you, Poppy.'

Poppy turned round, put her comb in her handbag and closed the clasp. 'You are not in competition with me, Kate, so get that right out of your head. I've only known Peter a couple of months, while you've known him years. I have no plans to court anyone at present, so count me out. I am very fond of Peter. He is a lovely man, and I always want to be his friend. I also want him to be happy. He was in love with you for two years, and as this is a girl-to-girl talk, I'll tell you what I really believe. If you take things slowly, give him time to get to know the real you again, then you'll win in the end. But give him time.'

'I will do whatever it takes to win him back, for I love him so much it hurts. Thank you for being straight with me. I appreciate your honesty. And I hope we can be friends.'

'Of course we can. And now we'd better go, before the men come to look for us.'

Peter seemed relaxed in David's company, and when the girls approached them his smile wasn't forced. 'I've told Kate the first slow-fox is with you, babe.'

Poppy tutted. 'I'd promised it to David, 'cos he needs to brush up his dancing skills. He doesn't come often enough, that's his trouble. He prefers playing cards. Still, Kate can give him a few pointers.'

While they were dancing they passed Kate and David, who were chatting in a friendly manner. 'I like your Kate,' Poppy said. 'She's very friendly, and easy to talk to.'

'I'm getting to the stage where I bear her no ill will for the hurt she caused. And we're talking. Not about getting back together, but talking. It's a year since I walked away from her, and she said she hasn't looked at another boy during that time.'

'I believe that, Peter, because she really loves you. Perhaps you don't appreciate it yet, but you will.'

'How are you, babe? Finished night school, have you?'

'Yes, no more lessons, but I've got to pick my reference up on Monday night.' Poppy thought about telling him what had happened that morning, but decided against it. It wouldn't help Kate if they were too friendly, because he would never walk away. Perhaps when things sorted themselves out, and he and Kate were back together for good, then she'd tell him.

They swapped partners for every dance, until the waltz before the interval, when Poppy told Peter, 'You have this with Kate. I want to have a word with David.' This wasn't a lie, for she hadn't told her mother or brother that she'd handed her notice in. She had intended to wait until Sunday, when the family had a lazy day, but then decided she'd tell David tonight and get his reaction. After all, if she didn't get another job for a while, she wouldn't be able to contribute towards the housekeeping, and her brother and mother would have to keep her. She wouldn't be entitled to unemployment money because of leaving Sutherland's of her own free will. She'd manage for a couple of weeks on the two weeks' wages she was entitled to, and the bit of money she had in her purse, but it wouldn't last for ever. And anyway, she didn't fancy the idea of being out of work.

David was twirling his sister around, and because he seemed to be enjoying himself so much Poppy hadn't found the right moment to tell him her news. And just when she thought the time was right, fate stepped in to take a hand.

'Oh, my God, I don't believe it!' Poppy pulled David to a halt. 'What on earth is she doing here?'

David followed her eyes to where a girl was waving from the edge of the dance floor. 'Who is she, Poppy? Do you know her?'

'Yes, she's a friend. At least, she's only recently become a friend, but I'll explain later. I'll have to go over to her, so come with me.'

'She's very pretty,' David said, as he was being pulled past the dancing couples. 'Where have you been hiding her?'

'She's also very posh,' Poppy told him, 'so you can practise your grammar on her.'

'Hello, Poppy.' Charlotte had never been in a dance hall before; she'd only been to dinner dances in classy hotels. The sight of so many couples filled her with excitement. 'I know it's a surprise, but aren't you happy to see me?'

'I'm always happy to see you, Charlotte, but I certainly didn't expect to see you here.' Poppy touched David's arm. 'This is my brother, David.'

'I'm Charlotte, your sister's friend.' Charlotte shook David's hand. 'She's told me all about you. And you really are as handsome as she said you were.'

David was delighted, as well as interested. 'Go on, tell me what else she said about me. There's nothing I like better than flattery.'

'Charlotte, now the introductions are over, and you've given my brother's ego a boost, will you tell me what you're doing here? You didn't come on your own, I hope? Do your parents know you're here?'

Charlotte giggled. 'So many questions, Poppy! I came because I heard you telling Jean you were coming tonight. I didn't come on my own; I would never have found it. Andrew drove me here, and I had my father's permission to come.'

'Is Andrew picking you up to take you home?' Poppy asked. 'I wouldn't be happy if I thought you were wandering around strange places on your own.'

'Don't worry so, Poppy. I'm not going to come to any harm. Andrew is taking me home, on Papa's instruction.'

'So your brother is coming back for you?'

Charlotte giggled again. It was infectious, and David found himself warming to the pretty young girl. 'He's not coming back, Poppy, he's waiting in the foyer for me.'

'You mean Andrew intends to stand in the foyer until the dance is over? But that's an hour! You can't leave him out there on his own for an hour. It would be really mean to expect that of him.' Poppy was torn. She looked for Peter and Kate, who were standing by the wall now the dance was over, and she waved before saying to her brother, 'Will you tell Peter some friends have turned up and I won't be away long. Then come into the foyer to meet Charlotte's brother. We can't leave the poor man out there on his own for an hour.'

Charlotte was delighted with the turn of events, but she was careful not to overdo her pleasure, or Poppy would suspect she was up to something. 'I did ask Andrew to come into the dance hall with me, Poppy, but he said he wouldn't because you must be getting sick of the sight of our family.'

David stood listening, fascinated by events. He wouldn't have moved if Poppy hadn't given him a dig. 'David, go and tell Peter, then follow us to the foyer.'

Pulling Charlotte by the hand, Poppy pushed open the door, and there she saw Andrew leaning back against the wall talking to Bill, the doorman. 'Why are you staying out here? Surely you don't want to stand in the one spot for an hour?'

'I promised my father I'd drive Charlotte here and back, otherwise he wouldn't have let her come.'

'You and your father are spoiling Charlotte, letting her have her own way so much.' Poppy smiled, causing Andrew's heart to flutter. And when she went on talking, it was her face rather than her words that he soaked up. 'Mind you, she does have a way with her that makes you give in, even against your better judgement. She's wormed her way into my life, but I never expected to see her here. She always pops up unexpectedly, like a jack-in-the-box, but the Grafton is the last place I expected to see her.'

David came up behind his sister, making her jump. 'David, you gave me a fright, you silly beggar. Did you tell Peter some friends have turned up?' She waited for his nod, and then introduced the two men. 'David, this is Charlotte's brother, Andrew.'

After the pleasantries were over, David said, 'Shall we go back in the hall now? The interval will be over soon.'

Charlotte thought she'd been quiet long enough. She brought a blush to David's face when she said, 'Will you ask me for a dance when the music starts, David? I really am not a bad dancer, and I won't stand on your feet.'

Andrew gasped, 'Really, Charlotte, that is very forward of you, and you should apologize. David may have a partner waiting for him and wondering where he is.'

It was slowly dawning on David who the couple were. He remembered Poppy telling him and their mother that the bloke who knocked her over was very posh, as was his sister. And these two just fitted the bill. He was about to ask, nicely of course, if that was how they met, but his sister could see by his face how his mind was working, and jumped in to head him off.

'No, David doesn't have a partner waiting, and I'm sure he would very much like to dance with you, Charlotte. We have two friends in the hall, so I think we'll join them. Will you come in and meet them, Andrew?'

'No, I won't intrude,' Andrew said. 'I really don't mind waiting for Charlotte. I can always go for a walk to pass the time.'

This wasn't in his sister's plan. 'Oh, I couldn't enjoy dancing if I knew you were walking up and down.' Her hands went behind her back and she crossed her fingers. 'I'll come home with you, Andrew, if you don't feel like dancing.'

'A charmer, and now a blackmailer,' Poppy said with a chuckle. 'You are a girl of many talents, Charlotte. I think I could learn a lot from you, but not tonight. I came here because I love dancing, and I intend to do just that. So come in, Andrew, and join our friends. You'll see plenty of pretty girls you can ask up.' She jerked her head. 'David, Charlotte, come on. The band is beginning to warm up.'

There was just enough time for introductions before the band struck up with a slow foxtrot, and Peter reached for Poppy's hand. 'Come on, babe.' He was leading her on to the dance floor when she turned her head and called, 'Pair off, David.'

'Let's do as we're told,' David said. 'Poppy will have my life if I'm still standing here next time she dances by. I'll take Charlotte, Andrew, and you take Kate. And after the dance is over, we'll compare notes on who won.'

Kate was shy when Andrew asked her to dance, but she soon loosened up when they got on the floor. She was the more experienced dancer and found herself leading, rather than being led. But it wouldn't have been noticed by other dancers, only by Andrew. 'I'm sorry. I'm afraid I don't dance often, and I'm quite stiff. We'll leave the floor if you wish?'

Kate thought what a nice polite man he was, and very attractive. 'We will not leave the floor! Think what it would do to my reputation. You are a little stiff, Andrew, that's all. Let yourself go and loosen up. It's only a dance; they can't put you in prison if you miss a step.'

'I used to dance a lot when I went to university, but I haven't done an awful lot since, just the odd one now and again. I'll have to get out and about more.' Andrew found Kate quite easy to talk to. 'Is Peter your boyfriend, or am I being nosy? I don't mean to be.'

'He was my boyfriend for two years, but we split up a year ago. It was my fault. I did something I really should have known at the time was wrong.'

This wasn't what Andrew wanted to hear. 'So is Poppy going out with him now?'

'They've only known each other a few months, and Poppy tells me she has no intention of courting anyone yet. She's nice, is Poppy, and she's helping me win Peter back.'

'Yes, she strikes me as being a really nice, fun-loving person. I don't know her very well, though,' Andrew admitted. 'She is more a friend of my sister.'

At that moment his sister was having the time of her life with David. Looking up into his eyes, she said, 'We dance well together. Quite professional, don't you think? I hope they play a tango. That is one dance I can't master, so you can teach me.'

David tried to look stern. 'If you would stop making me laugh, then we might look more professional. Look, you're pulling a funny face again. Will you stop it!' But David was enjoying himself. Charlotte was a real charmer. Childish and funny one minute, the next showing she was able to hold her own with any dancer on the floor. And she could be serious when the mood suited her. Tonight, however, she was out to enjoy herself on the dance floor, while remembering her reason for being there.

The music came to an end, and David acted the gentleman and escorted Charlotte to where the other two couples were standing. Poppy was doing the most talking, with Kate helping out to cover the silence of the two men. Peter was eyeing Andrew up, wondering who he was and why he was there. But when David and Charlotte joined the group, the atmosphere changed completely. 'Your brother said I dance very well, Poppy,' Charlotte said, her eyes sparkling. 'Actually, although I have no wish to embarrass him, he said he couldn't remember ever having a better partner.'

With all eyes on him, David chuckled. 'You little fibber! I never said any such thing! How could I, when you were pulling such funny faces I couldn't dance for laughing.'

'I was pulling faces because you were tickling me.' Charlotte was enjoying a freedom she'd never known before, and was making the most of it. 'I hope you don't tickle me when we're doing the tango, for the steps are very intricate and I could lose my balance. It would be very unladylike if I were to fall flat on my face.'

This brought laughter from the group, and broke the ice. 'I hope you are not leading my brother astray,' Poppy said. 'He's never been accused of tickling a dancing partner in the middle of a tango before.'

For the first time in weeks, Peter was roaring with laughter, and Poppy and Kate raised their brows and hopes. 'David,' Peter said. 'Are you not going to defend your reputation? You don't want to be known as the tango tickler, do you?'

'Oh, I don't know,' Poppy said. 'I think the tango tickler has a certain ring to it. If word got around, David would be much sought after, and have his own fan club.'

David wagged a stiffened finger at Charlotte. 'See what you've done now, you little mischief-maker? I'll be the talk of the town.'

Although Charlotte was laughing and playing the fool with David, she was keeping an eye on her brother. Andrew appeared to be relaxed and enjoying the banter, but if he didn't push himself forward, and make the most of the opportunity of being in Poppy's company, then the evening would be wasted and her hopes and plans in tatters. She started meeting his eyes, sending a message. But she had little hope of his responding, unless she did something to push him. She was in despair, until the band struck up with the strains of a foxtrot, and she moved nearer to Andrew, gave him a dig, and said, 'If you don't ask Poppy for this dance, I'll never speak to you again.'

Andrew's eyes shot open wide. 'Charlotte, keep your voice down and don't make a show of me.'

'If you don't make use of your chance, Andrew, I will make a show of you by falling flat on my face,' Charlotte hissed. 'And I'll pull David down with me.'

'Is this a conspiracy, or can anyone join in?' Neither brother nor sister had noticed Poppy behind them, and they were startled. Charlotte was the first to recover her wits. 'Andrew was just saying he would like to ask you to dance, Poppy, but he's afraid you would refuse because he can't dance to your standard. I told him not to be so silly, that you weren't the type to turn him down. But he doesn't know you as well as I do, so he doesn't know how kind you are.'

'I'm sure Andrew is quite capable of choosing his own partners, Charlotte,' Poppy said. 'And seeing that Peter and Kate are already on the dance floor, and David is waiting for you to fandango with him, Andrew will have to be a gentleman and ask me for this dance. Otherwise I'll be left alone, like a wallflower.'

Andrew thought his ship had come in. 'It will be my pleasure, Poppy, but I doubt if it will be yours. I'm not exactly the best dancer in the world.'

Charlotte, hands on hips, tutted. 'Really, Andrew, you're getting better than me at telling fibs. You and I often have a dance at home, and we do very well. And anyway, Poppy is my friend, and I'm sure she won't complain if you get a few steps wrong.'

David tapped her on the shoulder. 'Are you coming to dance, or not? Honestly, you aren't the size of six pennyworth of copper, but you can't half talk. Now come on, or I'll look for the next-best-looking girl in the room.'

When his sister had walked off with David, Andrew raised his brows at Poppy. 'Are you willing to take a chance? I'll quite understand if you want to sit this one out.'

'I'm not only willing, I'm determined,' Poppy said. 'If you can't tell your left foot from your right, at the end of this dance, then I'll take up ballet dancing.' She took his hand to lead him through the people standing at the edge of the dance floor, but quickly dropped it because it didn't feel quite right. And when he took her in his arms as they stepped on to the floor, she felt most uncomfortable. It was queer, she told herself, that each time he'd touched her she'd felt the same. She could even remember the first time it happened, on the day he'd knocked her over, when he'd given her his hand to help her to her feet.

They covered the floor without a word being spoken. Andrew thought he was walking on air, and told himself only heaven could be a better place to be, while Poppy kept her eyes glued to his shoulder. 'You are a good dancer, Poppy.' Andrew was afraid his lack of conversation would have her thinking him a very dull person. 'How well do you think I'm doing, or should I take up another hobby, like skydiving?'

Poppy chuckled. 'I don't think you're doing badly at all.' She raised her head to find herself staring into the deepest brown eyes she'd ever seen. She lowered her gaze quickly, as that feeling of discomfort returned. She was annoyed with herself, but couldn't understand why. He was a nice-looking man, but so were hundreds of other men. He came from a rich family, there was no doubt about that, but money wasn't everything. The one thing Andrew did have in his favour was a loveable sister whom Poppy had grown fond of. And for Charlotte's sake she would not be rude to him. 'If you came a couple more times, you would soon be as good a dancer as anyone here.'

'Do you come often, Poppy?'

'I haven't been coming as often as I used to, because of night school two nights a week, and doing homework a few nights.'

'My sister tells me you are now qualified to look for work as a secretary. She wasn't talking about you behind your back, I hasten to say; it's just that she seems very fond of you and likes to praise you. So, with night school finished, you'll probably be coming here more often?'

'I doubt it. I'll have to watch my pennies after next week, for I gave my notice in at work today. I haven't told the family yet, so please don't mention it to anyone.'

'That was rather impetuous, wasn't it?' Andrew regretted the words as soon as they left his lips. 'I'm sorry, that was out of order. I have no right to criticize what you do. You must have had a good reason.'

The music came to an end and the dancers were leaving the floor when Poppy said, 'Ask me up for the next dance and I can explain. I don't want you thinking I packed my job in on a whim, without good reason.'

Charlotte was delighted to see Poppy and Andrew talking, and was giving herself a mental pat on the back. David was curious, but not to the point where it interfered with the fun he was having with Charlotte. Kate wasn't concerned about how and why Andrew was there; she was just happy he was.

And Peter was trying to figure out who the bloke was, and where he fitted into Poppy's life.

And then someone else came on the scene, who didn't confuse Peter because he knew him, but caused David to look at him with curiosity, and Andrew with jealousy.

'How about the next dance, Poppy?' Jim sounded bright and cheerful. 'You told me I could ask, so here I am.'

'Oh, hello, Jim,' Poppy said. 'I'm sorry, but I've promised the next dance to someone. However, there's a nice young lady here who may fancy a change of partner. Charlotte, this is Jim, a good friend of mine and a smashing dancer.'

'But what about David, Poppy? He'd be left on his own.'

'The next dance is a "excuse me" quickstep, so we can excuse anyone we like.' This was Poppy's bright idea. 'Which means we all get a chance to dance with each other.'

'Oh, goody!' Charlotte was thrilled. 'I've never played that before, Poppy. How does it work?'

It was Jim who answered. 'If yer see someone you would like to dance with, then you just walk up to their partner, tap him on the arm, and he has to pass the girl over. And yer can keep on doing it until yer get fed up, or the girl's partner punches you and breaks yer nose.'

A strangled noise came from Charlotte, and all heads turned to see her eyes wide and a hand covering her mouth. 'What's wrong, sweetheart?' Poppy asked. 'You look as though you've seen a ghost.'

The girl was shaking her head. 'I don't want to dance in the "excuse me", Poppy, My father would be really angry if Andrew or I went home with a broken nose.' When the laughter came, Charlotte looked surprised. 'He would, Poppy, and Mother would be inconsolable. She would need the smelling salts to stop her from fainting.'

Andrew crossed over to his sister and put a protective arm across her shoulder. 'Look around at the men, my darling sister, and you will see there is not one with a broken nose.'

Jim was flabbergasted that his innocent joke had caused any trouble. I mean, he thought, how could anyone believe noses got broken because of a dance. 'I was only kidding, girl. It doesn't happen for real. I'm always excusing someone, and I've never had me nose broken, not once.'

Charlotte thought her acting deserved an award. Oh, she had such a lot to tell Papa. He would be really amused, and proud of her, of course. 'All right, Jim, I'll dance with you, and Poppy can dance with Andrew, while Peter dances with Kate.'

'Pardon me,' David said, looking down in the mouth. 'You promised this dance to me.'

Charlotte tossed her curls as she linked her arm in Jim's. 'Well, it is an "excuse me" dance, David. Just tap my partner on the arm, and then duck.'

When Poppy was led on to the floor by Andrew, she said, 'Your sister never ceases to amaze me. She acts like a child, but she has her head screwed on the right way. She's a really good actress when she puts her mind to it, and with such innocence you can't help falling for her charms.'

'Charlotte really is a little love, and the kindest person I know.' Andrew was back in heaven with Poppy so close in his arms. 'She is not as childish as she makes out, and has an intelligence that often surprises me.' He held her away and asked, 'Now, are you going to tell me why you gave your notice in? I really am interested.'

Poppy found she was at ease with him when she wasn't looking into his face, so her tale was told as she was looking somewhere between his chest and his shoulder. 'The man is a brute. I couldn't allow him to speak to anyone the way he spoke to Jean. So I gave my notice in when Jean did. And now you have the whole sorry tale. I don't regret it, and would do it again if such a situation arose.'

'I think you did the right thing,' Andrew said. 'I know John Sutherland, not as a friend but through business transactions. And he is not a man I could be a friend to. His father is a gentleman, but unfortunately the son is anything but. Anyway, you are better off away from him. And with a good reference, you will soon find other employment.'

Andrew argued with his conscience. Should he offer to help? For he could, and would love to offer her a position in his office. But he knew any offer would be turned down flat, and could even break their fragile friendship. 'I have no doubt you will not be long out of work.' He laughed, hoping what he was about to say would be taken as a joke. 'Have a word with my sister. She'll help. She's quite the little business-woman when it suits her. If she was the one looking for a job, whoever interviewed her would take her on just to stop her talking. My father is putty in her hands.'

'Peter could get me a job immediately, so I wouldn't need to be out of work at all. But I prefer to be independent. I do have my pride, you know.'

'Don't forget you promised to visit my office for tea and cakes,' Andrew reminded her. 'Come in with Charlotte one day, and let me know your news. I would like that.'

'I will, I promise.' For the first time since they'd set foot on the dance floor, Poppy looked into his face. 'And if I have landed a job, the cakes are on me.'

Chapter Twenty-Three

'Peter didn't seem very happy tonight, seeing you dancing with Andrew,' David said, hanging his coat up in the hall. 'He asked me who he was, and was he taking you out. I'd say Peter is very jealous.'

'What did you tell him?' Poppy asked.

'What could I tell him? I don't know much about Andrew, except he has a lovely sister. I really enjoyed myself tonight, thanks to Charlotte. She's really very funny.'

Eva came in from the kitchen. She'd had a kettle of water on the boil for twenty minutes, so there'd be a hot drink ready for when they came in. 'All I heard was that you had a good time, David, but Peter didn't. So while I'm pouring the tea out, fill in the rest of the story.'

David pulled out a chair and sat with a satisfied smile on his face, rubbing his palms together. 'I had a whale of a time. Charlotte is a great girl. She'd be the life and soul of any party.'

Eva put the cups of tea down in front of them, then drew out a chair for herself. 'Now, who is Charlotte, and who was the Andrew you said Peter was jealous of? It's all very confusing.'

'Andrew and Charlotte are the brother and sister who knocked me over that day when it was raining. I've bumped into them a couple of times. Our office is very near to theirs,'

Poppy said. 'I don't know Andrew very well, but Charlotte has become a friend of mine and Jean's, as you know.'

'And why didn't Peter like you dancing with this Andrew?' Eva asked. 'I thought he was back with his old girlfriend?'

'He's getting there, Mam, but it's not going to happen overnight. It'll take time, but Kate will win him round, and she deserves to. Peter is used to dancing with me, but he'll get over it. That's why I asked David to come with me tonight, so Kate could get a look in. I was surprised when Charlotte and Andrew turned up, but I was glad to see them, for it relieved the tension.'

'I wonder if Charlotte will come to the Grafton again, Poppy?' David asked. 'Let me know and I'll come along, just for a laugh.'

'I doubt she'll come again, David. And don't get too fond of her 'cos she's way out of our league. I've grown very fond of her myself, but I know it won't last, our friendship, 'cos I couldn't keep up with her social life.'

'Money isn't everything, sweetheart. It shouldn't come between friends,' Eva said. 'One person sits in the front stalls in the picture house 'cos that's all they can afford. Another person sits in the dress circle 'cos they can afford it. But there's no reason why those two people can't be friends.'

Poppy could feel her tummy churning as a voice in her head told her to get on with it. 'I've got some news, Mam and David, and it's not good news.' She saw her mother and brother look startled, and was quick to assure them, 'Oh, it's nothing serious. No one has died! But it's not good news, either. I gave a week's notice today, and I'm leaving my job next Friday. And as I haven't got another job lined up, I might not be able to put in the usual housekeeping money until something turns up. I'm all right for this week, and next, and

I'm hoping not to be out of work for long. But I can't say for certain.'

It was David who asked, 'How and why did that come about, sis? You've never given any hint you were thinking of leaving so soon.'

'I wasn't. It just happened. My pride wouldn't allow me to stay there.'

Eva put a hand over one of Poppy's. 'You must have had good reason, sweetheart. Why don't you tell us, and get it off yer chest. A trouble shared is a trouble halved. And me and David are here for yer. So tell us what brought it about.'

Poppy began her tale with standing outside the office block waiting hopefully for Jean to arrive with good news about her interview. There was no sound or movement from Eva or David until she came to the part where she'd decided she couldn't sit and listen to her friend being ridiculed, insulted and sworn at. Then David said, 'Good for you, Poppy. You did what any self-respecting person would do. If I'd been there, I'd have lost my temper and thumped him one.'

'David is right, sweetheart,' Eva said, 'except about thumping your Mr John. Violence never solves anything. But I'm glad you kept your dignity. I wouldn't have wanted you to work with such a dreadful man, so I'm glad you handed your notice in. And don't you worry about money. We'll manage fine.'

'I'll give extra every week so your money won't be missed, Poppy,' David said. 'I don't spend much on myself, and I'm on a decent wage.'

'It won't be for long,' Poppy said with determination. 'I brought the *Echo* in with me earlier, so I'll have a look down the job vacancies. And I'll go to the Labour Exchange and see if they know of jobs going.'

'Ask Charlotte's father,' David said. 'He may help. He must know plenty of firms.'

'No!' Poppy shook her head. 'I will not ask Charlotte, Andrew or their father for help. I'll get there on my own. I was determined to learn shorthand, and I stuck with it. And I'm just as determined to become a private secretary, and I'll do that as well, you'll see.'

'Of course you will, sweetheart.' Eva wasn't saying it just to bolster her daughter's feelings; she was certain in her own mind that Poppy's struggle to learn shorthand wouldn't be wasted. She wouldn't be out of work long, not if Mr Jones gave her a good reference. With that in her hand, and a smart appearance, she shouldn't have a problem. 'Put it out of your mind for now. It's time for bed. You've had a hard day, but yer'll feel better in the morning after a good sleep.'

'Don't you worry about me, Mam. I'm no shrinking violet, I'm tough. It's Mr John you should be worried about, because it will be all round the offices why we gave our notice in. His father is bound to know by now, and he's not going to be very happy about the way his son runs his office. I bet he gets a good ticking off, and he won't be able to answer his father back. He'll have to stand there and take it. Like Jean's had to for so many years.'

'That's enough now, sweetheart, because if yer go to bed with an active brain yer'll never get to sleep.'

'I'm on my way, Mam, and I will sleep because I'm tired.' Poppy gave her mother a kiss, then leaned over to David. 'Thanks for coming to the dance with me, our kid. It was a good thing really, with Charlotte and Andrew turning up out of the blue. I'm glad they did, because now when I talk about Charlotte you'll know what she's like. So here's a whopping big kiss to say thank you.'

'I should be thanking you, our kid, because a game of cards seems dull in comparison. And seeing as it's Saturday tomorrow, when you and our mam don't go to work and I only do a couple of hours, how's about me taking you both to the pictures? A little outing for the Meadows family.'

'Oh, that would be nice,' Poppy said. 'I'll look forward to it. What do you say, Mam?'

Eva chuckled. 'As soon as you two go to bed, I'll wash these few cups, then get the *Echo* out. I'll look down the list of cinemas, and see what's on. If we don't all favour the same film, we'll toss for it.' She waved a hand towards the door. 'Off you go. Goodnight and God bless.'

Sunday morning the family were having a leisurely breakfast while reading articles in the *News of the World*. Eva had the first few pages, Poppy the middle section and David the sports pages near the back. 'Liverpool got beaten yesterday,' he informed them. 'Lost by one goal.'

'Aren't you glad you weren't there, son?' Eva asked, a smile hovering around her mouth. 'It's bad enough reading that your favourite team lost, but it must be heartbreaking to have to stand and watch them.'

'Ay, just look at this,' Poppy said, holding the pages between her two hands. 'They're advertising television sets for thirty pound. They've come down in price from last year. The cheapest then was fifty pound, going up to a hundred. It would be nice to have one, to see what's going in the world. And they have plays and films on.' She lowered the paper. 'When I'm working, and getting a decent wage, shall we save up and buy one?'

'I'm all for it.' David sounded eager. 'They have football on as well. The day after the game, of course, but at least you can watch it in comfort. Standing in the Kop when it's cold or raining is no joke. It takes a very loyal fan to go to every home game. So I'm all for clubbing together to buy a television.'

'Whatever you two decide, I'll go along with,' Eva said, folding her pages of the paper. 'It will be nice for me when I go on part time, having the afternoons with me feet up and being entertained.' She pushed her chair back, passed the paper to David, and began clearing the table. 'We're having roast beef for dinner, and I'll do a Yorkshire pudding.'

Poppy rubbed her tummy. 'Goody, goody. I love Yorkshire pudding with plenty of gravy.'

When the knock came on the door, Eva looked down at the dirty dishes in her hand and the tablecloth littered with crumbs. 'Oh, dear, this is probably Marg. I'll take these out while one of you brings the sauce bottle and jam out. And the other, whip the tablecloth off the table and shake it in the yard.' When the second knock came, she shouted, 'Hold yer horses, will yer?'

'Look at the state of me in my dressing gown,' Poppy moaned. 'I don't care who it is, I'm opening the door in it. If they don't like it, they can lump it.'

'Ay, queen, I heard that.' Marg Boden brushed past. 'And I wouldn't care if yer were in yer nuddy. It wouldn't put me off me dinner.'

Eva poked her head into the living room to see her neighbour pulling a chair out for herself. 'Don't make yerself comfortable, sweetheart, 'cos you ain't staying for dinner. The piece of beef I've got will not stretch to four people.'

'Oh, I won't be staying until dinnertime, queen, 'cos I've got to get me own dinner on the go. We're having lamb with mint sauce, and veg of course.' She winked at Poppy and David before adding, 'I promised Ally I'd just have one cup of tea, ten minutes' chatter, then go home. Is that all right with you, queen?'

Eva came in drying her hands. 'Do I have any choice, Mrs Boden? It seems not, for we were all set to lounge around for the whole day.' This was a fib of course, but neither Poppy nor David contradicted their mother, as they sat and waited to be entertained by their neighbour. They only had to wait a few seconds.

'Say that again, Eva Meadows.' Marg narrowed her eyes to slits. 'Did you just say that the three of yer were going to hang around all day in yer dressing gowns?'

Eva nodded. 'That's what I said, sweetheart. There's nothing wrong with your ears.'

'Well, you lazy buggers!' Marg looked from one to the other. 'Yer should bleeding well be ashamed of yerselves! Not only do yer not go to church, but yer can't even be bothered looking respectable. The neighbours will think ye're running a house of ill repute.'

David managed to get an expression of innocence on his face. 'What do you mean, Marg? What is a house of ill repute? I never heard of that before.'

Poppy copied him. 'Neither have I! Do you mean like Florrie, over the road? I know her house is untidy.'

'Don't act the bleeding goat! Who do yer think ye're trying to kid!' Marg sat back in the chair and crossed her legs. 'If all this is because yer can't be bothered making me a cup of tea, and yer think I'll take the hint and slink back home, well yer've got another think coming, queen, because I came for a purpose, and I ain't about to move me backside until I've done what I set out to do. So now you know.'

Eva stood by the table looking thoughtful. 'I've forgotten what yer said yer'd come for now, so remind me.'

Joan Jonker

Marg held up three fingers of her left hand, and ticked them off with the index finger of her right. 'Cup of tea, ten minutes' chat, and ask Poppy if Sarah can go to the Grafton with her and David again on Tuesday. Now they are easy enough to understand and agree to. So get the ruddy kettle on, and stop messing about.'

'All right, sweetheart, keep yer hair on. I'll put the kettle on. That's number one and my job. David can keep you chatting until the tea's made. That's number two sorted out. And number three is Poppy's turn. She'll answer the question about Sarah and the Grafton.'

Marg let out a deep sigh. 'All that for a ruddy cup of tea. I ask yer, was it worth it?' She winked at Poppy before raising her voice. 'The least she can do is put a couple of biscuits on the saucer to make up for the time she's wasted.'

It didn't take Eva long to make the tea, and soon they were seated round the table with a plate of assorted biscuits in the centre. After dunking an arrowroot biscuit into her tea, and lifting it quickly to her mouth before the end fell off, Marg turned to Poppy. 'Would you mind taking Sarah with you to the Grafton on Tuesday? If it intrudes on yer love life, then just say so. Sarah won't be upset. I mean, yer don't want a hanger-on if ye're with a boyfriend.'

'I haven't got a boyfriend, Marg,' Poppy said. It had to come out sometime, so it may as well be now. But she wouldn't go through the whole saga of Peter and Kate, for whatever they decided it was their business, not a source of conversation for people who didn't even know them. 'And I've got another surprise for you. I handed in my notice at work on Friday, and I leave next Friday.'

Marg's eyes were like saucers. 'Go 'way! Ooh, where are yer going to work now, then? Is it a better job, with more money?'

'Calm down, Marg. I haven't got another job to go to.' Poppy gave a shortened version of what happened, and ended by saying, 'I wasn't going to put up with it any longer, and I went with Jean to give in our notice.'

Marg gave Poppy a slap on the back. It was meant to be a comfort, but it nearly toppled Poppy out of her chair. 'Yer won't be out of work for long, queen, not with your looks. And with yer learning shorthand, yer should walk into one.'

'Me and David have told her that,' Eva said. 'She'll have a job in no time.'

Marg rested her elbows on the table. 'Ay, I think I'll move in here. Yer have a lot more excitement than we do in our house. Have yer got room for a lodger?'

David asked, 'How would you consider sleeping on the couch for a mere thirty bob a week? That would include breakfast, but you'd have to be out of the house by seven thirty 'cos I need the bathroom to shave in.'

'Yer can sod off, lad. I do much better than that in me own home.' Marg was grinning at what she was about to say. 'I get me breakfast free, as long as I feed me family before they go off to work. Then I can go back to me lovely comfortable bed, which is still warm from me lovely husband. When I've rested, I go downstairs and blow the dust off the sideboard and mantelpiece, put the dirty dishes in hot water to wash themselves, put a few cobs of coal on the fire my feller lit for me, then stretch out on the couch until I feel refreshed. Then I stroll to the shops for something tasty for my lunch, like boiled ham for a sandwich, with a fresh cream cake to follow.' Marg yawned and put a hand over her mouth. 'I buy two tins of cooked meat, an onion and an Oxo cube. Mix them all together in a pan and heat it up just before the family are due in. I serve the dinner, but don't eat any meself because I can't stand tinned meat, it reminds me of cat food. Then I put a hand to me forehead, like this.' Marg took on her Ethel Barrymore role. 'And I let out a sigh before flopping full length on the couch and complaining about being tired out after cleaning the house from top to bottom. And it never fails. My Ally tells me to stay where I am, and he and the girls will wash up and make me a nice cup of tea.'

No one had spoken a word. They were all carried away, not only by the tale their neighbour was making up as she went along, but by her ability to tell a story to fit any occasion.

Marg still had a few words to say. 'So yer see, lad, you'd have to pay me money to sleep on yer couch. And I wouldn't come cheap.'

Eva felt like clapping. Who else could tell a story off the cuff like that? And with all the expressions and actions. 'Have you ever thought of writing a book, Marg? Ye're wasting yer time and talent.'

'Oh, don't think I haven't thought of that, queen, 'cos at school my teacher said the same thing.' Marg giggled. 'Well perhaps not quite the same words you used. I can't remember exactly, but what it amounted to, in a nutshell, was that if the number of words I used in a week were written down, it would take a crane to lift the book. Actually she didn't say book, 'cos she was posh, she said tome. I thought she meant a tomb, you know, like what they bury kings and queens in, and I laughed. And d'yer know what, I got the cane for laughing in the middle of a lesson. I didn't think that was fair, 'cos half the class were laughing, only they had lifted their desk tops so the teacher wouldn't see them. I got me own back on a couple of them at playtime, though. I pinched their ball and threw it into the boys' playground. The lads hung on to it until the bell went, so they got paid back for laughing at me.'

'I wouldn't have the nerve to laugh at you, Marg,' David said. 'I'd laugh with you, but never at you.'

'That's good thinking, lad.' Marg held an arm out and flexed her muscles. 'Mind you, I'd never hit a mate. That would be hitting below the belt, and against the Queensberry rules.'

'Before we forget what you came for, Mrs Boden,' Poppy said, 'can we get back to the Grafton on Tuesday. I may go, and I may not. I'll have to pull my horns in and watch what I spend, but I don't think I'll have to be so tight with myself. One night out a week won't break the bank.'

'I'll take you on Tuesday,' David offered. 'I haven't made any plans so I'm free. Sarah could come with us.'

Poppy's grin reached from ear to ear. 'I'm so glad I have you for a brother, David. You are one little love. I'd miss not going to the Grafton, but I didn't want to go on my own because of Peter and Kate. He'd be bound to ask me to dance, and if I was alone he'd naturally ask me to join them. I don't want to do that; it wouldn't be fair on Kate. But if I'm with my brother and a friend, it would be different. I wouldn't feel awkward. So if David is game, then you can tell Sarah to call for us at half seven.'

'She'll be over the moon, queen, and as soon as I tell her she'll be up those stairs like a shot, to choose which dress she'll wear.'

David grinned. 'How many dresses has Sarah got, Marg? Is she fashion conscious like her mother?'

'Yeah, she's got a lot of clothes has our Sarah. So has Lucy, come to that, but where Sarah is careful with her money and spends it on decent clothes, Lucy is more easy come, easy go. She loves chocolates and thinks nothing of going through a whole box in one night. She takes after Ally. He's got a very sweet tooth.'

Marg glanced at the clock on the mantelpiece and stood up so quickly she knocked the chair flying. 'Oh, my God, look at the time! I told Ally I wouldn't be long.' She picked up the chair and pushed it under the table. 'It's all your fault, yer know. Yer keep yapping away and I can't get a word in edgeways.'

'You cheeky beggar!' Eva said. 'I don't think I've been able to get half a dozen words in since you've been here!'

'Oh, I'm not blaming you, queen, and I'll tell my Ally that. It's Poppy what's done all the talking. What with her love life, and packing in her job, well, I don't know about me writing a book, she could sell her story to the *News of the World* and make a fortune. She'd have to spice it up, like, but she'd never have to worry about working again.' Marg forgot she was in a hurry as her imagination took over. 'I can see the headline now, on the front page in large letters. Wealthy Boss Has Wicked Way With Typist. You'd coin the money in, queen.'

'Marg, have you forgotten yer've got a home to go to?' Eva kept her face straight. 'And a family who will be expecting a roast dinner.'

'Oh, the dinner won't take me long, queen, 'cos I put the meat in the oven before I came here. And the veg are all washed and in the pan, ready to put a light under.'

'Marg Boden, you've got a skin as thick as an elephant. I'd call yer every name under the sun for holding me back with our dinner, if only I could bring meself to swear.'

On her way to the door, Marg turned. 'Seeing as ye're me mate, I'll swear for yer.' Stomping a foot, she snarled, 'Damn, blast and bugger the bleeding woman.' Then, all smiles, she asked, 'Now don't yer feel better getting that off yer chest, queen? I always say a good swear is better than giving someone a black eye.'

'I've got to my age without swearing or giving anyone a black eye, sweetheart,' Eva said. 'And I can't see me changing now. But if I ever catch one of me fingers in the mangle, or bang me head on the mantelpiece, then I'll give yer a knock on the wall and you can swear for me.'

'Will do, queen, will do.' Marg waved a hand over her head as she made for the front door. 'See yer tomorrow, queen.'

David came back into the living room after seeing their neighbour out. 'She's hilarious. Never lost for words. There were a few times there I wanted to breathe for her, 'cos she went on non-stop.'

'She can be serious when she needs to be,' Eva said, her head nodding in agreement with her words. 'There's a couple of elderly people in this street who have good reason to be grateful to Marg. If it's snowing or raining, she gives them a knock and gets their messages for them. And if they're not well she'll send for the doctor, or sit with them herself until they're better. Not many people see that side of Marg, because she never lets on. She's kind and thoughtful, and one of the best friends anyone could have.'

Poppy was nodding now. 'We've also got good reason to be grateful to her. She's always been there for us, hasn't she, Mam?'

'Yes, she has, sweetheart. When I had to go out to work after yer dad died, she was the one waiting for yer to come home from school, with a hot cup of tea ready to warm you up. I could never have managed without her. I couldn't have kept this house on, not without her help.'

'I know, Mam, and we'll make it up to her. Let her see how we've never forgotten her kindness,' Poppy said. 'When we're all settled, with me in a new job, we'll do something nice for Marg. I don't know what, but we'll think of something to surprise her.'

David was nodding. 'Very good idea, sis. When we're in the money, we could buy her a watch, or a necklace. Or take her to the Adelphi for dinner. She'd like that best, I think. She loves getting dolled up, so she'd love the Adelphi.'

Eva gave a low cough. 'Excuse me, but aren't you forgetting something? Just before Marg came, you were all set on buying a television when we'd saved enough money. Now you're talking of saving for a watch for our neighbour or a posh meal at the Adelphi! Before you make any plans, I suggest we forget all about a television, and a thank you present for Marg, until we're financially settled. Don't you agree?'

David and Poppy looked at each other and nodded. 'We got carried away there, Mam,' Poppy said, 'spending money we haven't got. But it was nice while it lasted.'

'We had good intentions,' David said. 'And it doesn't mean we have to forget the television, or Marg! Thinking of them will give us something to look forward to.'

'I get my reference from Mr Jones tomorrow night, so keep your fingers crossed it will be a good one. I'll start looking around in earnest once I've got that in my hand. And I've made up my mind that I'm going to ask Mr John for a reference as well. I don't think he'll refuse, because by Monday I'd like to bet any money he will have been ticked off by his father. I've worked there for over three years, never a day off, so I can't see how he can refuse to give me a decent reference. Then I'll have two to show any firm I apply to for a job.'

David patted her on the back. 'Well said, our kid. I'm proud of you.'

'I wish you all the luck in the world, sweetheart,' Eva said, 'both in your working life and in your love life. But don't worry over things that are not worth worrying about. The world isn't going to come to an end if yer don't get a job straight away. I know you have your pride and want to pull your weight in the house, but if me and David don't worry why should you? You'll find a job, maybe not as soon as you'd like, but it will happen. And when it does, we can start talking about what we're going to buy, and when we'll be taking Marg for the posh meal you mentioned. All it takes is patience, and my ma used to tell me that patience always pays off.'

Poppy jumped to her feet. 'Okay, Mam. Now let me help you get the dinner ready. You see to the beef, and I'll do the veg and potatoes. Then when it's on the go, we'll sit down while my dear brother makes us a cup of tea.'

'Ay, watch it, sis. You'd better be nice to me if you want me to take you to the dance on Tuesday.'

'I'm going to be very nice to you, David, in case you change your mind. In fact I'm going to give you one of my roast potatoes in appreciation.'

'A big one, sis?'

Poppy nodded. 'A big, golden, crispy one. And that is worth a slow foxtrot of anyone's money.'

Poppy couldn't help being apprehensive when she arrived at the office on the Monday morning. She'd told her mother she wasn't the least bit worried, but that had been bravado. It was easy to appear laid back with a piece of toast in your hand, and a cup of tea in front of you. But waiting by the entrance for Jean to arrive was nerve-racking. Several women from offices in the same block had stopped to ask if what they'd heard on Friday was true, and were sympathetic when told it was. One or two said they weren't surprised because Mr John was known to be a bully.

Jean came hurrying up, her face red with the exertion of walking very fast. 'I'm sorry I'm a few minutes late, Poppy, but the bus was full and had to stop at every stop.'

'You can tell me later. Let's get in. We don't want to give Mr John an excuse to contradict what we told personnel.'

The two women were in for a shock, though, for by nine thirty Mr John had not put in an appearance. Poppy got on dealing with the mail as usual, and typed a few letters, but still no sign of their boss. There was nothing else for her to do, or Jean, until clients' letters had been seen by Mr John, and answers to them dictated to Jean. This left the two women doing jobs that really didn't need doing, like making sure the files in the filing cabinets were in order. Which they were, for that was one of Poppy's responsibilities.

'I wonder where he is?' Jean said in a whisper. 'Perhaps he's not well, or he's had an accident.'

'That would be too much of a coincidence, Jean,' Poppy said. 'There's more to it than that, I'll bet. And I definitely think it has something to do with what happened on Friday. But I'm surprised that no one has come to tell us what is going on.'

Just at that moment the office door opened and a strange man came into the room. He was tall and middle-aged, with a receding hairline and a healthy complexion. The two women had seen him many times in the building, but didn't know who he was.

'Good morning, ladies. My name is Cecil Hammond and I work upstairs with Mr Sutherland Senior. He has asked if you would be kind enough to go to his office, and I am to take you. I believe you are Miss Slater and Miss Meadows?'

Poppy nodded, for Jean was looking uncomfortable. 'I'm Miss Meadows, and my colleague is Miss Slater. Can you tell us why Mr Sutherland wants to see us? Is Mr John not well?'

Mr Hammond waved them to the door. 'I will leave it to Mr Sutherland Senior to explain why he wishes to see you. Please follow me.'

The two women didn't speak as they walked up the stone steps to the floor above. They passed the first door, then Mr Hammond opened the second door with a flourish. 'Miss Slater and Miss Meadows, Mr Sutherland.'

The man seated behind the desk left his chair and walked towards them with hand outstretched. He looked to be in his sixties, with white hair, medium build and rounded shoulders. After shaking hands, he pointed to the two chairs set down to face him across the desk. 'Take a seat, please, ladies.'

When the women were seated, Mr Sutherland leaned his two elbows on the desk and made a temple of his fingers. 'I was given some unsettling news on Friday from the Personnel office. Two members of staff, both working in my son's office, had handed in their notice. The reasons I was given for this were garbled, and I would like to hear from the two members of staff involved what their reasons were for wanting to leave the firm. You have nothing to fear, I can assure you, but I really would like the truth. It is my firm, and I am therefore responsible for what happens to members of my staff. So, please, what is the real reason you have decided you no longer wish to work here?'

The two women exchanged glances, and Poppy saw that Jean was a bag of nerves. 'I will tell you, Mr Sutherland, and Miss Slater can interrupt if I miss anything out, or if she doesn't agree with any part of my version.'

Poppy started from the time she walked into the office on

the Friday morning, and told him everything. She saw Mr Sutherland slowly shaking his head, and there seemed to be sadness mixed with his bewilderment. Poppy felt sorry for him, but he had every right to know what was going on in what he called his firm. 'Miss Slater has been subjected to Mr John's temper and rudeness for the many years she's worked here, and I too have had reason to dislike much of his attitude. But I'm not as shy or gentle as Miss Slater, and I put up with it because I needed the job. However, I would never have tolerated the temper and bad language that my colleague had to suffer. And last Friday was the last straw. When Miss Slater told Mr John she was handing her notice in because she'd been offered a job elsewhere, with better conditions and a higher salary, he went crazy. I was in my own office and as I did every other morning I wondered how she could stand there and have insults hurled at her. Then he criticized her looks and her ability, and I couldn't sit and listen to a lady . . . and Miss Slater is a lady . . . being insulted. So I went in for her sake, really, and he bawled at me to get out. So I decided I'd leave when Jean leaves.' Poppy heaved a sigh. 'And that is it, Mr Sutherland, but you can ask Miss Slater for her version if you wish.'

'No, I've heard enough, and I can't tell you how sorry I am. An apology isn't enough for what you have suffered, especially Miss Slater, so I would very much like you both to withdraw your resignation. I can assure you there would be no repeat of the harsh treatment you were made to undergo.'

For the first time, Jean spoke. 'Oh, I'm sorry, but I have been offered a job elsewhere, and I start next Monday. I couldn't back out of the agreement now, not after my new employer was kind enough to take me on.'

'Then I can only apologize once again,' Mr Sutherland said, 'and wish you well in your new job.' He looked at Poppy.

'What about you, Miss Meadows? Can I coax you to stay on?'

Poppy didn't have to consider the offer, for she was quite sure she didn't want to come back into this building after Friday. She'd never been happy here. But she did have some sympathy for Mr Sutherland. He couldn't be held responsible for his son's actions. 'I'm sorry, Mr Sutherland, I had already made up my mind to move on. But I do appreciate your kind offer. Miss Slater and I are sorry you have become involved in a situation which must be upsetting for you.'

The two women would never know how hurt and disgusted Mr Sutherland had been by his son's behaviour. There had been strong words between father and son, and Mr John had been told to expect a large drop in salary, until he proved himself worthy of his father's trust. And for the foreseeable future a watchful eye would be kept on him.

'I wish both of you well, and hope you will be happy in whatever position you take.' He shook hands with both women. 'Mr Hammond will be taking over my son's office for the rest of this week, and I would be grateful if you would help him familiarize himself with the daily routine, and also our valuable clients. I am sure with your help the office will work as normal and none of our clients' business need be disrupted.' He waved a hand towards the door. 'I'm sure you will get on well together, for Mr Hammond is an old friend and colleague.'

When the two women returned to their office, Mr Hammond asked if Jean would acquaint him with the filing system. But Jean suggested it would be better to sort the post so the day to day running of the office would continue as usual. It was a priority to answer the day's correspondence, and they should start immediately so that the letters could catch the post that afternoon. She retired, with Mr Hammond, to Mr John's office, where she read each letter out to him and suggested what the reply should be. Having worked for years with the same clients, she knew their business inside out. Mr Hammond was amazed at her efficiency, and was quite happy for her to take over the day's work. Tomorrow he would start asking questions, but today he'd leave it to the two capable members of staff to get the office back on track.

The two women worked as a team, with Jean typing replies, and Poppy addressing the envelopes ready for posting that day. They wouldn't catch the lunchtime post, but the four o'clock collection would see them arriving at their destination the next morning.

'I've got two letters for Mr Fortune's office, Jean,' Poppy told her. 'Shall I run up with them now?'

Jean, her fingers flying over the keys, nodded. 'We're late for dinner, you know. It's half past one.'

'We can go out when I come back from Fortune's. The café is open all afternoon, thank goodness, 'cos I'm feeling peckish now.' Poppy slipped her coat on and picked up the letters. 'I'll be as quick as I can.' Once outside the building, she didn't dawdle. She took to her heels and walked as fast as her legs would carry her. When she reached her destination she was out of breath, and her eyes went to the ceiling when she passed the two letters over to Amy. 'It's hectic in our office, Amy, so would you take those up to Mr Simon right away, and ask if there's any reply?'

'Why, what's the panic?' Amy was disappointed. She'd been hoping for a chinwag to brighten up her day. 'Someone ill, or what?'

'Mr John didn't come in. He's got a cold, apparently,' Poppy lied. Amy loved listening to gossip and passing it on to all and sundry. If Poppy told her the truth, it would be round every office in Liverpool before the day was out. 'Me and Jean are running the office, and we're rushed off our feet. We haven't even had a dinner break yet, and I'm starving. So be an angel and see if you can get a quick answer from Mr Simon. If I don't get a drink or something to eat soon, I'll be passing out.'

'I'll try, seeing as it's you. Lean on the counter for support, 'cos I don't want to come back and find you passed out on the floor.'

Five minutes later Amy came back to say there was no reply. After thanking her profusely, Poppy set off back to Sutherland's and Jean. And it was a different Jean from the one she'd worked with for nearly four years. Allowed to work as she wanted to, without fear of being shouted at, the new Jean was confident and efficient. The change in her was unbelievable, and Poppy was full of praise for her. 'You could run this office on your own, Jean, as long as you had someone like me to help out. You'd leave Mr John standing. In fact you've been doing his job for years.'

'Thank you, Poppy. I've got to say I've enjoyed this morning, doing what I know needed doing, without someone bawling at me. If he were to walk in now, I wouldn't take orders from him. And Mr Hammond said I've done remarkably well. He's going to get more involved tomorrow, when we're back to normal.'

'Jean, will you shut up now, please, and let's go for something to eat. I'm absolutely starving! Put your coat on and let's go. Never mind straightening the papers and putting the cover on the typewriter. I warn you, I'm in danger of dying of starvation any minute.'

Feeling ten years younger, and lighter in heart, Jean linked arms as they walked out of the office door. 'Poppy Meadows, you don't half exaggerate.'

Chapter Twenty-Four

Poppy stood in the corridor of the school waiting for the lesson to be over. She could see through the glass that the pupils were closing their books and putting them in briefcases or handbags Tonight was the last night of the course, and all the pupils would be getting a reference from Mr Jones, the teacher. Poppy couldn't wait to get hers. But she couldn't just barge in and expect him to hand over her reference before the other pupils. So she waited, and as she watched she noticed such a difference in the atmosphere, she could almost feel it from where she stood. There were smiles on all the faces, and she could hear the good-natured banter. The ordeal was over now, and each one of the people in that room would be receiving a reference to say they had passed the course and could add shorthand to their list of qualifications when applying for a job.

While Poppy's main objective in coming tonight had been to pick up her reference, she did have another reason. She wanted to say goodbye to Joy and Jane, who had befriended her when she was feeling lonely, having joined the course when it was in its third week. They'd been really good to her, walking her to the bus stop and waiting with her to see she got on safely. She would have been lost without them.

Then Poppy saw some of the men and women walking towards Mr Jones's desk, so she pushed the door open, smiled as she passed him, and made her way to where her two friends were sitting.

'We were just talking about you,' Jane said. 'It's a wonder yer ears weren't burning.'

Joy chuckled. 'Why don't yer tell her the truth! We were calling yer all the lousy beggars going for not coming to see us to say goodbye.'

'I've been standing in the corridor for ages,' Poppy told them. 'I didn't like coming in until the lesson was over. You might have known I wouldn't miss seeing you for the last time. You've been good mates, and I don't forget people who have been good to me.'

'Ah, you're making me feel sad,' Joy said. 'We'll walk yer to the bus stop tonight for the last time.'

'Oh, dear, dear, dear,' Jane tutted. 'I hope you've got a hanky with yer, Joy, 'cos I can't stand people who use the back of their hand. Dirty beggars.'

'You'll soon cheer up when you read the good reference Mr Jones has for you,' Poppy said. 'You'll be walking tall with your shoulders straight and your head held high.'

Jane pulled a face. 'Didn't you hear him say none of the envelopes are to be opened in the school?'

'No!' Poppy shook her head. 'Why can't we open them?'

Joy piped up. 'I can understand why he's said that. Think of all the commotion if someone didn't get as good a mark as they were expecting, and the person next to them got good marks and started bragging. It would cause mayhem! I know I'll be mad if you get higher marks than me.'

Poppy agreed. 'I can just see this room looking like a battlefield. That wouldn't happen, I was exaggerating, but some of us might get a big disappointment.' She looked over to the teacher's desk, and there were only about ten people in the queue. 'We may as well join the line. I feel a bit sorry for Mr Jones. He's done his job, and it's not his fault if some of us don't make the grade.'

'Oh, you'll have made the grade, Poppy,' Jane said. 'You're his blue-eyed girl.'

'Listen, Jane, if I get a good reference I'll have deserved it. Ever since the first night I came here, I've spent all my spare time working on it. At least two hours every day, and all day Saturday and Sunday. I've worked ruddy hard and expect a good report.'

'I was only joking,' Jane told her. 'Don't be getting in a twist.'

'Some things are not funny, Jane,' Joy said, 'and that wasn't funny. I'm fed up telling you to think before you open your mouth.'

'Oh, for heaven's sake, don't let's fall out,' Poppy said. 'We've been good friends and I'd like to remember you as friends, and not scratching each other's eyes out.'

'Me and Jane are always arguing,' Joy said, smiling. 'If we didn't have a row every night, we'd think we were sickening for something. We never carry it over to the next day, though, because neither of us can remember what the argument was over.'

'We can remember what it wasn't about,' Jane said. 'And that's a feller, because we haven't got one. We are doomed to be old maids.'

'Don't be daft,' Poppy said. 'Anyone listening to you would think you were ancient. I've told you if yer went dancing you'd soon meet some nice blokes.' She noticed there were only three people at Mr Jones's desk. 'Come on, there's only three there now, let's get our results before the caretaker comes to lock up. And I'm not opening the envelope until I get home. My mam will have the kettle on the boil, and I'll sit by the fire with a cup of tea and read what fate has in store for me.'

Mr Jones looked over his glasses and smiled. 'Good evening to you, ladies. I hope you have found the course rewarding, and that it will help you in your careers.' He handed each of them a sealed envelope. 'There will be another four-month course starting in late autumn if you feel you would benefit from a refresher course. Not that I think you'll need it, ladies. I'm quite sure you are all capable of moving onwards and upwards. I wish you the best of luck for the future.'

Outside the gates of the school the three women stood holding the envelopes in their hands. 'I've a good mind to open mine now,' Jane said. 'I can't wait until I get home. I haven't got the patience.'

'Well, if you do, don't you dare read it out loud, or I'll clock you one,' Joy told her. 'Keep it to yerself because I don't want to know, not before I know how I've got on myself.'

'Me neither.' Poppy opened her handbag and slipped the envelope inside. 'When I do open it, I'll either jump for joy, or cry my eyes out. And I don't intend doing either in the main road with people going past.'

'Mine's going in my bag as well.' Joy's bag wasn't very big, so she had to fold the envelope. Then she began to chuckle. 'I'm just thinking. I wonder if I'll sleep better if I read the report before I go to bed, or whether I'd sleep better not knowing?'

'You'd get no sleep at all if you don't open it, soft girl,' Jane said. 'At least if you open it you've got a fifty per cent chance of sleeping, and a fifty per cent chance of being awake all night. So, like the saying goes, yer pays yer money and yer takes yer chance.'

'Make up your mind on the way to the bus stop.' Poppy slipped in between the two friends and linked their arms. 'And as it's the last time you'll be escorting me, let us part on a happy note, with smiles on our faces. For my part it's been a pleasure knowing you, and I wish you well in the future. And just for interest, if you ever do decide to take up dancing, I go to the Grafton at least two or three times a week. It would be a lovely surprise to see you there.'

'I've been trying to talk Jane into going to that Millington's place you told us about, but it's like talking to meself. I've mentioned it to a few people at work, and apparently Connie Millington is very well known. One of me workmates said if Connie Millington can't make a dancer out of yer, then there's no use in trying.'

They were at the bus stop now, and Poppy could see a bus in the distance coming towards them. 'Here's my bus coming, so I'll say my farewell.' She hugged and kissed both women. 'Take care of yourselves and never fall out. You've got a good friendship going, so don't ever let anything come between you.'

The bus came to a stop and Poppy hopped on board. 'Thanks again for looking after me. Ta-ra.' The bus started up and she stood on the platform waving until the two friends were out of sight. Then she took a seat, patted her handbag, and hoped the reference inside was good enough for her to start applying for a post as a private secretary. And until the bus reached the end of her journey, she kept her fingers crossed.

Eva opened the door to Poppy with expectation on her face. 'Well, sweetheart, how did it go? Did you get the reference yer were hoping for?'

Poppy kissed her mother's cheek as she passed. 'I don't

know, Mam. I haven't opened it yet.' She slipped her coat off and draped it over the arm of the couch. 'None of the pupils were allowed to open their envelopes in the classroom, which surprised me at first. Then I realized the school had to be locked up at a certain time, and if we were allowed to open our envelopes, we'd have stood around talking and the caretaker wouldn't have been able to lock up.'

'I've been on pins, waiting for yer.' Eva walked through to the kitchen. 'Kettle is on the boil, so tea will be up in a jiffy.' She popped her head into the living room to ask, 'Have you really not opened it up, then, sweetheart? I'd have thought you'd be really eager.'

David came bounding down the stairs. 'Well, how did you get on, sis?' He looked at her closely. 'I can't tell anything from your face. Come on, put me out of the suspense I've been in for the last hour.'

Poppy opened her handbag and took out the envelope, which she handed over to her brother. 'When our mam comes in, you can read what is written in there. If I read it out loud myself, I'll probably end up crying and make a fool of myself. So you can read it, and I'll know by the expression on your face whether I've passed with flying colours, or failed miserably.'

Eva bustled in. 'We'll have the tea in a few minutes. I'll let it brew for a while.' She pulled a chair out and sat down. 'I don't care who does what, but for heaven's sake get a move on. It won't be disappointing, I'm sure of that, but I'd like to know how good it is. The teacher said yer'd done well, sweetheart, and you've plodded on with homework when yer could have been out enjoying yerself, so let's hope you can now reap the benefits. Open the envelope, David, and be quick about it.'

David ran a finger under the seal and took out a letter-headed sheet of paper. He winked at his sister before lowering his eyes to the paper. Poppy and her mother could see his eyes moving along the lines, but could tell nothing from his expression.

It was only a matter of seconds, but to Poppy it seemed an eternity. She'd been so sure of herself over the last few weeks, but now she wasn't sure.

David didn't look up, or say a word. Then when he'd finished reading, he folded the sheet of paper and passed it over to his sister. His face expressionless, and his voice matter of fact, he said, 'Miss Meadows, if anyone came to me with this reference I would take them on immediately.' His face alive now, he told her, 'Poppy, that is a very glowing reference, and I am so proud of you.'

Poppy's laughter was mixed with tears of joy. 'Mam, can you pour the tea now, while I read what Mr Jones has said about me? Then you can read it and tell me what a clever daughter you've got.'

Poppy read that Mr Jones had no hesitation in recommending Miss Poppy Meadows to any employer who was seeking an employee who was capable, diligent, pleasant, and had all the qualities required of a private secretary. There was more about her speed at typing and shorthand, but Poppy couldn't take it all in at once, and passed it over to her mother to read while she sipped the hot tea, and hugged herself mentally.

'That's wonderful, sweetheart,' Eva said. 'And I am very proud of my clever daughter.'

'I've been going through the *Echo*,' David told her. He was so happy he felt as though he was the one who had achieved what his sister had. 'I couldn't see anything for a private secretary in the jobs vacant section, but they must come up some time. Now you've got that excellent reference, you can afford to be patient.'

'You know I'm not the most patient person in the world, David, so I won't be sitting on my bottom hoping that one night, perhaps in six months' time, there'll be an advert in the *Echo*!' Poppy was feeling a warm glow inside. She was now nearer to getting a decent job than she'd ever been. 'No, once this week is over, and I'm away from Sutherland's, I'll be active in looking for work. I can't just sit around and wait.'

Eva looked across at her son. 'Tell her you've got a little surprise for her, son, and make it two lots of good news she'll have had in one day.'

'Oh, you've been promoted!' Poppy said. 'That is good news.'

'That's not it, clever clogs,' David told her. 'Although that should happen within the next two weeks, I'm glad to say. No, what Mam is talking about involves not just me, but her as well. It's something we decided weeks ago, but we thought we'd leave telling you until you'd finished the shorthand course. You've been so good at sticking at it, which we never thought you would, that we planned to give you a little treat.'

'You shouldn't be talking about treating me! If I'm out of work for a long time, you might have to keep me! I told you I won't be entitled to any dole money.'

'And we've told you not to worry, sweetheart,' Eva told her. 'Me and David bring enough in between us to keep the house going. The treat was your brother's idea, so I can't take praise for that, but I have helped a little with money.'

Poppy's wide eyes went from one to the other. 'Now you've got me curious. A treat could be anything from a slab of chocolate to second house at the pictures. And I wouldn't say no to either of them if the chocolates are Cadbury's and Tyrone Power is in the film.'

'Ah, I'm sorry to disappoint you, our kid, but we never thought of those when we were trying to decide what you would like.' David pulled a face. 'Sorry about that, but me and our mam thought you'd be more likely to appreciate a new dress for when you go for an interview.'

Poppy was silent for a while, then she said softly, 'I couldn't let you buy me a dress. At my age, I should be capable of buying my own clothes. I love you to bits, both of you, for thinking of me, but I couldn't let you buy me a dress.'

'Oh, not just one dress, sweetheart, but two dresses!' Eva smiled at the wide-eyed surprise on the face of her beautiful daughter. 'One from me, and one from David. You'll need to look smart when you do go for an interview, and knowing you look the part will give you more confidence.'

'I don't know what to say.' Poppy was feeling very emotional. 'I could do with a decent dress, because the two I possess I wear for work and for going dancing. So I'll be more than grateful to accept your treat.'

'The envelope is in the drawer, David,' Eva said. 'Would you get it out and give it to Poppy, please? She might just see something she likes in her dinner hour tomorrow.'

When Poppy opened the envelope, there were four one-pound notes inside. 'I feel terrible taking money off you, but I know I need decent clothes. My coat will last me until the beginning of next winter, when I'm hoping to be in a position to buy myself another. However, I do need a couple of smart dresses if I'm to impress any likely employer. But I'm taking this money on the understanding that I pay you back when I get myself a job.'

'We'll discuss that some other time,' Eva said. 'Right now you need to have clothes fit for attending interviews. And the place I'd start looking, if I were you, is the shop where we bought our coats. The lady had two rails of dresses in the back room, and you have to admit she is very reasonable. You could nip up there tomorrow in your lunch hour.'

'Ooh, I don't know about that, Mam, 'cos I always go to the café with Jean. Besides, the office is upside down at the moment, with Mr Hammond having to learn so much.'

'I'm sure Jean wouldn't object to you going on a message, sweetheart. It would be mean of her if she did, because she's got a new job to start on Monday.'

'I was just thinking Jean might not get a full hour for her lunch, anyway. I know if Mr Hammond needs her, then she'll stay. She is very conscientious; she'd skip lunch to help out. So I might just get a chance to run up to that shop.' Poppy was feeling good, and very lucky. 'Well, all things considered, it's been a pretty good day all round for me. Let's hope my luck continues.'

'It will, sweetheart, you'll see,' Eva said. 'Don't forget, Rome wasn't built in a day.'

'Our Poppy's very late. I'm getting really worried about her.' Eva paced up and down the living room, clasping and unclasping her hands. 'She should have been in half an hour ago. Something must have happened to her.'

'Mam, will you stop worrying,' David said. 'You're going to turn me into a nervous wreck.'

'I worry about her every time she goes out,' Eva admitted. 'Ever since that night she got attacked.'

At that moment a knock came on the door, and David was off his chair like a streak of lightning. When he opened the door, his mother was at his heels. 'Where the heck have you been, Poppy? Our mam's been out of her mind.'

Poppy lifted the bags she was carrying, and squeezed past. 'Give me a chance to get in,' she said, 'and I'll tell you why I'm later than usual.'

Eva nearly tripped over her daughter's feet in her haste to get into the light to make sure Poppy was not hurt in any way. And no matter what David said, she would always worry about Poppy. Wait until he got married and had a daughter himself, then he'd understand that mothers always worried about their daughters more than they did about their sons.

'Oh, Mam, it's been a really lucky day for me.' Poppy's face was aglow. 'I'm sorry you've been worried, but I'm only a bit late.' She put two bags on the couch. 'Just wait until you see what's in those bags. I can't believe how lucky I've been in the last twenty-four hours. The good reference I got from Mr Jones, you and David giving me money to make myself look presentable, and wait until you see what I got for that money. I feel like pinching myself to make sure I'm not dreaming.'

'Can we have our meal before you show us your dresses, sweetheart? Me and David kept the dinner back waiting for you. We're hungry, and anyway, the meal will be burnt to a crisp if I don't take it out of the oven soon.'

'I can wait, Mam, even though I'm so happy I'd sing you a song, if I could sing. Go on, I'll give you a hand putting the dinner out. But we've all got to eat at double quick time. I can't sit still while those bags are unopened.'

The dinner was sausage and mash, and David helped to carry the plates in. 'You haven't forgotten we're going to the Grafton with Sarah, have you?'

'Of course I haven't! It's been a rare old day for me, one

way and another, but I haven't forgotten the Grafton. I might even wear one of the new dresses. That's if you don't mind?'

David raised his brows. 'Why should we mind? I can't wait to see what there is about them to make you so happy.'

'Then hurry and eat up,' Poppy told him with a chuckle. 'Ay, remember when we were kids, and we used to say that the last one to finish their dinner had to help Mam with the dishes?'

Like someone switching on the electric light, a picture came into David's head, and as clear as day he could see himself and Poppy facing each other across the table. She was laughing and waving a fork at him, telling him he was a slowcoach and would have to help Mam with the dishes.

'You were a bossyboots then and you still are, Poppy Meadows. Heaven help the poor bloke who marries you. I'll have to have a word with him before the wedding, to make sure he knows what he's letting himself in for.'

'You'll be married before me, brother, but I'll not be having a word with your intended. She won't need me to tell her she's getting a good deal when she gets you.'

'What makes you think I'll be married before you? I haven't even got a girlfriend yet.' David pushed his empty plate out of the way. 'Mind you, you must admit she'll be someone with good taste. And according to my boss, I'll be a man of means by that time.'

Eva collected the plates, saying, 'Don't count your chickens before they hatch, son, but it does look as though the Meadows family are going up in the world. I can see meself bragging about my son, who is a boss in his place of work, and my daughter the private secretary. I can just see Marg's face if she heard me saying that. "Getting above yer bleeding self, Eva

Meadows. Don't forget I knew yer when yer had sweet bugger all. So don't be coming over all posh with me."'

Poppy and David roared with laughter. 'Oh, Mam,' Poppy said, 'you sounded just like Marg.'

'I'm going to tell her what you said,' David grinned, 'and I'll add that we don't like bad language in this house.'

Eva carried the plates out to the kitchen, saying over her shoulder, 'I wouldn't bother if I were you. She'll only tell you to sod off.'

Poppy jerked her head sideways. 'Let's give Mam a hand, or we'll not be ready when Sarah comes. I'll help with the dishes if you'll shake the tablecloth in the yard and put the chenille one on. Then if you intend getting shaved do it after you've cleared in here. I'll get washed and clean my teeth in the kitchen, to save time, and then I want to show you and Mam the dresses.'

David stood to attention, clicked his heels and saluted. 'Yes, sir, three bags full, sir.'

Poppy rounded the table and threw her arms round his neck. 'If you weren't my brother, I'd marry you. If I can find someone like you, I'll consider myself the luckiest girl in the world.'

'You will, Poppy. It's just a case of waiting for the right one. It could happen tomorrow, or in a year's time. Cupid is very busy, but he'll get round to both of us eventually.'

Eva came to the door of the kitchen, holding her wet hands in front of her. 'I thought you two were in a hurry? Sarah will be here before we have a chance to see those new dresses. So will you get a move on, please?'

Poppy hurried out to help dry the dishes and put them away, while David joined the four corners of the tablecloth together and took it into the yard to shake the crumbs off.

Then it was all systems go, and in twenty minutes the room was tidy and Eva and David were sitting on the couch waiting for Poppy to come out of the front sitting room wearing one of her new dresses. And their wait was worth it. For the dress, in a medium beige, fitted her perfectly, and the colour set off the gold of her hair.

'Oh, sweetheart, it looks a treat on you. It fits perfect, as though you'd had it tailor made.'

David nodded. How proud he was of his beautiful sister. In his eyes, she knocked every film star into a cocked hat. Her figure was perfect, and the dress showed it off. 'You'll have every bloke in the Grafton after you tonight, and every girl green with envy.'

'Both dresses are quite plain,' Poppy told them. 'I had to remember they were to wear for going to job interviews, not to a dance. But they'll do for both, really, don't you think?'

'We haven't seen the other one, sweetheart, so we can't really say. That one looks lovely on you. It's very smart, and attractive. But let's see the other one, and we'll choose what you should wear tonight. That's only fair, isn't it, son?'

'I should be the one to choose,' David said, giving his mother a sly wink. 'Seeing as I'm the one taking her to the dance. But your opinion will be taken into account.'

Poppy disappeared to the sitting room, and mother and son spoke in whispers. 'Your sister is so beautiful, son. I just wish your dad could see her, and you. He would be so proud of you both.'

'Mam, you have always told us that when people die and go to heaven, well, only their body dies, not their soul. So you should know that our dad is looking down on us all the time, and he'll know that you are the one who has made me and Poppy what we are. Not in looks, because looks are not everything. Nice to have, but not the be all and end all. It's what's inside that counts.'

Poppy interrupted David's outlook on life by entering the room wearing a dress in a deep maroon colour, quite plain like the beige one, but fitting Poppy's figure like a glove. It had long sleeves and a fitted waist, and where the beige one had a round collar, the neck on the maroon one was square, without a collar, but with rows of stitching to set it off.

'That's the one to wear tonight, Poppy,' David said, nodding for emphasis. 'Don't bother taking it off. You look lovely in it. Don't you agree, Mam? The colour is perfect, and gives her a warm glow.'

'I agree she suits it, and the dress suits her. That is the most poetical I can get.' Eva smiled at her daughter. 'Turn round, sweetheart, and let's see it from the back.' She nodded. 'The calf length is just right for dancing, and also reserved enough to face a potential boss.' She chuckled. 'If he's young, and has got any sense, he'll offer you his hand in marriage, as well as a job.'

'I'll leave this on then,' Poppy said, 'seeing as you both approve. I'll take the other one upstairs to put on a hanger, and I'll put some make-up on while I'm up there. I'll be as quick as I can, 'cos Sarah will be knocking any minute.'

In the cloakroom at the Grafton, Sarah gazed in admiration when Poppy took her coat off. 'Ay, that's a smashing dress, Poppy. Is it new?'

'Yes, I only bought it this afternoon. My mam and David treated me. Does it look all right?'

'I'll say! It looks more than all right, it really suits yer.' Sarah put out a hand to feel the material. 'I'll have to get round me mam to treat me.'

'Wouldn't you be better getting round your dad?'

Sarah, who took after her mother in looks, grinned. 'It doesn't work that way in our house, Poppy. Me and our Lucy get round me mam, and she gets round me dad. And it never fails. I think he gives in to her to shut her up. Anything for a quiet life, that's my dad.'

Poppy gave her hair one last comb, then closed her bag. 'I can hear the music and my toes are tingling. Let's go before I do a slow-fox on my own in the cloakroom.'

Poppy was linking Sarah's arm as they walked towards the dance hall, but she stopped in her tracks when she saw Andrew standing by the door. 'What on earth are you doing here, Andrew? Don't tell me that sister of yours has dragged you along again?'

'Yes, Charlotte wanted to come. She's in there now, dancing with your brother. And she didn't have to drag me along. I enjoyed myself last week. My only concern is that we may be imposing on you. Interfering in your life.'

Poppy was grinning. 'So Charlotte is in there dancing with David? She's a little minx, she really is. Full of mischief and fun. But you can't fall out with her – she won't let you. Not that I want to – I'm really very fond of her. Anyway, what are you doing out here? Surely you don't intend to stand here all night?'

'Your friends Peter and Kate are here, and I really don't think I should intrude. I'm a complete stranger to them.'

Poppy pushed Sarah towards the door. 'You go in, Sarah. I'll only be a minute, then I'll introduce you.' When the door had closed on Sarah, Poppy looked up at Andrew. 'Do you want to stand out here all night? Is that what you prefer to do?'

'No, of course not. It's just that I'm not as outgoing as my sister, and not as pushy. I would like to be more like her because she has a lot more fun than I do. But one can't help the way one is made.'

'You can't help it, no, but you can at least try to change it.' Poppy held out her hand. 'Come on, you can dance with me until you see someone you take a fancy to.'

Andrew would have kissed his sister, had she been there. For she had set the wheels in motion for tonight. She even had their father encouraging him to get out and enjoy himself. And he could think of nothing he would enjoy more in the whole world than to have Poppy Meadows in his arms.

'You seem a lot more relaxed now, Andrew. Your dancing is smoother.' Poppy looked up and found him staring down at her with what looked like a half-smile on his face. She caught his eyes and quickly lowered hers, while at the same time asking herself why he had this effect on her. She didn't feel uncomfortable with any other bloke, so why? He had never said anything out of place to her; in fact he was a perfect gentleman. Then in a flash she believed she had the answer to her problem. And it was what had been bothering her since the day he'd knocked her over. He had been wearing a suit and overcoat that she could tell were handmade, while she was wearing a raincoat that had seen better days.

'What are you thinking about, Poppy? You're miles away.' Andrew squeezed her hand. 'I've been talking to you but you don't answer.'

Poppy pulled herself together. 'I'm sorry. I had something on my mind and didn't hear you. What were you saying?'

'It's too late now,' Andrew told her. 'Charlotte has been waving to you, trying to catch your attention, but her dance is over now, so she can tell you herself what she wanted you for.'

He hesitated. 'Do you mind my standing with your friends? My sister has taken a liking to your brother – they both enjoy telling and playing jokes. I'm not like Charlotte, I'm not good with strangers. I never know what to say. I'll look stupid standing on my own, so may I join you?'

'Of course you can! You don't have to ask.' In her head she was reminding herself of what her mother once said, that money didn't always bring happiness. 'You know Peter and Kate, and my next-door neighbour, Sarah. Who I see is having a conversation with Jim, who you'll remember from last week. So come on, and don't be shy.'

The next dance was a slow foxtrot, and Jim and Sarah were the first couple on the floor, followed by Charlotte, pulling a laughing David with her. Peter couldn't resist, and asked Andrew if he would partner Kate, just for this dance.

'That's naughty of you, Peter,' Poppy told him as he put his arm round her waist. 'It's an insult to Kate.'

'No it isn't, babe, because I'd already asked her if she'd mind me dancing with you. You said we'd always be friends, and Kate is quite happy about that. And there's nothing wrong with friends dancing together.'

'Have you and Kate made it up then, Peter? Oh, I do hope so, for anyone can see she is very much in love with you.'

'We're getting there, babe, slowly but surely. But you are still my slow foxtrot girl, and always will be. And as I said, there's nothing wrong in dancing with a friend. And talking of friends, where does Andrew fit in? Have you known him long, or is he new on the scene?'

'I've known him roughly as long as I've known you, and his sister, Charlotte. Actually, she is more my friend than he is.'

'Not a very talkative bloke, is he? He hardly says a word unless someone talks to him.'

Poppy found herself coming to Andrew's defence. 'He's probably quiet with strangers, but he talks to me all right, and to David. He hadn't danced for a long time until last week, and he's out of practice. So I'll be having the next slow-fox with him. I promised Charlotte I'd help him get his dancing feet back, 'cos, as she said, being his sister she can't tell him off if he doesn't follow her steps.'

'She seems a nice kid, always laughing. I'd say they come from a wealthy family. They both speak and dress very well.'

'I don't know about that, Peter. I don't even know where they live, though their father's firm is in Castle Street. I know Charlotte through bumping into her one day. Now we often meet up around lunchtime, and she and Jean and I have lunch together. Apart from that I don't know any more about Charlotte and Andrew. Except I get on with them and like them.'

The next dance was a waltz, and Sarah and Jim were once again first on the dance floor. They certainly seemed to have hit it off together. David paired off with Charlotte, and after giving himself a good talking to Andrew plucked up the courage to ask Poppy. He started to apologize for his lack of dancing skill, and she cut him short. 'Andrew, will you stop making apologies for your dancing? And why are you so shy around me? I'm not going to eat you. Why are you so different from your sister, who I get on fine with?'

'I thought you had made it quite clear you didn't wish to know me. Ever since that unfortunate accident, when you flatly refused to let me help, you have made it obvious I am not your favourite person. Several times I've met you in Castle Street and tried to strike up a conversation, and you have refused to even stop and talk to me. I'm not a shy person normally, Poppy, my job wouldn't allow me to be. But I can't get through to you. Even a simple invitation to my office for a cup of tea was turned down. So can you expect me to be anything but shy with you?'

'I fully intend to come to your office for a cup of tea. I promised I would and I don't break a promise. But you know I've been taking lessons in shorthand for nearly three months, and swotting at home for a few hours every day. Then to top everything, as I told you last Friday, I've packed my job in.'

'Yes, I remember. What is happening now?'

'Well, I leave on Friday, then I start job hunting.' Poppy didn't want him to think she was feeling sorry for herself, so she put some enthusiasm in her voice. 'I finished the shorthand course with flying colours, and received a very glowing reference. I am now qualified to apply for a position as a secretary, but I'll be lucky to find someone willing to employ a secretary without any experience.'

Andrew was holding her hand to his chest now, and was wishing the dance would go on for ever, he felt so contented. 'Every secretary had to start at the position you're in now, and they all found jobs. And seeing as we are speaking to each other in a friendly way, would you object to a compliment?'

Poppy chuckled. 'There's not a girl breathing who would object to a compliment.'

'Then may I say you look very beautiful tonight. The dress really suits you.'

'Thank you, Andrew, your compliment is very welcome.' Poppy looked up and saw a look in his eyes that sent a shiver down her spine. She was lost for words, and was glad when the dance came to an end. They were walking off the floor, Andrew with his arm round her waist, when he asked, 'Can we call a truce now, and be friends?'

Oh, dear, Poppy thought, I must be going soppy all of a sudden. 'Okay, truce called, and we are friends.'

Charlotte came to join them, pulling David behind her. 'I haven't had a chance to talk to you, Poppy, because your brother insists on dancing every dance with me.'

David's jaw dropped. 'Aren't you getting your facts mixed up, you little devil? I'm quite worn out, and will be glad when the interval comes.'

'He has no stamina, your brother. He tires very easily.' Charlotte, as always, was smiling and looking very happy. She was really enjoying her newfound freedom. 'You look very nice tonight, Poppy. That is a lovely dress.'

'A present from my mother and brother,' Poppy told her. 'A lovely surprise.'

'I'll be coming to lunch with you and Jean tomorrow,' Charlotte said. 'I'm looking forward to it.'

'Make the most of it, then, for it might not be possible after this Friday. Not for a while, anyway.'

'David has told me all about it, Poppy, and I think you are very brave, and a good friend to Jean. But you won't be out of work for long, and then we can begin our lunch dates again.'

Looking at his sister, Andrew wished he had her ability to talk without having to think first. And right then he decided he'd have to come out of his shell, or lose the girl he had fallen in love with at first sight. So he put his arm across Poppy's shoulder, and told his sister, 'Poppy has promised to come for that tea and cake she keeps putting off. And as she'll be free next week, I think we can coax her to name a day. In fact she'll be job seeking, so she can call in any time for a drink, and to rest her tired feet.'

'I don't know how to start job seeking, as you put it.' Poppy felt quite comfortable with Andrew's arm on her shoulder. In fact she found she liked it. 'But if Charlotte is with me, we'll call into your office. However, finding employment comes before tea and cakes. I need a job for the sake of my pride and independence. And I'm certainly not wasting what it's taken me months to learn. So, all in all, I don't really know what's going to happen in the near future. But I believe we'll all keep in touch somehow.'

Jim came up then, holding Sarah's hand. They both looked happy, and Poppy was glad, for she had a soft spot for Jim, and Sarah was a nice girl who wouldn't let him down.

'You're looking good tonight, Poppy.' Jim always had a cheerful smile on his face. 'The dress looks nice on yer. In fact yer look so good I'm almost afraid to ask yer for a dance.'

'Don't be daft, soft lad. It's not the dress you'd be dancing with, it's an old mate. We'll have the next dance together and everyone can have a change of partner.' Poppy turned her head to where Peter and Kate were standing. They were holding hands and had smiles on their faces as they talked. And seeing them so intimate, Poppy felt happy. Any guilt she felt about Peter disappeared.

'Andrew, would you partner Sarah? I think Peter and Kate would rather stay together.'

The dance was a quickstep, and Jim was in his element. He was a good dancer with a natural rhythm, and easy to follow. 'Sarah seems a nice girl, Poppy,' he said. 'We're getting on well together. Good little dancer, too!'

'She's a lovely girl, Jim. You wouldn't go far wrong with her. Nice family, too! You'd like her mother; she's a born comedienne.'

'D'yer think she'd mind if I asked her for a date? Sarah, I mean, not her mother.'

'No harm in trying, Jim. Tell her I gave you permission to ask. That might help.'

Jim swung her round, as happy and carefree as a bird. 'I'll ask her to come to the flicks one night, and keep me fingers crossed.'

Poppy waited for the next slow foxtrot, and made sure she was near enough to Andrew to say without anyone's hearing, 'Shall we, Andrew?'

He was delighted. They seemed to have made a lot of headway tonight. But there were two things he didn't know. One was that his sister was watching every move, every sign, for she had promised to report back to her father. And second, Poppy wanted to find out whether she really did feel a shiver run down her spine, or was it her imagination? Not that she was really interested, she told herself, she was just curious.

'How do you intend to set about looking for work?' Andrew asked. 'Will you put an advert in a newspaper?'

Poppy gaped. 'Oh, no, I couldn't afford to do that. And I don't think it's a good idea to try and sell oneself. No, I've started to read the vacancy column in the *Echo*, and I'll try asking the Labour Exchange if they know of any jobs going. Not that I think that will do any good, but anything is worth a try.'

'Poppy, can I ask you for a favour?'

'Of course you can, if it's not too personal.' Poppy looked him straight in the eyes, and then it came. A shiver down her spine that she felt sure he must have felt, for he was holding her close. But surely that didn't mean what her mother had told her? She hardly knew him, and they were not suited. They came from different backgrounds. 'What is the favour?'

'Look on me as a friend. I want that very much.'

'Well, I don't consider you an enemy, Andrew, I never have.'

'Then when you're in the city, whether shopping or job hunting, promise you'll call in and see me.'

'I promise. In fact I'll come in one day with Charlotte. I'll make arrangements with her, and she'll let you know which day it'll be. Does that satisfy you?'

'Not completely, Poppy, but it's better than nothing.'

When Andrew and Charlotte arrived home, it was to find their mother had already retired. 'I think I'll go straight up,' Andrew said. 'Are you coming?'

'I'm going to the kitchen for a drink first.' Charlotte didn't think helping her brother could be classed as a lie, so she didn't hesitate to go on. 'I'll boil myself some milk. You go up.' She made her way to the kitchen door but didn't go in. After hearing her brother's footsteps on the stairs, and then the closing of his bedroom door, she did an about-turn and made for her father's study, as arranged.

'Hello, Papa.' She avoided the cigar between his fingers and gave him a hug. Then she sat on the corner of his desk and set her legs swinging. 'A definite improvement tonight, Papa. Andrew has come out of his shell, and he's letting Poppy see he likes her. But I found out from Poppy's brother tonight that she has given her notice in at work, and she's leaving Sutherland's on Friday.'

George frowned. 'Why has she given her notice in? And what difference would it make regarding the situation between her and Andrew? It is all very confusing, my dear. I wonder if you could clear the air for me.'

'Well, from what David told me, Papa, Jean Slater went into John Sutherland's office to hand her notice in, and Poppy could hear him shouting bad things at Jean about her appearance, and he was using bad language and bawling at her. And Poppy couldn't bear to sit there and let Jean, or any woman, be spoken to in such a manner. So she went into John

Sutherland's office to defend Jean, and he screamed at her to get out. So she handed in her notice. Apparently John Sutherland was like a madman.'

'He does have a reputation as a bully, I'm afraid,' George said. 'His father, John Senior, is a member of the club, and you wouldn't meet a nicer person. He's a thorough gentleman, from the top of his head to the tips of his toes.'

'Then aren't you glad you have a son like Andrew, who is gentle and caring.' Charlotte slid off the desk. 'Poppy looked lovely tonight, Papa. She had a nice dress on that really suited her. She's very beautiful, and I do hope she and Andrew continue to become closer.'

'I can't comment on something I know nothing about, dear girl, and sometimes I can't keep up with your devious methods of making things happen. But I can agree on what I have seen with my own eyes. And I agree that Miss Poppy Meadows is a beautiful young lady.'

'She's promised to come with me to Andrew's office for tea and a cake. So would you like me to bring her to your office to say hello?'

'I would like that very much, my dear. And if things continue as you hope, then, in your devious way, you can try to arrange it so your mother can meet her.'

'Oh, I can do most things, Papa, but that is one bit of magic I can't pull off.' She hugged her father and kissed him before walking towards the door. Then with her hand on the knob, she turned. Her eyes filled with devilment, she giggled. 'I will try though, Papa, so listen for the big bang.'

Chapter Twenty-Five

When Poppy and Jean came out of the office building on Friday lunchtime, they were surprised to see Charlotte waiting for them. 'I know you weren't expecting me but I thought I couldn't miss coming for lunch with you today, the last time you'll be coming out of this building and walking to the café.'

'Oh, that was thoughtful of you,' Jean said, feeling like a free spirit for the first time in years. She'd been getting more confident each day, with Mr Hammond praising her efficiency. 'I think that's really sweet of you, don't you agree, Poppy?'

'Yes, it was thoughtful, and it's always nice to see you, Charlotte.' Poppy smiled at the young girl, who seemed to be part of her life now. How it had come about, she couldn't really remember. But she was glad to see her today, which wasn't really a day of rejoicing as far as she was concerned. Jean had reason to be happy as she was starting a new job on Monday. But the thought of being out of work was making Poppy nervous. She hadn't any idea how to go about finding a job.

After sighing inwardly, she told herself she mustn't put a damper on the day by being miserable. It wasn't Jean's fault she had given her notice in, and she mustn't be made to feel guilty. Without her help, Poppy wouldn't be in a position now to apply for a decent job.

Putting a bright smile on her face, Poppy linked arms with her friends. 'Don't let's make it a farewell lunch, eh? We'll meet again very soon. Once I've found myself a job, we can go back to our usual routine. And that is lunch every day at the café.' She chuckled. 'Soup and homemade bread in the winter, and salad or sandwiches in the summer.'

'That would be lovely,' Jean said. 'I don't want to lose touch with you, Poppy, because without your help I wouldn't have a new job to go to. And of course I do hope Charlotte keeps in touch.'

'This is just a thought,' Poppy said, 'but what if our dinner hours don't coincide? I know most offices close from one to two o'clock, but not all of them do.'

'The girls in Papa's office have a flexible lunch hour,' Charlotte told them. 'They take their lunch break to fit in with their work. Except for Papa and Andrew, who usually take their lunch break around two o'clock, or later. And of course they are not tied to time. Sometimes Andrew doesn't bother, if he's busy. He'll have sandwiches sent in.'

As she was pushing the café door open Poppy said, laughingly, 'That was very helpful, Charlotte. You have confused us now. So I think this Monday and Tuesday are out of the question, as I would probably be wasting my time. I'll wait until Charlotte tells me what time you take your break, Jean. Will you be at the Grafton on Tuesday, Charlotte?'

'Oh, yes, I'm really looking forward to it. And David is going as well. At least he promised he would.'

'Then you can tell me what time Jean has her lunch break, and I'll meet her here on Wednesday. Just to find out if she's settled in her new job, and if she likes it And being nosy by nature, I'll want to know about the people she's working with.'

'I'll go to the counter and order,' Jean said. 'I'm not going to ask what you want, because it's our last day and we'll have what we always have.' She took her purse from her pocket. 'This is on me, for you've both been very good friends, and I hope it stays that way.'

Charlotte pulled her chair closer to Poppy's. 'Can I meet you here on Monday, Poppy? I know you'll be wanting to look for a job, but you can spare an hour. I do enjoy being with you, and I'm lost at home. I don't know what to do with myself. So say you'll meet me, and perhaps Jean will be able to come. I could easily find out what her lunchtime is, but I know she wouldn't want me to get involved. I don't want our friendship to change just because of who I am. You wouldn't ever stop being my friend, would you, Poppy? I'd be very sad if I lost you. Heartbroken, in fact.'

Poppy looked into the beautiful face, and found herself being moved by the appeal in the brown eyes as big as saucers. 'You would make a fantastic actress, Charlotte. You have missed your vocation. You've brought tears to my eyes, that's how good you are.' She covered the girl's hand with one of her own. 'Of course I won't stop being your friend. I wouldn't care if you were the Queen, or as poor as a church mouse. I don't choose friends for who they are, Charlotte, I choose them because I like them and enjoy their company. And because we will be there for each other when times are hard. And yes, I will meet you on Monday for lunch, but after that I can't promise when I'll see you again. At the Grafton, of course, because I need some pleasure in life. But not lunch every day, for I need to look for work, and I won't be able to afford it. You can understand that, can't you?'

Charlotte nodded. 'Yes, of course I understand. I'll meet you here on Monday.' Her mind was working overtime, but she couldn't tell Poppy what she was thinking. Her best bet was to have words with Papa tonight. She'd wangle a way to get him into his study, and tell him all the things in her head and her heart. 'I don't think you'll be out of work long, Poppy. There must be plenty of offices looking for someone like you. Beautiful, intelligent, and kind.'

Jean came back carrying a heavily laden tray. 'I told the girl at the counter I'd wait and carry the order myself, but I didn't realize it would be so heavy. Would you take one of the plates off, Poppy, before I drop the lot?'

Poppy jumped to her feet. 'You should have given me a shout, and I'd have lent a hand. It smells good, though. My tummy can smell it too and it's starting to rumble. Mushroom soup is my favourite.'

Once the tray was emptied, Jean breathed a sigh of relief. 'I'll never offer to carry our lunch again. One of the waitresses can bring it.' She stood the empty tray by the leg of the table before looking at Poppy. 'Every soup is your favourite. If it's vegetable, onion, tomato or mushroom, you always say it's your favourite.'

'Well, it is on that particular day! As my mam always says, hunger is good sauce. Everything tastes good when you're hungry.'

'I'd like to meet your mother, Poppy,' Charlotte said. 'She sounds nice.'

'She's more than nice, she's lovely, and I love the bones of her. I was only nine when my dad died, and David was twelve, I think. So my mam had to be mother and father to us. She had a hard time, looking after us and working full time as well. We'd do anything for her, David and I, because, when money was scarce, there was always love and laughter to keep us warm.'

Charlotte was very moved. She'd never known what it was like to be cold and hungry, but she was learning that not everyone had the advantages that she had. 'Do you think I will ever meet your mother, Poppy? I'm sure I'd really like her. She must be someone special to have children like you and David.'

'Oh, dear, I can see you becoming a member of the Meadows family. You'll be turning up on our doorstep with a blanket under your arm. And I'd have to turn you away because we only have three beds.'

Charlotte chuckled. 'I can always sleep on your couch, or sit on a chair all night.'

'You've left somewhere out,' Poppy said, breaking off a piece of bread. 'You didn't mention the bath.'

'Oh, Poppy, you are funny. However, I imagine it would be very uncomfortable trying to sleep in a bath, so I'll settle for one of your chairs.'

'You'd be well advised to settle for your own bed, sweetheart, for I'm sure you live in the lap of luxury. Not that it makes you any different from me or Jean, just that you probably get a better night's sleep.' Poppy screwed her eyes up and thought for a few seconds. Then she announced, 'No, I make that sound as though my own bed is as hard as a plank of wood, and it isn't. It's really very comfortable and I snuggle up nice and warm.'

'Me too!' Jean said. 'I have a very comfortable mattress, and my pillows are filled with the softest feathers. Same with Mother. She is very comfortable in her bed.'

Poppy chuckled. 'Well, I must say this conversation is most interesting. It's going to brighten up our day and put a spring in our step. I bet there is no one else in the whole of Liverpool who is having lunch with friends and discussing subjects like sleeping in a bath, beds that are as hard as a plank of wood, and feather pillows! Only old women would think that an interesting conversation. We should be discussing the latest fashion in clothes, whether we prefer two-inch heels or three-inch. Whether to let our hair grow to shoulder length or have it cut in a bob!'

'There is one other thing we haven't talked about that I've heard is a very popular topic of conversation,' Jean said, 'and that is the price of fish.'

Every customer in the café turned their heads at the burst of laughter. And the three friends were still chuckling when they stood outside the office block. 'I enjoyed the lunch break,' Poppy said. 'It was like a happy farewell to Sutherland's and went off with a bang.'

'It was very funny, Poppy, about me sleeping in the bath, and the beds. And the price of fish was hilarious. I'm going over to see Papa now, and I'll tell him all that has been said. I bet he'll find it funny too.'

Before Poppy could stop them, the words came out. 'Will you tell Andrew as well? You might as well brighten his day too!'

Ah, thought Charlotte, now that is a step forward. 'Yes, I'll go to Andrew's office as well. I wouldn't visit my father without also seeing my brother. Shall I tell Andrew you were asking after him?'

'He won't be interested. He's probably got more on his mind. But if he does mention me, give him my regards.'

Jean looked at her watch. 'We'd better go in, Poppy, it's five to two. Don't want to be late on the last day.'

'You're right, Jean. We want to leave with a clean record.' Poppy squeezed Charlotte's arm. 'Whatever happens with

Jean's dinner break, I'll meet you at the café on Monday at one o'clock. Is that a date?'

'Oh, yes. I'm looking forward to it already. I'll be there on the dot. And if Jean can't be there, I'll see her in the office and sort times out for the future. I hope we can continue as we have been. I'd miss our lunches very much.'

After looking at her watch again, Jean practically pulled Poppy up the steps, and they both turned at the top to wave to Charlotte.

Charlotte stood on the edge of the pavement and waited until the road was clear before crossing to the opposite side. Then she turned into Castle Street and hurried to the Wilkie-Brook's office block.

'Shall I tell your father you are here, Miss Charlotte?' the receptionist asked. 'He does have a client with him at the moment, but he should be free any time now.'

'I'll wait here then,' Charlotte said, 'and if the client is still there in ten minutes, you can ring my father and tell him I'm here. That might hurry their meeting along.'

'Shall I make you a cup of tea while you're waiting?' the receptionist asked. 'It won't take a minute.'

'Thank you, but no, I really couldn't drink any more. I've just come from having lunch with friends. Don't worry about me, I don't mind waiting.' Charlotte accepted the chair offered to her, and let her mind wander.

Her life had changed out of all recognition since the day she'd first met Poppy, and she felt as free as a bird. Now she was going to see her father, and she was sure he would find the conversation between her and her two friends really funny. She loved to hear his hearty laughter, and he always looked much younger when he was laughing. His home life was happy, as it was for her and Andrew, but real laughter was seldom heard in the large house. And when she'd spent some time with her father, she'd climb the stairs to Andrew's office and cheer him up. And she had every intention of adding a few words to what Poppy had said. It was naughty, she knew, but it was in a good cause. She was hoping it would make him more daring next time he met Poppy. And that would be on Tuesday at the Grafton.

Charlotte noticed a gentleman passing the reception room, donning a hard hat before shaking his gloves and slipping his fingers into the soft kid. Then she heard the receptionist lift the telephone and dial a number. 'Your daughter is in reception, Mr George. Shall I send her in?'

Charlotte was already out of the door when the receptionist said, 'You can go in now, Miss Charlotte.'

Swivelling in his chair, George's face lit up when his daughter came into the room. She always looked so happy, it seemed the room was filled with sunshine. 'Well, young lady, what have you been up to that put that smile on your face?'

'I've been to lunch with Jean and Poppy, and, oh, Papa, we have had so many laughs. It started when Poppy was talking about her mother, and I asked if I could meet her. Poppy said she could see me turning up on her doorstep one day with a blanket under my arm.' Charlotte was in full flow now, and took George from sleeping in the bath to Jean's saying one topic they hadn't discussed was the price of fish.

Charlotte had a knack of impersonating people, and her facial expression changed to suit Poppy's way of speaking, then Jean's. George's chuckle gradually turned into hearty laughter, and behind the laughter was his pleasure at the change in his daughter. She was no longer tied to the house every day, which was stifling and unhealthy for a young girl with a love for life and friends of her own age. It had been a lucky day for her when her brother had knocked a stranger over outside their office.

'You really do get on well with Poppy, don't you, my dear?'

Charlotte nodded. 'I love Poppy, she's my very best friend. And she has had a lot of sadness, too, Papa. Her father died when she was only nine, and David was twelve. And their mother had to go out to work to earn money to keep them. She adores her mother, and do you know what she said? She said she loves the bones of her.'

'She must indeed be a fine woman, Poppy's mother. And I can believe that her two children must love her very much.' George nodded. 'Yes, love her bones indeed! What a wonderful way of expressing it.'

'Poppy has called me sweetheart several times, and when I told her I liked her calling me that she told me her mother has always called her sweetheart.'

George's thoughts were very deep. Since meeting Poppy his beloved daughter had learned more about the lives of people not as fortunate as herself than her private education, and her parents, had ever taught her. 'Would you like me to call you sweetheart? I would be very happy to, if you'll let me.'

Charlotte's eyes were like saucers. 'Oh, Papa, that would be lovely! I'll tell Poppy when I see her on Monday.' Then the smile left her face. 'But I don't think Mama would like it.'

'My dear girl, your mother would be delighted! I'm quite sure she will insist on being allowed to use the endearment herself.'

The sigh that came from Charlotte was one of happiness. 'It's been a lovely day, Papa, and now I'm going up to Andrew's office. I have some news which will make him happy. I'll add a bit to it, but it's not wrong if what you add is to cheer someone up, is it?'

'I'll have to give that some thought, my dear, but I'm sure what you say is right. Now off you go, and I'll see you later.'

Charlotte was humming as she climbed the steps to her brother's office. The tune was one they played at the Grafton for a slow foxtrot, titled 'I'll See You In My Dreams', and the girl thought it was very romantic. When she reached the office of Andrew's secretary she asked, 'Is my brother in, Wendy?'

'Yes, Miss Charlotte. I'll let him know you're here.'

'There's no need,' Charlotte said with an impish grin. 'He'll know I'm here when he sees me.'

Andrew was on the phone to a client, and with a finger he indicated that Charlotte should take a seat and not interrupt. Minutes later, his conversation finished, he set the phone down in its cradle and turned his attention to his sister. 'You are looking very much like the cat that got the cream, my dear sister. What have you been up to?'

'I've just come from Father's office. I've been telling him how much I enjoyed having lunch with Poppy and Jean. We had some fun, Andrew. Would you like me to tell you? I bet you would laugh as much as Papa did.'

Andrew closed the file on his desk and put it into a side drawer. 'Work is finished for this week, Charlotte, so go ahead and let the fun begin.'

Charlotte put on a better show for her brother because she was now word perfect, and went through all the actions. Next door, in her office, Wendy couldn't hear every word, or see any of the actions, but Mr Andrew's laughter was so hearty and infectious the secretary found herself laughing along with him.

'You've enjoyed yourself today, Charlotte.' Andrew was tapping the top of his desk with a pencil. 'There has been a big improvement in your life. Does Mother know where you go and what you do? She's never mentioned it in my presence.'

'Some of the things I tell her are true, Andrew, and others are not so true. You know she knows about Poppy, and has even said she would like to meet her. But you also know what Mother is like, and I'm not taking a chance on her spoiling my friendship with Poppy.'

'How is Poppy, by the way?' Andrew tried to make his voice sound neutral, as though her answer wouldn't be of great interest, but he couldn't fool his sister.

'Oh, she's fine. Except I think she's worried about her job. This is her last day at Sutherland's. But she did ask how you were, and say I was to give you her regards.'

Andrew sat upright in his chair. 'Did she really say that, Charlotte, or is it something you've made up?'

Charlotte was quick to answer. 'No, I did not make it up, and you can ask her yourself next time you see her.'

'No, I believe you. And I'm sorry she's worried about finding another job, but I'm sure she won't find it a problem. Her appearance alone will stand her in good stead.'

'Do you know what I think would be nice, Andrew, and I'm sure Poppy would love it. We could take her to the inn in the country. That would really take her mind off her worries.'

'I'd leave that idea alone if I were you, Charlotte. We are only just making friends and I don't want to rush things. It's a nice thought, but not for the time being. I've only just got to the stage where she's talking to me, and actually looking into my face. Please don't spoil things for me. I know I sound like a lovesick teenager, but Poppy is the only girl I've ever felt like this about, and I don't want to lose her.'

'You won't lose her, Andrew, because I believe she is really starting to like you. I can tell because she doesn't pull back now when you hold her hand. That is a definite improvement, and a good sign. I'm meeting her on Monday at the café, and as she's not working I'll try to coax her to come here to see you.'

'Don't overdo it, Charlotte, please, or she'll think I'm not capable of finding a girl without your help.'

'No, she won't. She won't see anything wrong in my wanting to see my own brother when I'm in the city. She'll be at a loose end, for she won't have found a job before one o'clock on Monday.'

Poppy hung her coat up and put her handbag down by the side of her desk. 'It won't be long now, Jean. Three hours and we'll have seen the last of this place.'

Jean nodded, but put a finger to her lips to warn Poppy not to say too much because Mr Hammond was in Mr John's office. He was a nice man, very polite and gentlemanly. Jean fleetingly wished that he had taken over Mr John's office years ago. How different her life would have been.

Both women turned when the office door opened and Mr Hammond came out. 'Miss Meadows, Mr John Senior would like to see you in his office if you wouldn't mind. Shall I take you, or can you remember your way there?'

Poppy frowned. 'Why does he want to see me, Mr Hammond? I thought we'd said all that needed saying on Monday.'

'I really can't discuss his affairs, Miss Meadows, but I'm sure there is nothing you need worry about.' He spied her handbag on the floor and nodded towards it. 'May I suggest you take your bag with you for safety. Miss Slater will be coming into the office with me, so this room will be unattended for a while.'

When Poppy bent down to pick up her handbag, she pulled a face at Jean, who was wearing a surprised expression.

As Poppy climbed the stairs to the top office, she was telling herself there was nothing to worry about. There couldn't be. They'd done everything above board. Given their notice in and worked the full week with no problems. But all the thinking didn't stop her from being apprehensive when she knocked on the door of John Sutherland Senior.

'Come in, Miss Meadows.'

Poppy closed the door behind her, and was taken aback when Mr John left his chair and came towards her. There was a chair in front of his desk, and he beckoned Poppy towards it. 'Please sit down, Miss Meadows, and don't look so scared, for I'm not going to eat you.'

'I'm not scared, just curious. I can't imagine what you would want to see me for. I leave here for good in a few hours' time, and I haven't neglected the office work while working my week's notice. The files are all up to date; you will find all is in order.'

Mr Sutherland laced his fingers and sat back in the brown leather chair. 'I know you and Miss Slater have worked very diligently this week. Mr Hammond has reported on this several times. In fact he's been singing your praises each day. But I didn't know you were also qualified to be a secretary.' He leaned forward and rested his elbows on the desk. 'Why did my son never mention this?'

'Because he didn't know. I only finished the course last week.' Poppy couldn't make out what was going on. But whatever it was she wasn't going to be talked down to. So she tossed her head, sending the golden curls swinging, and said,

'I'm happy to say I passed with flying colours.' She opened her bag and took out the envelope with Mr Jones's reference in. She placed it on the desk, saying, 'As you can see, Mr Sutherland, I did very well.'

John Sutherland scanned the words, then passed the letter back with a smile. 'Indeed you did, Miss Meadows. And the reference backs up Mr Hammond's praise for your work. So what I would like to do is offer you a position as a secretary with this firm.'

'Oh, no! I'm leaving here today. Thank you for the offer, but although it may hurt you to hear this, I could never, ever, work for Mr John. Not in any position, and not for all the money in the world. I have too much pride for that. I'll soon find a job. I'm not lazy.'

John Sutherland lifted his hand. 'I wouldn't expect you to work with my son again. The offer I'm making is for you to work in this office as my private secretary.' When he saw she was about to speak, he said, 'Please hear me out, and then decide.' Once again he laced his fingers. 'It is many years since I had a private secretary. We have many typists, and Mr Hammond has taken my dictation, for he has been a qualified secretary since I set up this firm. So we have managed between us very well all these years. The filing system is also one of Mr Hammond's duties, and one he enjoys.'

Poppy was confused, and asked, 'Then if your office is being run to your liking, why am I sitting here?'

'Because, my dear, Mr Hammond is wanting to retire. He will be calling in each day because he lives alone and would miss our daily chats. But he has reached the stage where he no longer enjoys getting up early every morning. As he says, he doesn't want a rigid routine, but he would like to come in and potter.'

'But there must be other staff you could use as your secretary?' Poppy said. 'They wouldn't take kindly to me taking over. Besides, I would still be in contact with your son; it would be unavoidable.'

'You have my word that would never happen. I can't say you will never pass each other on the steps or in the street, but I can say, without any doubt, that my son will never speak one word to you.'

'But why me?' Poppy was still confused. 'There are probably dozens of girls far more competent than I am.' She quickly added, 'Not that I'm incompetent, because I'm not. Neither am I lazy, and I don't take time off work.' John Senior chuckled. 'That is why I would like you to accept the position. It would be nice for me to have someone who wouldn't be afraid to say what she thinks.'

Poppy relaxed. He really was a nice man, and if it weren't for his son she would have accepted the job without hesitation. And he was right, she needn't see Mr John if she didn't want to. And she had a feeling he'd be in hot water if he ever did confront her. 'What are the terms, if I agree to take the job? Would it be the same hours, and the same lunch break?'

'Nine o'clock start, and one o'clock lunch break. The starting salary would be six pounds a week. Saturday, of course, the office is closed.'

Poppy was flabbergasted. That was double the salary she was on. And it was a pound a week more than Jean would be getting at her new job. 'That is a very tempting offer, Mr Sutherland, and I will be truthful and say I wasn't expecting such a good wage because of my lack of experience.'

'I get the impression you are a person who always speaks her mind, Miss Meadows. Am I correct?'

Poppy nodded. 'I was brought up to be honest and

outspoken, but not at the cost of hurting someone.' She chuckled, and a smile crossed her lovely face. 'I'm at a loss here, I'm afraid. I really don't know what I am to call you. I could not address you as Mr John, because it wouldn't fit comfortably with me.'

'So you are going to accept the post, Miss Meadows?'

'Tell me how I am supposed to address you, then I'll tell you.'

'Let me put my thinking cap on.' He tapped on his desk for a few seconds, and then came to a decision. 'How does JS sound?'

'A bit too familiar. The rest of the staff here would really think I was pushy. How about Mr S.?'

John Sutherland Senior was thinking how lucky he was that his friend Cecil Hammond had recommended Poppy Meadows. She was like a ray of sunshine in the room. He felt sure the office would never be dull again. 'We'll settle for Mr S. for the time being, until something more suitable comes to mind. And now to business. For the first week or so Cecil Hammond will be here every morning at nine o'clock. I am privileged; I come in a little later. I will contact Personnel as soon as you leave here and explain you will not be leaving the firm. I will fill them in as regards salary, and they will have all your particulars, anyway.'

'I was due to pick up my week in hand as well as this week's wages, so would you tell them I'm not entitled to it all, and ask them to make the necessary deduction?'

'I don't think I need to go through all that, Miss Meadows. You will take the wage packet handed to you without any comment. Your increase in salary will start next week. So I will see you on Monday morning. Perhaps not at nine o'clock, though.'

Poppy felt like jumping for joy, and had to control the urge to hug him. Oh, wait until she told her mam and David! They would be so proud of her. But she couldn't contain her joy until she got home: she just had to tell someone. Then she remembered Charlotte was going to see her father, and would probably still be in his office.

Poppy only gave it a second's thought. She'd burst if she didn't tell someone, and Jean would be busy with Mr Hammond.

'Mr Sutherland, I wasn't expecting this, and I've made arrangements to meet a friend on Monday for lunch. Unfortunately we don't have a phone at home, but I know where she is right now. Would you mind if I took time out to see her? Otherwise she will think I've let her down if I'm a little late, or even can't make it at all, since it will be my first day.'

'By all means go and see your friend. I realize this has come as a bolt from the blue. Off you go, but be back in time to pick up your wages.'

Poppy leaned over the desk. 'You are very kind. But don't be too kind or I'll take advantage of you.' She heard a low chortle as she closed the door behind her. Then she ran down the stairs, and opened the door to her old office to see Jean and Mr Hammond going through the filing cabinet. Taking her coat from the stand, she told a startled Jean, 'I won't be long because I'm walking on air. I've wonderful news for you later.'

The receptionist in the Wilkie-Brook's office smiled as she recognized Poppy. 'Can I help you?'

'Is Miss Charlotte still here?'

'Yes, she's with her father. Shall I tell her you're here?'

Poppy nodded. 'Yes, please, if you would.'

The receptionist passed the message down the phone, then

told Poppy, 'Will you go through? Miss Charlotte will open the door for you.'

'Oh, Charlotte, you'll never guess. My mind is all higgledy-piggledy, I don't know whether I'm coming or going. I've just got to tell someone my news, or my head will burst.'

'Come in, Poppy.' Charlotte opened the door wider, and Poppy saw her friend's father behind his desk. 'Oh, I'm sorry. I never thought I'd be interrupting. In fact I'm not capable of rational thinking right now. Shall we go outside, Charlotte, so your father can get on with his work?'

'Don't you dare leave this office.' George came from behind his desk. 'I am as eager as my daughter is to hear your news.'

'I've got a job! Just like that.' Poppy snapped her fingers. 'I've got a job! Isn't that wonderful?'

Charlotte was agog. 'I haven't long left you, and you've got a job! You clever girl, how did you do that?'

'Charlotte, you sit on the desk and Poppy can sit in the chair,' George said. 'I'm intrigued, Poppy. How could you have found a job so quickly? I'm very happy for you, though, and I can quite understand your excitement. But do put my daughter and me out of our misery and tell us how it came about.'

Poppy's words poured from her mouth in her excitement. There were lots of things she left out, things she didn't think important for now. 'I can't believe I'm so lucky! And Mr Sutherland Senior is so nice. I'm sure I'll get on with him.'

'If your job is with John Senior, I can assure you he is a world apart from his son,' George said, feeling happy for the girl who had made such a difference to his daughter's life. And looking at Poppy now, with her wide smile and eyes like saucers, he could understand his son's falling for her. 'You couldn't find a nicer or kinder man for a boss. You really are very lucky.'

'Come upstairs and tell Andrew,' Charlotte said. 'He will be so happy for you.'

'Oh, no, I can't disturb him. He'll think I'm behaving stupidly just because I've got a job.'

George, after telling himself he was getting as bad as his daughter for wanting to play Cupid, said with enthusiasm, 'There's no one with him at the moment, and I'm sure he'll be delighted to hear your news. Go with Charlotte and cheer him up.'

'I shouldn't really,' Poppy said half-heartedly. 'I should go back and finish the work with Jean, so the office is all in order for whoever takes over next week.'

'Five minutes won't make any difference.' Charlotte gave her friend no choice and dragged her out of the office and up the stairs, leaving George wishing he could go as well, to see how his son reacted to seeing the girl he'd fallen for. But his presence would hold his son back, so it would be best for him to keep away now and rely on his daughter to fill him in on her now nightly visit to his study. He'd get a really good account, for Charlotte was fast becoming an excellent impressionist. There wasn't anyone she couldn't take off, and he'd begun to wonder if she ever did an impression of him behind his back.

Andrew was sitting behind his desk when the door was flung open and his sister appeared, with a reluctant Poppy in tow. 'Really, Charlotte, do you never do anything quietly? Anyone would think you didn't have a minute to spare.'

'We came to give you Poppy's good news, Andrew. You'll never believe how lucky she's been. She was so excited she had to come and tell us.'

Andrew walked round his desk. 'Is that true, Poppy? You've come with good news?'

'Yes, yes, yes! I keep pinching myself to make sure I'm not dreaming.' Poppy's face was so alive, Andrew couldn't take his eyes off her. 'I thought I might be out of work for a long time, and I was worried.' The words rolled from her tongue. 'Then I get a job handed to me, and I can't take it all in. I am so lucky, I could cry.'

Andrew was taken aback. 'You've got a job, Poppy?'

'Yes, and I'm so happy. I can't wait to tell my mam and David.'

Andrew walked towards her, saying, 'That's wonderful news, Poppy. I am so pleased for you.' He put his arms round her, as though it was the natural thing to do, and she smiled up at him.

'It won't sink in, Andrew. Mr Sutherland was so nice to me, giving me the job without even an interview, on twice the salary I was on before.'

Andrew's smile faded, and he held her away. 'You're going to work for John Sutherland? That brute of a man? I'm disappointed in you, Poppy.'

'No, not John Junior – I would never speak to him again, let alone work for him. I'd starve first.'

'Come and sit down and tell me all about it. I'm astounded really, and can't wait to hear the whole story.'

'I can't stay now. I've left Jean to clear the office and tidy up. She doesn't even know what's happened, and I can't leave her to hear it from someone else. She's been a good friend to me. Charlotte will fill you in. I know it sounds childish, but I was so thrilled I had to tell someone, and I knew Charlotte was coming here.'

'When you're ready to go home, why don't I drive you there? I've finished here for the day, and you'd be home sooner to tell your mother the news.'

Before Poppy could reply, Charlotte stepped in. 'Oh, what a good idea! I could come with you, then go straight home with Andrew.' Charlotte had her own car parked by Exchange station, but that wasn't going to stop her helping her brother. 'Come here when you finish work, Poppy, and we'll run you home, save you waiting for a bus and getting crushed.'

The suggestion had brought Poppy down to earth. She couldn't take Andrew and Charlotte to her home. She wasn't ashamed of living in a six-roomed house, and certainly wasn't ashamed of her family. But these two were used to servants and heaven only knows what else. And her mam would be only getting home herself, and not ready for visitors. 'No, I don't want you to run me home, but I appreciate your offer. My mother won't be prepared for visitors, and it wouldn't be fair on her.'

'We wouldn't think of coming inside your house, Poppy,' Andrew said. 'Not without a prior invitation. We will drop you at the corner of your street, and you wouldn't have the discomfort of waiting for a bus, and being squashed. You'd be home in ten or fifteen minutes.'

The offer was too tempting to refuse. Friday night, when everyone was finishing work for the weekend, was a mad scramble to get on a bus. 'That would be fine, thank you, and now I really must go, or Jean will think I've deserted her.'

'We'll be ready and waiting for you,' Charlotte said, thinking that things were moving on in the love stakes. She gave Poppy a big hug. 'I am so happy for you.'

'Where on earth have you been?' Jean asked. 'I thought there was something wrong, the way you ran off.'

'I didn't want to say anything in front of Mr Hammond, Jean, although he knows why Mr Sutherland sent for me. But it wasn't his place to tell you my wonderful, unbelievable good news. I still can't get my head around it, Jean. Mr Sutherland has given me a job as his personal secretary. From Monday I'll be working in his office.'

Jean looked stunned for a few seconds, then she threw her arms around Poppy. 'Oh, that is wonderful news. Now I won't have to feel guilty. I have been worried that it was through you I was handed a really good job, away from the horrible Mr John, and you were out of work. That was the only drawback to my new position. But I can breathe easy now, and sleep without a guilty conscience. Tell me how it came about.'

Poppy took her friend through the whole meeting with Mr Sutherland, except for her salary. That would sound as though she was bragging. She'd tell the truth one day, but not now. She ended by saying, 'Same lunch hour, so if yours is the same we'll meet every day.'

'Are you not worried about Mr John making trouble for you? He's wicked enough.'

Poppy shook her head. 'His father has promised me that Mr John will never exchange one word with me. And I believe him, for he's not a bit like his son. He's kind and a proper gent.'

'Well, it's been quite a day,' Jean said. 'But I'm so happy that on Monday you and I will be going to work in a good mood, looking forward to it. I never looked forward to coming here every morning. I've been living on my nerves for years.'

Poppy looked over to Mr John's office. 'Is Mr Hammond still here?'

'No, he's finished. Everything is ready for Monday morning. He said when you came back, we could both collect our wages and go home. So shall we make tracks?' The women looked round the office for the last time, then they closed the door on the way out.

Sitting on the back seat of the car with Charlotte, Poppy had been giving directions to Andrew. When they were nearing her street, she leaned forward and tapped him on the shoulder. 'The second street on the right is where I live, Andrew, but you can stop here and let me out. I've only got to cross the road and I'll be home in no time.'

Andrew indicated to warn the car behind he was turning. 'I may as well see you to your street, save you crossing the road.'

'You're spoiling me,' Poppy said. 'I only live six doors down.'

Andrew stopped the car by the first house. 'We want to spoil you today, for it's been a good day for you.'

Charlotte put her hand on her friend's arm. 'Are you going out tonight, Poppy?'

'No, I hadn't planned to.'

'Then why don't you come with me and Andrew?' Charlotte was delighted Poppy had no plans, for if she had they would spoil her own cunning plot. 'Come out with us to celebrate your achievement. We're only going for a drive and a drink, but we'd like you to come, wouldn't we, Andrew?'

Poppy didn't wait for Andrew to answer. 'That's very kind of you, but I won't come. I don't have the right clothes to go to the places you two probably go to, and I'd feel uncomfortable.'

Andrew turned in his seat. 'Poppy Meadows, I never thought you were a snob! You do surprise and disappoint me.'

'I'm not a snob!' Poppy told him. 'I'm just being truthful! And I'd rather be truthful than feel out of place.'

'Poppy,' Charlotte said, 'we're only going to a pub for a drink, and neither Andrew nor myself will be changing out of the clothes we're wearing now.'

Poppy felt stupid. She'd really had the wind taken out of her sails. 'You two are going to a pub for a drink? You're pulling my leg.'

'Actually it's an inn,' Andrew said, 'but most people would call it a pub. Charlotte and I went for a run in the country one night, and we came across this place. It looked like a picture postcard, so we went inside out of curiosity. And we fell in love with the place. It's hundreds of years old, stone floor, log fire, lantern in the window, and the only customers were farmers just in from the fields. They were drinking jugs of ale, and they made us very welcome. The landlord told us the history of the inn, and it's unbelievable. There are no mod cons, and they don't sell fancy drinks, but we loved it. So much so, we took our father, and like us, he loved it. It's just as it was hundreds of years ago, so if you do come, don't expect comfortable chairs, or posh glasses, because you'll be disappointed.'

'It sounds wonderful,' Poppy said. 'And do you really not have to dress up?'

'You'd be out of place if you did. The farmers come in straight from the fields, smelling of earth and animals. But they make us welcome, and are happy to see us.'

'I go one day through the week,' Charlotte said, 'to buy fresh chickens and eggs that my father has ordered for our kitchen. And the order is appreciated, because farmers don't earn much money.'

'You've talked me into it,' Poppy said. 'It sounds wonderful, and just the right way to end a perfect day. But how do I get there?'

Andrew's heart was beating fast, and although his sister had lied about them going out that evening, for they'd never even discussed it, he could have kissed her. 'It's half past five now, so shall we make it half seven? We'll meet you here if that suits you?'

'That gives me plenty of time to tell my mam and David my good news, have my tea and make myself look presentable. But I warn you, Andrew, if I see anyone in this place tonight wearing a tiara, I'll never speak to you again.' With that Poppy scrambled out of the car, blew a kiss and ran the few yards to her front door, leaving behind a very happy man, and his cunning, but loveable, sister.

'You're just in time, sweetheart. I've made a cup of tea for meself and there's enough in the pot for you.' Eva reached for a cup hanging from a shelf in the kitchen. 'You're a little early tonight, aren't you?'

'A bit, that's all. Is David in yet?' Poppy didn't want to tell her news twice; she wanted to see the reaction on both faces at the same time. 'Actually, I got a lift home, Mam. That's why I'm early. Charlotte's brother drove me.'

'Ooh, ye're coming up in the world, sweetheart, I hope all the neighbours saw you.'

'I shouldn't think so, Mam. He just stopped the car at the top of the road and I jumped out.' She heard a key in the lock and said, 'Here's David, so I'll put a drop of water in the kettle and he can have a cuppa with us.'

'It's not worth it, sweetheart. I'll have the dinner ready soon.'

'No, I'll make a full pot of tea, Mam. Leave the dinner for now, I've got something to tell you. And I talk better with a cup of tea in front of me.'

David poked his head in. 'I'm with you, sis. I could murder a cup of decent tea. And while you're making it, tell us what the something is you have to tell us.'

Eva was setting the cups and saucers on the small table in the kitchen. 'Yer sister came home in a car tonight, David, right to the top of the street. She'll be the talk of the neighbourhood.'

David raised his brows. 'Who was the knight in shining amour?'

'Just carry the cups through, David, and once we're settled I'm going to give you and Mam a shock.'

'Oh, not a shock, sweetheart,' Eva said, pulling out a chair with one hand, while trying not to spill the tea in her other. 'A pleasant surprise I'd like, but not a shock.'

They were all seated when Poppy said, 'Well what I have to tell you is a bit of both. So make yourselves comfortable, and I'll begin at the beginning.'

Poppy was halfway through her tale, and there'd been various exclamations from her mother and brother, when there was a knock on the front door. 'Oh, no, who the heck is that.' David scraped his chair back and made for the door. 'I'll get rid of whoever it is.'

'Oh, no, you won't get rid of whoever it is,' Marg said, pushing David out of the way. 'First Poppy gets out of a posh car at the top of the street, and has all the curtains twitching. Then we hear screams and shouts coming through the wall. So I've come to see what's going on.'

Eva couldn't contain her pride and pleasure. 'Our Poppy's got herself a new job, Marg. She's a private secretary now, earning good money.'

'Ooh, er,' Marg said. 'Was that her new boss what brought her home in a posh car?'

Poppy got in before her mother could answer. 'They were two friends who drove me home, Charlotte and Andrew. Your Sarah knows them. And so the neighbours will have more to talk about, they're picking me up in the same place at half seven. They're taking me for a drink to celebrate my good fortune.'

'Oh, I'm delighted for yer, queen, and yer deserve it. I won't stay, seeing as you'll need yer dinner making if ye're going out later. But before I go, just out of motherly concern, what's this bloke like that our Sarah keeps talking about? She calls him Jim, and she seems smitten. Is he a good bloke?'

'Marg, he's lovely. I'm very fond of Jim. You certainly don't need to worry about Sarah where he's concerned.'

'That's good enough for me, queen. And I'm delighted for yer, I really am. Enjoy yer night out. Ta-ra.' Marg went out as quickly as she came in.

'I'll see to the dinner while you get yerself ready, sweetheart. It's good of your friends to take you for a drink to celebrate.'

'I don't think they'd mind if you came along, David,' Poppy said. 'Unless you've got something else to do?'

'I won't come tonight, sis,' David told her. He'd known for a while that Charlotte had high hopes for her brother and Poppy. And he'd seen for himself the longing in Andrew's eyes when he looked at his sister. So he wasn't going to hinder the flow to true love. 'I've promised to go for a game of cards.'

'I'll hog the bathroom for half an hour then, save me rushing at the last minute.' Poppy got to the bottom of the stairs, remembered something and backtracked. 'Oh, I got my week in hand, plus my wages, so I can pay you the money back now.'

David reached for a cushion off the couch and threw it at

her. 'It's very bad manners to return a present. An insult, in fact.'

'I wouldn't insult you or Mam for the world. But I will treat you when I've saved a few pound. The Meadows family is spreading out. Tomorrow, when my feet are back on the ground, we'll decide whether our first buy will be a television or having a telephone installed. So give it some thought before then. Right now it's me for the bathroom, then our dinner, and then out to celebrate.'

'Do you want to sit in the front, Poppy,' Charlotte asked, 'or in the back with me?'

'So there's no sign of favouritism, I'll sit in the front going, and the back on the way home. Sitting in a car is a novelty to me, and I'll see more sitting in the front.' This cheered Andrew and his sister, and the drive to the country inn was a pleasant one. It certainly was for Poppy, who couldn't take in the many events of the day. There was too much happening at once. But she'd go over it all when she was snuggled up in bed later.

Andrew came to a stop outside the inn, and turned to Poppy to see her reaction. 'Well, Poppy, what do you think?'

She grabbed hold of his arm without thinking. 'Oh, it's like a picture of a magic house, the kind you see in fairy tale books.'

'Wait until you see inside.' He helped her out of the car, then opened the back door for Charlotte. 'I don't know how the landlord keeps it going. They don't get enough customers to make it pay.'

'It's been in his family for generations, he told me,' Charlotte said. 'I had a good talk to him when I came to pick up the chickens and eggs last Wednesday. He can remember his grandfather, who lived to be ninety, and then his dad took over. And he's got a son of fourteen, who will take over when he retires.'

'Come on, let's go in,' Andrew said. 'I'm sure Poppy will find it very interesting.' And he wasn't disappointed when he saw the expression on her wonderful face. 'It is just like a fairy tale,' she said softly. 'Like the ones I remember from the books my mam used to read to me when I was a little girl.'

Then the silence was broken when the farmers and landlord welcomed them with smiles and raised tankards. Andrew ordered sherry for Poppy and Charlotte, beer for the farmers and landlord, and just half a pint for himself, because he'd be driving home in the dark and he wasn't used to the strong ale.

Poppy was glad she'd agreed to come, for it was so relaxing, with the log fire, the lanterns and the happy, friendly farmers. And hearing of the history of the inn, she was very impressed. But what struck her most of all was the ease with which Andrew and Charlotte mixed with the farmers, drank from glasses that seemed as old as the inn itself, and sat on seats that were worn with age. Andrew was like a different person from the one she thought she knew. The farmers, with their country accents, and jokes about the antics of their pigs and chickens, had them all laughing. But it was Andrew who held Poppy's attention. With his head thrown back and his hearty laughter, she was seeing him in a different light.

When it was time to leave, Poppy was sad, but Charlotte told her they'd bring her back very soon. And before they left Andrew ordered a round of drinks for the farmers and the landlord and thanked them for their hospitality.

When they were outside, Andrew held the car door open, and asked, 'Well, Poppy, are you glad you came?'

'Oh, yes, I wouldn't have missed it. How stupid I would

have been to have turned down your invitation.' To his delight and surprise, she kissed his cheek. 'Thank you for taking me.' Then she hugged Charlotte. 'You have given me a perfect end to a perfect day.'

'Are you sitting in the front or back?' Charlotte asked. 'I don't mind where I sit.'

'We'll both sit in the back, eh?' Poppy said. 'I want to go over everything that has happened to me on this wonderful day, and I'm sure Andrew would be bored by my voice going on non-stop. It would put him off me for life.'

'Oh, I don't think you could do anything that would put my brother off you,' Charlotte told her.

'Well, I'm not taking any chances, so I'll sit with you in the back. I won't be so talkative after today, for there'll never be another day when so many nice things happen to me.'

Andrew slid into the driver's seat. 'Oh, yes there will, Poppy,' he said. 'I can promise you that.'

Chapter Twenty-Six

Poppy came down the stairs on the Saturday morning rubbing the sleep from her eyes. 'Ooh, you should have called me, Mam. I didn't hear the alarm going off.' Yawning, and stretching her arms over her head, she said, 'I slept like a log. I don't even remember putting my head down on the pillow.'

'It was an exciting day for yer yesterday, sweetheart,' Eva said. 'And you were late getting to bed.' Bustling into the kitchen, she called, 'I did look in on yer earlier, but yer were sleeping like a baby and I didn't have the heart to disturb yer. Sit yerself down and I'll make yer a cup of tea before yer get washed and dressed.'

Poppy pulled out a chair and sat down at the table. 'David must be in a good sleep. There's no sound from his room.'

Eva came to stand at the kitchen door. 'David went out at half past seven this morning, sweetheart. You remember him telling us his boss was planning on opening a new depot? Well, they've been a while getting it ready, but there's some equipment being delivered today, and his boss asked David if he'd work this morning to organize the setting up of the office. Once it's open, and the depot stocked, then David will be in charge.'

The kettle began to whistle, and Eva hurried to turn the gas off. 'I'll make the tea, then we can talk.'

Poppy went to stand by the kitchen door. 'It's been a good week for the Meadows family, Mam.' She yawned again, before chuckling. 'The way we're going on, we'll be able to afford a television *and* have a telephone installed. That would give Tilly Mint across the road something to talk about.'

'I don't care what Florrie Lawson says about us, as long as she doesn't knock and ask to use the phone, or come and watch television.' Eva poured milk into the cups, then passed one to her daughter. 'Sit down, and we can have a natter. It'll do you good to wind down after the hectic day yer had yesterday. You enjoyed yerself last night, I could tell when yer came in. And I got to thinking how funny it was that after being knocked over by a bloke, and calling him for everything, yer should end up being friends with him and his sister. Life can be very unpredictable when fate steps in.'

Poppy nodded. 'The day it happened, and my raincoat got torn, I was as mad as hell with both brother and sister. But I have to admit that my vanity brought on the temper. They were dressed like toffs, and they'd ruined the only coat I possessed. My pride was hurt. And if anyone had told me then that I would one day be friends with them, I'd have said they were mad.' Poppy smiled as she continued, 'How Charlotte wormed her way into my life, I will never understand. But I'm glad she did, for she's a little love, and I'm very fond of her. You would love her, for she's always got a smile on her face, and her eyes are filled with mischief.'

'And her brother, Andrew?' Eva had heard from David that there was romance in the air. 'Do you get on as well with him as you do with his sister?'

There was a slight hesitation before Poppy answered. 'I was wrong about both of them, Mam. They are toffs, and they do wear clothes we could never afford, but they are not snobs.'

She drained her cup before steering the conversation in a different direction. 'Do you feel like coming into town with me? I want to look around the shops and I don't fancy walking round on my own. I'll mug you to a cup of tea in Reece's.'

'What do yer want in town?'

'I was thinking I'll need a couple of skirts and blouses to start my new job. I need to look smart all the time, and ring in the changes every few days. At the moment I haven't got a skirt to my name, or a decent blouse. So will you come with me for company? And two heads are always better than one.'

Eva nodded as she reached for her daughter's cup and saucer. 'Yeah, it'll be a change for me, and the fresh air will do me good. You get ready, sweetheart, while I make us a couple of rounds of toast. They'll keep us going until dinnertime. But I don't want to be out too long, for David will want a meal when he gets home. We're having bacon, sausage and egg today, a nice quick meal. And I've got a piece of lamb for tomorrow.'

'I'd better put my skates on then,' Poppy said. 'I'll just have a wash and clean my teeth. I can have a bath and wash my hair later.'

Eva went to the bottom of the stairs and called up, 'Have yer got enough money for the things yer need to buy? If not, I can let yer have a few bob.'

'I've got plenty, Mam. I don't intend buying any expensive clothes. More along the lines of cheap clothes that look expensive.' Poppy came out on to the landing, and was laughing as she looked down on her mother. 'As long as I look like Miss Efficiency, no one will know my clothes came from a stall in Paddy's market.'

'Don't knock Paddy's market, sweetheart, because I was

glad of it when money was tight.' Eva waved a hand. 'Will yer stop talking or we'll never get out.'

David heard the key in the door and quickly sat down and opened the paper he'd bought on the way home. He'd only been in five minutes, but he was going to pretend otherwise, for a bit of fun. 'Where on earth have you two been? I've been home for ages, and I'm starving with hunger. It's coming to something when a working man's been slogging his guts out for hours, and he comes home to an empty house.'

'I'm sorry, son.' Eva slipped her coat off and hung it up in the hall. 'I went into town with Poppy, and we didn't notice the time flying over. But I'll soon have the dinner on the go, and as we're having an easy meal, with bacon, sausage and egg, it'll be ready in no time.'

Poppy gripped her mother's arm. 'Just a second, Mam. I think someone is pulling our legs.' She raised her brows at her brother. 'Don't you be having Mam feeling sorry for you. I can read you like a book. It's the twinkle in your eyes that gives the game away. Just how long have you been home?'

David chuckled. 'Five minutes before you.' He folded the paper and threw it on the couch. 'If you can read my face, Poppy, why can't I read yours?'

'Because I've got an open and honest face, that's why. And for your cheek, you can make me and Mam a cup of tea. I've been dragging her all round town, and I bet her feet are killing her. So be a gentleman, and make the ladies a cup of tea.'

'No, I'll make the tea,' Eva said. 'David's been out since half seven this morning. He must be worn out.'

David was out of his chair like a shot. 'I'm not tired, Mam, honest. When the equipment was delivered, all I had to do was tell the men where to put it. It was more boring than tiring. So let me wait on you. I'll make the tea while you put your weary feet up. Then we can sit for half an hour, talk about life in general, and Poppy's shopping in particular. I can't wait to see what's in the bags.' David hesitated at the kitchen door, then turned to face his sister. 'And I want to know what she got up to last night. What with the promotion, and coming home in posh cars, well, I'm having trouble keeping up with my sister.'

'I'm not the only one on the ladder of success, dear brother. I was saying to Mam this morning that the Meadows family are on the way up. So, on the bus going into town, we decided that we should start to enjoy our first taste of luxury. Beginning, perhaps, with a television, then following on with having a telephone installed so we can keep in touch with our friends.'

David looked blank. 'But we don't have any friends who have a telephone.'

'Oh, but we will have. When your office is up and running, I can ring you. And we can both ring home to ask Mam what we're having for dinner.'

'Don't mind me,' Eva said, 'pretend I'm not here. I won't be here to answer the phone when you ring up to ask what's for dinner. Because like you two, I'll be at work. I'm not packing my job in just to answer a blinking phone! I've made up my mind I want to keep my job on because I enjoy it, and I'd miss the women I work with. And also because I want to have some money of my own. I'm determined to have a holiday this year, come what may. I've never had a holiday in me life, and neither have you. There was never any money for such a luxury.'

Poppy met David's eyes, and they silently agreed what the

answer to that should be. 'Now that is the best idea you've had yet, Mam,' Poppy said. 'Better than a television or a telephone. Let's have a family holiday, eh? You say where you'd like to go, Mam, and me and David will go along with wherever you fancy.'

'I wouldn't know where to start, sweetheart, since Liverpool is the only place I've ever known. The women in work talk about going to Wales, or Blackpool.' Eva shrugged her shoulders. 'You choose, and I'll fit in with you. But don't forget, it might be difficult for us to get the same weeks off. The big factories close every year for the last week in July and the first week in August, but I can take a week any time, as long as I give plenty of notice.'

'I don't think working for Mr Sutherland Senior will make any difference to the holidays,' Poppy said. 'The office doesn't close down, as you know, and the staff stagger their holidays. I suppose being solicitors they can't shut down completely. So that only leaves you, David, but I'm sure you can fix it so we can all go away together.'

'I'll work something out, don't worry,' David said. 'And now, before I finally make that much talked of pot of tea, can I make a little suggestion?'

'We are all equal in this house, brother, and we all have a say. So out with it, what is this little suggestion?'

'Why don't we have a weekend away next week? There's nothing to stop us, and it would be a nice break. We have never been outside Liverpool, and now we can afford to spread our wings a little, let's go mad and have a weekend in Blackpool. We could get the train there on Friday night straight from work, and come home on the Sunday night. We could go to the Tower, where there is the best dance floor in the country, and Reginald Dixon plays the organ.'

'But where would we stay for the two nights?' Eva asked.

'Mam, the *Echo* is full of adverts every night for bed and breakfast houses,' David told her. 'And there's always a phone number for them, so I could ring from work and make enquiries. Anyway, I'll see to the tea while you two make up your minds. I'd be delighted to go away for a break, but it's up to you.'

'I'd be happy with Blackpool, Mam,' Poppy said. 'I believe there's plenty to do there, with the Tower and the fun fair. And the sea air will do us good, blow all the cobwebs away.'

Eva nodded. 'Yeah, let's go mad and let our hair down, eh? As you say, it will do the three of us good to have a change.'

David had a huge grin on his face as he carried the tray in. 'I can't wait to get on that dance floor and trip the light fantastic.'

'I believe they've got a zoo in there, as well,' Poppy said. 'That should be interesting. We won't be short of something to do to pass the time.'

David handed the cups round, then sat down at the table. 'Last but not least, Poppy, what have you got in those bags? I presume it's clothes, and I'm surprised you've let them stay in the bags for so long. Aren't you pleased with your purchases?'

Poppy jumped to her feet. 'D'you know, I'd forgotten about them.' She took two blouses out of one of the bags, and opened them up for her mother and brother to see. One was in white cotton, with pearl buttons down the front and two on each sleeve. It was tailored, ideal for a secretary. The other was in a light beige, with a winged collar, pearl buttons and three-quarter-length sleeves: also ideal for a secretary. Then came the skirts, one in black, the other in navy. Straight, calf length, and held against the blouses they matched up well.

'I know I'm a male, and supposed to be stupid where

women's clothes are concerned,' David said, 'but I can see they are going to look very smart, Poppy. Your new boss will think himself very lucky.'

Eva nodded, her heart filled with pride. How lucky she was with her children. Her beloved husband had left her a wonderful legacy. 'Are yer going out tonight, sweetheart?'

'No, I'm having a night in, Mam. I'm going to brush up on my shorthand, ready for Monday.' Poppy tilted her head as she smiled at her brother. 'I'm hoping you're not going out, David, because I'd like you to give me some dictation. Just a paragraph out of the paper would do, then see if I can read it back without making a mistake. It wouldn't take very long, and you could still go out if you've made arrangements.'

'I've nothing planned, so I don't mind helping you. Then we could have a game of cards to pass the time.' His handsome face lit up. 'I know, why don't we start living the high life tonight? I'll go to the shops when we've had our dinner, and get a bottle of sherry and a big slab of Cadbury's chocolate. How does that sound?'

'Sounds like the best thing you've said today,' Poppy told him as she laid the new skirts and blouses over her arm. 'I'll hang these up, then give you a hand with the dinner, Mam.'

'When are you seeing Charlotte and Andrew again?' David asked.

From the bottom stair, Poppy told him, 'I'm seeing Charlotte on Monday for lunch. She'll want to find out how my first morning has gone. Then I suppose she and Andrew will be at the Grafton on Tuesday.'

'Just out of interest,' Eva said, 'will Peter be there?'

'I don't know that, Mam.' Poppy stepped down off the bottom stair and came back in the room. 'I can't hold a conversation from out there. But as for Peter, I imagine he and Kate will be there. And I've got a feeling Sarah will, as well. I can see a romance blossoming between her and Jim. I hope so, because they seem good for each other.' She looked from her mother to David. 'Now have either of you got any more questions before I go upstairs to hang these clothes up?'

'I can't think of anything, our kid,' David said. 'If I do, I'll write it down.'

'Do I look all right, Mam?' Poppy was wearing the new black skirt and white blouse. 'Is the skirt too tight, d'you think?'

'You look a treat, sweetheart, so don't be worrying.'

'My nerves are shattered. I can't stop my hands from shaking.'

'You'll be fine,' Eva told her. 'David said to tell you to walk into your office as though you haven't a care in the world. And he told me to give you this.' Eva stretched her neck to plant a kiss on her daughter's cheek. 'He was sorry he couldn't wait to see you, but he's in a new job himself and he didn't want to be late.'

'I bet he's not as nervous as me.' Poppy had a habit of pulling one of her golden curls and watching it spring back. She was doing it now, until her mother slapped her hand. 'I can't help it, Mam, but I will give myself a good talking to on the bus going into town. Or I'll hum a happy tune. Anything to keep my mind occupied.'

Eva tutted. 'I've never seen you so nervous since the first day I took you to school when you were five. I had hold of your hand and had to push you through the gates. You had me so worried, I went back to the school halfway through the morning, only to find it was playtime, and you were running and skipping with all the other children, as happy as could be. You were having the time of your life. And today will be like that day. After an hour, you'll be asking yourself what you were worried for.'

Poppy managed to put a smile on her face. 'I'll go to work like a little lamb, if you'll come with me and hold my hand.'

'You're a young lady now, with a very important position, so just remember that. And yer can also remember how yer felt about learning shorthand. You never thought you'd get your head round it, but you did. And I'll bet you any money you'll come in tonight from work with a smile on your face as wide as the River Mersey.'

'Oh, I'll do that, Mam, even if I'm a nervous wreck inside. I'll be smiling because I've got through the first day all in one piece.'

'Come on, put yer coat on and we'll walk up the street together.' Eva patted her daughter's cheek. 'You'll be fine, sweetheart.'

Mother and daughter linked arms and walked to the top of the street, where they parted company to go their separate ways. Poppy reached the stop just as the bus ground to a halt, and she hopped on board. At least she wouldn't be late on her first day.

The conductor was on the platform, chatting to the driver, and Poppy paid her fare before walking down the aisle seeking an empty seat, so she could sit by a window. She thought if she gazed out on the passing scenery, it would take her mind off the day ahead. However, she had her mind taken off the scenery, and the ordeal ahead, when a woman came and sat down beside her, complaining loudly about the lazy, ill-mannered conductor. Groaning inside, Poppy forced a smile in reply. And this was her undoing, for the woman didn't stop at the conductor. In fact she didn't stop talking at all, not even to take a breath. Her neighbours were so noisy she couldn't hear herself think. They had the radio on so loud, it was affecting her hearing. The rowdy family had no consideration for anyone.

By this time everyone on the bus was listening, and Poppy could see them cocking their ears in case they missed anything, then putting hands over their mouths to silence their titters. The woman's next target was her landlord. He should be made to paint all the houses in the street which he owned, because they were a disgrace. He was quick enough to take the rent money every week, oh, yes, but too mean to spend a penny keeping the houses looking neat and tidy.

When Poppy looked out of the window, she saw the next stop was hers, and she stood up. 'Excuse me, please,' she said. But the woman took no notice, still rambling on. The target of her complaints this time was the manager of the local shop. While Poppy sympathized with the poor man, she had no intention of allowing the woman to make her late for work. Not on this day of all days. 'Would you let me pass, please?' Poppy could see her office building looming up and squeezed past the woman, who still hadn't once stopped for breath.

The conductor was just about to ring the bell to tell the driver it was clear to move on, when Poppy caught his eye. 'Yer nearly left it too late, love.'

On the pavement, Poppy let out a sigh of relief. Another couple of seconds and she'd have been on her way down to the bus depot at the Pier Head. She happened to glance up at the bus as it was moving away, and a smile came to her face when she saw the woman moving to sit by another lady, her mouth still working. She pitied the poor unfortunate victim, but one good thing had come out of the episode for Poppy. She wasn't nervous any more. And surprisingly, she didn't have an earache, either.

Poppy mounted the steps, and the only time she felt her tummy turn over was when she was passing her old office. In her mind's eye, she could see Mr John's face, and he was sneering. But she rubbed the image from her mind as she climbed the steps. She wasn't going to let him spoil the day for her. He wasn't worth it.

When Poppy opened the door of the room that was to be her office, she was met by a smiling Mr Hammond, and she could feel a difference in the atmosphere. There was no tension, just a smiling welcome. And she knew then she was going to enjoy working there.

'Good morning, Miss Meadows.' Cecil thought that just the sight of the new secretary's face was enough to brighten any day. 'I think we should take things slowly today, at an easy pace. Just until you get used to the routine running of the office. I know you are used to the filing system, so we won't touch on that today. You can hang your coat in the room next door, which will be your office. There is a typist in there who will share the office with you, and I will introduce her to you when we've had a little chat.'

Poppy lifted the arm she'd draped her coat over. 'Hang coat first, Mr Hammond, or little chat first?'

Cecil Hammond smiled. 'Good question, Miss Meadows. I think coat first, and I can then introduce you to your colleague, Miss Simpson.' He came from behind the desk. 'Come with me.'

There was interest in Lorna Simpson's eyes when the door opened, for she was eager to know whom she'd be working with. She left her desk to take Poppy's coat. 'Let me hang it up for you.' Then she held out her hand. 'Lorna Simpson, and I believe we'll be working together.'

Poppy shook her hand. 'Poppy Meadows.' She instinctively

knew she would get on with her new colleague. She seemed friendly, was smartly dressed, and at a guess was about ten years Poppy's senior. 'I'll be looking to you for help in the first few weeks, but I'll try not to be a nuisance.'

Lorna smiled. 'I'm always here if you need assistance.'

Cecil Hammond turned towards his office. 'I'm going through the morning routine with Miss Meadows. Would you collect the morning post, Miss Simpsom, and bring it to my office? Then, if you have time, a cup of tea would be much appreciated.'

Lorna nodded. 'Do you take sugar, Miss Meadows?'

'One spoonful, please.'

The next hour passed over smoothly, with Mr Hammond explaining that each morning Miss Simpsom would bring the post into Mr Sutherland's office, and it would be opened by himself, or Poppy when she'd had time to settle in. The letters would then be left on the desk in a neat pile, until Mr Sutherland arrived. He would read the letters through before dictating the replies. Then he would read the typed replies before signing them and handing them over to be put into envelopes and taken downstairs to the post room.

It was turned ten o'clock when Mr Sutherland came in, and Cecil vacated the chair to allow his friend and boss to sit behind his desk, with the correspondence laid out ready for him to read. 'I'll leave you with Miss Meadows, John, and I'll be next door in the filing room.' Cecil added, 'Give me a call if you need me.'

Mr S. sat back in his chair with a letter in his hand which he'd taken off the top of the pile. As his eyes were scanning the lines, he asked, 'Do you think you'll enjoy working here, Miss Meadows?'

'If I didn't, I'd be a very hard person to please, Mr S., for

Mr Hammond and Miss Simpson have been very kind, friendly and helpful.'

He picked up a second letter and read it through. 'These two letters need an immediate reply, so are you ready to take dictation?'

Poppy lifted the pad that had been on her knee for ages, and from her mass of curls she produced a pencil from behind her ear. 'Ready, willing and able.' She chuckled. 'Well, I'm ready and willing. But the big question is, am I able?'

Both Cecil Hammond and Lorna Simpson heard the hearty laugh. And because they were both very fond of the older Mr Sutherland, they smiled.

Poppy might have sounded light-hearted and confident on the outside, but inside she wasn't so sure of herself. She was praying she could keep up with him, and wouldn't have to keep asking him to repeat himself, or slow down. But her fears were groundless, for Mr S. spoke slowly and clearly, and her confidence was soon restored. In fact she was doing so well, she dared to say, 'You don't have to make allowances for me being new, Mr S. I'm having no problem keeping up with you.'

The lined face broke into a smile. 'I'm always slow at the start of the day, my dear. And at my age I'm allowed that. The only time you will hear me growl is if a letter from a client annoys me. Then you will see me come to life, and my dictation will be somewhat faster.'

'I'll still keep up with you.' Then Poppy had a thought. And because he seemed to have a sense of humour, she decided to share the thought with him. 'However, it has just crossed my mind that if one letter can make you angry enough to dictate at speed, then what about when you have two such letters? I must remember to have an extra pencil within easy reach, sharpened and at the ready.'

'That will not be necessary, Miss Meadows, for I have mellowed a lot over the last few years, and I rarely lose my temper.'

Poppy settled into the routine easily, and several times she thought how lucky she was to have been given this job. Mr Sutherland was easy to work for, and a perfect gentleman. A far cry from his son. There were no orders snapped at her, no leering eyes, no touching of hands. In this office there was peace, perfect peace. And it was run like clockwork. Poppy finished taking dictation, typed out the replies to the letters, and gave them to Mr S. to read and sign. Then they were passed over to Lorna Simpson, who addressed the envelopes and made sure the letters caught the lunchtime post. And it was all done in a pleasant atmosphere, without a voice raised in anger.

When Poppy was putting her coat on at lunchtime, she was feeling very happy. She couldn't wait to tell Charlotte – and Jean, if she could join them – how lucky she felt. And, of course, she wanted to know how Jean had fared on the first morning of her new job.

Poppy's feet had barely touched the pavement when she was smothered by Charlotte's arms wrapped round her neck. 'Oh, Poppy, I've been thinking about you all weekend. Do you like your new job? Were they kind to you?'

Her voice muffled, but her heart singing with happiness, Poppy said, 'If you'll give me room to breathe, sweetheart, I'll tell you.'

Charlotte linked her arm and squeezed. 'It seems ages since I saw you, Poppy, and I have missed you, even though it's only been two days. But I can see you every day now and we can have lunch together. Jean is meeting us in the café, and

'I've had strict instructions that I am not to ask you any questions about your job until she's with us. She doesn't want to miss one word.'

'And I'm eager to know how she got on,' Poppy said, as they walked towards the café. 'I've got so much to tell you both, and then we've got Jean's news to listen to, so it's going to be a busy lunch hour. We'll have so much to talk about, we'll have no time to eat.'

'You must eat something, or you'll make yourself ill.' Charlotte nodded in agreement with her words. Then she thought she'd better put into action the plan she'd drawn up that morning. It wasn't something she wanted Jean to hear. 'Andrew and I are going to drive you home tonight, as a little celebration of your new job. We'll drop you at the corner of your street again, so don't worry about your mother not being prepared for visitors. Then on the way, you can tell Andrew how your day has gone, for he will be interested. Will you come up to our office when you finish work? It's very difficult to park outside your office, with it being such a busy street.'

Poppy nodded before pushing open the café door. 'Thank you. It's kind of you, and I do appreciate it. Don't mention it in front of Jean, though, 'cos I'd feel embarrassed. And it had better be the last time, or I'm going to be spoiled for getting on a crowded bus.'

Jean got up from where she was sitting at a table for three, and the two women, who had worked together for several years in an office where the atmosphere was always tense, smiled before holding out their arms and hugging each other.

'I can tell by your face you've hopped in as lucky as me,' Jean said, looking relaxed and years younger. 'I still can't believe how quickly it's all happened.'

'You two sit down and I'll go to the counter and order,' Charlotte said. 'Soup as usual, with bread, and a cream cake to follow by way of a small celebration.'

It was a noisy lunch, with Poppy and Jean telling excitedly of the difference in their new jobs from working for Mr John. And they both agreed they were stupid to put up with his temper and rudeness for so long. They should have had the courage to walk out long ago. 'Yes, we should,' Poppy said, 'but in this case it's all well that ends well. We could have found other jobs, I suppose, but I'm sure I'd never have found a nicer boss than Mr Sutherland Senior. He is quiet and gentle, but can be businesslike when he feels like it. I get on with him like a house on fire, and we've had a few laughs already. I'm not afraid to speak to him on a level, and he seems to appreciate that.'

'Ooh, I'm not that sure of myself yet,' Jean admitted. 'My boss is very pleasant and friendly. But it'll be a while before I can get Mr John out of my system, and be more outgoing.'

The lunch break passed quickly, and when it was time for them to go their separate ways, they agreed to meet the next day at the café. After kissing Poppy, Charlotte said she might not make it for lunch the next day. 'But Andrew and I will see you at the Grafton tomorrow night. I'm looking forward to it.'

Jean was standing at the edge of the pavement, waiting for a break in the traffic, when Charlotte said, 'I'll walk up to the office with you, Jean, because I want to have a word with Father.' She blew a kiss to Poppy. ''Bye for now.'

Poppy watched for a while as they walked up Castle Street, then turned and ran up the steps to her new office. She was humming softly, and felt lighter in heart than she ever had.

★ ★ ★

Charlotte rapped on the door of her father's office. 'Can I come in, Papa?' Without waiting for an answer, she opened the door and walked in.

George raised his brows. 'It's manners to knock on the door and wait to be invited in, my dear.'

'I knew you weren't with a client, Papa, because I asked at reception. I wouldn't just walk in if you had someone with you.' Charlotte put her two hands behind her and lifted herself on to the desk. She shuffled her bottom so she could look her father in the face. 'I've just had lunch with Poppy and Jean, and it was wonderful to just sit and listen to them talking about their new jobs, and what a difference there was from working for John Sutherland. Jean is very happy here; she can't believe her luck. And Poppy, well, she's beautiful all the time, but today her eyes were shining, and she was full of life. She praised Mr Sutherland Senior, and said he was lovely to work for, and they got on very well together.'

George sat back in his chair. 'Anything new to report in the romance department? Does she mention Andrew at all?'

'Poppy was too excited today, talking to Jean. I knew she wouldn't mention Andrew, for her head was too full of other things, so I said we would run her home after work, just to the top of her road, so she could finish the day off in style. But I'm afraid I've been a bit naughty. I led her to believe I'd be with Andrew, otherwise she would never have agreed. But I won't be here when she comes, because I believe they would get on better if they had some time on their own. Andrew doesn't know what I've arranged yet, but I'll go upstairs when I've finished here. He can make an excuse for my absence by saying Mother rang for one reason or another.'

George leaned forward. 'Let me get this straight. Poppy has

agreed to accept a lift home with you and Andrew, but what she doesn't know is that you have no intention of being with them. And Andrew knows nothing about it! I know you love your brother, and you are fond of Poppy, my dear, but why do you have to be so cloak and dagger about it? And why don't you invite Poppy to our house, so your mother can make her acquaintance? That might help matters along, and I believe your mother has every right to be involved if Andrew is really serious about the girl.'

Charlotte's eyes were like saucers. 'Oh, no, Papa! I wouldn't arrange a meeting because I think it could be disastrous. If Poppy was made to feel she was on show, it would put an end to any hope Andrew has.' She slipped down off the desk. 'I have to go up to Andrew's office now, and put him in the picture. Then I'll nip off home.' She kissed her father before heading for the door. 'I'll see you later, Papa.'

When the door had closed on his daughter, George pushed his chair back, so he could cross his legs in comfort, and began to think deeply. He was sure his wife would approve of Poppy, for it would be hard not to like the girl. And if they became acquainted, it could only help Andrew's cause. Then George had a brilliant idea. If his daughter could plan, then so could he. He lifted the internal telephone and asked his secretary to have him put through to Mr John Sutherland Senior. Then he sat back and chuckled as he waited for his telephone to ring.

'John, old boy, I hope I find you well and prospering?'

'Can't complain, old boy,' John Sutherland replied. 'I'm not as rich as you, but I'm making enough to keep heart and soul together.'

'It's ages since we met, John, so how about lunch at the club tomorrow? I would like to see you again; we don't meet often enough. But as there is something I want to ask of you, lunch is on me. Not to mention the odd glass or two of single malt. How does that sound to you? Say two o'clock at the club?'

'Sounds excellent, George, old boy. I'll look forward to it. See you then.'

George placed the receiver back in its cradle, then sat back with a very satisfied expression on his face. And he said softly, under his breath, 'I believe that's as good as anything my beloved daughter has come up with so far. If what I've got planned in my head bears fruit, then I really will be helping the course of true love.'

Later, as he was leaving the office, he lifted his hard hat as he bid the staff goodnight. And they could hear him whistling as he ran down the steps outside. The receptionist jerked her head at one of the typists. 'Mr George is in a very good mood. Perhaps he's got a dinner party to look forward to.'

'I was going to say some people have all the luck,' the typist replied, 'but I won't, 'cos he's a good boss.'

Andrew was standing outside the office building when he saw Poppy turn the corner. She waved to him, and his heart flipped. Even at that distance she looked adorable, and he wished she was his girlfriend so he could run towards her and greet her with a kiss, as lovers do. He had never felt like this before and wished he had the nerve to tell her so. As for anyone who said there was no such thing as love at first sight, he would tell them they were wrong. For he'd lost his heart to her the minute he'd held out his hand to help her up off the ground.

'I'm not late, am I?' Poppy asked. 'I got away as quickly as I could.'

'No, you're not late,' Andrew said, 'but I'm afraid I have a disappointment for you. Mother rang to ask Charlotte to go home, as she needed her for some reason or another. That's all Charlotte could tell me. I did say you wouldn't be happy coming in the car with just me for company, but she said she would apologize when she sees you tomorrow at the Grafton.'

Poppy looked up into his face, and asked, 'Why wouldn't I be happy in the car with just you for company? Because Charlotte said the drive home was to celebrate my first day in the new job, I had made up my mind to sit in the passenger seat anyway, to make the most of it. So, unless you have any objection, I'd be delighted to sit in the front seat and enjoy your company along with the scenery.'

'I would never have any objection to you sitting beside me, Poppy, you should know that. It will be my pleasure to drive you home and set you down safe and sound.'

'Are you ready for the off, or do you have to go back to your office for any reason?'

'No, I'm finished for the day. My office is closed.' Andrew was so happy he became daring, and cupped her elbow. 'My car is parked by Exchange Station, but it's only a few minutes' walk.'

'It'll do me good to get some exercise, and stretch my legs,' Poppy said. 'The only exercise I get is when I go dancing.' They reached the car and Andrew opened the passenger door. As she slid into the brown leather seat, she added, 'With you and Charlotte spoiling me like this, I'll be getting fat.'

Andrew looked at her before starting the car. 'You don't need to lose weight, Poppy. You are perfect as you are.'

'Oh, you wouldn't be saying that if you saw me first thing in the morning, bleary-eyed and bad-tempered.'

Andrew chortled. 'I don't believe that for one minute, but I'd like to see it. Just out of curiosity, of course.'

Poppy snuggled back into the soft leather. 'I've had a wonderful day, Andrew. A day of peace, with no one shouting, snarling, and looking down his nose at me and Jean as though we were peasants. John Sutherland Junior is an uncouth, big-headed rotter, and I feel free and happy knowing that I'll never have to see or speak to him again. But his father is just the opposite, and I'm going to enjoy working for him.'

Andrew steered the car into the street where Poppy lived, and he had his hand on the ignition key to switch the engine off when she said, 'Six houses down, Andrew. You might as well do the job properly. I won't invite you in, though, because my mam will only have been home from work for about a quarter of an hour. And as soon as I get in, she and David will be firing questions at me, about how my day has gone. But I will ask you in soon, just to prove that I do have a mother, and she's wonderful.' She stepped out of the car, then turned and put her head back in. 'Thank you, Andrew, you really are a love. Will I see you and Charlotte at the Grafton tomorrow night?'

Andrew was in his seventh heaven. 'Of course we'll be there. I particularly am looking forward to it. Until then, take care, and give my regards to your mother.'

Poppy's wide smile had Andrew driving home humming softly to himself. He definitely seemed to be making progress. And he vowed that tomorrow night at the Grafton, he'd come right out of his shell and let her see how he felt about her.

And if Andrew was in a happy mood, so were Poppy's mother and brother as they eagerly listened to how wonderful her day had been. How kind and gentle Mr Sutherland Senior was, and how well they got on. 'I couldn't be any happier, Mam, for everything seems to be going my way right now.'

David tried to look serious when he asked, 'Does your happiness lie solely with your new boss, or does being driven home by Andrew have a part to play in it?'

'Not a big part at the moment, dear brother, but who knows what the future holds?' Poppy saw the knowing looks exchanged between her mother and brother, but she was so happy she didn't care.

In the smoking room at the club, George Wilkie-Brook sat facing his old friend, John Sutherland. George was smoking a cigar, while John preferred his old faithful pipe. And on the table in front of them were two glasses of the best malt whisky. They had discussed business for a short while, then George had talked at length about his son's wish to become more than just a friend to John's new secretary. 'I have met her, and I can understand Andrew's being captivated by her. You must agree, old boy, she is very beautiful.'

John nodded. 'Yes, indeed. And while this is only her second day as my secretary, I find her intelligent, efficient, and also full of life. She certainly brightens my office with her presence, and she's put new life into myself and Cecil. If Andrew captured her heart, he would be a very lucky man.'

'I wholeheartedly agree, old boy, and my daughter, Charlotte, dotes on her. We are all hoping there is a happy ending to this story.'

'What does Harriet say?' John asked. 'Is she of the same mind?'

'Ah, well, you see, Harriet hasn't seen the girl yet. Not because she doesn't want to, for she does. The thing is, she's not allowed to. Charlotte is the matchmaker in this, and has done much to bring the couple together. But she is keeping Poppy from meeting Harriet, for she believes my wife, being of the old school, will frighten the girl off. And this is where I come to the part where I'm asking you, as an old friend, to do me a big favour. And remember, it's all in the cause of true love.'

John knocked his pipe on the huge crystal ashtray. 'As long as you are not planning to take my new secretary away, then I'll do what I can to help. I have to say, however, that I can't see how I can.'

George uncrossed his legs and sat forward. 'I'll tell you what I have in mind, then we'll go through to the dining room for our meal.'

Poppy and David were surprised to see Andrew and Charlotte in the foyer of the Grafton, waiting for them. 'We got here early,' Andrew said, as Charlotte hugged Poppy. 'We've got your tickets, so we can go straight in.'

'You shouldn't have bought our tickets,' David told him. 'Let me pay you for them.'

'You pay next time, eh?' Andrew couldn't wait to get on the dance floor so he could hold Poppy close as they danced together. But the girls had to go to the cloakroom to hang up their coats and comb their hair.

'I'm sorry about last night, Poppy, but it couldn't be helped,' Charlotte said. 'However, according to Andrew I wasn't missed. He said you enjoyed the ride home.'

Poppy smiled at her through the mirror. 'Yes, I did! Your brother is very gallant. It's nice to be treated like a lady.' She gave a curl one last twist, then linked Charlotte's arm. 'Let's go, my feet are itching.'

The first couple Poppy saw when she pushed open the

door to the dance hall were Sarah and Jim. They seemed to be enjoying themselves, and waved when they saw her. Sarah had told her over the weekend that Jim would be calling for her to take her to the dance. It seemed Jim had found the right girl at last.

Then Poppy spotted Andrew and David, in conversation with Peter and Kate. 'Come on, Charlotte, let's join the gang.' The first thing she noticed when approaching the group was the easy manner in which Peter stood with his arm round Kate's shoulder, and the couple looked very happy. Love was definitely in the air there, Poppy thought, and was very happy for them. Peter greeted her with a kiss on the cheek, and asked her to put his name down for the first slow foxtrot.

'I'm sorry, Peter, but I promised Andrew the first. Make it the second, eh?'

'That's okay, babe. We'll swap partners for the next one. Kate doesn't mind, do you, love?'

Kate turned her head and winked at Poppy. A wink that said, thanks to you, Peter and I are fine now. 'If Andrew can put up with me.'

As soon as the band started up, Andrew's arm went round Poppy's waist and he led her on to the dance floor. Holding her close, he whispered, 'Has Peter made it up with Kate?' When Poppy nodded, he told her, 'I'm glad. I don't have to be jealous of him any more.'

Poppy leaned back to look into his face, but found those deep brown eyes played havoc with her heartbeat, so turned her head to look over his shoulder. 'You haven't been jealous of Peter, have you? There was no need, for there was never anything serious between us. We're good mates, we're fond of each other, but there was never any romance involved. Does that satisfy you?'

'Yes, it is a great relief. But can I ask you a personal question? You won't get angry or think I'm being forward?'

'You can ask, Andrew, but whether I answer or not depends on the question. So out with it, before the dance is over.'

Andrew held her close, his cheek touching hers. He wasn't to know it, but his nearness was causing her to feel a sensation she had never felt before. It took her breath away. And the sensation came again when he whispered, 'Do you think there is any possibility there could be a romance between you and me?'

'I don't know you well enough to answer that honestly, Andrew. My mam told me she knew my dad was the man for her the first time he kissed her.'

'And did she say that was the sign of true love?'

Poppy nodded. 'Yes. She told me there were other signs, but I'm not repeating them to you in the middle of a dance floor.'

'Would anyone notice if I stole a quick kiss now?' Andrew asked. 'If it was the right sign, it could be the start of a romance, don't you think?'

'Oh, I think a few people would notice a couple kissing as they danced past. Let's have a night out on our own, to get to know each other better.'

'That would be wonderful,' Andrew said, his tummy doing somersaults. 'How about tomorrow night?'

'Yes, that would be fine. You can call for me at home. Then you could meet my mam.'

'I can't wait,' Andrew told her, 'so I'm going to steal a sly kiss. And I don't care if every person in the room sees me.' He put a finger under Poppy's chin and raised her face. Then, softly, he brushed his lips against hers. Neither knew the effect on the other, but later, Andrew admitted to seeing stars, while Poppy said she felt as though she was floating on air.

'Would your mother say that was a good sign?'

'That I don't know, and I won't be asking her. But if you were to ask me, then I'd say that was a very good sign.'

'I am so looking forward to meeting your mother. I'm eager to know every little thing about you, Poppy, and meeting your mother is a good start.'

Little did they know what the next day was to bring.

John Sutherland, or Mr S., as Poppy called him, put his signature to the last letter, then handed them over to her. 'See that they get the lunchtime post, Miss Meadows.'

She smiled at him. 'I'll see to it right away.' She was halfway to the door when he called her back. 'Before I forget, would you ask Miss Simpson to organize tea and biscuits for later? I'm expecting a lady visitor, and would like to offer her some light refreshment. She's the wife of a friend of mine, and rang last night to say she had shopping to do in town, so would call in to see me. If need be, tell Miss Simpson to send one of the juniors for cakes or biscuits. My friend knows her way up to my office, and I'll give you a ring when she arrives.'

He was used to Poppy's playful ways by now, and found them refreshing. So he smiled when she said, 'Your friend will be treated like royalty. I shall make the tea with my own fair hand. And I'll make sure there are no broken biscuits.'

It was a quarter past two when the phone on Poppy's desk rang. 'Would you come through, please?'

Poppy stopped by Lorna's desk. 'I think his visitor has arrived, so better put the kettle on.' Then she patted her hair, smoothed down her skirt, and made sure the seams on her stockings were straight.

When the door opened and Poppy came in wearing a smart white blouse, a figure-hugging black skirt, and walking like a model, Harriet Wilkie-Brook was taken aback. Her husband hadn't exaggerated when he said the girl was stunning. Apart from a face that was perfect, and an outstanding figure, the girl held herself well.

'Miss Meadows, this is a friend of mine, Miss Harriet.'

Harriet inclined her head in answer to Poppy's smile. Then, as planned, she feigned surprise. 'Meadows, that sounds familiar. Your name wouldn't be Poppy by any chance?'

It was Poppy's turn to show surprise, but hers was genuine. 'Yes, my name is Poppy Meadows.'

'Well, I do declare! My son and daughter often speak of you. And I believe you have met my husband?' Harriet was almost as good an actress as her daughter. 'What a coincidence, John! I am so glad I called in, for I have heard so much about this young lady from Andrew and Charlotte.' She left her seat to shake Poppy's hand. 'I am delighted to meet you, my dear. My son and daughter speak of you so warmly, and they'll be delighted when I tell them how I came to meet you this afternoon. Do please come and visit us sometime in the near future, so we can become acquainted. Will you do me the honour of calling one day? Andrew would bring you. Or Charlotte, who is forever singing your praises. Promise you will pay a visit very soon?'

Poppy was in a dilemma, and looked to Mr S. for guidance. She worked here, he was her boss! But he seemed to be quite pleased about the turn of events, and there was no help coming from that quarter.

'I will try to visit you, Miss Harriet. When I next see Andrew or Charlotte, we'll talk about it.' She gave a wide smile, which made Harriet hope her son would claim this extraordinary girl before someone else did. She was quite enchanting, and would be so good for her son.

'Shall I ask Miss Simpson to bring the refreshments through, Mr S.?'

'If you would, Miss Meadows. And don't forget the sugar. Both Mr Hammond and myself have a sweet tooth.'

Before turning, Poppy said, 'It was nice meeting you, Miss Harriet.'

'We'll meet again soon, my dear, I'm sure.'

Poppy was a bag of nerves as she went over the events of the day with her mam and David. 'I didn't even know what to call her, because I can't remember their second name. I know it's a double barrel one, but that's all!'

'What are yer getting yerself in a state for, sweetheart?' Eva asked. 'She didn't eat you. She's not an ogre.'

'I know. She was very nice, actually. But it was in my place of work, and here she was, treating it like a social event. It was embarrassing, to say the least. Anyway, I'd better make an effort and get myself ready. Andrew will be here soon.' She noticed there was a sly smile on her brother's face. 'What are you looking so pleased about?'

'I've had a feeling for a long time that Andrew was going to be part of your life. And it looks as though I was right. And Charlotte! She says a prayer every night that you and Andrew fall in love.' David wasn't often serious, but he was now. 'And I don't think you could find a better bloke if you searched the whole world over. I've said to Mam, he's someone who is sincere and you could trust him with your life.'

Eva asked, 'Do you love him, sweetheart?'

'I'll tell you later tonight, Mam. Right now I'd better put a move on. I don't want to keep him waiting.'

Poppy was coming down the stairs when she heard the car pull up outside. 'I'll go, Mam!'

Andrew looked at her and their eyes locked for a few seconds. Then he held his arms out and Poppy stepped down into them. 'You know what happened today?'

'Yes, Mother told me. You're not upset about it, are you? She meant no harm, and she's never stopped singing your praises since she got home. She told the housekeeper and the cook. They all know Andrew has a beautiful friend. Mother's last words to me as I left the house were, "If you let that girl get away, you'll have me to answer to."'

Poppy looked up at him, her arms round his neck. And without a word being spoken, their lips met. It was their first real kiss, and they parted only to sigh with happiness. Then Andrew claimed her lips again. This time it was a lover's kiss and left both of them light-headed. Andrew broke the spell long enough to ask, 'Is this what your mother meant?'

Poppy didn't answer. She took his hand and pulled him up the steps and into the living room. 'Mam, David, this is my boyfriend, and we love each other.'

Liking Andrew on sight, and having heard from David that he was a good man, Eva was delighted. She kissed her daughter, and hugged Andrew. 'You make a lovely couple.'

'We'll be back later, Mam, and you can get to know Andrew. But first I want him to drive me to his home so I can meet his parents properly. And most of all, I want to see my very best friend, Charlotte. I want to thank her for bringing me and Andrew together. She did it by fair means or foul, but she did it, and I love her for it.'

Half an hour later, and without giving advance warning, Andrew walked into the house with Poppy on his arm. And never had the Wilkie-Brook house known such joy and laughter. Frances and Jane were brought in from the kitchen, and they were taken aback when Poppy kissed them. They weren't servants to her, they were people like herself, who were working for a living. She'd known from the minute she'd set eyes on Andrew and Charlotte that they came from a rich family, but she didn't care, because her own family had riches of a different kind. She would have loved Andrew whether he was rich or poor, and it showed on her face when she looked at him. And Andrew was in a world of his own. He couldn't take his eyes off the beautiful girl he had thought he would only see in his dreams.

George and Harriet were so overjoyed, there were tears in their eyes as they hugged each other. But the happiest of all was Charlotte. She stood between her brother and her very best friend, and she clung to both of them. She told herself God must have forgiven her for the lies she told, for had He not granted her wishes? Poppy would always be in her life now, and that was the best present that anyone could give her.

Six months later, George Wilkie-Brook and his friend John Sutherland sat in the smoking room of the club. The smoke from George's cigar and John's pipe swirled around them. 'Well, old boy,' George said, looking happy and contented. 'It's been a very interesting six months, don't you think? And one I have enjoyed immensely, I have to say. From the moment Poppy set foot in our house, on Andrew's arm, we have known nothing but laughter and happiness.'

'Your son is a lucky blighter, I have to say,' John told his old friend. 'There are not many girls like Poppy. Prince or pauper, everyone is equal in her eyes. I was afraid she would be leaving me to get married soon after she and Andrew declared their intentions, but she is determined to carry on working, for which I am very thankful. I never much enjoyed going into the office every day until Poppy came along. Now I look forward to it.'

George chortled. 'She soon put Harriet in her place, and that's something no one else has ever done. My wife thought it wrong that her son's fiancée should do anything so lowly as go out to work, but Poppy said she would carry on working even when she and Andrew are married. And on her twentieth birthday, last month, when they got engaged, she loved the ring he bought her, but refused a very expensive watch. She intends to continue living with her mother, who, by the way, gets on like a house on fire with Harriet. Like Poppy, she's down to earth and doesn't pretend to be something she's not.' George raised his hand to a waiter standing near. 'Two glasses of your best claret, please, Joseph.' Then he turned back to John.

'My son is the happiest person in the world. He idolizes Poppy, and she feels as strongly about him. Harriet and I are well pleased with our life, now there is more to interest us. And, of course, it is much more lively. Poppy has a very remarkable sense of humour.' Then George remembered he had something else to tell his old friend. 'Oh, another thing Poppy has done, which I shall be eternally grateful for, is bring my beloved Charlotte into the real world. She never knew what it was to work for her money, but all that has changed. She helps in Andrew's office almost every day now, so she can go to lunch with Poppy and another friend, Jean. And she has a boyfriend. He is the son of one of Andrew's clients, and a very likeable young man. He had never been to a dance in his life, apparently, until he met Charlotte. Now he goes dancing with her, Poppy and Andrew. And I have to admit, John, that while I am a wealthy man, like yourself, I do think we missed out on life when we were their age.'

'One can't go back, old boy,' John said. 'We spent years of our youth sitting exams, in order to make money in later life. You can't have it both ways.' He looked pensive for a while, then asked, 'When will Poppy and Andrew be getting married? I'll be sad to lose her.'

'From what I've heard, John, you won't be losing her for a while. She has said she will only stop working when two things happen. One is when they start a family. And the other is when her brother David gets married and he and his wife live with Eva. Poppy has stated in no uncertain terms that she would never leave her mother to live alone. David has a girlfriend now, but he wants to get on in his job and be earning a decent salary before he thinks of settling down. So Poppy will be with you for some time yet.'

'That makes me feel very happy.' John looked at his watch. 'I'd better be on my way, or Poppy will say she can tell by my breath that I've had one drink too many.'

George chortled. 'The wench has us all in her spell, and loving it. And it all came about because of one rainy day.'